To my cousin Brayden,
Who showed me how to choose yourself. Always be free.

Freed by Destiny
Lost Queen Chronicles Book 6

USA Today Bestselling Author
S.A. McClure

Freed by Destiny

The Lost Queen Chronicles Book 6

Written by S.A. McClure

Edited by Rainy Kaye

Cover Art by Jennifer Munswami

Cover Art Elements by Francesca Michelon

Lunameed Publishing

lunameed@gmail.com

Indianapolis, Indiana

This is a work of fiction. Names, places, characters and incidents are either the product of the author's imagination or are used fictitiously, and any resemblance to any actual persons, living or dead, organizations, events or locales is entirely coincidental.

Special Thanks

Scott Thomas
Jazlyn Christine Renee Knapp
Torey
Mimi Nguyen
Sarah Biglow
Karpov Kinrade
Sara Collins
S. R. Bishop
Anij Fallows
Mom & Dad
Paula Dawson
Jason Templeton
B. Snowy
L.E.Custodio
Emma Morris
snir kolodni
J. Leigh James
Lauren
Seamus JV Sands
David Berkowitz-Tech-newszone.com
S. L. Puma
Raphael Bressel
Ondine, Donnie and Anais
Erik Skoog
Jules Grable
Lenka B

Melora Sundt
Michael Bishop
Rachel Daley
Russell Nohelty
Beth Barany
Belinda Crawford
DeMarco Family
Audra
Matthew Cooper
Katherine Flood
Alisha T.
T. W. Townsend
Rubiee Tallyn Hayes
Arioch Morningstar
Nathan "Kyundi2" Stocking
C.L. Shoemaker
Jo Jo and Sophie Hoffman
Stacie V. Henderson
maileguy
Wade G. Sullivan
J. Lim J. K.
Felicia T
Russell Ventimeglia
Katie L
Johanna H.
Jon
Geoffrey Willmoth
I'm at your mercy!

Thank You

Chapter One

All Astrid had was tonight. Tomorrow, she planned to turn herself over to King Renard.

Her life, as she knew it, would be over.

All her dreams. All her plans. Everything she had worked so hard to achieve for her people. Yet…

Sighing deeply, she nestled deeper into the grass. Dew soaked into her back as she peered into the heavens above. Wisps of clouds roamed through the skies, dimming the brilliance of the stars. They were said to be the essence of her ancestors. She wished, more than anything, she could seek their advice.

Although she prayed to the Light, the stars, and the sister moons, she did not receive guidance.

"You shouldn't be out here alone," Max said from behind her.

She whipped her head towards him and frowned. "I will never understand how you move so quietly."

He shrugged. "I'm an elf. What else would you expect? We're stealthy like that."

"A stealthy elf. Classic." She rolled her eyes at him.

She didn't know how to make him understand. Here they were, fighting a war against the tyranny of a king who would rather see their entire species destroyed, and the only thing she had to say to him was 'a stealthy elf.' It was no wonder they were all doomed.

A sliver of silver light filtered through the clouds, illuminating his face in a soft white glow. She peered at him expectantly. Her heart sank. There, in the place she had hoped would be a smile, rested the gnarliest scowl she'd ever seen. His teeth, partially bared, made his face appear more beast than man. Furrows creased his brow, and his eyes were hooded as he sank into the grass beside her.

Leaning back, he dropped his hands onto the ground, his fingertips grazing hers, as he stared into the sky. Although tension clung to his muscles and a vein in his jaw twitched, the scowl slid from his lips as he basked in the sister moons' glow.

The warmth of his touch jolted her. She was reminded how comfortable she was around him. How he made her feel as if she wasn't alone in the world.

But, when she closed her eyes, it was not his face she saw.

"Why are you here?" she asked.

Wind whistled through the trees and stirred her hair as she waited

Freed by Destiny

for him to respond. Her heart, beating rapidly, thrummed against her chest. His long, low sigh sent a shiver racing down her spine. Was he just as weary as she was? She wet her lips, preparing her response.

Without warning, he placed his hand atop hers and squeezed. The sudden warmth was like a sunburn searing across her flesh. It physically hurt to have him this close. To know she could only disappoint him further. Before she could attempt to extricate her hand from his grasp, he finally spoke.

"You deserve to know the truth."

She waited. This was not what she had been expecting.

"All those months I was unconscious, I could still hear the world around me. And try as I might to break through the manacles holding tight around my mind, I fought to return to you." His voice quivered, jumping an octave lower as he angled his head towards her. "I thought it was over, that I would forever be trapped in a state caught between life and death."

"I know," she whispered.

He held her gaze. His caramel eyes brimmed with adoration as he craned his neck ever closer to her. Closing her eyes and breathing in, she let the scent of him wash over her. He had become as familiar to her as her own hands. She cherished him. Loved him.

But not the way he wanted.

Splinters of darkness cracked through her heart as the thought struck her again. She pulled away from him and shifted her gaze skyward once more. Through her periphery vision, she caught him cocking his head at her. Confusion and pain clouded his eyes.

"Things are... different now." Her voice quivered as she said the words, even as they clawed at her throat, desperate to be kept locked inside.

Saying them meant they were real.

And if this was real, it meant she might lose him forever.

He grunted, his gaze still locked on her. The hair on her arms stood on end, even as she avoided looking at him. She didn't trust herself to have this conversation with him. If she let herself, she knew it would be the easiest thing in the world to give into the warmth and love he offered.

Love was a fleeting, ambiguous thing. Something she didn't understand but desperately wanted to.

And he was offering it to her on a silver platter. All she had to do was accept.

The way she had before.

Except.

Everything was different now. *She* was different.

Swallowing hard, she forced herself to meet his eyes. A lump formed in her throat as she opened her mouth to speak. What could she tell him? He already knew. She could tell from the anguish in his eyes that he'd already guessed what she was about to say.

"Max, I..."

"Don't," he rasped.

The shortness of his tone brought tears to her eyes. They stung as they leaked down the sides of her cheeks.

Freed by Destiny

Biting her bottom lip, she reached across the space between them and squeezed his hand.

"You are so special to me," she said. His hands were clammy in her grasp.

And cold.

Colder than she'd ever felt him before.

"You almost died. And I couldn't save you," she whispered.

He cupped her cheek and used his thumb to wipe away the tears that rolled down her skin as she wept for the girl she used to be and the promise she'd made of tomorrow.

"I don't want to lose you." Her body shivered, as she attempted to keep herself from telling him how she was feeling without using words.

A cavalier smirk crossed his lips. "Go on."

She cleared her throat again. A tightness spread across her chest, as if she were being stretched beyond the tearing point of her ligaments. She gulped in a breath, her lungs swelling and shuddering as she released her hold on it slowly.

"I have only loved a handful of people in my life," she said. Part of her desperately wanted to cling to his hand. To feel his warmth comforting her as she explained how she had formed an attachment to another man.

She was being a coward. The sweat soaking through her armpits and the ache in her chest and shoulders were enough to alert anyone of her distress, and yet, she still could not form the words.

Her teeth chattered. Grinding down on them, she set her jaw into a tight line as she said, "You have been there for me from the start. I cannot imagine my life without you..."

He placed his hand upon hers. His thumb traced circles across her skin, leaving a trail of fire in its wake.

"I know what you're going to say," he said.

Chewing on her bottom lip, she turned towards him. His eyes flicked to the ground. Although every inch of her itched to know what his thoughts were, she forced herself to remain silent. She owed him the space to speak his mind. After everything he'd done for her, he deserved someone who would love him beyond worlds. Beyond comprehension.

But that person couldn't be her.

"I had a lot of time to think during my coma."

She nodded, not trusting her voice to respond appropriately.

"It gave me time to process the type of predicament I placed you in."

She squeezed his hand gently. She didn't know if she wanted him to stop or continue.

He dropped her hand. The sudden loss of his warmth made her shiver. Even in the darkness, she could see the tightness in his jaw as he shifted his chin ever so slightly towards her.

"You didn't grow up in this world," he said. "You didn't know the pitfalls of being a royal. Or the hardships."

"Max, I..."

He placed a single finger against her lips, stilling the words on her tongue. Her eyes widened as he snatched his hand away from her.

Freed by Destiny

"I'm sorry," he murmured, his shoulders shaking.

"It's alright."

"No, it's not," he said. "But I appreciate the sentiment all the same."

He sank back, the tension in his shoulders easing as he leveled himself on the ground. He released a soft sigh as he knit his fingers beneath his head and stared into the sky.

Astrid waited for him to say something—anything—that would settle the fluttery feeling in the pit of her stomach. As the seconds passed and still, he did not say anything, she began to wonder if he would. Dampness seeped into her bones, and she shivered as a gentle gust of wind drifted through the trees. If this was to be her last night of freedom, she was glad she was spending it here, beneath the stars and sister moons, in the company of someone she loved.

Max cleared his throat. The sound jolted her, sending her hand flying to the blade belted on her thigh.

"Your first instinct is to reach for a blade instead of your magic," he whispered, without cracking an eye.

She shrugged, knowing he could sense her movements.

"Whatever you decide, Astrid, I am with you."

His words stirred the fluttering in her stomach into a frenzy.

"What are you saying?" she asked.

"Whether it is me or... him... or someone else entirely, my loyalty to you..." He sucked in a deep breath and held it for several seconds—almost long enough for Astrid to become worried, but

.

not quite. "I will remain loyal to you," he finished.

Astrid's throat constricted and she felt as if she couldn't breathe. Resisting the urge to yank the grass from the ground and scream into the heavens, she turned towards him and asked, "Why?"

Still, he did not open his eyes. He did not look at her. Or reach for her. Or give her any sign that he desired her to touch him. She bunched her hands into the loose fabric of her shirt and waited for him to say something. His nostrils flared and his chest rose and fell in a quick, staccato fashion.

"You saved my life," he finally replied. His voice was monotone, his hands resting on his stomach as he spoke. The only indication that he was struggling was the continued rapid rise and fall of his chest. "You and I share a common goal: we wish to free the magical world from the tyranny of King Renard. And, despite everything, I love you."

Her lips parted to say the words back to him. To confirm that she cared for him just as he did for her. And yet, she couldn't bring herself to give him false hope. She *did* love him. She always would.

"It was my fault you were injured in the first place," she said. "It was the least I could do to save you."

"I know what you gave up," he whispered.

The hollow place deep inside her where her healing magic should have been reared back. It was completely void. An empty carcass of what it used to be. She shivered, a sudden coldness seeping deep into her bones, and wrapped her arms tightly around her.

"I couldn't lose you," she whispered. Tears leaked from the corners of her eyes.

Freed by Destiny

They sat in silence as the stars twinkled above them and weight of her choice hung between them. Astrid did not regret giving up her healing magic to save Max. If she could go back and make a different choice, she would choose saving him every time. He had put his life in danger countless times to try and keep her safe. He had saved her. From Kaden. Renard. Even herself. And he deserved to be given the same. Having him awake again— alive—was worth more to her than her healing magic ever could.

"I don't want you to do this," he said, breaking the silence between them.

"I know."

"There's nothing I can do to change your mind."

"There's not."

Astrid stole a glance at him. His face was scrunched into a sour look, as if his head were stuck in a barrel of trash on a hot day.

"Could he?" he asked, his voice barely above the hum of the wind.

Her lips pressed into a thin line as she considered his question.

"No."

Although tension remained locked in his jawline, the rest of his features slackened at his words. He nodded once, his eyes still closed.

She wished he would say what he was truly thinking. A part of her knew it would break her, but at least then it would be in the open. And, even if they argued, they could get past it. Couldn't they?

She sighed heavily. Despite his revelation that he would always be there for her, a part of her still doubted him. She knew he loved her and wanted to protect her. But did that extend beyond not being the person she wanted to spend her life with? He'd been jealous of Bear. She couldn't envision a scenario in which he would sit ideally by while she fell deeper in...

She stopped herself before the word "love" applied to Kimari.

"I should return to camp," she said abruptly.

The comfortable silence between her and Max suddenly felt stifling.

Max sat up and stared straight into her eyes. His fingers trembled as he reached across the space between them and tucked a stray strand of hair behind her ear. His fingers trailed across the curve of her earlobe, sending electricity coursing through her veins. His hand came to rest on her shoulder. He leaned forward ever so slightly, his eyes never leaving hers.

Sweat clung to her palms as the fluttering in her stomach intensified once again. Whether from anticipation or anxiety, she couldn't decipher. Even as his lips brushed against hers, that swirling uncertainty pulsed within her. She allowed the kiss to linger for longer than she should have before shoving away from him and dashing back towards camp. She did not look back. She couldn't. She didn't trust herself to continue moving forward if she did. She didn't trust herself to leave in the morning if she did.

And staying here, with Max and Bear and the rest of her friends, would mean the destruction of them all.

Chapter Two

Astrid nestled into the pillows and cushiony mattress of her bed. Her limbs were stiff and heavy as she brought a blanket up to her chin. Although she closed her eyes and willed herself to sleep, thoughts galloped through her mind. Sighing, she unraveled herself from the blanket and lifted her hands above her face. Tiny sparks flickered between her fingers as she rotated her wrists.

Tomorrow, Renard would be her captor. She knew he would inhibit her magic. Stop her from being able to defend herself. Reduce her down to a powerless little girl. The sparks grew brighter as her agitation grew. Losing herself to appease the king was a fate worse than death, but condemning her people was unforgivable.

Kimari's face filled her vision. He'd met her gaze with baleful eyes after hearing his father's declaration. Even before her friends and allies had gathered around her, he'd known her answer.

As Bear, Kali, and Max pled with her to fight against Renard, he'd remained locked in place. His caramel eyes brimming with anguish. Whatever doubt might have seeped into the back of her mind and gnawed at her had fled. Renard would never let her. He would kill everything and everyone who stood in his way.

She only had one choice.

She tried to tell herself that her sacrifice would be better for her people. That being alive and oppressed was better than being dead.

But now, as she watched the flickers of her magic dance in the darkness, she wondered if the peace she would create would be as fleeting.

A soft tap on her bedroom door drew her attention away from her hands. She extinguished her flames as quickly as she had summoned them. She wasn't in the mood to converse with anyone. Especially not one of her friends, who she knew would attempt to convince her to stay.

"Astrid?" Kimari's voice filtered through the darkness. "Are you still awake?"

She clutched her arms around her chest and stilled her breathing, hoping he would walk away. Her mind and her heart were too muddled with the kiss she'd shared with Max and her anxiety over turning herself over to Renard—his father—in the morning.

"I saw the light glowing from beneath your door," he said. "Will you invite me in?"

She considered feigning sleep. If he asked in the morning, she could lie. It would be a simple one. She'd fallen asleep before he stopped by.

"I can tell you're awake," he said. "If you were asleep, you'd be breathing deeply instead of this strange silence of holding your breath."

Groaning, she sat up and called across the room, "Just because I'm awake doesn't mean I want to be disturbed."

His chuckle reverberated through the air.

"Really?" she asked, miffed that he found pleasure in her dissatisfaction at him inviting himself over to her room on her last night of freedom.

"Look, a guy's gotta try, ya know?"

Rolling her eyes, Astrid climbed from her bed and stomped over to her door, where Kimari had already cracked it and stuck his head inside her room.

"If you would rather be alone, I get it," he said, holding up his hands innocently as she pulled the door wide open. "But really, princess, it is a bit of a shame that you want to sequester yourself away when we could be talking strategy."

"Strategy?" she asked, dumbfounded. And here she had thought he'd come all this way to see if he could seduce her. She shook her head. That was not what she wanted either.

"Yes, strategy," he said with a nonchalant shrug. He leaned in close to her ear. "Unless there was something else you would rather be doing."

The heat of his breath on her neck made gooseflesh cover her arms. She stepped away from him and busied herself by turning on the lights set up in her tent.

"Look," she said, "I appreciate that you don't want me to be alone. I do. But... how, exactly did you escape the guards?"

"Nice attempt at a dodge," he said. "I asked nicely."

She cocked an eyebrow at him, her lips pursing as she waited for him to continue. He didn't. Sighing, Astrid plucked an apple from her snack cabinet and bit into it. Juice ran down her chin as she took another bite. At least when her mouth was stuffed, she couldn't say or do anything she would regret later. She hated how confused she felt when she was around him. Especially since she still had her doubts about what he was actually doing here. Why he had actually agreed to come to their base. It couldn't be just a coincidence that his father knew exactly where to send his armies.

"How did you really get out?" she asked, wiping her mouth with the back of her hand before settling into one of the chairs close to her bed.

"I told you. I asked nicely." His cheeks turned a surprising shade of purple when she glared at him. He sighed performatively and said, "And Maya might have had something to do with it."

Astrid scowled. "Maya? But she doesn't like or trust you. Why would she help you get out of your cell for the evening?"

"Maybe because you have a best friend who actually understands what you need and is willing to help you get it."

Her scowl deepened. "And I suppose you think you are what I need, huh?"

He shrugged.

"Well, let me tell you something. You're not."

Freed by Destiny

Kimari didn't bat a lash at her tone of voice as he strode forward and sat on the side of her bed.

"I know you don't trust me right now. And, maybe for good reason." He lifted his hands as flames burst into life around her fingers. "Alright, for very good reason. But that's not the point. I know you want what's best for your people. And I think there's a part of you who believes that I want peace, too. Otherwise, you wouldn't have reached out to me to begin with."

"Yes, but that was before your father announced that he would begin murdering innocent magicals if I didn't turn myself in. I want to trust you, but…" Her fire flickered as her hands shook. She balled them into fists as she spun towards him.

Only to find their faces mere inches from one another. Releasing a small yelp, she leaned backwards and glared at him.

"I am trying to help you. To help this country. What do I have to show for my efforts?" He leaned back, a look of pure disgust clouding his expression. "You can barely look at me without cringing."

Her heart lurched to a stop at his words. She couldn't explain her feelings to herself. For months, she'd loathed him and everything he stood for as a member of the Titus line. And yet, she wanted to trust him. After everything, she was still drawn to him.

"Besides, if I really wanted to fight with you, I would bring up the kiss you shared with lover boy," Kimari said.

She jolted.

"About that," she began. Her tongue was heavy and dry in her mouth. Sweat coated her hands and her heartbeat thrummed erratically in her chest. Dizziness crawled through her. "Max and

17

I… you know we were engaged. He… I…"

"It's okay, princess, I know you love him, and you wish you could be with him instead of me. I get it. Trust me. But, if we want our ruse to work—and it has to, if we're going to keep you alive—then you'll need to be a bit more careful when it comes to showing your affection to him."

Cold numbness kissed the tips of her fingers. She wanted to tell him he was wrong, but the bitterness and disgust in his tone gave her pause. He'd been so careful with his emotions before. So calculating. But the man who sat on her bed now was a torrent of emotion, ready to burst at the slightest provocation. She didn't know how to remedy the two sides of him.

"I can't help that I have a history with him," she said slowly. "But I want you to know that I am committed to our partnership. As long as we remain allies, we can—we will—make this world a better place. I know it."

Although his eyes remained hooded and his smirk carried just the slightest tinge of angst within it, Kimari began to slow clap.

"And there she is," he said. "The girl we all know and love. The Queen of the Fae. Astrid Stormbearer."

Glaring at him, Astrid pushed herself from her chair and turned her back on him.

"If you only came here to goad me, I think you should leave," she said. She hated that her voice trembled as she spoke to him. She was the draking queen of the fae, a warrior in her own right, and she was not going to let some pig-headed, spoiled, sexy as sin prince stop her from owning who and what she was. She'd fought too hard and for too long to be cowered like this. So what if his father had the means to destroy the entirety of her people. Wasn't that the whole reason she'd chosen to fight against him in the first place? The longer she stood there, with her back towards him, the more resolved she became.

"You want to be mad at me? Fine," she said as she turned around. She met his gaze head-on. "Think what you want, Kimari. I chose to trust you. I chose to take that risk because I saw something in you on that hill when your father sent his robots to destroy us. I chose that. Me. Just like I am choosing to overlook your childish, toxic, profoundly incomprehensible attitude towards me right now. You do realize that Max fought to save my life on countless occasions, right? That he has been my constant friend? That he has loved me, even when I found it difficult to love myself? And what have you done? Insulted me? Made my life more challenging? Kissed me on a livestream to our entire country?"

His lips parted as if he were about to interrupt her, but Astrid held up her hand as she continued to glare at him.

"I'm not done yet," she said. "I know who I am. And I will not stand by while you and your father continue to pillage this nation. Our people deserve more."

Astrid panted when she finished her speech, her skin glowing slightly from the exhilaration of saying exactly how she was feeling. Kimari paused until she nodded, giving him the indication that it was finally safe for him to respond.

"I am sorry to have caused you such distress," he said simply.

Astrid considered prolonging their argument but couldn't see what that would do for either of them, except form a rift on the eve of their reunion with his father. That would be all she needed.

"I'm sorry I thought you might have played a role in your father calling for your return to the castle."

He shrugged. "If our roles had been swapped, I would have considered the same possibility."

She nodded once, accepting his statement.

"So," she said, stepping towards him, "what did you really come here for?"

"Ah, well, that," he fumbled over his words. "I guess the real answer to your question is simple: I'm not sure how much time we'll have alone together once we're in my father's court. I've known him all my life and even I can see how petty and demanding he can be. He will watch us. He will want to assure himself that you aren't able to escape again."

"And you?" she asked. "What will become of you once your father has you in his grasp again?"

Although his features remained smug and a little cocky, an uncertainty lingered in his eyes as he said, "Let me deal with that one."

"But... won't he punish you?"

"He will. I am the crown prince. I'm supposed to be the jewel in his cap. The apple of his eyes. The feather..."

"Okay. I get it. You're supposed to be his legacy. But doesn't that mean that the punishment for leaving him will be even harsher? I don't want to return you to him only to have you killed."

"He won't kill me," Kimari said. "He can't. Or, didn't you know, I am extremely popular with the ladies."

Freed by Destiny

"Can't you be serious for even a minute?" She punched him in the arm, then settled back into the chair. "I don't want you to get hurt."

"I was being serious. I am popular among the people. And, after the entire world saw our kiss, he would have to be blind not to see that the two of us together is a greater asset than either or both of us dead."

"Uh huh." She toyed with a frayed thread on her shirt. "And if you're wrong about him?"

"I'm not."

"I wish I could believe you," she whispered, yanking the thread free from her sleeve and twirling it between her fingers. A small hole began to unravel around her cuff. It was strange how something so miniscule and insignificant as a single thread had the ability to destroy an entire garment.

"Look, I don't know what will happen once we join my father at court, but I do know this: we will be watched. And he will do everything in his power to turn us against one another. Which is why I want to create a solid plan now. Establish a code. That way, even if we're in a situation where we have to say or do something that might be hurtful to the other, we can give each other a sign."

"Kimari," she began, her head swimming. It had been a long, confusing day. She'd given up her healing magic to save Max. She'd witnessed her friends' and allies' reactions to Renard's proclamation. She'd effectively ended her relationship with Max only to have him say he would wait for her. That he would never stop hoping they would end up together in the end. And now, here she was, sitting in front of the very person who had caused much of her confusion and he was telling her he wanted to create a secret code.

She wasn't a spy.

Or afraid.

"We don't need a code," she said. "We just have to trust one another. I'm giving up everything—putting everything on the line—for you. For you to prove to me that I haven't misplaced my trust in you. That should be enough to carry us through anything your father throws our way."

Kimari didn't speak, move, or even blink in reaction to her statement. The only giveaway that he was still alive was the steady rise and fall of his chest as he stared her down.

Then, as if setting upon a decision he could live with, he said, "I know you don't want to hear this, princess, but you can be a real pain in the ass sometimes, you know that?"

She feigned horror. "Oh, the great and terrible pain of having you call me a a pain. Why don't you go take a look in the mirror?"

"I have." His lips curled in a delectable smile. "All I see is a handsome, talented, incredibly intelligent prince."

"And you're definitely not full of yourself at all."

He laid his hand across his heart. "Ouch. You hurt me, my lady."

She slapped his hand from his chest. "You're always so difficult to read. One minute you seem to be the most serious person in the room. The next, you're cracking jokes and pretending like nothing matters. Well, which is it?"

Her hand lingered on his, electricity surging between them.

Freed by Destiny

"I have a role to play, just like you, Astrid. I know you might not understand it—how could you when you've never lived the life of a royal?—but it is one I've learned to play to perfection. The world expects me to a certain way. Playboy. Warrior. Future king. My entire life, I have lived in my father's shadow, always fearful of stepping out of line. Of inadvertently harming his master plan. When I snuck out of the palace and met you in the meadow... that was the first time I had ever truly rebelled against him. So when you ask me how he'll react once we're back in the capital, I can honestly say I have no idea."

Although a part of her yearned to wrap her arms around him and console him for the things he'd endured as a child, she knew it would only serve to confuse her even more. Her head pounded and her throat felt thick and dry.

"I need sleep," she said, switching gears on their conversation with no explanation as to why.

He raised his eyebrows at her before his expression settled back into its usual slack, smug veneer. "You really don't want to establish a way for us to communicate then?"

She shook her head. "Not tonight, Kimari."

"And if we get to tomorrow and there's not time?"

The exhaustion of the day shoved against her, causing her temples to throb and her mind to go blank as she stared at him.

"I'm sorry," she said again. "I can't focus."

He rose from her bed and stormed across the room. Just before he disappeared through the tent flap, he turned back to look at her as he said, "In case we don't have an opportunity to establish something better in the morning. Just know that if I say to you,

23

'you're nothing more than a filthy winger,' what I'm really saying is: I love you; trust me."

Before Astrid had time to process the slur, he'd swept from her room into the darkness beyond. Nothing about this day had gone how she'd anticipated. And tomorrow she would surrender herself to the wolves.

Chapter Three

Sunlight filtered through the speckled windowpanes of Astrid's room in the ruined castle. How, after centuries of warfare, weather, and looters, the glass had survived was a complete mystery to her. Little specs of rainbows danced across her cover as she let the reality of the day process in her recesses of her mind. She'd agreed to turn herself over to Renard. Within the hour, she would portal to the designated spot with only Kimari at her side. Whatever the fate that awaited her, she could only pray that it didn't result in her death.

Filthy little wingers.

The audacity of his decision to choose that phrase to describe her left a bitter taste in her mouth. It didn't matter that he'd been hurt by her rejection or that she knew Renard would be looking for any crack to slam a wedge into. He would attempt to drive them apart. To make them question if they could trust one another.

That was, if he even allowed her live. At this point, she wasn't certain he would.

Pressing the heel of her palms into her eyes, Astrid groaned as she swung her feet off the bed. The stone floor was like ice, and she yelped as she hopped onto the t-shirt she'd left on the floor from the night before. Gooseflesh covered her skin as she rummaged in her pack to find a change of clothes. She sniffed her favorite black V-neck and, after determining it passed the smell test, pulled it on.

Thoughts raced through her mind as she selected a pair of black jeans to complete the look. After Renard's announcement and her conversation with Max—and then with Kimari—she'd been too exhausted to consider the vision she'd had of Penny.

She had not dreamt of her the night before.

She didn't know if that made what she'd experienced more real or less. Part of her didn't care. But she was left feeling baffled by the change in Penny's demeanor. Gone was the worrying, mothering friend she'd known her entire life. She'd been replaced with something much more… cold. And calculating. And yet, there was a part of her that knew Penny still cared about her. That she was worried about her. That she loved her.

Closing her eyes, she rubbed her temples in an attempt to alleviate the tension throbbing there. She couldn't think about this now. She couldn't consider what it meant that her mother had worked with Renard to develop her PEA. Or that they had tried to recreate the mythical queen.

Freed by Destiny

She trailed her fingers across the leather jacket with the Fairy Godmother's patch sewed into the back of it. She had morphed into something so different from the girl she'd been when they'd rescued her from Kaden all those months ago. She was stronger now. She trusted people more. But she also had more to lose.

A rap on the door was the only warning she had before Maya and Nalia pranced into the room. Without saying a word, Maya enveloped Astrid in a tight embrace.

"You don't have to do this," she whispered. "There has to be another way. We can run again. We can fight. We can—"

"Maya," Astrid said, cutting her friend's rambling off. "There's not another way. You worked for him. You know what he's like. If we don't surrender, he will kill every last magical in his quest to destroy or possess me. I'm surprised it took him this long to make this threat."

She squeezed her friend and held her that way until she felt the dampness of Maya's tears soaking into her hair.

"Stop that," Astrid chided as she extricated herself from Maya's embrace.

Nalia pawed at her legs and stared up at her, her eyes nearly bulging from her face.

I have to agree with Maya on this one, the dragon hissed in Astrid's mind. *If you go there, you will not return to us. I can feel it in my very essence, Astrid. He will consume you, just as he has countless others.*

What other choice do I have? She reared back at her. *Do you want me to willingly sacrifice innocent magicals in order to what, protect myself for just a bit longer? Well, I won't do it. I refuse to*

29

let him use me as a scapegoat for his heinous actions.

And if you go now, what is to stop him from killing those same magicals just because he can? Think about it, Astrid. Surely you can see that with you out of the way, he will have total reign to continue kidnapping, torturing, and killing magicals. All so that he can possess our magic. So that he can continue ruling—making himself an all-powerful god among men.

Astrid sighed heavily and turned her back on both her friends. She had been hoping no one would attempt to convince her stay. She'd already made her decision and there was nothing anyone could say or do that would persuade her change her mind. Her hands were already coated in the blood of humans and magicals alike. She would not stand by and let Renard continue to terrorize her people under the guise that he was searching for her.

She would not allow him to turn her people against her. If he killed her now, she would become a martyr to them. It might be enough to push them to rebel in earnest against him. Max, the rest of the E.L.Fs, the FGs, Layla—everyone who stood united against Renard would have a rallying cry to push forward.

She wouldn't be alive to see it, but at least her people would have a fire in their belly to fight for freedom.

Her death would have meaning.

"There are fates worse than death, Astrid," Maya said, her eyes wide as she stretched out a hand towards her.

Astrid took a good, hard look at her friend. Her cheeks were sunken, as if she hadn't been eating well, and there were deep bags beneath her eyes. Her skin was uncommonly pale. And her pink tipped hair lay flat and stringy against her skull. Gone was her contagious smile and her bubble gum. Gone was the feisty, vivacious woman Astrid had known this entire time. All that stood before her was a husk.

"Maya?" Astrid stammered. "Are you alright?"

She accepted her friend's hand and clung to her.

"Is Eldris…" She trailed off, uncertain how to finish that question.

"No," May replied. "It's nothing like that. I just… I couldn't sleep last night I was so worried about you. I can't shake the pit in my stomach screaming at me to force you to stay. To convince you that accepting Renard's terms and conditions now will ruin our chances of defeating him. We need you, Astrid. We need you to lead us. To unite us."

Astrid's chest tightened, and she desperately wanted to acknowledge the risk she was taking. But, although she wanted to, she couldn't bring herself to say that she was having her doubts as well. If she opened the door for doubt to cloud her decision, even if by just a little, she would chicken out of going with Kimari to surrender herself to the king.

"What other choice do I have?" Astrid asked. "If I stay here, you know as well as I do that Renard will not stop. At least when I'm there, I might be able to work from the inside. I might be able to stop him."

Maya's cheeks paled, her skin taking on a dim glow as she lowered her eyes. A swell of shame washed over Astrid.

"Even after all this time you know nothing of the king," Maya whispered. "You want to see the good in people. To believe that they can change. But Renard isn't capable of that. He doesn't have the capacity to feel empathy for others. Or to care if he hurts them. And I don't want you to end up in his web."

"Can't you see?" Astrid's lower lip trembled as she spoke. She closed her eyes as she let the truth settle into her. "I already am."

"And can't you see that you've been lying to yourself? Drak, Astrid, all we want is to protect you. And all you do is continue to sacrifice yourself—or try to. But why? Why can't you just let us help you?"

"I have!" Astrid screamed. Heat coursed through her body, and she couldn't stop her hands from twitching as she stared at her friend. "I have asked for help on numerous occasions. And I've given you each opportunities to shine. But... the weight of this crown doesn't rest on your brow, Maya. You're not the one the king is demanding to come to his court. Your hands won't be drenched in the blood of countless innocent magicals. I cannot—I will not—sit idly by when I have the chance to do something good. Why can't you understand that?"

She hadn't intended to become so angry, and now that she was, she didn't understand how she had gotten here. But she couldn't stop herself from continuing.

"I grew up believing my parents—the Diones—were actually my parents. Do you have any idea what it feels like to discover that your entire life was a lie? It was for my own protection. That's what everyone keeps telling me. That the Diones were heroes for sacrificing their only child and taking me in instead. But you know what that decision did to them? It destroyed them. They made that choice at the bequest of my mother. And their entire lives were ruined because of it. Drak... I don't even know if they did it willingly or if, because my mother was their queen, they felt like they had no other choice."

Her heart thrummed in her chest. There it was. The real reason she was so reticent to let anyone help her. To let anyone get too close. Maybe it had started out from the trauma she'd experienced as a child: from her adoptive parents' deaths, to the loss of Penny soon after discovering who she really was.

She'd been able to develop close friendships with many of the individuals trying to create a better world. She loved them all like she had never loved anyone else. It was the type of love forged by common experiences, trust, and the knowledge that they were all working towards the same goal.

But none of that changed the fact that she was their queen.

She could ask them to do anything.

And they couldn't really say no.

Not if she commanded it.

She hadn't done that to them. But still. She could never be sure that even her closest friends understood that she never would. That her requests were because of their friendship and their shared mission, not because of her status.

No one deserved to live under the thumb of a ruler, even if that ruler treated them like friends. Even if they would never abuse their power. That dynamic was always present. Always infiltrating her thoughts. Always limiting her ability to connect with them.

She held up her hands, cautioning Maya from responding. "I love you, Maya. But I could never forgive myself if I stayed here and let my people die. Their lives are my responsibility. Maybe one day, if we're ever able to take down Renard, we'll have a chance at creating something new. Something entirely different from what we've ever known. But right now, in this moment, I am the Astrid Shadowcrest, Queen of the Fae, the Firebird. It is my duty to protect my people. Even if you can't understand that."

The room went cold as shadows erupted from Astrid's body. They swarmed around Maya. Astrid's skin glowed a vibrant silver as more and more of the shadowy smoke poured from her. She couldn't think. She couldn't move. She couldn't react to Maya's screams as she was utterly consumed.

Chapter Four

What did you do? Nalia screamed. *Stop! Stop it!*

Astrid's entire body shook as she fought to rein in the power seeping from her. She stared straight at the ceiling as she clawed at the black, oily cloud spilling from lips, her fingertips, her toes. Silently she screamed as she watched Maya's skin turn a withered gray. She couldn't make it stop. She couldn't get control of her powers.

Something hard slammed into the back of her head, knocking her to the ground. She groaned as the oily cloud sucked back into her body like a pull cord on a toy. Gingerly, she touched the spot where she'd been struck. Her hand came away damp with silver blood. Closing her eyes, she fought off the nausea that threatened to overwhelm her.

"Maya," she groaned, crawling towards the last place she'd seen her friend.

"What the drak were you doing to her?" Max growled.

Astrid cracked an eye open to see him kneeling beside Maya. His eyes were hooded, and his jaw quivered as he gently lifted her limp body into his arms.

"Maya?" he whispered. "Can you hear me?"

Pressing his ear against her chest, Max went still as he listened for a heartbeat.

Astrid held her breath as she waited for any sign that she hadn't killed her friend. She didn't know what had happened to her. One minute she'd been in perfect control of her emotions, the next, the anger had billowed within her without any sign of ebbing. She'd exploded, her contempt for her circumstances pouring out of her in the form of her dark magic. She hadn't intended to harm Maya. She would never.

And yet, she had.

"Is she okay?" she asked, crawling closer to where Max cradled Maya in his arms.

Why did you attack us? Nalia asked, her voice quiet and timid in her mind.

Astrid turned towards the baby dragon. All she wanted was to wrap her in her arms and explain that she'd lost control. That she'd hadn't meant to hurt or scare anyone. Instead, all she could think about was the terror etched into Maya's face as she was drained of her life force by Astrid's magic.

"I'm sorry," she said out loud.

Freed by Destiny

Max lifted his head and met her gaze.

"She's still alive," he whispered. "But barely."

"Thank the Light," Astrid said. She took one of Maya's hands in her own and cradled it to her chest. "I swear I didn't mean to hurt her."

The air in the room became stifling as she waited for Max to respond. She didn't know which she wanted more: for him to chastise her for letting her emotions get the better of her, or show her grace, mercy, and forgiveness.

"I know you didn't mean to hurt her," Max said. "If there's one thing I know about you, Astrid Shadowcrest, it is that you are a lot tougher than you seem.

"Oh." She didn't know what else to say. Her mind was muddled from the blow he'd delivered to her head.

"What happened?" Maya asked. Her cheeks were gaunt, and her lips chapped. She looked as if she had visited the eternal after and returned all within a few minutes.

"Astrid lost control of her powers," Max explained slowly. "You were injured—nearly killed."

Astrid's hands went limp at his words. He hadn't even given her a chance to explain or apologize. He'd just dived right in without considering how much Maya would hate her if she knew the truth. She swallowed hard, unable to release Maya's hand as Max continued.

"I had to knock her out for a moment to preserve your life. She wouldn't—couldn't—stop herself," he corrected himself. His jaw tightened as he glanced between them. "You need to tell me what you were talking about before she lost control. We can't stop her from doing it again unless we know what triggered her."

"I'm sitting right here," Astrid said. "If you have something to say to me, you can."

Max glared at her with such contempt that she nearly fled the room. Instead, she forced herself to meet his eyes. Her internal core turned to ice.

"Haven't you done enough damage for one day, Astrid?"

A burning sensation filled her eyes as she stared at him, completely at a loss for words. She hadn't meant to hurt Maya. She never would.

She squeezed Maya's hand and whispered, "I didn't mean to, Maya. I'm…I'm so sorry." Her voice cracked with each of those last three words.

Maya's head lolled backwards as her body went limp.

"I think you should leave," Max said sternly.

Astrid lingered. She couldn't figure out the words to say. They all tasted of ash on her tongue.

Scrambling to her feet, she rushed towards the door.

"I'll make sure she's okay," Max said.

She glanced back at him. At Maya still cradled in his arms.

"I'm sorry," she whispered again before she dashed from the room.

Tears streamed down her cheeks as she ran through the castle. Her watch buzzed, reminding her of the time. Of her rendezvous with Kimari. Of her return to Renard. All her nightmares about harming the people she loved most were slowly coming true. She'd hurt Maya. Whether intentionally or not, she'd released her magic on her as if she were nothing more than a fly to swat.

And she wouldn't even be around to explain what had happened. Why she had turned on her. How she'd ended up in this position. She didn't know if she would ever be able to explain.

Turning a corner, she slammed into something sturdy and hard. She stumbled backwards, tripping over own feet as her arms flailed, trying to keep herself from falling.

A strong hand caught her beneath the armpits and heaved her upwards.

"Whoa there, lady," Bear said as he steadied her on her feet.

The rampage of thoughts battling within her stilled at his warm, gentle voice. She peered up at him, her cheeks stained and her hair disheveled.

"I did something horrible," she whispered, clinging to Bear's shirt.

"I can't believe you've done something so terrible as all this," he said, wiping away a tear before it fell from her cheek. "Come on then, tell me what happened."

Although she wanted to tell him, she didn't want the last image of his face to be a look of horror. She didn't deserve more than that, but she desperately wanted to remember him like this: looking at her with love in eyes—and a touch of concern. But mainly love. She couldn't risk seeing the light disappear from his smile. Or the fear and disgust replace the warmth emanating from him. She was about to turn herself over to a world full of darkness.

She couldn't—wouldn't—have the last memory of her friend and protector degrade into just another nightmare.

"I can't…" she stammered. "I'm sorry."

She hugged him tightly.

Pulling back, she kissed him gently on the cheek. "No matter what anyone says, I love you."

"What's all this about then?" Bear asked. He scanned her face, his eyebrows rising, but Astrid simply shook her head.

"Tell Maya I love her. Tell her… tell her I didn't mean for any of this happen." She started to hug him again but knew that if she allowed herself to continue receiving comfort from him, that she wouldn't be able to leave. Not until she'd resolved the tension between her and Max. Not until she knew if Maya was going to be alright or not. The longer she waited to leave, the more difficult it would be to carry through with her plan.

Grinding her teeth together she turned her back on Bear.

"Don't turn your back on me," he said. "It won't do."

She ignored him. She was too exhausted from little sleep, the physical drain using the dark magic had taken on her, and the emotional toll of seeing Maya on the ground.

Broken.

She had broken her. And she refused to do that to anyone. She didn't deserve their compassion. Or their love.

Bear gripped her shoulder and yanked her back. "When I tell you to stop, I expect you to at least acknowledge that I'm speaking to you."

"Yeah, well." She wiped her hand across her face to hide the fact that she was an emotional wreck.

"Whatever has happened can't be as all bad as all this."

"But it is."

He hunched forward so that he was at eye-level with her. "Why don't you tell me what's going on? At least then I can at least try to help."

Her watch buzzed again, a message from Kimari popping on the screen.

The deadline to arrive is in ten minutes. Where are you?

Bear's eyes trailed down to her wrist. His cheeks gleamed a brilliant silver for the briefest of moments. "I know you think you need to do this, but you don't."

She shook her head. "I've already explained myself to you—and the rest of the council. I'm not doing it again."

She lifted her chin and squared her shoulders, forcing herself to appear the regal, resolute queen she wanted to be. Even if she didn't feel that way on the inside.

"I am doing this, Bear. Whether you think this is a necessary decision or not, that choice doesn't belong to you. And I am so exhausted by having to explain myself. Is it that you don't trust me to make the right decisions? Is that it?"

"No! Of course not."

"Then why? Why do you always try to convince me to choose a different path? Why do you—"

"Because I love you! We all do. And we don't want to see you put yourself in harm's way. It has nothing to do with your capabilities. If anything, you're the most capable of us all. But darlin, you have to understand. You feel the burden to protect us, but we feel it too. Every single one of us would die for you."

She shook her head. Those were the exact words she had been dreading hearing. She wasn't willing to sacrifice him or anyone else. It was why she'd given up her healing abilities to save Max. It was why she was choosing to turn herself over to Renard.

"It doesn't matter. I'm leaving. Kimari is waiting." Flames danced between her fingers as she glared at Bear. "Don't try to stop me again."

"I won't try to stop you," he said softly. "But I won't let you go believing that no on here loves you. Just tell me what happened."

"You want to know? Fine. I'll tell you. I lost control, Bear. I got angry, and I couldn't stop the darkness from seeping out of me. I couldn't stop it from attacking Maya. And she…" She broke into a sob. "I hurt her."

Without a word, Bear enveloped her in his arms, cradling her to his chest, and she sobbed against him.

"I didn't mean to," she whispered.

"Hush," Bear cooed. "You didn't mean to. Maya will understand."

"How can you say that?"

"Did you forget that you hurt me once before?" He held her at arms' length and peered into her eyes. "Whatever this power is within you, it something that cannot be contained once it's unleashed. And I promise you, Astrid, Maya will understand. You just have to give her time."

"I don't have time." Her watch began vibrating incessantly. Sighing deeply, she tapped the answer button and Kimari's face projected into the space between her and Bear.

"Where are you?" he asked. "We don't have much time left."

Closing her eyes, Astrid steeled herself for the inevitable. She was leaving this place. Her friends. The world she had come to know. She wasn't certain she could save them, but she would draked if she was going to give up without a fight.

"I'm coming," she said, then ended the call before Kimari could respond.

Turning her attention back to Bear, she slid her hand into his. "Promise me you'll try to explain what happened to Maya?"

He nodded once. A single tear escaped the corner of his eye. Its silvery glow disappeared into his mass of beard.

"Tell the others…" she began. "Well, I honestly don't know what you should tell them. Words cannot explain…"

"I know," Bear said. "Leave it to me."

She squeezed his hand. "You're still the best Fairy Godmother a girl could ask for."

"And you're still a giant pain in my arse." Bear grinned at her.

She shoved him in the shoulder playfully. "And here I thought…"

"But also my favorite charge, in the history of charges," he added.

"You're definitely not the cheesy type at all."

"Me?" Bear feigned dismay. "Cheesy? Why, I've never been accused of a more delectable adjective before. Keep 'em coming."

Her laughter filled the hall before she sobered again. "I should go."

"Whatever you do," Bear said, "stay alive."

"I can't make any promises."

"I know. But still. Try."

She didn't say anything as she turned from him. If this was the last time they spoke, she wanted to remember the humor and the tenderness with which he interacted with her. She wanted to remember that she had at least one friend left in this world who didn't care what mistakes she'd made in the past or how weak she was now. He loved her. He wanted to see her thrive.

She just hoped she would survive long enough in Renard's court to see him again.

Chapter Five

"You certainly made it here just in the nick of time," Kimari growled at her from the corner of his mouth as Astrid joined him by Janae. They stood in a small courtyard. Bees filled the air with a low hum as they bounced from one flower to the next. Although it was a serene setting, Astird couldn't help but feel as if it were a mask for the horrors she was about to face.

Janae nodded to Astrid, her features serene and nearly expressionless. If it hadn't been for the wrinkles around the corners of her mouth, Astrid might have missed how tense the queen was.

"Once you turn yourself in, we may not be able to get you back," Janae said. "So you must be sure this is what you want to do."

"It is," Astrid said. "Trust me, if I saw another way out of this, don't you think I'd take it?"

"I'm not exactly keen on returning to my father's court, either," Kimari said. "You think being his enemy is bad, try being his son. I've seen what he's like when he's displeased. I can't imagine the wrath my betrayal will incur."

"Then why return?" Janae asked coldly. "Why not stay here and live in the mess you've made for the rest of us by accepting Astrid's foolhardy plan?"

"Maybe because I believe things can be better."

"Maybe? That doesn't sound like a resounding acknowledgement that your choice to return to your father's court is a good idea. In fact, it smacks of indecision."

Kimari's back straightened. He turned steely eyes towards her and said, "At least I am putting my actions where my mouth is. All you do is sit back and let others fight for you. What kind of leader does that? And I believe in Astrid. If anyone can get us out of this debacle, it'll be her."

Astrid smiled at him. Although she was still furious with him for using the slur against her last night, she appreciated that he was standing up for her in front of Janae. Not many could stand up to the elf's rigid countenance, but he had.

"Thank you," she whispered.

He cocked his head towards her. "About last night…"

Before he could continue, one of Janae's elves stepped forward and summoned the portal. Astrid barely had time to blink before the portal ripped a hole through time and space before them.

"I'll see you on the other side," Kimari said with a wink before he stepped into the portal.

Astrid glanced behind her. Several elves stood in a semi-circle around her, their faces somber as she continued to linger at the entry to the portal.

"What are you waiting for?" Janae asked. "Either go or remain here. The choice is yours, no matter what the consequences."

She stepped into the portal just as the door leading into the chamber swung open and Maya came rushing into the room. Her eyes widened as Astrid felt herself begin to disappear. Maya lunged towards her, her blonde hair flouncing as she stretched out a hand to take Astrid's.

"I'm sorry," Astrid whispered. "I'm so sorry."

Darkness tugged at the corners of her vision as the familiar frenzy of sensation pulled at her navel. One moment she was standing in a large room with the elves and fae surrounding her. The next, she was slammed into the cold, hard stone of Renard's throne room.

Robotic guards swarmed around her, their pistols pointed straight at her heart. She didn't fight against them as they cuffed her hands and forced a collar around her neck. She didn't speak as they turned their backs on her and stood at attention.

Her eyes darted around the room, searching for any sign of Kimari. There was nothing to indicate where he had gone or if he was still alive. Digging her nails into the palm of her hands, she forced herself to focus. To think. If she was going to survive whatever darkness Renard had in store for her, she would need to be alert. No matter how much she wished she could return to the dilapidated castle and throw herself into Maya's arms, she knew that wasn't possible.

Footsteps echoed from across the hall, drawing her attention away from her thoughts. She swallowed hard, steeling herself for a confrontation with the king. Lowering her head, she assumed a bowing pose as she waited. It was better to start with reverence and lure the king in with honey before striking. At least then he might not immediately order her execution. She was a traitor to the crown, after all. She would deserve nothing less.

Sleek leather shoes stopped before her. Lifting her gaze, Astrid noted the pistol holstered to his hip and the dagger on his thigh. She assessed the way his fingers curled into a tight fist and the way his eyes narrowed at her as he stared her down.

She hadn't seen Renard in person since the day she'd saved his life from Layla's assassination attempt. She wondered if he was also thinking of that day or if he would even care that she had shown him that kindness.

It hadn't been for him. Still, she hoped he would honor the traditions passed down for millennia. She had saved his life. Would he spare hers in return?

"You have been a royal pain in my arse," he said.

She almost chortled. Why would he think she would be anything else? He had murdered her entire family. He had attempted to murder her, too. How much blood was on his hands? The amount was unfathomable to her. And yet, she couldn't think of a quip to respond with. Instead, she chose silence.

"I seem to recall you being a lot chattier the last time you were here," Renard continued. "I think I like you better this way."

He walked around her. Astrid remained completely still as he made his assessment. She couldn't use her magic. If he had been able to block her abilities in the field where she'd met Kimari, she had to believe he was blocking them now. And, with her hands manacled, there was little she could do to fight against him. She needed to be smart about how she approached their conversation. She needed to figure out a way to convince him that she wasn't a threat as long as she was within his walls.

"I should have killed you then."

He kicked her in the back of the knees, sending her crashing to the floor. Her chin slammed into the floor, scraping her skin. Warm blood seeped from the wound as she rolled over and sat up. She stared at him as he smirked down at her.

"Such a waste," he said, almost as an aside.

"Father." Kimari's voice carried on the breeze. He smirked at Astrid as he stepped into the circle formed by the robots. He placed a hand on Renard's shoulder. "See how I have served you."

"No," Astrid whispered.

The fluttering sensation in her stomach intensified and she wretched on the stone before their feet. Kimari and Renard stepped backwards, their shoes scuffling on the floor as they avoided being splattered by her vomit.

Renard's bellowing laugh overpowered her whimpering.

"You have done well, my son," Renard said, clapping Kimari on the back. "One day, when the time is right, I will look forward to leaving the kingdom in your capable hands."

"Thank you, Father," Kimari said.

He sounded robotic, as if he were just going through motions. He avoided Astrid's gaze, always looking just past her whenever she looked at him. She'd been such a fool. She'd trusted his sister.

And been betrayed. Now, she had hurt Max.

And for what?

Empty promises Kimari never intended to keep. She bucked against her restraints. If she had been in control of her magic, she would doused them both in flames and left nothing but bone and ash.

But she couldn't.

She was bound. She was their captive.

And, for the first time in a long time, she was afraid.

Chapter Six

Soldiers prodded at Astrid's back as they led her, blindfolded, through the castle. She tried to count the turns as they guided her, but quickly lost count when one of them picked her up and flung her over his shoulder. She could tell from the way she bounced that they climbed at least one flight of stairs.

When they finally came to a halt, the soldier plopped her onto the ground with all the grace of a sack of potatoes and withdrew her blindfold. She blinked into the sudden brilliance of sunlight filtering through large windows. A door creaked open behind her and she spun around, half expecting to see Kimari waiting for her.

Instead, she found herself staring into a lavishly furnished room. A large bed with posts shaped like tree branches and gilded in glittering gold consumed most of the space. Green and gold tapestries shrouded the stone walls, creating a warm, earthy vibe.

Without a word, they removed the manacles around her wrists before patting her down. They collected her watch and blades and then shoved her to the bedroom. The soft click of the lock sliding into place was the only indication that she had been left alone. For a moment, Astrid wrapped her arms tight around her shoulders and let the weight of where she was settle into her bones.

She was a prisoner, albeit in a gilded cage, but a prisoner nonetheless.

Tears cascaded down her cheeks as she flung herself on the bed. Doubts swirled within her as she replayed the encounter with Renard. Had Kimari been lying to her the entire time, or was this what he had been talking about? At every turn, he seemed to give her more and more reasons to doubt him.

A soft knock on the door drew her attention. Lifting her head ever so slightly, she spied a maid enter the room and come to stand at the foot of the bed.

"I'm here to collect the rest of your things, miss."

She glared up at the maid. "The soldiers already took everything. What else could you possibly want?"

The maid's cheeks flushed a deep red as she bowed her head and mumbled, "I was told to take everything, including your undergarments."

Pinching the brow of her nose, Astrid sucked in a deep breath. It was one thing for Renard to demand her watch and her weapons, but to take her skivvies. That was too far.

"You most certainly will not take them."

If it was possible, the maid's cheeks deepened even further as she said, "King Renard instructed me personally, miss. If you don't comply... he told me to offer you this choice: either I take them or the soldiers waiting outside do." She clasped her hands tightly in front of her as she trembled. "If I could be so bold, I am, quite frankly, the better option."

Astrid didn't doubt it. "Fine."

She stripped her clothes off and left them crumpled on the floor. Taking a throw blanket from the bed, she wrapped herself in it. "What am I supposed to wear?"

The maid motioned towards a wardrobe resting against one wall that Astrid hadn't noticed before. "Everything you need can be found in there." With that, she picked up the articles of clothing and dashed from the room without another word.

The moment the door shut, Astrid flung open the wardrobe to reveal an array of dresses, blouses, and pants, all in neutral tones. She cringed when she saw them. She hated them all. Hated what they represented.

The door creaked behind her as it swung open.

"Queen Astrid!" A woman gasped from behind. "What are you doing?"

Cold hands landed on her shoulders, sending a shiver down her spine. The same maid from before made tsking sounds as she grabbed a random dress from the wardrobe and shoved it into Astrid's hands.

"Why are you here?" Astrid asked. "Surely, there is something else for you to be doing."

The maid slapped her across the cheek. It was gentle enough

not to leave a mark, but the sting kindled fire in her belly as she regarded the maid with a keener eye.

"What was that for?" she demanded.

"Stop being such a child," the maid said. Gone was pretense of her timidity from before.

"Who are you to speak to me like that?" Astrid growled through clenched teeth.

Although she'd experienced pain on numerous occasions, her healing magic had always acted quickly. Without it, she was coming to realize just how painful even the most minor of blows could have. She winced as she gently touched her cheek.

"King Renard has ordered me to prepare you for the ceremony. And to ensure you know your place here in the palace."

"What are you talking about? What ceremony?"

The maid didn't respond as she went to the wardrobe and selected a dusty pink blouse and tan trousers to go with it. Laying the outfit on the bed, she then went to the dressing table and opened one of the many jewelry boxes. Astrid hadn't noticed them before. Now that she had, the faintest hint of what was to come whispered at the back of her mind.

The maid picked a simple, rose-gold necklace with a delicate star pendant dangling from its chain. She pulled the matching earrings from the stand next to the jewelry box and laid both of them on table.

"You will wear these. Come on now. You don't have all day."

Astrid considered fighting against these orders, but a part of her was curious to see what Renard had up his sleeve. She also couldn't help feeling the slightest bit anxious about seeing Kimari again. He'd lied to her, yes, but surely he had advocated on her behalf. How else would she have ended up as a guest instead of in the gallows?

"We don't have all day," the maid prodded.

Sighing, Astrid forced herself to wander over to the bed. She trailed her fingers across the clothing. They were simple, soft, and well-made. They were the type of the clothing she'd seen the royal family don when they'd appeared on the broadcasts. But they were not something she would have ever chosen for herself.

"I can't wear these," she said.

"Well, unfortunately, my dear, you don't exactly have a choice. King Renard employed his personal stylist to select these items for you. And you will wear them without argument."

Without permission, the maid ran her fingers through Astrid's hair. Astrid flinched at the touch. In response, the maid pinched her, hard on the fleshy part of her underarm. Wincing in pain, Astrid turned on the woman.

"My role is to ensure you look presentable—more than presentable. You are to be Prince Kimari's wife, after all. What a love story it is."

Her voice was cold as she spoke. There was no flutter of awe or excitement, just a hardness that underpinned each syllable.

"Why are you doing this?" Astrid asked.

The maid shook her head. "I don't understand what you mean, dear. My aim is to serve my kingdom and my king. Even if that means taking care of a traitorous winger, like yourself."

The insult stung more than it should have. She had known, when she'd chosen to come with Kimari, that she would face insults and backhanded compliments meant to tear her down. But, the choice had been either come here with Kimari and delay Renard's attacks on her people, or watch as the king released a scourge upon her people. She had vowed to protect them, even if it cost her everything else.

She smiled sweetly at the maid. "I love the prince and I do want to please his majesty." The words tasted bitter on her tongue. "But, you cannot force me to wear something I don't want to," she said.

The maid laughed.

"You really think you still hold power here, don't you?" She twirled a lock of Astrid's hair between her fingers, her lips pulling down into an expression of pure disgust. "Your magic has been taken from you. You have no friends here. What do you expect to be able to do? You either play your role or King Renard will see to it that you are punished. And trust me, my dear, you do not want to know the extent of his power."

Searching the maid's face, Astrid noticed the scars running down her left cheek and spreading across her neck. Burn scars. The flesh was pulled taunt and was shiny as it molded over what would have been blisters and sloughed off flesh.

"What happened to you here?" she asked before she could stop herself.

The maid shook her head. "Come. Before you get into those nice clean clothes, I need to get you properly bathed. You are a mess."

Although Astrid did not want to follow the maid's commands, she couldn't help but feel that perhaps she, too, was a victim of this place. This kingdom. Astrid knew firsthand that learning to put on the mask of a loyal servant was one of the many ways someone could survive in this world. Maybe the maid was too uncomfortable to reveal her secrets now, but Astrid made a vow to herself to keep trying. She could befriend her. Learn her story.

The maid led her through a door at the back of her bedchamber and into a large, modernized bathroom. A walk-in shower lined the entire back of the room with a double vanity and mirror set on one side and a full-length window on the other. Natural morning light filled the room, making flecks in the white marble sparkle. Bottles of perfumes, lotions, and makeup were arranged in neat rows on the sink.

"I don't understand," Astrid whispered. "Why is he doing this?"

"What else would you expect our king would do for the woman who is to marry his son?"

She cocked at eyebrow at the maid but said nothing as she ran her fingers along the smooth surface of the vanity. Everything in this space was immaculate. It was insane to her. The king wanted her dead. She had zero doubt about that. Was he attempting to lure her into a sense of security before flipping the switch and becoming the cruel, brutal tyrant she knew him to be? He was like a cat toying with its prey before delivering a fatal blow. And, like a cat, she had every reason to believe that King Renard was enjoying the game.

"What should I call you?" Astrid asked, turning her attention back to the maid. "It seems strange to keep calling you 'maid' in my head."

"You may call Miss."

"Is that your real name?"

Miss sighed heavily. "I wouldn't expect you to know decorum, but no. It is the title all the royal maids are given."

"And what if I want us to be friends? You don't have to serve me…"

"I am happy with my station in life. Thank you, but I would prefer if you maintained a sense of professionalism when addressing me."

Stung, Astrid simply nodded.

She may have appeared young, but Miss was certainly comfortable standing up for herself.,

Astrid stepped into the shower and turned the knob. Warm water cascaded on her, easing the tension in her muscles and washing away the grime.

She showered quickly. She still wasn't convinced Miss wouldn't step into the shower when Astrid was least expecting her and stab her in the back with a blade. It was exactly the type of thing she would expect Renard to do. Give her a false sense of security and then strike. She would have to remain vigilant.

She didn't fight Miss as she wrapped her in a pre-warmed towel and sat her in front of the vanity. Miss applied a natural looking application of makeup to Astrid's face before leading her back into the bedroom to dress her. Briefly, Astrid considered telling the maid she didn't need help getting ready for whatever Renard had planned for her but decided against it. If she was going to survive, she needed to learn how to play Renard's game. If dressing like this, looking pretty, and acting grateful for the chance to save her people from genocide was what it would take, then she was willing to do it.

Freed by Destiny

When Miss had finished dressing her, she stood back and regarded Astrid with an assessing eye. Her lips twisted into a small scowl.

"What's wrong?" Astrid asked.

"There's something missing."

Astrid examined herself in the mirror. She looked clean, fresh, and dainty. The pink tones of the blouse complimented the undertones in Astrid's complexion. Her skin shimmered slightly from the powder Miss had applied as a finishing touch. It would mask any faint embarrassment—or anger—Astrid experienced. She wondered if that was a conscious decision on Miss's part or if this type of makeup was common among the nobility. It wouldn't surprise her if the higher-ranked humans both coveted her people's magical gifts as well as their bodies.

Miss rummaged around in a few of the jewelry boxes on the dressing table.

"Ah ha!" She clutched a small broach in her hand and pinned it onto Astrid's blouse.

Astrid curled her hands into fists at the sight of the signal. The dragon eating its own tail. Ruby eyes gleamed back at her.

The emblem of the king.

Her stomach twisted in knots. Resisting the urge to wrench the adornment from her clothing, Astrid peered at her reflection. *You have to make them believe you're madly, undeniably, and incandescently in love with Kimari.* She waited for Penny to respond. To tell her she'd brought this upon herself. To give her a boost of confidence. But all there was, was her.

Through gritted teeth and choking bile, she smiled at the maid as she brushed her fingers over the brooch.

The maid patted her on the head and whispered, "You can survive here."

Astrid's heart thundered in her chest. She struggled to find a response as the maid slipped through her bedroom door without another word. Breathing in deeply, she attempted to clear her mind from her racing thoughts. She needed to be calm. Clear headed. And, more importantly, alert if she was going to survive.

A set of guards tapped on her door before entering without permission. They blindfolded her again before leading her through the palace's corridors. With each step, another thought floated through her mind. So many questions nipped at her heels. Was this all a ruse? Or did the king really intend for her to marry his son? And for what purpose? She desperately wanted a moment alone with Kimari so they could talk, but she knew she wouldn't have an opportunity to.

He'd tried to warn her. Tried to tell her they'd be kept apart. That he would be forced to play his part. That she would start to doubt him because of the role he needed to play. Uncertainty coiled within her belly.

When they finally stopped and removed the blindfold, a set of large doors carved with emblems of Lunameedian and Szarmian history loomed before them. Astrid scanned the intricate designs as she waited for the doors to swing open, allowing her entry into whatever lay on the other side. The carvings depicted stories she'd read about since joining with the elves. Histories of the creation of the world. The battle between the gods. The chaos of darkness. The sacrifices made by countless heroes through the ages. Her eyes lingered on a panel near the top of the door. It depicted Queen Amaleah—the woman Penny claimed to have been modeled after. Her story was so ancient it was more myth than history.

For generations, she'd been spoken of as the savior who would return. Who would bring and spread light unto the world. Different tales provided different lenses from which to view her. Astrid doubted anyone would ever know her true history. Many of the first-hand accounts of her era had been destroyed during the Great Darkness. Those that had been kept safe were difficult to understand. Not even the top scholars of their age had been able to decipher them entirely. So, what they had were fragments of a life, mostly told from the perspective of those had lived some three hundred years after her death.

Still, there was a chance Renard had more manuscripts and artifacts from that time period than what were easily accessible by the general public. Perhaps, if she were lucky, she would be able to convince the royal librarian to grant her access to read and research to her heart's content. She doubted it, knowing Renard's penchant for cruelty. She doubted he would allow her any of the comforts she longed for.

The doors vibrated before silently sliding open to reveal a small table adorned with countless platters of food sitting in the middle of the room. Chairs wrapped around its edges. All but one were occupied. Neither Kimari nor Kali met her gaze. She glared at them, her skin taking on a shimmering glow.

A few other members of the extended royal family dined on the elaborate meal. Notably, Renard's wife was not present. Although Astrid found that odd, she decided it wasn't worth the effort of asking after her.

"Ah, Astrid," King Renard said as he rose from his chair. "It is a pleasure you were able to join us, albeit a little late."

He nodded towards the empty chair.

She clenched her fists as she regarded him. Here he was, feasting on an assortment of cheeses, meats, fresh fruits and vegetables, and desserts. It made her want to gag.

"Sit. Eat. You are our guest, after all." Renard swept his arm towards the dining table. "We have everything you could ever possibly desire. The chicken is especially good tonight."

Although Astrid desperately wanted to flee from this room, she knew doing so would ruin her chances of getting out of here alive.

Play the game.

Forcing a smile onto her lips, she sank into the empty chair. It was situated on the opposite side of the table from Kimari and Kali, closest to Renard. An elderly man with wiry glasses and a slim, lanky frame sat to her left. He smelled of sweet cigars and the musty, old-man scent she remembered from some of the patrons of The Wand. It was familiar and made her have a fleeting sense of nostalgia as she turned towards him and said, "Hello."

He shifted his gaze towards her, his glasses tripling the size of his eyes.

"You are shorter than I imagined. And not as tough looking." He jabbed his index finger into her arm. Hard. When she jerked back in surprise, he sniffed at her. "Here I thought I would meet a warrior queen. And what did Renard bring me instead?"

He grimaced as he looked above her head towards the king. "You brought someone I couldn't imagine defeating a single soldier, let alone demolishing some of your armies."

Astrid curled her fingers around the fabric floating above her thighs. If Renard hadn't been blocking her abilities, she would show this man exactly how powerful she could be. As it was, she had to contend herself with the fact that the man, presumably one

68

of Renard's advisors, didn't see her as a threat. As long as Renard believed he had the upper hand, she would remain relatively safe.

Still, his tone of voice and assessing gaze made her want to throttle him.

Renard pointed a nearly clean drumstick at them. "This one is a lot more vicious than she appears, Cyrus."

Cyrus leaned towards her until she could smell the fish on his breath. "Tell me why, out of so many, you were the chosen one. What makes you so special?"

It took everything within her not flinch away from him. Deep down, she knew he was attempting to psyche her out—but she'd had her fill of traitorous men taking what they wanted from her and leaving her behind in their wake.

She smiled at him sweetly. "Whatever do you mean?"

She batted her eyes at him, even as her frustration roiled within her.

His lips twitched, and Astrid was certain he was going to erupt in a torrent of curses at her. His cheeks flushed such a deep crimson she almost became concerned for his wellbeing.

Almost.

His cheeks sucked in, hollowing out his face in a way that made him appear more skeletal than human. She waited patiently for him to respond.

Eventually, Cyrus turned his attention towards Renard and said, "You will have your hands full with this one."

She rolled her eyes at him. "All I did was ask a simple question."

Delicately, she laid her hand on his arm. She reveled at his flinch. She knew exactly what he'd meant. It was the same thing so many humans had either outright said to her growing up or insinuated with their snide comments and harsh glares.

She was a fae. She was less than nothing. She did not deserve to exist.

She couldn't understand why, after all these years, this man refused to see her or her family as anything other than chattel.

He pointed his fork at her, and a bit of lettuce fell from it. Astrid covered her mouth to hide the smile.

"Listen here, girl. You should learn to show some respect for your elders."

"And did my 'elders' ever wonder what became of me? Did my elders ever stop to consider the impact this whole ordeal is having upon me? No. They just try to kill me. Or imprison me. Maybe both. But I don't care." She turned her attention to Renard. "I am not some pawn that can be used whenever the need arises and then discarded again when it's not convenient to have me around."

"I think you're mischaracterizing," Cyrus began.

"I assure you, I am not 'mischaracterizing' what my life has been." She jabbed her finger into his arm.

His eyes widened, trailing her finger back to her side as if he couldn't believe she'd actually touched him. His lips quivered.

"Magicals have been treated with the greatest of respect," Renard cut in. His voice sliced through Astrid. She shivered as she regarded him with a cold glare.

Freed by Destiny

"If you call being forced to work for unlivable wages, captured and killed in your pursuit for more power, and being hunted down like chattel, well, I would like to see you live in the conditions you have forced my people into."

She did not look away from him as she finished her reply. She wanted to see him squirm under the pressure of being confronted with the atrocities he had ordered. She'd had a vision of him apologizing for what he'd done to her people.

Instead, he smirked at her as Cyrus said, "You see? What did I tell you?"

Cyrus rose from his seat and straightened his tie.

"I am in awe of you, Your Majesty." He gestured towards Astrid. "Although I can see the appeal of bringing in one of her kind, I am afraid I've had my fill of conversation for the evening."

Renard slammed his hands on the table. A loud boom reverberated through the dining hall. Gooseflesh covered Astrid's arms. She looked down at her hands, not wanting to see the anger deepening the lines on the king's face.

"Sit down." Renard's voice was cold and calculating. Hidden beneath the calmness, a thread of anger laced its way through his words. "I have not dismissed you yet."

Astrid thought Cyrus would risk leaving the king to stew in his anger. His cheeks flushed a pale crimson and his hands balled into tight fists at his sides. He cleared his throat once, twice, and then a third time before finally sitting back down in his chair.

"Excellent," Renard said, his voice more relaxed now. He lifted his glass towards Cyrus and bowed his head slightly. "You will see what bringing her here will mean for our future."

Although his words did not contain malice, his tone did. Astrid stole a glance at Kimari, who was busily chatting with his sister. Neither of them looked at her, even as she attempted to catch their eyes.

"You will forgive me for saying this," Renard said.

Astrid shifted her attention back to the king. Crumbs from the biscuit he'd bitten into tumbled down his beard and onto the table. He didn't seem to notice them as he took a second bite before gulping wine from his glass.

"I have wanted you to belong to our family for such a long time now, I can't believe you're really here." He smiled at her, as if they were friends, and Astrid's stomach roiled with disgust.

"Was that before or after you wanted me dead?" she asked, cocking one eyebrow at Renard.

It was a ballsy move, but it was one she was willing to take if it meant seeing the look of utter disbelief and shock cross Renard's face.

Even if it was fleeting.

"You are an ungrateful little winger, aren't you? After all that I've done for you. This is how you repay me?" He sneered at her. "I never should have agreed to this idiotic plan."

"Father," Kali said sweetly.

Astrid turned her attention to the woman who had betrayed her. Despite everything that had transpired between them—or maybe because of it—she longed to have a moment with her. It could never happen. Kali had made her choice. And she'd chosen her father.

Freed by Destiny

Kali yawned behind her hand. "It has been a long few days, hasn't it?"

Renard's features softened, the purplish-red color in his cheeks fading back to their usual tan.

"I'm sure Queen Astrid has a lot to think about given her new circumstances." She yawned again and Astrid began to suspect this was more ruse than reality. "Perhaps we should all retire for a while. Give our...er... guest a chance to acclimate to what her life will be like moving forward."

"Gee, thanks," Astrid said. It took everything within her not to slam her hands on the table and release the frustration building within her. She was nothing but a puppet to them all. A plaything to be used and discarded at will. As it was, she ground her teeth in silence and waited for the king to react to his daughter's request.

Renard's lips twitched and his nostrils flared as if he were fighting a battle against himself about what to do and say next. He glanced between his children, his brow furrowing. "Fine."

Astrid released a breath she hadn't realized she'd been holding. The tension in her shoulders subsided, leaving her feeling drained. She smiled, timidly at Kali, but stopped when she realized the princess was pointedly looking away from her.

"Guards, take our guest back to her quarters to rest." Renard pointed a meaty finger at Astrid. "I expect you to show some gratitude for our hospitality when you join us for dinner."

Astrid kept her moth sealed shut as one of the guards placed his hand beneath her elbow and steered her towards the door. As they passed by Kali's chair, the princess abruptly pushed her chair back from the table, knocking into Astrid. She sneered as she stared down at her.

"You need to learn manners befitting your new station in life." Kali's voice dripped with venom. Her eyes narrowed and drifted downwards before snapping back up. "Father, would you allow me to train our new... friend... on the etiquette of court life? I don't want her to embarrass our family when she and Kimari make their debut."

Renard's body stiffened. His eyes took on a paranoid, mischievous glint as he stared at his daughter. "Do you really that's wise, Kaliope?"

She batted away his concern with a tinkling laugh. Her voice was far too cheerful and soothing to be natural. Astrid had heard her during their time together and this immaculate, polished air she was portraying was nothing like the rough and tumble warrior Astrid knew. Unless she was a supremely more accomplished actor than Astrid was prepared to give her credit for, this was a display for her father's benefit.

"I can take care of myself, Father. But, if you're worried a powerless, broken, little speck of a fae can hurt me, then, by all means, send a guard to protect me."

Renard tapped his finger on his jaw as he considered Kali's proposition.

"So be it," he said with a sigh, "but you'll take a guard with you. And Kimari."

"Father, I really don't think..."

Kali's words deadened on her tongue as Renard lifted a hand.

"Astrid will be your brother's wife and therefore, a representation of him. He should have a hand in her training."

Kali's jaw tightened and her back stiffened. "Yes, Father."

Freed by Destiny

Astrid scrambled to her feet only to be yanked towards the door by the guard.

"We will send someone to collect you when Princess Kaliope is ready for your training," Renard said. "And Astrid?"

Her back stiffened, but she did not turn to face him. Her head pounded at the thought of training with Kali. Of being in the same room with her for countless hours. How many times had she betrayed her? How many times had she used her most precious secrets to hurt her? The iron band around her heart tightened as she set a resolve to play the part of a forgiving queen, but to never let Kali get close to her again.

"I will expect you to cooperate with them."

She nodded but didn't say a word as she followed the guard from the dining hall. All she had was a glimmer of hope that Kimari would stay true to his word and find a way to help her.

Chapter Seven

Astrid stared at the ceiling above her bed, counting cracks in the stone. She'd been laying there for hours, her thoughts leaping from one nightmare to the next. Images of her friends' bodies, mangled by the war, lay across a battlefield. Fae hung from gallows lining the streets—worse than the hostile takeover twenty years before. The sunken eyes of magical creatures stared lifelessly at her as their carcasses were discarded in mounds. They smoldered, wisps of smoke curling from the fire kindled beneath them.

Would this be the fate of the magical world?

She'd thought coming here might give her people a fighting chance. That it would give Max and Janae time to recoup and plan a strategy that would work against Renard.

But she knew he would never give up. He wasn't just cruel.

Or power hungry. He hated magicals. Hated them for having something he could never truly possess. Hated them for their traditions and their connection with the world.

Hated them for having more power, influence, and support than him.

She should have let Layla kill him when she had the chance.

It was that dawning thought that made her stomach clench and sweat bead on her brow. She wrapped her arms around her waist and curled her legs up to her chest as she rolled onto her side. She had been so stupid to come here. She'd risked everything to keep her people safe, and it had been a mistake.

Her survival was a mistake.

Tears leaked from the corners of her eyes as she tried focusing on her breathing, slowing her heartbeat. She counted the seconds between each breath, holding her air deep in her chest, feeling the gentle pressure building before releasing it as she drifted into a fitful sleep.

Sun-soaked sky filtered through the small window by her bed. Crackles of salt crumbled from her eyes as she wiped away the sleep. Her head pounded as she pushed herself into a sitting position and centered herself in the present moment. She was Astrid Bluefischer Shadowcrest, Queen of the Fae. The Fireborn. Protector of the forsaken. The Great Equalizer. These were the names the magical world had gifted her. And she was beholden to them.

A knock on the door drew her attention away from her thoughts.

"Yes?" she asked.

Freed by Destiny

She glanced down at her attire. She'd been so exhausted and angry from her encounter with Renard and his advisors that she'd thrown on the first nightgown she'd found in the closet. It was a skimpy piece of lace, barely covering any part of her. Sighing heavily, she didn't even attempt to cover herself as the door swung open. If this was how Kimari and his father wanted her to be presented, there was no point in fighting against it.

Her eyebrows rose as she saw the person who'd entered her room. Kali stood awkwardly midway through the entry to her quarters.

"Oh! If you are still getting dressed, I can come back." Kali's cheeks turned a deep rose as she averted her gaze. "I didn't realize you were still in your lingerie."

"And here I was thinking you'd helped your father and brother select my clothing," Astrid replied through gritted teeth.

"I would never have selected something like that for you."

"No?" Astrid cocked an eyebrow. "And what would you have made me wear? Rags?"

She wrapped a lightweight throw around her shoulders as she wandered towards the closet.

"Well, for starters, your bedclothes would be comprised of the softest pants and lightweight sweaters to sleep in. Comfy, breathable, and certainly less revealing."

"Uh huh." She crossed her arms over her chest and stared at Kali.

Kali sighed as she swirled one of her braids between her fingers. "You know, I didn't have to ask my father to let me train you in proper etiquette. If you would prefer, I could have one of the governesses teach you instead."

"They would probably be preferable to you," Astrid muttered.

It didn't help that she had this nagging, constant voice at the back of her mind whispering that Kali was, most likely, one of her father's pawns. As much as she wanted to believe that both Kali and Kimari were on her side and that they were both fighting for the good of the kingdom, she couldn't bring herself to fully accept this ideal. Not when so much was at stake. The fate of the entire magical realm rested on her every move. She would need to be precise. Calculating.

"I know what you're thinking."

Astrid spun around, her shoulders tensing as she peered at Kali, who was inspecting her nails. Kali scrunched up her nose as she noticed a small chip in the gold arching across her tips.

"Then tell me, what am I thinking?"

Kali dropped her hands to her sides and stared Astrid straight in the eyes. She didn't waver. Didn't blink. She only stared at her with a penetrating gaze that made Astrid feel as if she could sense even the faintest hint of her heartbeat. It was unnerving. This sense that someone she didn't even know if she could fully trust saw her. The real her. The version of herself that she meticulously hid beneath the facade of "queen." It made her insides chill to a burning ice.

"You're thinking you know how this ends." Kali took a step forward, her gaze still unwavering. "Yet, you're unsure if you could be incorrect. If, perhaps, I am telling you the truth when I say you can trust me."

Astrid released a small breath, the relief in her lungs swelling as she attempted to gulp in air without allowing her chest to move all that much. Sweat coated her palms, turning them slick and yet strangely sticky as she balled them into fists.

"You know nothing, Kali."

Kali smirked at her, a small dimple forming in one cheek. "I know that my father will use you as a pawn if he doesn't kill you first. I know that you will never submit to him. And, I know that, even after everything we've been through and the mistrust I've sowed between us, you are still debating about whether or not you can trust me. Or, at the very least, if you can trust that I am your friend."

Kali halted her advance. She was a scant few inches from her, close enough that Astrid could feel the heat radiating from Kali's skin, although they were not touching.

Astrid took a small, almost imperceptible step back, breaking the tension. Kali blinked, and Astrid was set free from the spell of her gaze. She cleared her throat and crossed her arms over her chest. Kali's cheeks darkened as she abruptly looked in the opposite direction. During their conversation, Astrid had nearly forgotten what she was wearing. The lace nighty. Frantically, she turned towards the dresser and pulled out the first garment her hand touched. She didn't even look at it as she pulled it on over the lace.

Reaching out a tentative hand, she grasped Kali on the shoulder and turned her towards her. Where only a moment before there had been uneasy tension, now all she could feel was the warm smile radiating from Kali.

"I know you won't understand what I'm about to tell you, but I…" Kali swallowed hard, her cheeks sucking in as her shoulders shuddered slightly.

Astrid dropped her hand from Kali's shoulder and stood back so she could assess the princess. Her caramel skin glistened with a soft shimmer. Gold liner smudged her lower eyes, and her dark locks were capped with golden beads. She was stunning. Still, there were hints of the king all through her features. The furrowed brow. The slightly crooked nose. The cunning in her eyes.

And yet, there was a gentleness to her expressions that softened her. Made her more kind.

"I love my father," Kali finally finished her statement. "When I was a little girl, barely older than maybe three or four, I remember him carrying me around on his shoulders. Laughing as the sun danced through the trees shading us. He was happy, then, Astrid. And he made me believe that we always would be."

Her eyes narrowed. Her lower lip trembled, and Astrid knew Kali was remembering a time when Renard was not blood and power thirsty. When he still had the capacity to care for anyone other than himself.

Silver lined her eyes as she shuddered and turned her attention back to Astrid. "I—"

Her words were cut short by a curt knock on the door. Knots writhed within Astrid's stomach as she glanced between Kali and the door. If they'd been heard… she didn't want to consider what could become of Kali. Or herself.

Her heart raced. All thoughts fled her mind as she moved past Kali and pulled the door open only wide enough for her face to be visible through the sliver of a gap. A guard stood on the other side. His nostrils flared as he took a step back and cleared his throat.

"Prince Kimari is requesting your presence in the gardens, ma'am."

Freed by Destiny

He didn't meet her gaze. Astrid wondered if his timidity was a sign of respect or the exact opposite.

"And why would the prince send you instead of coming to fetch me for himself?" She narrowed her eyes at him, assessing how much he'd heard through the door before knocking. She wouldn't put it past Renard to spy on his own daughter, even if he did trust her.

The soldier clenched his hand, his arm shaking slightly as he kept his gaze locked on the tile floor. "I wouldn't suppose to understand the prince's mind, ma'am."

Astrid seethed at the formality of his tone. She was used to the members of her court treating her as their equal. They shared respect, of course, and she had the final say in most matters, but they challenged her. They held her accountable. There wasn't any of this "ma'am" business to contend with.

"You can tell my brother that if he wanted alone time with the queen, then he should have arrived here earlier," Kali drawled as she pried the door from Astrid's hand and threw it wide. "And, while you're at it, you can remind him that we are supposed to be training her on etiquette, not the art of lovemaking."

The guard's eyes bulged at the term "lovemaking," but to Astrid's surprise, he didn't give away his discomfort more openly. Instead, he jerked in a barely passable nod and turned on his heel to stride down the hall. Astrid watched him go, wondering what he'd heard and if he would tell the king his daughter was on the cusp of conspiring against him.

At least, Astrid hoped she was.

She turned back to Kali, who walked over to the jewelry stand and selected a delicate chain with a single pearl dangling from it.

Extending her hand towards Astrid, she said, "Here, wear this."

Tentatively, Astrid accepted the necklace. The pearl glistened with iridescent color. Pink swirled with ivory. Silver flowed in tiny rivers across the smooth stone. Her lips puckered into a small 'oh' as she held the necklace against her skin and peered at herself in the mirror. She looked like a fae tale queen.

"Kimari will love it," Kali murmured from behind her.

"And why should I care what he thinks?" She dropped her hand from her throat and turned towards Kali. "I am not some prize to be won and this is certainly not a love story, Kali." She didn't care if her outburst would be reported back to Renard. For just a moment, she wanted to feel like herself.

Kali lifted her hands in a placating fashion, her head bowing deeply as she took a step away from her. "I know. I'm sorry."

Astrid dropped the necklace back onto the jewelry stand. "I don't think I shall. I don't need your family's adornments to know who I am."

"Of course not."

Kali bit her bottom lip and stared at her feet. Astrid considered whether she'd been too brittle with her. There was still so much she didn't know about Kali. So many lies. Lies that formed a chasm between them that she wasn't sure could ever be breached.

"We should go," Kali said, finally looking up at her. "Kimari will be waiting for us. And, if there's one thing I know about my brother for certain, it's that he doesn't like to be kept waiting."

Astrid followed her from the room without another word. Whatever the moment between them had been earlier, it was gone. But she couldn't help but wonder if there was a sliver of hope for her to find a way out, even if it was with a different royal than she had been expecting.

Chapter Eight

Kali slapped Astrid's hand.

"Not like that," she said. "Like this."

She tilted her hand in a delicate, graceful salute as she sank low and bowed her head.

They stood in a garden on the eastern side of the palace, where golden morning light poured over them and the murmur of the nearby fountain provided a hum of white noise.

Astrid attempted to mimic the movements, but she ended up in an awkward mess of bent legs and elbows that made her look like a straw tied into a knot. She sank to the ground and stretched her legs out in front of her.

"I really don't understand how this," she said, gesturing with her hands, "is going to help me be a fair and just leader."

She tossed her hands behind her and shifted her weight so that her face arched towards the sky, taking in the sunshine. She couldn't remember the last time she'd allowed herself to just enjoy being in the outdoors like this.

"Because it's tradition," Kali said. She extended her hand towards Astrid. "Come on. I promised my father that I'd train you to be a proper princess. And here you are, ruining your dress in the mud."

Astrid shrugged. "You know, for someone who used to go gallivanting about and marching in the mud, I'm surprised that you buy into all this...fluff."

"Fluff?" Kali stared at her, her mouth slightly ajar.

"Perhaps, she just needs a break," Kimari said as he emerged from the shadow of a giant flowering tree a little ways down the main path.

"How long have you been standing there watching us?" Kali crossed her arms and stared at her brother with a scowl on on her face.

"Long enough to know you should never go into teaching as your main profession."

She narrowed her eyes at him. "And you think you could do any better?" She tapped her foot on the ground. "Please, oh great and mighty teacher, please show us how you would get her to follow the rules of court etiquette."

Kimari rolled his eyes. "Considering the fact that I've been waiting for you to get here for over an hour, I would think you would be a bit more gracious towards my benevolence."

"Benevolence?" Kali's face broke into a wide grin. Then she began laughing. "You have got to be absolutely insane to believe that you have a benevolent bone in your body."

Despite her best efforts to remain stoic, Astrid couldn't help but smile at the the clear fondness Kali and Kimari shared with one another. They were so different. Kali, despite her stately poise and girly demeanor, was tough as nails and well-versed in the art of fighting. She'd been trained to be one of Renard's top soldiers. A member of his elite force. Yet, here she was, as comfortable in a form-fitting sparkly dress as she was in body armor. Astrid had never been comfortable in dresses.

A shadow fell over her and she jolted from her thoughts. Shading her eyes with one hand, Astrid stared up at Kimari. He was breathtaking. Dark locks dangled at his shoulders. His white shirt was unbuttoned deep down his muscled chest. His jeans were tucked neatly into a pair of black boots. He was dashing, handsome, and, by all accounts, a rogue.

And yet, even with him convincing her to become betrothed and kissing her on a livestream, she couldn't help but wonder how much of her interactions with him were a charade and how much of them were real. It was so difficult to know where she stood with him.

"My lady." His deep voice brushed over her like a breeze, caressing her.

Gooseflesh prickled across her skin. The corner of his mouth tugged into a lopsided smirk as he waggled his fingers at her. Astrid slipped her fingers into his hand, heat radiating up her arm as he squeezed them.

"You really are the worst," Kali said, breaking the moment between them.

Kimari tugged Astrid to her feet. She stumbled a step when her feet hit the ground, but she recovered quickly.

"Shall I leave you to it?" Kali asked.

"Leave us to what, exactly?" Kimari replied. His features darkened as he regarded his sister.

"Look at the two of you. Madly in love." She wiped away a nonexistent tear from the corner of her eye. "If I didn't know the both of you so well, I would almost be convinced you actually were in love."

She closed the gap between them. "Father won't be able to hurt you if you are with child."

Astrid gasped. Whatever she had been expecting Kali to say, it certainly had not been that she would recommend she... become with child. She couldn't even bring herself to think about what it would be like with Kimari. Her skin illuminated as her thoughts drifted towards what Kali was proposing.

"And once I produce an heir?" She ground her teeth, her jaw clenching.

"Then you will have demonstrated you understood the assignment," Kali said pointedly. "And, perhaps, he will show leniency towards you."

"Great, so you think his plan is to kill me if..."

"Not if, Astrid. When," Kali corrected. "When you produce an heir. There are few people in this world who know my father better than me."

Freed by Destiny

Kimari's lips parted as if he were about to object. So aware of his body was Astrid that she felt his muscles tighten.

"And what I can tell you is that he will not hesitate to kill you if he thinks you will pose an insurmountable threat. He wants you to concede. To pledge yourself to us... to him."

"I will not yield." Even as the words poured from her lips, the tingling of her power spun around the core of her magic. Yet, she couldn't feel her powers stretching up from deep within her. It was as if there was an impenetrable wall separating her from her abilities. They called to her, their fragmented echoes escaping through the tiniest of cracks in Renard's design. Perhaps there was a way to break free from the shackles he'd placed upon her.

Kali sighed. "You don't have to yield who you are, Astrid. I see how you look at my brother. How he looks at you. There's no reason to fight it. The two of you can marry. Have children. Live."

Kimari remained silent as his sister spoke. Astrid wasn't even sure he was still breathing, there was so little movement or sound coming from him. Glancing at him from the corner of her eye, she saw his hand flexing between a balled fist and an outstretched palm. Despite herself, she couldn't help but feel a tinge of disappointment at his reaction to Kali's words. After all his persuasive ramblings, she would have thought he would be on board with Kali trying to convince her this was the best course of action. Instead, tension lined his jaw.

"Is that what you want?" Astrid dropped her gaze to her hands. "A magical you can show off at gatherings and children you can use to convince the world that you're not as bigoted as your father?"

"What?" Kimari stuttered. He took a step back from her. His eyes roamed erratically between the trees, flowers, and fountain.

Everywhere except for at her. Or his sister.

Astrid was surprised by his lack of composure. He was normally so good at masquerading. Half the time, she didn't know what he was thinking, much less what he was feeling. But now it was if she was catching a glimpse of a part of him that she had never seen before. He had trusted Kali enough to bring her into his plans to make a treaty with her, but here he was, presumably doubting her.

Unless this is a trick.

Her head twitched as she attempted to rid herself of the thought. She was exhausted from the constant feeling that she didn't know who to trust. Or how much.

"Can't you see?" Kali asked. Her lower lip trembled as she spoke. "If he has to force her into marriage with you, there will be nothing to stop him from killing her once she bears an heir."

His jawline tightened, his eyes turning hard and distant. "At that point, she would have served her purpose."

Astrid's breath caught in her chest. She couldn't believe what he was saying. She couldn't feel her toes, her fingers, not even her own heart beating in her chest. Everything was numb.

"You don't care if she dies?" Kali pressed.

"Why would I?"

She closed her eyes, not wanting to see the coldness in his expression. He was like a gargoyle, bereft of any real emotion. She'd been such a fool to trust him. To believe that he wanted anything more than to control her. To lure her into his trap. The perfect predator.

"I…" Her lips barely moved as she struggled to speak. A

whooshing sound filled her ears, drowning out their conversation. Still, she felt nothing.

"Did you say something?"

Astrid blinked rapidly, her pupils adjusting to the light once more. Kali's face filled her vision. She placed a firm, warm hand on her shoulder.

"I thought I heard..." She trailed off.

Kali frowned slightly.

"I'm fine." Astrid swallowed hard. She didn't dare a glance at Kimari. If she did, she knew she'd break all over again. And she couldn't—wouldn't—let him have the satisfaction of knowing that he'd hurt her in a way she hadn't even been expecting. She'd doubted his intentions from the moment he'd first agreed to her plan. Everything he'd done since then had all been a lead up to convincing her to become his father's prisoner. Even after everything, she'd cradled the glimmer of hope that he had genuinely wanted to forge an alliance with her. That he truly wanted to build a better world with her at his side.

She'd ended up in manacles anyway.

No, she wouldn't let him see. Wouldn't let him know.

She straightened her back. If surviving the slums had taught her anything, it was how to be tough. No matter what the situation was, she wasn't going to let him grind her down into pulverized particles.

"Are you sure?" Kali squeezed her shoulder gently. "I can call the guard to bring you some water."

"I said I'm fine." She shrugged away from Kali and forced herself to stare straight into Kimari's eyes. "An heir will not suffice. You can tell your father that if his plan is to rid himself of me the moment we have a child, it will not stop my people from continuing to rage against him. I am one person. One part of the machine that is rising up against him. Against you. And if there is to be any chance of peace, then he will remove the suppressor and allow me my freedom. He needs to swear that he will stop torturing and experimenting on magicals. You can tell him that if he does this, I will... I will concede to him. I will... lower myself to ensure his reign."

He blinked at her, his nostrils flaring. Then he nodded. Once. Almost imperceptibly.

"Astrid." Her name on Kali's lips was little more than a whisper on the wind. The sound of it made her breath catch.

Tears burned her eyes, threatening to spill down her cheeks. She willed herself to remain stoic. Calm. She would be everything Renard wanted. She would convince him that she could be controlled. That she could play the role of princess, wife, and mother to the bridge between the human and magical worlds. His family would inherit the gifts bestowed upon the fae—without requiring any more death. She would do this to save them. Even if it cost her everything.

Kimari stared at her with those baleful eyes that hardened with each passing second before mumbling something to his sister and disappearing behind some shrubs. Astrid picked at the spiky leaves of one of the shrubs to occupy her hands as her thoughts raced from one idea to the next. She couldn't believe she'd actually declared she would submit to Renard. She didn't know what had possessed her to do so. She hadn't planned on it. And yet, when she'd been confronted with the idea that he would kill her following the birth of an heir, she couldn't fathom any other way to at least attempt to survive. To give her people even a modicum of hope.

Hope.

Was it really worth the sacrifices she'd made? So many lives had been lost. Potts. Kilian. More would follow. It was a never-ending cycle. This death and destruction. And yet, that kindling of light, sparking in the darkest of places, was enough to rally them together. To push them through the cold. The mud. The death. It fed them when they were hungry, and nourished their souls when they were bereft.

She couldn't help but wander if it sometimes did more damage than good.

Hope.

It was all she had. And she didn't even know if it would be enough.

"Astrid?" Kali stood behind her. "I think we've had enough lessons for today. I should return you to your rooms."

Astrid shuddered against the thought of returning to that room, laden with all the finery. It was a prison. One that she doubted she would ever be able to escape, especially now.

"I would like to stay here a bit longer, if you don't mind," she said. She tugged on a fistful of leaves, ripping them away from their plant. Bits of green fluttered on the wind as others drifted to the ground. The sharp ends of the needles pricked her palms as she squeezed what remained into a fist.

Kali took a step forward and wrapped her arms around Astrid's shoulders. Astrid heard a distinctive click before a burst of lime green light exploded around her.

"We don't have much time," Kali said, dropping her arms. "It's a big enough risk that I'm doing this here."

"I don't understand." Astrid spun to face her. "What are you doing."

"I've activated a frequency that will distort any listening devices my father has placed on us—or around us." She waved her hand around them. "And this green light is just the underpinning of a high-end holograph. If anyone is looking at us, all they will see is me embracing you. But we can't stay like this for long without raising suspicion."

Astrid cocked an eyebrow at Kali. She didn't understand what was happening or why.

Kali clicked a button on her wrist. "I've just set a timer. When it goes off, I need you to turn around and assume the exact position you had before I activated the device. That way, when I end the frequency, we will go back to embracing."

"I still…"

"We don't have time for this. Look, I know I haven't given you much reason to trust me. And, in all honesty, I don't think I would trust me either, if I were in your shoes. But I need you to at least try. After everything we've through, I need you to at least give me the benefit of the doubt here. I saved you from my father's court once. And I am determined to do so again."

"Why?" She couldn't help the question erupting from her lips.

Kali had no reason or incentive for helping her. If anything, she was putting her own life at risk to aid her. It didn't make sense.

"Because, whether you believe it or not, I am your friend. And…I love you. I know you just promised Kimari that you would submit to my father… that you would bear him an heir and pretend to be the dutiful queen-to-be, but it won't be enough for my father. You're too much of a threat and he will kill you the moment he thinks he can get away with it."

"Why are you telling me this?" She didn't care if they didn't have time for long explanations. If she was going to trust Kali, she needed answers. Explanations. Something to help her reconcile the betrayal she'd experienced when Kali had left them.

"Haven't you been listening?" Kali shook as she closed the small gap between them and took her hands in her own. "I am not my father, Astrid. I want there to be peace. And… I don't think I realized how far he'd go to secure his power—his dominance—until I was with you in the laboratories. Until I witnessed him deploying that bomb…He is not a good leader. He is not the leader we need. You are."

Her alarm buzzed.

"Do you trust me?" Kali asked.

Astrid didn't know what to say. If she was being honest with herself, she didn't know if she could trust Kali. Not now. Perhaps not ever.

"Astrid, do you trust me?" Kali repeated.

Astrid breathed in deeply and swallowed hard, trying to give herself time to formulate a response. Before she could answer, Kali spun her around and wrapped her arms around her shoulders, just as the lime green light faded into nonexistence.

"Come on," Kali whispered against her ear, "let's get you ready for dinner."

She pulled away from Astrid and began the trek towards the palace. Astrid lingered.

Did she trust Kali? Her mind and body told her no. And yet, there the smallest sliver of doubt wedged into her soul.

She just didn't know if she was brave enough to trust it.

Chapter Nine

Astrid stood in front of the mirror. Her long, dark hair flowed over her shoulders. She hated the dress Kali had selected for her. It was form fitting and basically transparent. She felt like her entire body was on display. The sheer, gold fabric was molded to her like a second skin. Jewels studded the fabric, giving the whole outfit the appearance of being wet, as if she'd emerged from the ocean to stand before them. Tiny golden roses with ruby centers were linked together by shimmering, delicate chains and woven through her hair. She scowled at her reflection.

"Everyone will be enthralled by you," Kali said as she pushed a pin into place to secure a lock of Astrid's hair away from her neck. The arrangement displayed the sharp point of her ear. "They might even forget how savage you are."

Astrid snarled softly.

"Exactly," Kali said. "Look at you, unable to stop yourself from responding in such an uncivilized manner. Didn't you learn anything from our lesson this afternoon?"

Astrid couldn't tell if she was joking or not. The moment they'd arrived back to her room, dozens of servants had entered to prepare Astrid for the dinner. They'd primped and preened her, turning into a vision of what they believed she should be. Beautiful. Seductive. A hint of magic. But nothing more. Nothing powerful.

During all that time, Kali had given no hint as to what she'd done in the garden. She acted as if it had never occurred. In some ways, Astrid wasn't even certain it had. It could have all been just a dream.

"Leave us," Kali ordered, jerking her head towards the door at the few servants remaining in the room.

They scurried out of Astrid's room without another word. Kali stalked across the room and pressed her ear to the door.

"What—" Astrid began.

Kali held up her hand, stilling Astrid's questions before they even had time to emerge. After another few moments of listening, Kali tilted her head towards her and said, "My brother can be quite convincing when he wants to be. I have no doubt he has persuaded my father that you can be tamed."

Astrid scoffed. She was not some wild beast to be ridden until she could be controlled. Balling her hands into fists, she held back her anger as she regarded Kali. These humans did not deserve anything the magical world could offer.

Freed by Destiny

"I know it has been difficult for you being here, not knowing who you can trust," Kali said, "but I wanted to offer that you can trust me. I am not a foe, Astrid. In fact, I believe that we can do so much good for one another. For this world. But... you have to trust me."

Astrid shook her head. "How could I ever trust you, Kali? After everything we've been through. After you helped your brother into tricking me to come here? You knew when I met him in that clearing that your father would find out what we were doing. You had to. You... set me up. You lied me to. All those times I put my faith in you. You. Lied. To. Me."

"I know." Kali didn't provide an explanation or an apology. They both knew it would be tempered with excuses. She couldn't turn against her family, just as Astrid couldn't turn against her people.

"You should have warned me."

Silence hung between them. Dense. Foreboding.

"My father always gets what he wants," Kali said. "And, right now, he wants you. He wants you to be a part of this family. To prove that you can be. That you will... submit."

"And when I don't live up to his standards? Then what? He kills me? Tortures my people? He has all the power here, Kali. Your father is forcing my hand. And I do not want to be here. Like this. Without hope for a better future."

"Why can't you see that we are literally offering you a better future? Kimari has agreed to marry you. He's vouched for you. I am putting my reputation on the line by befriending you. By teaching you the ways of our court. And here you are," Kali said, sweeping her hands across the room, "living in luxury for the first time in your life. This should have been... It was your birthright.

And yet, you are begrudging us for what we are trying to do for you."

She shook her head. "Sometimes I wonder if it wouldn't have been better for my brother to set aside his curiosity about you. But no. You invited him to meet with you. To form a treaty behind our father's back. And he, the pigheaded, romantic, foolish boy that he is, decided to try. To see if there was a chance. And now you blame him for what has happened after." Her features sharpened as she struck Astrid with an angry gaze. "You should be thanking us for not killing you on the spot."

"And should a pig thank its butcher?" Astrid spat. Anger coursed through her veins. She couldn't believe Kali was standing before her, having the audacity to tell her she should be grateful that Renard was giving her this opportunity. Thankful that she was being treated like a queen. A captured queen, but a queen nonetheless.

"You are not a pig going to slaughter, Astrid."

"Aren't I?"

"Of course not!"

Astrid rolled her eyes. "You know, I would be a draking lot more likely to believe you if you weren't so blind to who and what your family is, Kali."

"I know exactly who and what my family is!" Kali sucked in her cheeks as she glared at Astrid. "They are the only family I will ever get. Don't you understand that? I figured you, of all people, would understand why I am so unwilling to give them up. Why I am willing to accept their faults."

"Me of all people? Your father is the reason I don't have a family. My parents are dead because of him. The real Layla Dione was left to the wolves… because of him. Everything that has ever gone wrong in my life is because of him!" Astrid panted as she finished speaking. Her body hummed with the energy of the argument. She fiddled with the bracelet clasped around her wrist because she couldn't stay still.

"I am sorry you feel this way. I had hoped…" Kali sighed heavily, her shoulders sinking as she exhaled. "I had hoped that perhaps you would come to see that we can be stronger together than apart. But I see now that I was wrong."

"I can never forgive your father for what he's done. And it's not just me who has been impacted by his lack of leadership and cruelty. What about all the magicals he's killed in his pursuit of their abilities? Your technologies are based on the talents of my people. He stole from us. And tortured and killed us in the process."

Kali turned her back on her. "It is unfortunate you cannot see beyond your rage for my family. Perhaps, if you are able to survive within our court, you will come to realize that not all of us want to see you harmed."

She strode from Astrid's room without another word. Astrid listened to her heels clacking on the stone floor, becoming quieter and more echoey the farther she moved down the hall. Her fingers fell from the bracelet as she turned to stare at herself in the mirror.

If you can hear me now, please give me a sign. What am I supposed to do?

She waited for Penny—Amaleah—to answer. When all she was met with was silence, she turned towards the open door. This family was giving her whiplash.

She wasn't sure how much more she could take.

Astrid lingered at the top of the stairs leading into the banquet hall. Tables laden with food crowded the room. She wasn't sure what she had been expecting, but it wasn't this. Twinkling lights were streamed around white marble columns. An orchestra played in the background.

The cacophony of voices and music stifled her thoughts as she looked upon the scene of revelry before her. Couples openly caressed one another, their clothes askance and their bodies melded together. Wine sloshed over brims as attendees swooshed their drinks back and forth to the music. It was disgusting to her how much waste there was. In the slums, so many magicals—and impoverished humans—lived without knowing where their next meal was going to come from and here these people were gorging themselves on high end food and too much wine.

"We should talk." Kimari's breath danced across her skin, sending a shiver down her spine.

She jolted. She hadn't heard him approach her from behind.

"Really?" She gripped the marble banister of the staircase leading to the main floor. "I take it from all of this that your father has agreed to my terms?"

She didn't dare look at him. She didn't know if she would kiss him or scratch his eyes out.

"Do you want an honest answer or one that will make you feel better?"

His words turned her stomach to ice. Her breathing became shallow. Her heart raced.

"So there's no hope," she whispered. Although her eyes burned with unshed tears, she did not allow them to trail down her cheeks. She would not give him—either of them—the satisfaction of knowing they'd broken another chunk from her soul.

"I didn't say that," he said.

His warm hand hovered above her shoulder, radiating against her without actually touching her. She flinched away from him, and he shoved his hand into his pant's pocket.

"I know you don't want to hear this, but you're already our prisoner, Astrid. You lost what little room for negotiation you had when you came here. In his eyes, you are already his prized possession."

"I am not something that can be owned," she shot back.

He sighed. "I know that."

Her back stiffened as the distance between them closed. He pressed against her and waved at a group of onlookers.

"Smile," he hissed in her ear. "Give them what they want. Make them believe you're in this whole-heartedly."

She gave a quick stomp on his foot as she smiled down at the crowd. The sharp release of his breath against her hair and the tightening of his grip on her arm was enough for her to know she'd hurt him.

"Play nice," he said.

"Or what?" she asked through gritted teeth. "You'll threaten to kill me? I'm sorry to say that threat doesn't have as much meat to it when my life is already on the line."

He didn't say anything. She began to worry if she'd actually rattled him, but, when she cocked her head towards him, his lips pressed against her cheek and he pulled her more tightly against him.

"What the drak!" She panted as she attempted to pull away from him without making it awkward. It didn't help that every place he touched her sent electricity spiraling through her body. She was also hyper aware of how the members of court watched their every move. She knew they would be searching for any sign she wasn't fully committed to their prince. Any reason to beg for her blood.

"We really need to work on your showmanship. Here I am, trying to help you, and what do I get in return?" Kimari stared down at his injured foot. "Stepped on. Intentionally so. Do you have any idea how painful it is to have a pointy heel jabbed into the top of your foot?"

Despite the tension between them, she couldn't help but laugh at the disgruntled, yet playful, expression on his face.

"Has anyone ever told you how adorable you are when you're half-mad?"

"Adorable?" He repeated flatly. He pulled her tight against him. "I believe the words you were searching for were dashing. Debonair. Powerful. Maybe even a dash of seductive."

She laughed. "You wish."

He growled and gently shoved her against the balcony. His body pressed against her. Heat radiated from him. Every part of her tingled as he leaned into her. Their breath mingled and she waited for him to kiss her. Their eyes met as his lips hovered just above hers. Part of her longed to close the gap between them. To feel his tongue brush against hers. To know he desired her just as much...

"I know you," he whispered. "We haven't been acquainted for very long, but you and I cut from the same cloth, Astrid."

He chuckled as he straightened, leaving her gasping at the sudden lack of warmth pressing into her body.

For a moment, they just stared at each other. Him, with the confident smirk she'd grown to know so well plastered across his face. Her with her heart leaping in her chest.

"What did I miss?" Kali asked as she crested the last step onto the same level. She looked between them. "Everyone is watching you. And people are beginning to talk."

"Good," Kimari said before Astrid had a chance to really process what Kali was implying. "Let them talk."

He reached for Astrid's hand and interlaced their fingers. "She is to be my wife and if I want to revel in her for all to see, well, then I don't see an issue with that."

Kali glared at him but said nothing as she turned her attention to Astrid. "My father has requested that you join him at his table."

Astrid's gaze trailed past Kali and to the throne set upon a platform on the opposite end of the banquet tables. His golden crown gleamed in the soft light. A table laden with exquisite food rested before him. Only two other chairs were on the platform. Astrid sucked in a sharp intake of air when she saw the queen seated at the right hand of the king. She'd seen pictures of her, of course, and watched video clips of her conducting charity events or speaking with young children, or even cutting the red ribbon at the start of construction for public buildings. In each of those instances, she'd always appeared regal, elegant in a way Astrid had always envied.

But the woman at the table was none of these things. Her fraying hair was disheveled and, although her head bobbed in time with the music, there was a glazed, almost medicated look to her expression. Not even her dress fit appropriately. It hung in strange angles and gave the queen a frumpy air.

"That's your mother?" Astrid whispered from the corner of her mouth as she linked arms with Kali and began descending the stairs.

"She… wasn't always like that."

Music drowned out the words that followed. Astrid leaned in closer to Kali, hoping to catch what she was saying, but it was impossible with the hum of chatter and music all around them. They reached the dais just as the musicians finished the final crescendo of their song. Renard clapped slowly. All the partygoers joined him, their conversations stilled for the time being.

"Welcome, Astrid Bluefischer, Queen of the Fae, betrothed to my son."

Astrid resisted to urge to flinch against his assignment of ownership to Kimari. Still, she knew she needed to play a part. She had given her word that if he accepted her terms, she would be the dutiful daughter. A prisoner without chains. She planted what she hoped was a winning smile on her face and curtsied.

When her gaze rose to his face, the curve of his lips were twisted into a sly smirk, as if they were in on a joke that only they knew.

Freed by Destiny

Co-conspirators in a never-ending game for power. She hated that he made her feel this way.

"Come, sit next to me." He gestured towards the empty seat to his left. "Let us celebrate together."

As she climbed the steps to the platform, her heart hammered in her chest. Sweat coated her palms, turning them slick as she sank into the chair next to him. Whatever happened next, she was determined to not let him see the terror lurking beneath her veneer of servitude. He could strip her of her magic. Her titles. Her friends. But if there was one thing he could not take away from her, it would be the fire raging within her.

"You will have to forgive our earlier interactions," Renard said as he stripped a hunk of meat from the turkey leg he held in one hand. Juice coated his fingers as he shoved the meat into his mouth.

Bile burned the back of her throat as specks of his food coated his bottom lip.

"It has been such a long time since I've met anyone who challenged me quite as much as you have," he continued. "I rather thought you would be more like your father than your mother."

He drained a full goblet of wine and lifted his glass in the air, calling a servant forward to refill its contents.

Astrid studied the plates. The juicy, sweet fruits covering one of the plates before her tempted her, but she refrained from joining in the meal. She knew it would all turn to ash in her mouth. Besides, she wanted to be alert and listen for any sign that there might be another way forward.

"You knew my mother well?"

He shot her a curious glance as he ripped a chunk of bread from the loaf in the middle of the table. It stretched the entire length of table so that they could all share it. Astrid leaned forward to see what the queen was doing, but she remained focused on the meal before her.

"Did no one tell you the history? I'm surprised Janae never told you the truth of your parents."

Her breath caught in her chest. She knew many of the stories about her parents. Theirs was a story of love. They'd been friends since childhood. And, when the time came for her mother to choose her consort, the decision had been easy. They loved one another. Everyone said so.

"Before your mother decided to wed your father, she and I courted."

Astrid gasped. This didn't make sense.

"No."

The single word hung between them, filling the space with an uneasy tension that she desperately wanted to dispel.

"I can assure you, it is the truth."

"My mother would never…"

"Child," he said, "you never knew your mother. And yet here you are, telling me what is and is not the truth."

She ground her teeth, trying to keep herself from screaming at him.

"It was a shame your mother chose a different path. She was the best drak I've ever had."

Freed by Destiny

Astrid leaned forward to see how the queen reacted to her husband's words. Her eyes were glazed over, and she didn't acknowledge him at all. Frowning, Astrid lifted her chin towards Renard.

"I might not know much about my mother, but I know she would never stoop so low as to…"

Renard sighed. "I had hoped, given your current position in life, that you would accept the truth of the matter. But I can see now that you are unwilling to understand how the world works. This life is a series of threads, Astrid. Each one is a memory, a specific instance in time. And they are woven together into an intricate pattern. Yours and my tapestries have been combined since the beginning."

Bile churned in her stomach.

"Of course they have," she growled. "You had my parents assassinated because you couldn't bear the thought of the fae having more power than you. You tried to kill me. And, when you discovered your failed attempt to eliminate the last of my mother's line, you sought me out to kill me."

"Tsk, tsk, Astrid. You really have it all wrong. I don't want to kill you. I want you to join us. To be a part of this family. We can work together."

"Tell me about the project you were working on with my mother before I was born." The words escaped her lips before she considered if it was wise to reveal how much she knew.

He eyed her carefully. "How did you know about that?"

"There were rumors," she said, enunciating each word deliberately to give herself time to think through what to say next. She didn't not want him to checkmate her into revealing Penny had survived

113

for over twenty years. "You might have killed the majority of the fae nobles, Renard, but you didn't get them all. I've spoken to them about their memories."

"Your mother never would have revealed what we were working on to them."

"Because you knew her so well," Astrid countered. "Remember, Renard, she stole the technology containing what remnants of Queen Amaleah you could recover."

"Shut your draking mouth!" Renard slammed his fist on the table and peered around the room. His eyes darted towards his wife. He sneered at the drool slipping from the corner of her mouth.

Astrid wanted to cower away at the anger. Yet, another, bolder part of her couldn't resist pushing him just a little bit further.

"How did you recover her essence? I've been wondering this for some time."

"I said, shut your draking mouth," Renard repeated, this time with a cold, calculating tone that sent a shiver down Astrid's spine.

She knew she was treading on dangerous ground, but she didn't care. Maybe it was the events from earlier in the day. Maybe it was the anger pouring from his eyes.

But she felt bold.

Chapter Ten

"You couldn't handle the fact that she took the PEA before you had a chance to use it?" Astrid asked. She picked a grape from its stem and plopped it into her mouth. "Is that why you assassinated my family? Or is it because you will never be anything more than a sniveling, weak, little boy who's jealous of everyone else's gifts?"

She knew it was a mistake to goad him. Dangerous, even. But she couldn't help but feel like she needed to push his limits. He'd taken everything from her, was still taking everything, and all she had at her disposal was her ability to insult him.

Renard blinked at her, his cold eyes calculating. Astrid held her ground without wavering. He was a monster.

"You will never know what the PEA was capable of," she growled.

"You want to know why? When you sent your precious Kaden to capture me, I still didn't know who I was. My PEA couldn't access my memory files, so I let the elves extract my memories. Everything on the PEA was destroyed."

In a flash of crimson and gold, Renard gripped her hand firmly in his own. He squeezed until her fingers went numb. She winced in pain.

"It would be prudent of you to stop. Now."

Despite the pain crippling her hand, she laughed. "You don't deserve to know what secrets it held"

Astrid didn't feel the impact of his hand slamming into her cheek. Or his ring slicing her flesh open. It happened too quickly. Her head jerked to the side from the impact. Her eyes fluttered open then closed. Swelling distorted her features. When the pain did come, it was a stinging, burning force that sent her reeling.

A collective silence filled the room as every guest turned to face them. Astrid felt their eyes on her. Predator eyes. They wanted to see her suffer. Hated her for who she was. What she was.

There was pity, too. She didn't know which was worse: the hate or the pity.

"Father?" Kali said, emerging from the line of guests pushing closer to the table. She approached the dais. "Our guest of honor has arrived."

She held her gaze on her father, unwaveringly, as if tempting him to rebuke her in front of all these people.

Everyone knew of Renard's cruelty. How could they not? Yet, Astrid doubted they cared whether he hurt a fae. Even if she was a queen, and betrothed to his son. She was his property.

Freed by Destiny

He nodded and Kali bowed her head in return. Lifting her hands, she clapped them twice. The crowd parted as several servants ushered the bystanders to the sidelines.

Smoked curled around them as the lights dimmed. A spotlight pointed at the staircase, where a woman painted in gold stood in the middle of the stairs. Loose curls formed a halo around her face. She wore a loose, impossibly sheer gown. Astrid's skin shimmered slightly as she realized what this woman was.

A nightingale.

One of the king's concubines. His to use whenever he wanted. Astrid stole another glance at his wife, wondering how she must feel at this display. She sipped from a goblet of wine, her cheeks taking on a ruddy complexion. She did not look up or acknowledge the nightingale.

The nightingale's hips swayed as she made her way down the stairs and came to stand before the king.

She began singing, her movements sultry as she swayed her arms above her head and twisted her body to the orchestral sounds. Renard stared at her, completely transfixed. Astrid watched, too, unable to draw her eyes away from the graceful, smooth movements. To yield that much power, without having magic, astonished her. In that moment, Astrid vowed to determine a way to transfix the king like this. To convince him she can be an asset instead of a detriment. Even if it crackled her soul to do so. She at least had to try.

The dance ended with the woman bowing deep before the dais. She peered up at the king through her eyelashes, her lips pouting slightly. Renard clapped loudly, spurring his guests to follow suit. It was as if the entire room has forgotten he'd slapped Astrid only moments before. A stinging heat still lingered across her cheek and silver blood dripped onto the tablecloth. Astrid didn't dare press a napkin to staunch it. Not until she was sure the king was finished harming her.

Placing a hand on Renard's arm, she whispered, "I am sorry, my king, for how I reacted to you earlier. I've been thinking about how we can come to better understand one another."

He drew his eyes away from where the nightingale had started another dance to stare at her. His lips twitched between a smirk and a scowl.

"I mean it," she said, squeezing his arm gently. "I don't want us to quarrel."

"If you don't want to quarrel, then do not fight against me, child. I know it can't be easy for you, being raised as a peasant. Living in the slums without any hope for the future. Kaden told me the state of the bar you worked in. How it was full of drudgery." He brushed his finger across her cheek where he'd struck her. "That will leave a scar without the use of your healing magic."

Astrid swallowed hard. How did he know she'd given up her ability to heal? Biting her tongue to keep herself from asking, she bowed her head towards him, hoping it came off as demur and ashamed, rather than an attempt to hide her confusion.

"I'll have a servant bring you the healing injection later. I wouldn't want my son's wife to be disfigured."

Balling her hands into fists, Astrid forced herself to smile sweetly up at him. "Thank you, my king."

He cocked an eyebrow at her, clearly not convinced this newfound sweetness was sincere. "Kaden told me many things about you, and so did my daughter."

She couldn't tell if he was trying to goad her into another fight or if he was genuinely trying to form a connection with her. First with the revelation about his relationship with her mother. And now this.

"Oh?" She sipped from her wine glass to mask her expression. She desperately wanted to search the crowd for Kimari and Kali's familiar faces, but she was afraid to divert her attention away from the king. He demanded it. Needed to feel as if he were the sole person of interest in the room. She wondered if that was part of the reason he'd been gruff with her earlier. She had stolen the limelight and yet she was not fully his to control.

Not like the nightingale who was still dancing seductively before them.

"I was sorry when Kaden died," she said.

"Dead?" He gave her a confused look. "Kaden didn't die."

"But I thought…" She trailed off. She had seen him die, hadn't she?

Renard shook his head and pointed to a spot in the crowd. "He's standing right there. Unless you think I have somehow found a way to bring the dead back to life."

Astrid looked to where he was pointing, her jaw dropping as she saw the man who'd haunted her nightmares for months standing surrounded by a gaggle of women.

"How… I could have sworn…"

"That you murdered him when you helped those traitors escape their deaths?" Renard sneered. "Come now, Astrid, you should know better than that."

Her thoughts snapped into place. *Of course.* After all his years of research, Renard had finally been able to develop a device that could bring health back to even those on the precipice of death. An iciness numbness crept through her body as she watched Renard waggle his finger at Kaden, who extracted himself from the circle of admiring women to come before king like the dog he was.

"My King." He bowed deeply.

Renard watched Astrid carefully. She could feel his eyes on her as she regarded the man she'd sworn she'd killed. She was certain the king had kept him out of her sight until just now just to toy with her. He was like a spider, spinning an intricate plot of webs to lure her closer to him. To ensnare her so deeply, she would never be able to escape. How he'd known she would feel remorse at killing Kaden, she could only assume Kali had shared enough of her experiences with him. Or perhaps Kimari.

It didn't matter. She refused to let the king see her squirm.

"Lady Astrid." Kaden said her name quickly, as if even the taste of it on his tongue was like consuming ash.

She leaned towards him and smiled. "I'm glad to see you looking so well."

He met her gaze. Despite the hardness of his expression, she thought she could sense the man she'd seen in his apartment lingering just beneath his surface. He was a murderer. She'd known that since the first time she'd met him and witnessed him kill patrons of The Wand. He could be cruel. Harsh. And yet, she also couldn't forget the way he'd spoken to her then. How he'd described being an orphan much like herself. How the king had taken him under his wing. Raised him as a son. A peer to the crown prince.

Freed by Destiny

She couldn't entirely fault him for his loyalty to the royal family. She understood him in a way she couldn't the others. Renard had offered him comfort and a way to survive. He would have been a fool to reject him.

"That is not the impression you gave the last time we met," he replied in a monotone tenor.

Astrid blinked at him. She couldn't tell if he was angry, goading her, or something else.

"No. I suppose it's not."

Renard slammed his glass on the table, sloshing wine over the brim and onto the tablecloth. It splattered on Astrid's hand. She scowled as she quickly wiped it off with her napkin. She had never taken the king as a sloppy drunk before. Then again, she'd never seen him at a party.

"Enough of all that," Renard said. "I want to see the two of you make up. It won't do for the two of you to quibble over past grievances. Come on now."

Astrid cocked an eyebrow at the king. She didn't quite understand what game he was playing. Why insist that a rival monarch and his most trusted soldier make amends for their previous entanglements?

Regardless, she smiled at Kaden and said, "I'm sorry for trying to kill you and leaving you for dead."

Kaden's eyes flitted towards the king, as if checking to ensure himself that this was, indeed, the path the king wanted him to take. He must have found an answer because he turned his attention back to her with a huff. "I'm sorry for killing the old man in your bar."

"And?" Astrid pressed, knowing it was dangerous. The king's mood shifted so quickly she could never be sure how he was going to react from one moment to the next.

Kaden bared his teeth, his eyes flashing dangerously. "I won't apologize for anything else. Everything I've done has been in direct service to my king. You would do well to remember that."

Resisting the urge to lunge across the table at him, Astrid contented herself with scowling at him instead.

"See," Renard said, completing ignoring the tension swallowing the space between them, "he's sorry for killing your friend. Accept his apology, Astrid."

The anger bubbling just beneath her surface was enough to burn her alive from the inside out. Coupled with the slightest twinge of empathy she felt towards Kaden for the circumstances that led him down this path of hatred, the emotions battling within her were almost overwhelming. It took all of her self control to keep herself from lashing out at both of them. She'd lost control enough times that evening and could not afford to risk another misstep.

"Thank you, Kaden. I accept your words."

He narrowed his eyes at her, as if anticipating more. As if sensing her internal struggle. But he didn't goad her. He simply nodded at her, his lips pressed into a thin line and his brow creased into a deep V as he regarded her.

"Come now!" Renard continued. "I think you can both do better than that."

He scanned the room and his eyes stilled on a distant corner of the room.

Freed by Destiny

Astrid followed his gaze, her stomach squirming as she realized what he was looking at. A couple swayed together, locked in a sensual dance meant only for them.

Please, no.

She curled her fingers around the tablecloth, clenching it to keep herself from attacking the king.

Clapping his hands together, he motioned towards the couple. "That is how you show just how much you forgive one another. How much you care. Dance."

A haze filled Astrid's mind as she lingered in her chair. Although she was determined to show him she could be trusted—broken— just the thought of Kaden's hands wrapping around her waist and drawing her close filled her mouth with bile.

"I said, dance."

Startled, Astrid jerked her head towards the king, a grimace already forming on her lips. She blinked at him. He nodded towards Kaden.

"I can't be so undesirable that you would refuse to a single dance with me, My Lady," Kaden said. The sound of voice jolted her into action.

"No, of course not." She pushed herself from her chair and descended the few steps from the dais to the floor. She glanced around the room, searching for any sign of Kimari, but he was nowhere to be seen. She briefly wondered how he would react to his father forcing her to dance with another man—his best friend, by all accounts—during their betrothal party. She doubted he would care at all.

Kaden gripped her hand in his own and led her into a slow waltz.

Although he led, she stumbled over her feet during transitions in the music. Her foot stomped on his foot, making him grimace in pain.

"Are you intentionally trying to hurt me to show your displeasure at being forced to dance with me or are you truly this bad at dancing?"

"What makes you think it's not both?"

Kaden pressed his hand into the small of her back and dipped her. Clenching his shirt into her fist, she clung to him until he pulled her back up into a standing position.

"What the drak!"

He leaned in close, his lips brushing against her ear lope as he whispered, "Just imagine if my grip had slipped and you'd gone tumbling to the floor. How embarrassing would that have been?"

"So glad to see nothing has changed you."

"What? I'm still as dashing and powerful as ever?"

"Try savage and you might have yourself on the right track."

He smirked at her. "Awe, and here I thought you'd been wasting away with your guilt at killing me these past few months. Come to find out, you were perfectly happy to let me rot."

His words stung, leaving a knot in the pit of her stomach. She arched an eyebrow at him as she considered how to convey the complicated emotions she'd experienced after believing she'd killed him. She didn't even know if he deserved an answer.

"May I cut in?"

Kimari's voice was a welcome reprieve.

"Thank you," she mouthed when she spun around to look at the prince. He smiled down at her with nothing but adoration in his eyes.

No, not adoration. *This was all a game to him*, she reminded herself. Even if she was wrong, she needed to treat him like a villain.

"Of course," Kaden said, his voice gruff as his hands dropped from Astrid's waist. He stepped away, giving Astrid space to begin the dance anew with Kimari.

"You have some explaining to do," Kimari hissed into her ear as he pulled her tight against his body.

Chapter Eleven

"I don't know what you mean?" Astrid gasped as Kimari's fingers dug into the soft spot on her side.

"Why is it that every time I believe we've come to an agreement, you have to go and drak it up?"

Doubt swirled within her at his words. She hadn't intended to cause any type of issue for their plans. Or to anger him.

"I'm sorry…"

"Sorry?" He barked out a laugh, followed by an adoring smile.

The quick transitions between love and seething anger left her unsettled. She knew he could switch his behaviors with a snap of his fingers, but still, she couldn't understand why he would be so angry with her now.

"Do you have any idea how difficult it was for me to convince my father that you could be molded into the perfect princess? That you were willing to make an attempt at being malleable. And yet, on the very first night my claims were put to the test, you walk in here as if you were dead set on proving me a liar."

His voice was low in her ear. The hushed tones sounded all the more sinister as he pulled her closer. To everyone else, Astrid was sure it appeared as if they were sharing intimate conversations with one another.

"I...couldn't help myself," she replied softly.

He spun her away from him, his expression a mask of smiles as he gazed upon her. She returned his smile and laughed as he drew her back into his arms.

"I know how challenging it will be for you to act with decorum while you're living here," Kimari said once she was tight against him once more, "but we have to come to an understanding, you and I."

The pace of the waltz increased, their steps becoming faster. Astrid missed a step and accidentally stomped on his toe. He winced, the corners of his eyes watering.

"I think the first order of business should be getting you some dance lessons." He stared at her sternly before bursting into a fit of laughter. "Honestly, Astrid, have you never danced like this before? You're terrible."

"Well, not all of us were raised in a palace, you know. My dancing consisted of techno music in clubs where everyone moved like this." She pulled her hand out of his grasp and then began flailing around, her hips swaying. She closed her eyes as she lifted her face to the heavens above.

Several people around them gasped as she dropped low and then swayed her way back up. Peeking from a cracked eyelid, she glanced over to where Kimari stood. His lips were slightly ajar as he watched her dance. His eyes smoldered as they trailed her every move. She winked at him as she slowly advanced towards him.

"This is how you danced?" he asked. He stood, ramrod straight, as she danced around him, pumping her body to the nonexistent bass within the orchestral waltz.

"What?" she purred at him. "You never had an occasion to dance like this?"

His cheeks turned a deep plum as she pressed her back against him and continued swaying and pumping.

"I would have thought you'd spent countless hours in the clubs. You were a party boy, after all. Or did the headlines get it all wrong?"

"Um…"

"Maybe I should hire you some dance lessons, too."

"Oh, you think I can't dance like this?" he said.

Astrid smirked at him. She'd anticipated that he wouldn't be able to hold himself back from rising to the occasion. Still, she appreciated that he had tried.

"Do you even know how you look right now?"

"Do you?" he countered.

She liked this side of him. Carefree. Snarky. A bit cocky, but it only added to the fun of the conversation. She found herself wanting him to let go with her. To show her his true self rather than the mask he wore for everyone.

"Dance with me." Spinning around to face him, she took his hand and began to pump it with her own. She knew they must look ridiculous to everyone else. Whispers swarmed all around them like gnats, but she didn't care. Let them talk.

As he stared down at her, a warmth settled over her like nothing she'd ever experienced before. Not even with Max. She doubted they'd ever been fully honest with one another. Doubted they ever could be, if she was being truthful with herself. And yet, in that exact moment, it felt as if the only two people in the entirety of the world were them. That the smiles they shared with one another could last an eternity. That they could live and love and die all right here in this very spot and know that they had existed. That they had loved.

For a moment.

She felt seen.

"What are you doing?" Renard's voice cut through the room like a dull knife in a bone.

Astrid released Kimari's hand and turned towards the king, dropping her eyes to the ground. If nothing else, she could at least feign deference.

She trembled slightly, hoping Renard would take her hesitancy to respond as a sign of respect and abashment at dancing in such a lewd way. In reality, she was trying to come up with a way to explain what style of dance she was doing.

"Queen Astrid was demonstrating how she used to dance in the city," Kali said.

Freed by Destiny

She stepped into the space between Astrid and the dais. Astrid released a small sigh of relief as the king's face softened.

"It's a modern dance that I've danced to when I've gone out with my friends in the city," Kali added.

Astrid cocked an eyebrow at the princess. This was news to her. Since when had the darling princess of Lunameed go out to bars? Sure, she was a member of a secret and elite fighting force tasked with protecting the king at all costs, but still. Astrid couldn't envision her moving her body in such provocative ways.

Renard tapped his finger absently against his chin as he regarded her. "I don't remember your guards telling me about these... excursions."

Kali shrugged. "I snuck out."

"You snuck out?" Renard repeated, as if hardly believing it himself. "How in the almighty darkness did you sneak out?"

Her eyes widened and her lips pouted as she stared up at her father. Astrid barely contained the smirk tugging at the corners of her mouth as she watched Kali wind her father around her finger like string. She was like a cat begging for attention. Those baleful eyes. The way she silently begged her father to listen to her. To give her what she wanted.

"Call it my rebellious teenage years," she said softly. "I doubt many of my guards knew. And those who did know were paid off handsomely for never telling you."

"Is that so?" he growled, eying the guards lining the walls.

"Oh, don't blame them, Father. You know I've been fascinated by the secret passages in the palace since I was a child."

He narrowed his eyes as he considered Kali's words.

Kali directed her attention towards the orchestra. "I know this might be a challenge for you, considering the types of instruments you have, but... could you play anything more modern?"

There was a rustling of paper and quiet chatter as the musicians debated in hushed tones. The conductor tapped his baton several times on the music stand in front of him, his rotund body shivering as he lifted his hands and gave the direction for the first notes of the song to begin. The hall filled with heavy beats, so close to what was played on the dance floors at the clubs downtown that Astrid wasn't convinced they weren't the same musicians.

Kali began mimicking the movements Astrid had performed only minutes before. Her hips swayed, her hands reaching high above her head as she slowly twirled in a circle. Eye darted towards Astrid with a look that conveyed, 'what are you doing' and 'you're in so much trouble,' all at the same time.

Astrid resumed her dance, pressing against Kimari as she moved.

For the briefest of moments that felt like an eternity, Kali and Astrid were the only ones dancing. Their bodies drew closer together, until their hands were clasped as they shimmied and rotated to the music. Then, as if an avalanche had been released from its peak, the thunder of feet tapping on the waxed, marble floor erupted.

As more guests joined them in the free flow dance, Astrid stole a glance at the king. His gaze was zeroed in on her, as if he were scoping her out, ready to attack at a moment's notice. It was a hunter's gaze. A predator.

Astrid looked away almost as quickly as their eyes met. A cold, sinking sensation swelled within the pit of her stomach as she turned her back on the king. Kimari's face filled her vision. He leaned into her, his scent and touch permeating every facet of her being as he nestled his head against her cheek.

"Don't think I've forgotten your earlier missteps," he whispered. "We will discuss it later."

The muscles in her stomach clenched, and her breathing hitched. After the moment they'd shared, she couldn't believe he was still angry with her. That he still thought they needed to have an argument.

"For now, let's just enjoy the moment."

His breath against her ear sent gooseflesh racing across her skin. Even in her most vulnerable moments with Max, she'd never felt… She couldn't even find the word to describe the electricity racing up and down her body, urging her forward. Convincing her that she was…

"I won't say it," she whispered.

"Huh?" Kimari cocked an eyebrow at her. "Won't say what?"

Love. The word hung on the tip of her tongue, begging her to utter it. To make it real. She squashed it down, unwilling to let herself feel the way she did right then. Besides, what was love other than a mechanism to get hurt? She didn't care to find out.

Chapter Twelve

By the time Astrid had removed her makeup and gown from the evening's festivities, she was completely wiped. Every part of her body ached as she peeled back the covers and snuggled into her bed.

Memories of the evening danced before her. They were like snowflakes falling from the sky. Each one unique. Each one fleeting as she tumbled into sleep.

Gooseflesh covered her skin. She'd delved into these dreams so many times before, they were starting to become commonplace. Yet, she wasn't sure she could trust them. She stood in a courtyard with tall stone statues surrounding her. Nine in total, each one depicting a different person. Five women and four men. As Astrid gazed upon them, she wondered who they were. What great deeds had they done to land themselves here? Vines wrapped around them and moss blanketed their bases, covering their legs in a thick, green tapestry.

Penny's body materialized out of the smoke swirling around her. Her eyes shimmered with an opal glimmer as she met Astrid's gaze.

"I've been waiting for you."

Astrid sank onto the ground. Gone were the aches and pains that wracked her physical body. Here, she was eternal.

"Yeah, well, I had places to be tonight," she said. Drawing her knees up to her chest, she threaded her fingers together. "I have to ask you something."

She'd been thinking about it all night—ever since Renard had mentioned that he and her mother had been lovers, once upon a time.

"You want to know if Leilani and Renard were ever in love." It wasn't a question.

Astrid hugged her legs tighter. If she was being honest with herself, she wasn't sure she wanted to know the full story. Her mother had been a complicated woman. She'd engaged in questionable scientific research. And then, she'd stolen the results from her partner in order to ensure they didn't fall into his hands.

That Penny didn't become his.

"You're unsure," Penny said.

Astrid swiped her fingers under her eyes. Dampness clung to them as she bowed her head towards Penny to keep her from witnessing her weakness. They settled into an uneasy silence.

Freed by Destiny

"Leilani had a very complicated relationship with Renard," Penny finally said. "She first encountered him when she was very young. Before she met your father. Before she even knew who she was."

"And she fell in love with a monster?"

Penny's features slackened as she regarded Astrid. "You have to remember, my memories of that time are not firsthand, Astrid. Everything I know comes from implanted data from your mother. She provided me with context. And, in her memories, Renard was not a monster."

"How could she have ever thought he was anything but a villain?" Astrid shot to her feet as she stormed towards Penny, who didn't even flinch as they came nose-to-nose with one another. "He is manipulative and cruel. Those things don't just develop overnight, Penny. They're bred. They're forged through countless altercations that always end in the perpetrator's favor."

She released an exasperated breath. Her fingers twitched uncontrollably as she attempted to remain calm.

It didn't work.

"She helped create him."

Penny's features didn't change with each passing word. All Astrid wanted was for her to demonstrate some emotion. Some signal to prove to her that her PEA was still capable of processing human emotion. She could mimic emotions. She could pretend. But she couldn't experience them. Not in the same way those who could walk, and run, and be intimate with their partners could.

"Astrid," Penny began. Her voice was methodic, as if she had been practicing this speech for an eternity and only just now realized that it would be a perfect time to share it. "Leilani was only a teenager when she met Renard. And he wasn't that much older than herself. It was but a summer romance. Nothing more."

"Then why did Renard describe it like it was some epic romance? Like my mother intentionally broke his heart when she chose my father?"

"I can't answer that one. Your mother did not provide additional context."

"Great."

"I do not believe your mother ever anticipated you finding out about her romance with Renard," Penny said matter-of-factly. "She didn't provide a lot of context around how they met or what their arrangement was. There was just a jumbled mess of images of the king bathed in golden sunlight, wearing swim trunks and racing into the ocean."

"Well, that's just stellar, now isn't it?" Astrid said through clenched teeth. "I can't imagine he would have been any different than he is now."

Penny shrugged. "Circumstances change people."

"True..." Astrid paused, contemplating Penny's words more intently. She didn't understand how someone could change so drastically.

Penny motioned for Astrid to take a seat on a tree stump located between several of the pillars. Astrid sank onto the damp wood, surprised she could feel the wetness in the seat of her pants. This was either the most realistic dream she'd ever had, or she was still awake. Somehow, she knew she didn't want to find out the answer.

"'All I know is that she loved history. The magical world. Your father. And you. Perhaps not in that order."

"Not power?" Astrid cocked an eyebrow at her PEA. "You're going to sit there and tell me that she didn't crave to be in control. To dictate what would be coming next."

"There was probably an element to what you're describing," Penny conceded. "But honestly, no. Leilani sought knowledge, not power."

Words were too inconsequential to describe the emotions flooding through Astrid's body. The idea of her mother having any type of romantic relationship with Renard made her insides crawl. Sure, there had been moments when she'd considered that they'd formed a bond beyond rulers searching for a way to bring one of the most powerful magicals to ever live back. Some said she was just a powerful queen, granted magic beyond all other magicals. Others believed she was a Creator herself.

But who among men and magicals would ever want the gods to return?

She didn't know why that phrase rang through her mind at that exact moment. She'd forgotten the author's name a long time ago, but she remembered the sentiments they'd written about. Maybe it had been in one of her history courses in school, or a video she'd watched on some channel. It didn't matter. The heart of the idea was the same. The Creators had been powerful. They could create life with only the whim of a thought, and eradicate life with the snap of a finger. If they had wanted, they could have forced all who were beneath them to bow.

All her life, Astrid had believed they were myths, some piece of ancient lore that her teachers spoke about in analytical tones. They weren't real. Yet, the entity she'd known her entire life could have very well been one. Whatever or whoever Penny was based on, she manifested powers within Astrid far greater than what she should have naturally been gifted with. Still, Astrid couldn't seem to bring herself to believe that the entity who had been her greatest friend for the entirety of her life was based off an ancient queen.

"How did you die?" The question tumbled from her lips before she could stop herself.

Penny ran her fingers through her hair absentmindedly as she stared at Astrid. "What do you mean? I am not dead. I am right here, with you. Though, if you are searching for how I came to exist in this... fractured state..."

"No, I don't mean you as the PEA," Astrid said, exasperated. "I mean, how did you die? Your physical body?"

Penny's eyes glazed over as they flicked from left to right as if reading a body of text more quickly than Astrid could ever imagine. Her body twitched, her eyes never stopping their movement. Astrid considered interrupting her but stopped herself just as her fingers were about to graze Penny's arm. She'd never seen Penny react like this before. Never felt her delve past her breaking point and continue in a frenzied state she couldn't control.

What if interrupting her sequencing broke her again?

Astrid had only just gotten Penny back. And, although this version of Penny was slightly different than the one who had existed before her extended coding had been unlocked, she was still the entity who had cared for Astrid her entire life. Who had loved her. Who had been a friend.

Astrid wasn't about to risk losing her again. She'd fought too hard and for too long to figure out a way to fix what had been broken by the extraction process. She didn't even know if the spell would work a second time if she broke her PEA again.

With a loud whirring noise, Penny came to a halt. She blinked several times, her lips turning into a deep frown.

"There is no record of my death."

"What do you mean? There has to be."

"There are thousands of references to my name. There are stories, little more than myths. But, when the Dark Age of King Lian fell upon us, any written records of my life and death were destroyed. Nothing was saved. Nothing except the oral traditions, the stories passed down by hundreds of voices joining together to spread my history. That is why you know who I was."

The Dark Age had reigned for nearly three hundred years. During that time, written records and technologies had been wiped from the world, leaving the survivors to piece together what they could into some semblance of the world they'd known before the fall. Before the darkness had consumed them.

Astrid curled her fingers into tight fists as she regarded Penny. She couldn't understand how someone would want to literally destroy every piece of their history.

"Then how do you exist like this?"

Penny shrugged. "Honestly, your mother pieced together the oral histories. She tracked down artifacts, remnants of things I'd owned during my lifetime. And, with Renard's help, was able to create a sequencing algorithm."

"You're not really Amaleah, then."

"No. My base programming was based on what Leilani could piece together about Amaleah's personality and abilities. The algorithm did the rest."

"Then how can you magnify my abilities? Or create new ones that I should never have possessed?"

"Whatever she found in that cave was enough to produce a model of what her powers were. Renard was the one who figured out how to make the PEA gift powers to its owner."

Astrid stood without moving. She didn't even know if she was breathing during that time, her mind was racing so quickly as she attempted to make sense of what Penny was telling her. Part of it made sense to her. She'd seen what Renard's technologies were capable of, and she could only imagine what having one of his devices would do to a person if it had been implanted in them at birth and allowed to seep into them. She hypothesized that, even if the device were to be completely removed from her body, she would still retain some of its effects.

"I wish you could be with me when I'm awake," Astrid whispered. "I miss you. So much."

"And I, you."

"Isn't there a way for you to come back?"

Penny's eyes glistened as she said, "The spell is slowly repairing me, but I'm not sure I will ever be capable of things I was before my programming was deleted. Even now I am so different than who I used to be. Yet, I am also not the cold, calculating monster Renard made me to be. I refuse to be."

"You're not a monster."

"That may be true, but I am lonely. Alone in a world full of lonely souls. And I don't want to live like that anymore. I don't want to exist in a world where I am expected to hide my true self just for the sake of another's comfort. Leilani and Renard created me, Astrid. They gave me this life. This drive to succeed. To be of service."

"But what if you could choose something else?" Astrid pressed. "What if there was an opportunity to be more than an AI trapped in a PEA?"

Astrid's entire body buzzed with excitement as a single thought ripped through her: what if she could devise a way to remove Penny from her entirely? She could have a body. A life, separate from Astrid's. She could continue to learn and grow and become something more than just a PEA. She could be free.

Penny shook her head, her eyes hardening as she regarded Astrid with a sad smile. "I know you mean well, Astrid, but there's nothing you can do to make me more whole. I am fragmented shards of a former self I never even knew. And I will keep on shattering into smaller and smaller pieces as my memory files deteriorate."

"But what if we stop that from happening? What if we turn the whole world upside down and show them artificial intelligence is possible?"

"I love you for trying, but my darling girl, it will never work. PEAs have never successfully been implanted to a robotic body before. I have run the scenarios countless times. It just doesn't work."

"That's because no one else has ever had a PEA like you before. You're one of a kind, Penny." She took Penny's hands and threaded her fingers through the PEA's. "Listen to me, Penny. All my life, you've been my constant companion since before I can remember. You made it possible to believe. You deserve to live a life that is full of opportunities to just... be. And that's what

I want to offer you. A chance to dive into data, synthesize the results, and come up with a solution."

"And what if it fails?" Penny whispered, her voice cracking. "What if you successfully remove me from your subconscious only to destroy the data? You used the recovery spell on me once. I'm not convinced this plan will work, Astrid."

"Don't you think it's worth the risk?"

They stared at each other in stony silence. Astrid wobbled back and forth on her toes as she waited for Penny to say or do anything to indicate that she understood. A tingling sensation crept up her fingers, starting at her tips and spreading up her arm, past her elbow, before ebbing away. She flexed her fingers as she waited, working off the nervous energy flooding her system.

"The healing spell is working," Penny said at last. Her voice cracked as she spoke, though Astrid couldn't understand why. "But I'm not sure if removing me from your body will work. How could it?"

"A chance at a real life is worth it, Penny. It has to be."

"Because you make the assumption that seconds and minutes are just as important as hours and days and years."

"No, I make the assumption that it is better to live in freedom, realizing your true self, than it is to whither away without trying."

"Fair point. But I'm afraid I cannot—"

"If you don't accept this chance, what will my pursuit of the draking spell to bring you back be worth?" Astrid interrupted. "I risked so much to have you returned to me and now I'm offering you the opportunity to have your own space. Without me."

Freed by Destiny

Penny took Astrid hands in her own. Warmth encompassed her fingers as Penny trailed circles across her skin with her thumb.

"I have loved you since the moment Leilani first put programming into you, Astrid. But, until today, I didn't realize how sure of yourself you've become. I barely recognize you."

"Yeah, well, the last time we really and truly spoke you were begging me not to go through the extraction procedure." Astrid snapped her fingers. "Poof. Gone. And I have been searching for a way to bring you back ever since."

"And now you've seen me in your dreams on countless occasions. But it's not the same, is it? Not the same as having me constantly by your side for emotional and mental support."

"No."

"I have to confess I've always wondered what it would be like to have a body. To live among the world. To fall in love and to care for children. But that is a fantasy."

"No, I refuse to believe that," Astrid growled. "There was a way to bring you back when everyone told me it was impossible. Including yourself. And now, you're asking me to trust you again. What would make removing you from my PEA and placing you inside a robotic body any different than keeping you with me?"

"Listen to me, Astrid. Please. You have it in your head that if you can get me into a new body that my healing process will continue. But what if it doesn't?"

"We'll find a way."

Storm clouds formed all around them, lightning striking out in all directions, illuminating the sky in a blaze of silver light.

"I hope we can," Penny whispered before her body exploded into a cascade of glittering light.

Astrid screamed as she tumbled to the ground.

Penny was gone.

Chapter Thirteen

Sweat soaked Astrid's bedsheets as she gained consciousness from her dream. Her pajamas clung to her drenched body, making her shiver as a cool breeze swept over her. Panting, she leaned her head between her legs as she waited for the nausea to pass.

Seeing Penny, hearing her voice, feeling her touch—it had all felt so real. It had been real. She kept reminding herself that this was the spell working. Penny was coming back to her in stages, one part of her at a time. And, although she wasn't exactly the same entity that had consoled her and kept her company all the days of her life, this new version was somehow stronger. More resilient and powerful than Penny had ever been. She hoped that she didn't lose that spark along the way. That whatever coding had been unlocked by the spell was permanent. She rather liked this more confident and powerful version of her oldest friend.

"I promise you," she whispered to herself as she wiped the sweat dripping down her brow with the back of her hand. "I promise I will find a way to give you a body. A life of your own."

She had zero idea how she would pull off such a feat, but she was determined. This was something she could give her truest friend that would make her life significantly better. If there was even a modicum of potential Penny to have a body of her own, Astrid would find a way to make it happen.

A soft tapping on her door drew her attention. Groaning slightly, she stood from the bed and wrapped a robe around her shoulders as she crept to the door.

"Who is it?" she asked. Her throat ached as she spoke, and the copper taste of blood coated her tongue. She caressed her chapped lips, cringing as she found the bleeding cracks.

"I heard you screaming," a male voice from the other side said. One of her guards, she was sure.

"I had a bad dream," Astrid said. It was the truth.

"Would you like for me to call one of the servants to bring you a warm glass of milk?"

Leaning her head against the door, Astrid let the chilled wood ease through her body, clearing her mind. "No, I don't think that will be necessary."

"Just so," the guard replied. "But, if you change your mind, just let me know."

"Thank you." She walked towards the window on the opposite side of the room and stared out at the twinkling lights of the cityscape beyond the gardens. She missed her home. She missed The Wand and how things used to be, before she discovered who she was. Before she decided to push forward with her destiny.

She wondered what Bear and Max and Maya were doing at that very moment. Were they looking out at the palace, thinking about her? They were her family now. She hoped, with every fiber of her being, that she would be able to see them again, even if it was only to tell them what they meant to her.

Her door creaked open and she spun around, drawing the robe tighter around her body. She was half expecting the guard to be standing in her doorway. Or Kali.

Instead, Kimari stood there, his face a mask of annoyance, anger, and something else she couldn't place.

"What are you doing here?" she demanded. Her hands shook as she held her robe closed.

"I couldn't sleep." He glanced over his shoulder, as if checking to see if the guard was listening in before slamming her door shut behind him.

"I wouldn't call this a proper meeting, would you?" She pressed her back against the window to keep herself from shuffling her feet. Why was he here?

"I don't care," he said. He closed the gap between them with three large steps. His face was so close to hers, she could feel the heat of his breath mingling with her own. "We need to talk."

"And this couldn't have waited until morning?" She quirked an eyebrow at him.

He leaned into her ever so slightly until there was less than a finger's width between them.

"No." His voice had taken on a husky tone, deeper and raspier than it usually was. With her back pressed against the window, there was no place for Astrid to go. She was trapped by him. As if sensing her thoughts, he placed his palms on either side of her body, his fingers pressing into the stone of the wall. "Do you have any idea what kind of danger you put us both in tonight?"

Peering into his eyes, she recognized one of the emotions coursing through him: desire. If she leaned forward just slightly, their lips would caress one another. There was no one here to see them. No one to stop them. No one to judge her for wanting him and despising him all at the same time.

He blinked and leaned away from her. The sudden loss of heat and tension between them made her bold. She reached for his hand. He didn't fight against her as she interlaced her fingers with his.

"I didn't mean to cause a scene. I just... couldn't help myself. There are so many secrets between your father and my...past." She couldn't bring herself to tell him the truth. "I need answers. He is the only one left who can fill in the gaps."

Kimari squeezed her fingers before tugging her closer to him. Wrapping an arm around her shoulders, he nuzzled his face against her neck. Every part of her was set ablaze. She wanted more. Desire swelled within her as his breathing changed. She needed to kiss him, to feel his hands gliding over her skin. A shiver ran up her spine at the thoughts parading through her mind.

"I'm sorry there are so many secrets. So many gaps in your story," he whispered. He cradled her against him.

She thought she'd felt safe with Max. He'd been her protector. He'd helped her learn who she really was. He'd supported her as she'd stormed towards claiming her throne. And she did love him, but in the way someone loves their best friend. How Kimari made her feel was different. More passionate. More driven by the pairing of two souls into one. They had been raised so differently, and yet they were so similar.

"It's not your fault." She trailed her fingers down his back, feeling him tense beneath her touch. His breathing hitched as her hand came to rest on his hip. "Unless you're withholding information from me, in which case, I will have to demand that you share your intel."

Chuckling, he positioned his head from her neck to hovering just above her once more. "Astrid, I…"

She didn't give him a chance to finish. She pressed her lips against his. He stiffened, then his lips moved against hers, caressing, tasting, savoring. She moaned slightly as he wrapped his hands around her waist, drawing her even nearer to him.

She'd kissed Kimari before, but this kiss exploded like fireworks through her body, igniting every part her. All the doubts, the worries, and the insecurities she'd been experiencing since choosing to come here with him seemed to melt away the longer they lingered in each other's arms.

When, at last, they separated for longer than a breath, Kimari sighed contentedly and tugged Astrid towards her bed. She glanced between him and the still damp sheets and shook her head.

"No." The single word escaped her lips before she could stop it. But, once she'd uttered it, she knew it was true. If they cuddled together, she didn't know if she would be able to maintain her self control. And, despite his words, she still doubted him.

He tucked a strand of her hair behind her ear, his fingers grazing her cheek and lingering on the side of her head as he peered down at her. Although her room was dark, the sister moons gave off just enough light that she could see his expression. His brow furrowed into a deep V as he searched her face.

"Do you want me to go?" he asked. Although his words said one thing, his eyes and body language told a completely different tale.

She leaned her forehead against his, soaking in the heat of him as she whispered, "No."

He folded in around her. Unsure where she ended and he began, Astrid clung to him. Every part of her felt as if she were on fire, electrified by his touch. Energized by the love she felt pouring from him. All her doubts about his loyalty melted away. There was only the two of them. No one to hurt them. No one to break them apart. No one to stop them from surging forward to a new beginning.

Together, they were infinite.

He cupped her cheek, his fingers caressing her as he tilted her face upwards to press his lips against her. She did not hold back as she returned fire with passion. He slid his other hand beneath her robe, trailing circles up and down her back as he pulled her tightly against him. They stumbled backwards as a pair until they fell onto her bed, cradling each other.

"Astrid," he murmured each time they pulled apart just long enough to catch a breath. "Astrid."

Each time her name cascaded from his lips, she yearned to hear him say it again. She didn't know if it was the wine, the fear she'd felt during the dinner, or the darkness still looming over her from the dream, but all her hesitations and inhibitions sloughed from her with each kiss and murmur.

Although she knew he wanted more, he didn't pressure her. Didn't move past cuddling her close to his chest and kissing her. For now, the comfort of knowing there was a spark of hope between them was enough. It was the kindling she needed to trust him. To believe him when he told her he would stand by her, even against his father.

The sister moons slid beneath the horizon. And still Astrid remained locked in his arms.

Astrid breathed in deeply, savoring the spicy scent of his cologne as she dug her face into his chest. Her breathing shifted as she drifted into sleep.

"Astrid." Kimari's voice was urgent as he nudged her. "You have to wake up."

He kissed her brow. "Please."

She stirred, her body aching as she shifted her head to stare up at him. His back was pressed against the headboard and his arms were wrapped tightly around her, still cradling her to his chest as she slumbered.

"How long have I been asleep?"

His lips curled into a half-smile. "Long enough."

Realization dawned on her. He'd spent the night in her room. Despite the fact that all they'd done was kiss, she was certain Renard would find some way to twist this to his gain. Force her into the marriage sooner, hoping for a child. An heir born of both magic and human blood. Only then could he be secure to execute her. The thought sent a shiver coursing through her body.

"You have to leave. Now." Even as her body longed to remain close to him, she pushed herself away from him. She couldn't believe she'd let him stay. Memories of the night before shoved their way to the forefront of her mind. Desire quickened her heartbeat.

He stared at her with a wolffish grin stretching across his face. "Last night..."

"Shh," she said, placing her fingers against his lips. He kissed them, closing his eyes as if savoring the taste of her once more. "You can't be here when my maids arrive."

She glanced at the time illuminated on the watch wrapped around his wrist. It was already an hour past when the servants Renard provided to her normally there to help her prepare for the day.

"Astrid." Her name on his lips once again sent a whoosh of fire through her.

She wanted nothing more than curl up beside him, but she couldn't let Renard have this win. Not when she was so afraid for her safety. Her life. She didn't have any power here. Not really. Sure, she should say no. She could put up a fight. But, at the end of the day, she didn't have her powers. She'd been separated from her friends and family. And the only people in this forsaken place that she had any type of relationship with had betrayed her on so many occasions she wasn't sure she could trust them.

That included Kimari.

"You need to leave," she said again.

He searched her face. He must not have found what he was looking for because he stood from the bed and walked towards the door. His fingers lingered on the handle as he turned back to her.

"I know you don't understand, and that I have given you every reason to doubt me. But I do care for you, Astrid. And I want to build a life together. I don't know if you believe me, or if you even care. But I can't go another day without you knowing I will fight for us. I will fight for this opportunity to build a bridge between our two peoples. And, if you just give me a chance, I know I can convince my father that you aren't a threat to him. That you can be content living by my side."

He slid through the door without another word. She stared after him, her heart racing as she attempted to piece together what he'd just told her. He cared for her. He wanted to build a life together. And yet, even as she mulled over his words, one phrase stood out to her. Could she be content to live by his side? The very thought of giving up the power she'd fought so hard to achieve rocked her world. She was a queen in her own right. A hero to her people. And here was this human, this man, trying to take away her power.

She cared for him. She believed she might even be falling in love with him. But she would drakked if she would let him steal the very things that made her whole. That made her herself.

Tears leaked from the corners of her eyes as she leaned her head back against the headboard. Beyond anything else, she wished she could talk to Penny. The old Penny. The one who had given her counsel on countless occasions and who loved her exactly as she was. But she couldn't. She'd been left with this new version of her oldest friend, with the unlocked memories and the history that had been locked away from her coding for years. Grinding her teeth, Astrid forced herself to get up.

She didn't have time to cry, or to mope. Or to wish that she had been born in a different era. One where she didn't have to fight so hard to protect her people. That wasn't her reality and all she had was now. She'd made a promise to herself and to her people. She would keep fighting. She would stop at nothing to protect them. Even if it cost her everything.

Still, as she slipped out of her robe and selected a new gown for the day, the memory of his caress haunted her. He was a part of her now, whether she liked it or not. She just hoped he'd been sincere in the other things he'd said to her. That he cared for her. That he wanted her by his side, always.

His word was all she had to go on.

Chapter Fourteen

Her days spent in the palace jumbled together. Not once did Renard allow her access to her magic. The same routine happened every day. Get up. Eat breakfast. Practice etiquette and womanly virtues. Break for reading. Prepare for an evening spent in either the family dining room or the grand banquet hall. Return to her rooms for sleep.

Throughout each day, Astrid hoped Kimari would give her a sign that the night they'd spent together was real. That he did, indeed, love her. That he would fight for her to stay alive. Yet, he did not return to her rooms, nor did he bring up their time together to her. Sometimes, Astrid caught herself wondering if it had all been a dream and he'd never come to her at all.

The same was true with Kali. Each day, Kali would spend hours teaching her another skill she would need as Kimari's wife, as the

Lunameedian queen. Yet, not once did Kali bring up the idea of escaping again. She didn't attempt to disrupt any listening devices or send Astrid hidden messages. It was as if the entire experience in the garden had been a figment of Astrid's imagination.

Yet, Astrid knew they had both happened. She knew they had plans they weren't sharing with her. She just couldn't figure out a way to prove it.

Kali pressed her hands into Astrid's back before lifting one of them to straighten Astrid's chin.

"Back straight, eyes forward," Kali said as she dropped her hands from Astrid's body. "You need to practice your posture, Astrid."

Rolling her eyes, Astrid did as Kali directed.

"Good."

Her back ached as she made a tour about the room. It felt awkward to keep her back so straight as she walked. Her hips groaned against each step, but still Astrid forced herself to place one foot in front of the other.

"How much longer do I have to do this?" she asked when she came to stand before Kali once more. "I've been practicing walking, dancing, talking, and so many other mundane things for weeks now. Surely, I have made enough progress that your father sees me fit to be done with this."

Kali's braids bounced as she shook her head. "Unfortunately, there is just so much that you don't know yet."

Astrid scowled. This princess training was tedious and not at all what she thought she would be doing when she'd agreed to come here. Sure, she'd believed that Renard might kill her on the spot, but some things were worse than death. She was convinced this was one of them.

"I don't understand what the end game is here," she said. "I know your father intends to kill me once I bear an heir for his precious throne. You told me so yourself."

Kali's eyes darted around the room as her skin turned ashen. In an almost imperceptible movement, she shook her head.

"What? You don't want Renard to know I know his plans? Well, that's too bad."

Releasing an exasperated sigh, Kali stormed towards Astrid and swung her hand across her face, backhanding her with enough force to send Astrid reeling backwards. She stumbled, her feet tripping over themselves before she fell to the floor in a heap. Kali knelt to help her up. As her arms linked with Astrid's, a strange hum filled the air around them. Just like in the garden, time seemed to still.

"What the drak are you doing?" Kali growled. "Do you have any idea how much risk I've taken over the past two weeks to prepare an escape plan for you? And here you are, moaning about improving your posture. Why would you ever say 'you told me so yourself?' *Drak*, Astrid! I told you to trust me."

"Trust you! Don't make me laugh, Kali. How could I ever? You and your brother are the reasons I'm in this predicament to begin with."

Kali sighed. "And I told you that I was working on a plan to get you out of here. I've seen the writing on the wall, Astrid. My father won't stop until he's consumed the entire world. And the only person who has even come close to stopping him is you."

Tension clouded Astrid's thoughts as she tried to come up with a retort, but everything soured on her tongue.

"We don't have much time," Kali said. "I can't risk doing this again, but I need you to say it. Tell me you trust me. That no matter what, you will understand why I have to do the things I do from here on out."

"Any hint as to what those things might be?"

"Great and terrible things."

"Oh, well, in that case."

"I'm not joking, Astrid. If I have to do something… unsavory to convince my father I am still on his side, I will. Even if that means hurting you. I just need you to trust that I won't harm you beyond repair and that I will figure out a way to protect you. To free you."

Astrid contemplated what Kali was saying. Part of it made sense to her, yet she couldn't stop the nagging voice at the back of her mind pleading with her to reconsider putting her faith in Kali. She'd already betrayed her once.

"You have to believe me."

"How can I?"

Kali shook her head, a defeated sigh slipping through her lips. "We're out of time."

The haziness around them evaporated and time seemed to move at a regular pace once more. Kali gripped a chunk of Astrid's hair and pulled her head back.

"Don't ever disrespect me again. Do you understand?"

Glaring at her, Astrid spat silver blood. She bared her teeth but didn't say a word as Kali released her hold on her.

Freed by Destiny

"Maybe next time you'll think twice before insinuating that I would ever betray my father," Kali said. She propped one hand on her hip. "You should know by now that attempting to flee is futile.

Astrid rubbed her cheek where Kali had struck her. Although her flesh was tender and ached to the touch, she did not let herself cry.

"Just remember what I've told you," Kali continued. "As long as you do that, you'll be fine."

Astrid didn't know if it was a threat or a masked clue to trust her. She was tired of trying to figure out the motives of this family. Tired of trying to please them. They held her life in their hands and did not give her any hope that they would let her forget it.

"You should take a break," Kali said as she strode past Astrid. "Reflect on what's happened here today. And remember your place."

She left without another word. Astrid listened to the clacking of Kali's shoes against the stone floor. When the sound faded into silence, Astrid leaned back against one of the walls and slid to the floor. Drawing her knees to her chest, she let the tears she'd been holding in slide down her cheeks.

Remember who you are.

That voice. She hadn't heard it like this for so long.

Penny? She closed her eyes and breathed in deeply, hoping to hear Penny's voice again.

Remember.

Pressing the heels of her hands into her eyes, Astrid forced herself to stop crying.

S.A. McClure

I am Astrid Bluefischer. Queen of the Fae. Protector of the Weak. The Firebird. And I will not forget.

A sense of calm washed over her as she repeated her title over and over again. Her heart rate slowed, her mind clearing. She didn't know if she'd heard Penny's voice or if her subconscious had created it for her. It didn't matter. It didn't change who she was or what she had come here to do. She was a fighter. Had been her entire life. Just because this was a particularly rough period in her life, it did not mean she would let them—any of them—tear her down.

Picking herself up from the floor, Astrid walked to her bedroom window. City lights illuminated the sky, casting a haze over the ground. As she watched, fire began to burst to life all throughout the city. Their blaze rose above even the highest skyrises, yellow and red flames licking at the sister moons. Astrid gasped, her heart thrumming painfully in her chest. She knew it was them. Her friends. Her soldiers.

Her rebels.

Sirens began to wail, signaling the fires had reached well beyond what the automatic sprinkler system within the city could handle. She gripped the window's ledge, trying to ground herself in the reality of what was happening. Her people were attacking the city. There were only two outcomes possible: they would be destroyed by Renard's armies or they would be held as captives. They would be used as pawns against her, forcing her hand more than it already was.

Her chest tightened as, in the distance, the dark shadow of a swarm of robotic soldiers advanced on the city.

Chapter Fifteen

Astrid's door flung open as two soldiers rushed into her room. One of them grabbed her by the arm and yanked her away from the window.

"It isn't safe for you here," he bellowed as he half-dragged her towards the door.

"Where are you taking me?" She struggled against his grasp, her mind racing through all the possibilities. Would she be taken to Renard? The dungeons? Somewhere else in this light forsaken palace that she hadn't discovered yet? The possibilities were endless, but the magnitude of horror each one presented increased as each idea leapt into her head.

"To safety," another one of the soldiers said.

The guard holding onto her arm dug his fingers into her wrist. She winced, the first blossoms of a bruise forming beneath her skin. She longed for her powers, the magic deep within her. If she had access to it, these soldiers wouldn't dare treat her like this. Even if she was still forced to follow their commands, they wouldn't subject her to pain or humility in the same ways they did now.

"You don't have to be so gruff," she said.

The guard tightened his grasp even more. Astrid groaned.

"Lay off her," the other soldier said.

Astrid did a double-take of the second soldier. With her flat chest and stocky build, she'd almost mistaken her for a man. But, now that she looked more closely, she noticed the subtle curves, tight ponytail, and softer features the soldier had.

Astrid continued to struggle against the one carrying her. He smacked her across the head as one of her feet slammed into his stomach. Stars danced in her eyes as she wobbled and nearly collapsed onto the floor. Only his grip on her wrist stopped her from sinking to the ground entirely.

In a flash Astrid barely saw, the female soldier flung her arm into the other one's neck and shoved him backwards. He dropped Astrid's wrist as he was pinned. He gagged as she cut off his airstream, his face turning pink as he struggled to free himself from her grasp. She did not budge.

"If you ever lay a hand on the Queen like that again, I will cut your cock off and feed it to the dogs. Do you understand me? Blink twice if you understand."

He must have followed the female soldier's command because she stepped back and removed her arm from his gullet. He gingerly touched the spot where she'd throat punched him. Tears leaked from the corners of his eyes as he glared at her.

Freed by Destiny

"Do we have an understanding?" The female soldiers placed herself between him and Astrid.

Although Astrid could tell he wanted to spout off at her, wanted to attack her, it was clear he was also afraid of her. He nodded.

"Good." She turned towards Astrid. "There's an attack on the city. We've been ordered to escort you to the safe room with the rest of the family." She placed a firm hand on Astrid's shoulder. "You'll be safe with us. I promise."

Safe. Astrid didn't know if she knew the meaning of that word anymore. If Renard's own soldiers weren't afraid to beat on her, then how could she expect any different from their master? She swallowed hard and ground her teeth.

The soldier bent down to eye level with her. "I promise I won't let him hurt you anymore. And he'll be reported to our commander." She shot a glance at him, her lips curling into a vicious snarl. "Don't think for a second you're getting out of this with a slap on the wrist, Gustav."

"Drak you, Anne. I mean it."

Anne rolled her eyes at him and refocused on Astrid once more. "He's a lot more talk than he is bite."

"Tell that to my head."

Anne chuckled before her expression turned serious again. "People are setting fires throughout the entirety of the city. We don't know who's responsible yet, but until we can determine what the threat is, you have to be kept safe."

She nodded. "Let's go."

Smiling, Anne motioned for Gustav to go first. His eyes narrowed at her and his shoulders hunched up close to his ears, as if he was considering attacking her back, but he seemed to think better of the prospect. He strode from Astrid's chambers without a word.

"You next, I'll bring up the rear," Anne said.

Astrid looked both ways down the hallway before leaving her room and following Gustav towards an unknown location within the palace. She prayed her people would be successful. That they would be able to breach the palace walls. That they would find her. It was a long shot, especially with the robotic soldiers already dispatched. Still, she couldn't help the small flame of hope kindling deep inside her.

Her friends wanted her back. They wanted to know she was safe. And they were willing to fight—and die—to make it happen.

Astrid followed Gustav through a series of hallways she didn't remember ever walking before. They changed direction several times and Astrid wasn't sure if he was doing this on purpose to confuse her or if the way to the safe room was really that convoluted. Shots fired, in the distance. The sound of the explosives popping grew louder with each passing minute. Anne pressed against her back, urging her to go faster.

They entered a glass hallway. Dozens of trees lined either side of the walkway, their trunks wrapped in twinkling white lights.

Astrid gasped. "Where are we?"

She'd never been to this area of the palace before, but its beauty was breathtaking.

"The princess's promenade," Anne said.

Astrid spun in a circle. Everywhere she looked were twinkling lights.

Freed by Destiny

"The king had it built for Princess Kali when she was a young girl after they took a trip to the Borganda. When they returned to Lunameed, she wouldn't stop talking about how beautiful the wrapped trees were or how the delicate strings of lights turned the world into an enchanting dream. So, the king replicated the gardens here."

The windows rattled as an explosion went off close enough for the blast to reverberate through their bones.

"We have to go. Now!" Anne growled as she shoved Astrid forward.

Gustav glanced back at them, his eyes full of fear as he raced down the hall.

The blasts became louder. It seemed as if every step Astrid took, another one went off. And they were close. Streaks of light and hazing smoke were visible through the glass panes. She could see streaks of light and a haze of smoke on the other side of the glass panes. Cracks formed in the glass as the concussive blasts continued to break against them.

"Run!" Anne yelled.

Gustav bounded forward. Astrid covered her eyes with her hands as the shards of broken glass cascaded all around them. Slivers of glass, sharper and thinner than any blade, sliced through her skin. She gasped in pain, silver blood coating her arms and matting her hair as she continued to blindly charge forward.

Gunshots, so close they made her ears ring, formed a cacophony all around them. Astrid stole a glance through the trees. A group of figures fought against robotic soldiers no more than forty paces away. It was too dark and hazy for her to tell who was in the fray, but somewhere in her heart she knew Bear and Max were there, doing everything within their power to reach her.

Anne scooped Astrid into her arms and shoved past Gustav as she charged through an open doorway at the end of the walkway. Her breathing came quick and shallow as she hugged Astrid to her chest. Anne turned down another passageway, this one full of doors. Midway down, she skidded to a halt and dropped Astrid on the floor. She fumbled with a keypad next to the door.

As Astrid waited for Anne to input the correct code, a chill filled the hallway. She glanced up at three figures standing at the end of the hall. Their faces were shrouded in darkness. Her stomach dropped.

They weren't her friends.

"Anne," she whispered.

Her guard punched in the last digit of the code and waited for the door to swing open. A loud squawking blared from the keypad, its keys flashing red.

"Drak. Drak. Drak…" Anne muttered as she leaned her head over the keypad again.

But Astrid wasn't watching her guard. Her eyes were firmly locked on the figures still standing at the end of the hall. They turned toward the blaring keypad.

"Anne," Astrid said again.

"What?"

"Look." She pointed towards the figures, her arm shaking.

Anne looked up from the keypad and froze. Her cheeks sucked into her as she stared at the figures, her eyes widening.

Freed by Destiny

"Drak," she murmured.

"Who are they?" Astrid asked.

"I… thought they were only rumors. Myths to scare new recruits." Her hands shook as she punched in the code again. The entire pad lit up with white light and an electronic door slid open.

The figures screeched in unison before charging towards her.

Chapter Sixteen

Anne grasped Astrid under the shoulders and heaved her through the door just as the creatures leapt on the spot she had been laying in. The door slammed shut behind them, locking the figures on the other side.

"What the drak were those things?" Astrid shouted. She scrambled away from the door and pressed her back against the wall. Peering around the room, she realized that Kali and Kimari were both there, along with their mother. Renard was nowhere to be seen.

"What was what?" Kimari asked, leaping to his feet and coming towards her, a look of confusion mixed with concern plastered on his face.

They're barely talked since their night together. He'd been careful to keep his distance from her. And yet, here he was, standing before her as if no time had passed at all. She glared at him. He shirked away from her.

"Astrid." Her name on his lips made her yearn to feel his arms wrapped around her, but she couldn't forgive him. Not yet.

"Lieutenant Anne." Kali approached the soldier. "What is on the other side of these doors? Have the rebels breached our defenses?"

"They...yes, My Lady. They've breached our perimeter. There was fighting in the promenade. And..." She glanced at the door behind her. "I'm not sure what those things were."

"That's not true!" Astrid growled, forcing herself to stand.

Kimari took her hand, his warmth giving her the resolve needed to continue.

"You said you thought they were just myths. Rumors. So don't stand there and say you don't know what they are. You do."

Anne licked her lips, her hands flexing as she stared at Astrid with a hard look in her eyes. "There were rumors in the training camps. I didn't think they were real. I..."

She paused as the sound of something clawing at the door drew all of their attentions towards whatever was on the other side of the lock.

"Just spit it out already," Astrid said.

"Soldiers have been going missing from the training camp for years. Decades some say. But all the stories share a common element. A trio of wraiths coming to steal their light."

Astrid cocked an eyebrow at her. "And you think that's what's on the other side of this door?"

Freed by Destiny

"Yes."

She shook her head. "How could there be wraiths here?"

Anne glanced at the Queen and then from Kali to Kimari. Her lips trembled slightly, but she didn't say anything.

"Renard wanted to be able to control death," Queen Lianna said.

Astrid swung her head towards the queen, her jaw dropping slightly. She hadn't heard her speak so coherently the entire time she'd been a captive in the palace. For a month now, all she'd seen the Queen do was nod, drip food down her chin, and stare off into space.

Lianna strode towards the door and pressed her palm against the metal. She did not balk when the screeching sound of a claw dragging across the metal on the side reverberated through the room.

"My husband fears death above all else, and so he sought a way to control it. He searched for the wraiths for nearly a decade. And then he programmed them to follow his commands. There were... issues with the training, of course."

"The soldiers being taken from the camps," Astrid whispered. Realization sank into her bones. This king had so many more secrets than she knew. What would be next?

Lianna nodded. "Them. And others. But... I had thought he'd finally figured out how to master them. To bring them to heel. There had been so few reports of them attacking anyone over the past three years."

Astrid narrowed her eyes at the queen. This version of her was so drastically different than the one she'd witnessed so far. She wondered if the public version of herself was just an act or if she had moments of clarity.

"Why would Father keep them here?" Kali said. "If he knew they were a threat."

"I don't know."

"Where is Renard?" Astrid asked. She was surprised he wasn't locked in their room with them.

"He has his own secure room," Kimari said. "Only his personal guards know where it is, and they stay inside the room with him."

"And you don't think it's rather convenient that the night there's an attack on the city his soul-eating minions just happen to be waiting outside the room where his family is being kept?"

The three royals shared a look between them.

"Are you implying my husband sent them here to… to what, exactly? Kill his own family?"

It was exactly what Astrid was thinking. Or, at the very least, sent to kill her. She wouldn't put it past the king to have her assassinated during a time of strife and confusion and then blame her death on the very people out there trying to save her.

Oh, creators, she thought. *What if they find their way to this hallway? What if the wraiths catch them unawares and kill them?*

She couldn't bear the thoughts of Max or Bear being killed by those things.

"There's another explanation," Kali said. Her voice wobbled. "What if he lost control of them? What if they're here, not because Dad sent them to… to kill us… but because he's not ordering them to do anything right now."

Freed by Destiny

"You think they're using the attack on the city… on the palace… as a way to break the manacles around their necks?" Kimari dropped Astrid's hand and closed the gap between him and his sister. "It honestly makes more sense."

"You're assuming that wraiths are more than mindless creatures searching for their next meal," Lianna said. "Renard described them to me on countless occasions. They are little more than dogs. Beasts who kill anything in sight when set loose."

Anger bubbled within Astrid as she stared at the queen. She'd felt sorry for her, for how Renard treated her and looked at her with contempt. But hearing her now, talking so lowly of a specific type of magical creature, made her wish she'd never given the queen the benefit of the doubt. She was just as bigoted and vile as her husband.

"They are innocent creatures who are just living by their nature. You can't fault them for acting out when I'm sure all they've experienced since they've been in Renard's captivity is pain and suffering."

"Who are you to tell me how my husband treats the creatures who come under his domain? He is the king, you pointed-eared little…"

"That's enough, Mother," Kimari cut in. His jaw twitched as he stared at his mother with contempt. "Astrid is my fiancée. I am marrying her. I love her. So it would be prudent of you—"

Lianna smacked him on the shoulder with a loud crack. "Who are you to disrespect me so? I am the one who brought you into this world, Kimari. And you best believe that if you don't start acting like you know it, I will make you."

Curved protrusions exploded on the door as the wraith struck the

183

door again with its clawed hands. Astrid trailed her fingers over the jagged metal, slicing one of them open. Shaking her hand, she sucked on the wound until it stopped bleeding.

"We can't stay here much longer. The door won't hold." Anne glanced towards Lianna. "Is there another way out?"

The Queen shook her head. "I don't…" Her lower lip trembled as she sputtered on her words. "Why are we here?"

Kimari and Kali exchanged a glance. Astrid's heart dropped as she realized the moment of clarity within Lianna had vanished. She was the frail, confused woman once more.

"How long as she been like this?" Astrid whispered to Kimari.

He shook his head. "Now isn't the time."

She wanted to understand everything there was to know about Lianna's condition, but before she could ask another question, the creatures began slamming their bodies against the door. The door cracked down the center, beginning where the claws had nearly punctured it and expanding outward.

"Drak, drak, drak," Kali whispered under her breath.

She raced to the other side of the room and slammed her hand against a painting hanging on the wall. It glowed blue before popping open to reveal a laser pistol. She wrenched it free from its case and pointed it at the first wraith as it was midway through the door. She struck it in the chest, creating a blazing hole in its center of mass, before firing a second shot straight through its skull.

It shrieked, falling backwards as a second one was already crawling through the hole. Kali fired again. The wraith lifted its arm, blocking the shot from striking it in the chest. It shrieked as it lunged forward and slammed into Anne. She struggled beneath its mass, her arms flailing wilding as she tried to pull the dagger holstered to her thigh from its sheath. Gripping the hilt, she stabbed the wraith multiple times in rapid succession. Black smoke curled from its body, winding upwards with each new blow. It didn't even flinch.

Before Astrid had time to react to Anne's struggle with the wraith, the third one dove through the hole and ambled towards Kali. She fired rapidly at the creature. Many of the shots struck the it, but the only sign that it was injured were the jolts to its body with each hit. Still, Kali continued to fire.

"Tell me you know how to get out of this," Astrid yelled at Kimari.

He drew his sidearm and placed himself between the door and Astrid. Sweat coated his brow as he pointed his gun at the opening. "It won't stay down for long. They can't die."

Anne stabbed the wraith in the head several times until it fell backwards. She scrambled to her feet and rushed to do the same to the one advancing on Kali. It, too, collapsed.

"We need to go. Now," Kimari said.

He pressed his hands on either side of the hole and peered through the opening. When nothing attacked him, he leapt through the hole and then called for the others to follow. Astrid glanced at the wraiths on the floor. The first one to fall twitched as it began to reanimate.

Kali took her mother's hand and dragged her towards the opening. She whispered coaxing words in her mother's ear as she guided her through the opening. Anne slammed her dagger into the twitching wraith's head, making it stop moving, before motioning for Astrid to follow the others out of the room.

"We can't stay here," Anne said. "These things will just keep arising. There's nothing we can do to stop them."

Astrid didn't argue as she stepped through the hole. With the dampeners around her wrists, she couldn't access her powers. Couldn't protect them with her magic.

The hallway was shrouded in smoke, making it difficult to see anything.

"Kali? Kimari? Where are you?" she whispered.

"Astrid? Is that you?" Bear's voice echoed through the hall.

Her heart hammered in her chest. She'd nearly forgotten the sound of his voice. "Bear? Is that really you?"

A figure stepped through the shadows. His leather jacked fitted over his broad shoulders and his neatly trimmed beard with wisps of grey mixed into its dark color were all Astrid needed to see to know that he was.

She flung herself into his arms.

"How did you find me?" She pressed her face into his shoulder as he wrapped his arms tightly around her. "I thought I would never see you again."

"You have Kali to thank for this," he whispered against her hair.

"What?"

"She got a message to us. Well, to Maya. When they realized that Renard planned to kill you immediately after the wedding. We've been working on this plan ever since."

"But…" She couldn't understand how it had happened. Renard watched everything. Saw everything. Heard every word that was spoken in the palace, if he chose to. There was no possible way Kali could have gotten a message to Astrid's friends without the king knowing.

"Don't question it," Bear said. "We're here now and we're going to get you out."

"The robotic soldiers," Astrid said. "They were heading to the city. We have to stop them. They'll kill everyone."

"Don't worry about all that. Not now. Come on, we can't stay here." He scooped her into his arms and carried her to the other end of the hallway.

"Stop right there!" Anne yelled from behind them. "Let Queen Astrid go, and I promise I won't kill you."

Bear dropped Astrid to the ground and gripped a potion ball hanging from his utility belt. It pulled away from the link attaching it to his person easily.

"Just let her leave, lass. No one needs to get hurt."

"What have you done with Prince Kimari and Princess Kali? Where are they?" Anne demanded.

"They are unharmed," Bear said, his back still turned towards Anne. "And they will remain that way. We didn't come here for them. Just let us leave with Astrid."

Anne's fingers curled around the pistol in her hand. Astrid didn't know where she'd gotten the weapon and it didn't matter. It was pointed directly at the center of Bear's back. He wouldn't survive that kind of blast.

Astrid turned towards Anne, her eyes pleading as she said, "I want to go with him. Please, just let me."

"You know I can't do that."

Her stomach dropped as she watched, as if in slow motion, as two things happened at once. The wraith on the floor squirmed and then lunged on top of Anne. The hole where its face should have been latched onto her neck. Bear threw the potion bomb over his shoulder. It rolled across the ground until bumped, against Anne's twitching leg before exploding into a mass of pink goo. It covered the wraith, immobilizing it. Anne's legs were caught in the goo as well. She struggled against it, trying to break free, but couldn't budge.

Frantic energy coursed through Astrid. She turned her attention towards Bear and said, "There are two more of those wraiths in the other room." Her eyes darted towards Anne. "We can't leave her like that. The other two will regenerate. And, when they do, they'll kill her. Please, Bear. We have to do something."

He grunted, but pulled two more potion bombs from his belt, one in each hand, as he headed back towards the broken doorway. He tossed the bombs through the hole before making his way back to Astrid.

"Where are Kali and Kimari?" she asked as she gathered herself from the floor.

"They're safe. I had to knock 'em out to make it look more realistic, but they'll be fine once Renard uses one of those healing contraptions on them."

She glanced back to where Anne was still struggling against the goo holding her legs in place. The wraith was completely coated in the substance, unable to even twitch a finger. It was then that she noticed two bodies slumped against the floor. Their backs were pressed against the walls and their heads were resting on one another.

Freed by Destiny

"You promise you didn't hurt them?"

"I swear."

"Okay. Let's get out of here."

She glanced over her shoulder as she followed Bear to an exit at the opposite end of the hallway from where Kimari and Kali were unconscious on the floor. A third body, who must have been the queen, was slumped on the floor as well, just a little distance away from her children. Kali had been the one to set this whole thing up. That was what Bear had told her. She'd put herself at risk to get her out of the palace. Away from Renard.

Her chest tightened as her gaze traced the outline of Kimari. What was his role in all of this? Was he genuine in his care for her, or had it all been some cruel game to him? She doubted she would ever know.

She raced after Bear, the tightness in her chest increasing with each step. She couldn't shake the feeling that something really bad was about to happen. To all of them.

Chapter Seventeen

Cold air hit Astrid's face as she emerged from the palace and into one of the gardens. Her breathing hitched and her side ached. After a month of little exercise other than dance lessons, she supposed she should have expected to be out of shape. Still, the stitch in her side made her gasp for air.

They hurried around a tight corner.

"Our transport vehicle is just on the other—"

Bear didn't get a chance to finish his statement as he was flung backwards by a robotic arm.

Astrid screamed and rushed towards him. "Are you alright?"

He wiped blood from his mouth with the back of his hand and pushed her behind him. "I'm fine. Just stay outta harm's way."

He unclipped two more of the potion bombs.

"Turn yourself over to us and we will not harm you further," the robot said in a gravelly voice.

Bear peered around the garden and shrugged. It was him against a single robotic soldier. Astrid knew he could take it.

"And how, pray tell, are you going to make me do that?"

The robot's arm morphed into a spinning series of barrels, all pointed directly at Bear.

"Um, Bear... what do you think you're doing?"

"Just trust me."

There that word was again. Trust. Unlike her feeling associated with Kali and Kimari, she trusted Bear more than anyone else she'd ever met, except for maybe Penny. He had always been caring and loyal. Even before all this started, he'd been her friend.

The robot fired. Hundreds of bullets streamed across the sky. Astrid screamed.

Bear dropped another potion ball directly in front of them. A crystalline shield stretched around them, protecting them from the shots.

"This was your plan?" she growled. "Seriously? What are we going to do now?"

"Just wait."

A boom followed by a concussive blast slammed into the shield, obliterating it. Astrid slammed her fist into Bear's knee, bringing him to the ground. She threw her body over him, shielding him with her own. She squeezed her eyes shut, anticipating the bullets shredding her muscles.

To her surprise, nothing happened. No more bullets. No intense pain. Nothing. She cracked her eyes open to see a smoldering crater where the robot used to be.

"What the drak are you doing?" Bear grumbled as he shifted his shoulders, trying to knock her off him.

"Trying to protect you. Isn't it obvious?"

"Alrighty then, well, you can get off now. Don't let me forget to argue with you later about putting yourself in so much danger."

"Um, right. Sure." She rolled off him and stumbled forward. Only bits of metal remained of the robot.

"What happened to it?"

Bear came to stand behind her. "Maya has been working on a targeted explosive that can be used to destroy specific robots. It doesn't work so well when there are hoards of them, but when it's just a couple, they don't stand a chance."

"Great. So, I see we have a lot to discuss."

"Once we get out of here." He stepped forward, heading towards a hole in the stone wall.

She'd imagined what leaving the palace again would feel like. But now that it was finally happening, she just felt numb. She was leaving Kali and Kimari behind. She still wasn't sure what their motives were or why they were so loving and kind to her one moment and then cruel the next.

But, she did understand. The thought oozed through her like sludge. *They were both afraid of their father.*

"We can't leave them," she whispered, grabbing onto Bear's arm and squeezing.

"Leave who?" Bear stopped in his tracks and turned to face her.

"Kali. Kimari. You said they helped Maya figure out how to rescue me. We can't leave them. Not now. Renard will hurt them. Maybe even kill them."

Bear shook his head. "They weren't part of the deal."

She planted her hands on her hips and stood as tall as she could. "Then change the deal. I won't leave here unless they come, too."

"We can't bring them with us."

She dug her feet into the ground. "Bear, I love you and I am so excited to be leaving this draking place, but I cannot leave them here to face the consequences. I can't. I won't."

"We don't have time for this. We have to go. Now. Kali knew the risks when she reached out to Maya about setting this plan up. She asked me to knock them out to make it look like they challenged me. They will be fine, Astrid. Now, let's go."

"I said no."

He sighed heavily, his eyes drooping as he regarded her. "You're really not going to let this go, are you?"

She shook her head.

"You are literally more stubborn than an ox, aren't you?"

"I don't understand that phrase, really."

"Yeah, well. Just know you are the most stubborn person I think I've ever or will ever meet."

Freed by Destiny

"Great. Glad to hear it. Now, can we please go get Kimari and Kali?"

He checked his watch. Even from the distance between them, Astrid could tell there was a timer counting down.

"What happens when the timer goes off, Bear?"

"We lose our window."

The idea of running out of time and having whatever Maya had planned for occur made gooseflesh cover her arms. She did not want to be here to see what was in store. "How much time do we have?"

"Less than ten minutes."

"We should get moving then."

She raced back towards the hallway. Bear's heavy footfalls pounded behind her. She was thankful he was willing to follow her. No matter how crazy her plan was, he had always been willing to support her in the end.

She skidded to halt as she stepped into the hallway where they'd left the royals and the wraiths, her breath catching in her chest. A pair of robotic soldiers bent over the queen. They jabbed a syringe into her arm and released a glowing blue liquid into her. Lianna stirred, her eyes fluttering open.

"W-what happened?" she murmured as she sat up. She rubbed the side of her head.

The robots didn't answer as they moved onto Kimari. They injected him with the same substance as his mother.

He locked eyes with Astrid when he revived. His jaw tightened as he stole a glance at his mother and then at Kali. Almost imperceptibly, he shook his head. Astrid glared at him and ducked behind an artistic column. She held up a hand, indicating for Bear to stop before stepping into the hallway. He stared at her, his chest heaving. Holding up one finger, she motioned for him to wait for her command.

Kali had been revived and the robots were making quick work of incapacitating the wraiths with a stab to the head. They chipped away at the hard material holding the wraiths and Anne in place.

"Lieutenant Anne, give a report." Renard's voice sounded metallic as it emanated from one of the robot's bodies.

"Sir, although I successfully got the fae queen to the safe room, we were attacked by three wraiths. They managed to break through the door. I incapacitated them. We were then attacked by the rebels. One of them was able to trap me with some sort of bomb. I was encapsulated in a material I could not break through."

"I see. And where is the fae now?"

"Gone, sir."

Silence.

Astrid closed her eyes, hoping he wouldn't explode in a fit of anger. Static noise whooshed through the stereo as he breathed heavily into the microphone. The image of his face, purple with anger, bloomed within her mind as she waited to hear his response. Renard did not like when his plans failed.

"You mean to tell me that she just what? Disappeared?" There was a loud snap on the other end of the call. "I put you in charge of ensuring she was kept safeguarded. You failed me."

"I am sorry, sir. It won't happen again."

Freed by Destiny

"You're right. It won't."

The robot shot Anne straight through the heart. Astrid covered her mouth to keep herself from screaming. She didn't know why she was surprised. He'd been willing to sacrifice an entire town to thwart her. Why would she think that he would have any reservations about killing a single soldier who had failed him?

"Kimari, I expect you to give me a full report when you arrive at my council chamber. I need to know exactly what happened."

"As you wish, Father."

"Kali, take your mother to her rooms. Keep her company until a nurse comes with her sleeping pill. Now that Astrid has been taken from us, the rebels are retreating. This gives us an opportunity to find their location and attack. But we have to act quickly."

"Yes, Father." Kali trailed her fingers over the necklace of three interlocking circles hanging from her neck as she stared down the hall, right at where Astrid was hiding.

The soldiers lifted the wraiths and threw them over their shoulders. To Astrid's horror, they began walking towards where she and Bear were hiding at the end of the hall. There was no place for her to run. No place to hide.

"The faster route is to go this way," Kali said, drawing their attention to her.

"This is the most direct path," one of the soldiers said.

"It might be, but with the extent of damage to the hallway, I can only imagine what it looks like outside. The path will be easier and safer to go this way." She nodded towards the opposite direction of where Astrid knelt behind the column.

The robots jerked their heads from the direct path back to Kali. "Is this an order?"

"Yes," Kali stated simply. She wrapped her arm around her mother's waist and helped her rise to her feet.

Lianna stumbled over her own feet as she took steps with Kali's help.

The robots paused, but then followed Kali and Lianna down the hall. Astrid breathed a sigh of relief, but she was also worried about Kali. She doubted she would see her again that night. If ever. She wouldn't put it past Renard to lock her away—or worse—if he thought she had been involved in Astrid's escape.

She waited until the sound of the soldiers' feet disappeared before stepping from her hiding place. She pointedly avoided looking at Anne's body as she walked towards Kimari.

"What are you doing here?" He growled. "You were supposed to be gone by now."

"I couldn't…. I didn't want to leave without you."

He shook his head, his eyes flashing.

"Do you have any idea what Kali risked to ensure you had this chance?" He glanced towards where his sister had disappeared down the hall, as if half-expecting the soldiers to return. "If my father discovers our betrayal, he will hurt us."

"That's why you have to come with me. Please, Kimari."

"Do you remember what happened last time I went with you? My father literally threatened to kill magicals…his own citizens… until he got me back. He is obsessed with controlling you, Astrid." He took her hands in his as he closed the gap between them. "I can't let him crush you."

"Astrid," Bear said from behind her, "if we don't leave now, we won't make it back to our vehicle. We need to leave."

She peered into Kimari's eyes. "All this time, you really were trying to help me."

His lips curled into a small smirk. "Well, of course, silly. What did you think? That I was actually trying to hurt you? To control you, just like my father?"

She shrugged. "Well…"

He kissed her. Deeply. Fiercely. And in that kiss, she knew, beyond anything else, that he loved her. He was willing to sacrifice everything to protect her, including his own life.

Defying his father like this was certainly enough to earn him that consequence.

"I love you, Astrid. And I am so sorry for all the times I made you doubt… made you think I wasn't on your side. My father…"

"I know."

He pressed his forehead to hers and breathed in deeply as their breath mingled. "When we get to the end of this battle, I promise I will find you. And we will spend a lifetime making up for all the misunderstandings and confusion between. We will build a life we always dreamed of."

She squeezed his hands. "I promise, too."

He kissed her again.

"Until then. Be safe." He turned his attention to Bear. "Keep her safe."

Bear just nodded.

Kimari brushed a strand of Astrid's hair behind her ear, his fingers lingering on her cheek one last time before turning and dashing in the opposite direction. Astrid's heart cracked as she watched him disappear. She was amazed at how quickly she'd grown to care for him like this. How deeply she wanted to see him every day. Even after everything he'd done over the past month, she could understand it was his way of keeping her safe. The risk he and Kali had taken to secure her passage out of the palace was enough to prove that they wanted her to remain safe. To remain alive. She just hoped she would have a chance to show them her gratitude in the future. That she would be able to repay them.

"Come on," Bear said.

Astrid sprinted after him as he led the way to the vehicle parked just a short distance from where they'd battled against the robotic soldier. She laughed a little as she climbed onto his bike. A burst of glitter exploded from its exhaust when he kicked it into gear.

"Hold on," he said as he raced down the narrow path. The bike lifted from the ground as they jumped from the hill, soaring higher than she ever remembered before. She held on tightly as Bear steered them away from the palace.

She twisted around to catch one last glimpse of the city. Dozens of robotic soldiers returned to the stone fortress. In unison, they pointed both of their arms at the gardens surrounding the structure and fired missiles. Explosives streaked across the sky before exploding in an array of color. Columns of fire and smoke billowed towards the sky. Fluttering embers danced on the wind, like falling stars. All was the chaotic beauty of fire and rampage, colors mixing with one another and brilliant light illuminating what seemed like the entirety of Lunameed.

Freed by Destiny

But then, the light show faded into darkness. Silence, save for the rumbling of Bear's bike as he sped through the skies, was the only constant as they sped away from the destruction. In the distance, the cracking began. Buildings on the outskirts of the palace crumbled as the ground beneath them dissolved into nothing. Astrid held her breath, praying that Kimari and Kali would survive this attack. Praying that Renard wouldn't but knowing he would. He was like a cockroach. He could survive anything.

When the cracking finally stopped, all that was left were ruins.

Chapter Eighteen

Astrid and Bear flew in silence. She was still grappling with the idea that Kimari and Kali had risked everything to free her but hadn't thought to do the same for themselves. They had known, just as she did, that if they left with her, Renard would become even more vicious than he already was.

Still, the thought of them having to face their father, of having to lie to him, made her bones quake. What if he discovered their role in all of this? What if he locked them up? Hurt them? Worse? She wouldn't put it past him to kill his own children if it meant securing his throne. His power. He didn't care about anyone or anything other than what he could control.

When she finally emerged from her thoughts, she realized that she didn't recognize a single shred of the scenery around them. During the months she'd traveled with Max to find the remainder of the fae nobles who had survived the massacre, she thought she'd seen the entirety of Lunameed. Apparently, she'd been wrong.

Or they weren't in Lunameed anymore.

"Bear?"

"Hmm?"

"Where are we?"

He mumbled something about not being at liberty to say just yet. He landed his bike and pulled to a stop on the side of a narrow road.

"Let's see those bracelets you got on there," he said, pointing to the cuffs still suppressing her powers.

He clutched up a scanning device and held it over the bracelets, letting it examine them. Astrid ground her teeth. Renard most likely had planted a listening device—or worse, a tracking one—within the bracelets, which was why Bear was being so cagey, but she wanted answers. She wanted to know what had happened over the past month that had pushed him to drive such a long distance away. She still couldn't believe they'd successfully attacked the palace. Or that Maya had been able to hack into the robots' operating system again to seize control. She truly was a wizard when it came to electronics.

"Maya, are you getting all of this?" Bear asked.

Astrid jerked her head towards Bear. She wanted to hear Maya's voice. Even though she would see her and be able to hug her soon enough, that didn't stop her from wanting a piece of that reunion now.

Freed by Destiny

She held out her hand. "Let me talk to her."

Bear shrugged and turned his back on her as he spoke in a low voice she couldn't understand. Fuming, Astrid tucked her hands behind her back and waited for Bear to finish his conversation with Maya.

"I understand." He turned back to her. "Alright. It seems Renard created a failsafe on these. If anyone tries to remove them without some sort of specific key sequence, they'll release a poison into your blood stream. Without access to your healing ability, it'll kill you within minutes."

"Oh." She dug her nails into the palms of her hands. Surely this wasn't the end of the road. "So, what do we do?"

"Well, we can't take you back to our base without revealing its specific location. The cuffs definitely have some sort of tracking device within them. So… we have to wait. Here. And hope that Renard doesn't send his soldiers to come find us before Maya can get here to deactivate the cuffs herself."

Astrid folded her arms over her chest. "How long will it take for her to get her?"

The ground shook beneath her feet, rattling loose stone on the road as a portal erupted before her. Maya stepped through with an elf Astrid had never seen before. The portal closed behind him with a loud snap. Her heart sank as she realized Max hadn't joined them. It'd been a month. She missed him. The ache inside her chest revealed how much she had been hoping he'd missed her, too.

Rushing forward, she wrapped her arms tightly around Maya.

Maya nuzzled her face against Astrid's shoulder, hot tears soaking through her shirt.

"I thought we'd lost you forever," Maya whispered.

"We don't have time," Bear said. His head was lifted towards the skies, watching. Searching. Waiting for the inevitable.

"Right," Maya said softly. "You're right."

She unzipped the pouch strapped around her waist and rummaged through an assortment of tools. Metal clanked against metal and glowing light emanated from some of the tools. Astrid recognized a one or two of them.

Maya plucked one of the tools from her pack and turned a dial on its side. Deciding it was calibrated to the correct level, she pressed it against one of Astrid's cuffs.

"This might pinch," she said just as the cuffs contracted, cutting off the circulation in Astrid's hands. The device tightened around her flesh.

"This is your grand plan to not have them release poison into my system?" She winced in pain. "Take my whole hands off and you won't have to worry about it?"

Maya shook her head. "There won't be any lasting damage to your body. I just have to…"

Intricate lines within the cuffs began to glow a brilliant blue. Despite how tight the cuffs were against Astrid's skin, they vibrated quickly. There was a mechanical whir as they broke into several pieces along the illuminated lines.

"What was that?" Astrid asked as she rubbed her raw and bloodied skin. Her flesh stung.

The elf stepped forward with a few petals of a star flower. He dropped them into a small cup and poured water in with them before offering it to Astrid. She gulped down the contents. Instant relief flooded her senses as the magic of the flower worked its way through her system. The cracked, bloody skin around her wrists smoothed and healed before her eyes. Sighing in relief, she handed the cup back to the elf and smiled at him.

"Thank you."

He bowed his head and backed away from her, his eyes leveled on the ground.

Maya was busy scanning the rest of Astrid's body. She discovered several tracking devices embedded just beneath Astrid's skin in various places of her body, including ones she didn't remember any of Renard's people touching her. She squirmed as she realized they must have drugged her at some point—or multiple times—to implant them.

And she hadn't even known.

The thought of his researchers knocking her out and experimenting on her, implanting things within her and doing who knows what else to her made her stomach clench. She rushed to the side of the road and emptied her stomach onto the ground.

Maya ran to her side and pulled her hair out of her face as she continued retching. "It's okay now. You're safe. You're safe."

Astrid didn't feel safe. Although she was thankful to be reunited with Maya and Bear, she couldn't wipe away the feeling that Renard had violated her personal space. That he had allowed his people to experiment on her without her knowledge or consent. He was a monster. He deserved whatever came to him. At the end of it all, some people were incapable of love or empathy. Renard was one of them.

For the first time in over a month, she felt the surge of her power grow, igniting into an inferno that she couldn't contain. Her fingers began to glow, their tips blazing with fire as she flexed them outwards.

Maya backed away as more fire consumed Astrid's body. Her wings erupted from her back, springing outward and pumping towards the sky. Shooting upwards, she closed her eyes, letting the feel of the wind cool the feverish tinge caused but the sickness she'd encountered only moments before. She twirled and dropped, letting the wind carry her. She soared above it all. For the briefest moment, she forgot about her fears and everything she'd been through. She forgot about the losses she'd experienced.

She was free.

That was what she was fighting for. That was what she would continue fighting for until she drew her last breath, not only for herself but for all who lived within this world.

Dropping to the ground, she landed not as herself, but as the firebird. Bear held his hand to his eyes, blocking her brilliance. The others turned away. She diminished her flames and strode towards them, feeling more like herself than she had since first arriving at the palace.

"Feel better?" Maya asked, cocking an eyebrow at her as she came to stand beside Bear.

Astrid nodded. Words were too much. She still needed time to process. To grieve. To plan.

"Then I think we should show you who's been helping us this whole time."

Wordlessly, the elf threw a handful of portalling dust in a cloud before them. A portal formed, revealing a cityscape on the other side. Tall skyscrapers crested the clouds. Ships, laden with heavy machinery and guns, filled the harbor. Several flags flew from a single pole, the top one bearing the sigil of a golden bull crowned with an ornate circlet.

"The Golden City," she whispered.

"Turns out, they're not just a myth."

"But... how?"

Maya shrugged. "They reached out to me two weeks ago and said they wanted to help. They're the one who supplied the fire power to confront Renard tonight. They're the ones who are training our newest recruits to be soldiers."

Nervous energy zipped through her veins as she considered what Maya was telling her.

The Golden City was a myth magicals told their children to coax them into slumber. It was said that many centuries ago, there had been a queen who could turn anything she touched to gold. Her nation became of the wealthiest in the world. But her gift did not come without its limitations. She resided on a small island off the coast of Mitier. Although they boasted a large population, they did not have fertile ground. And so they needed to trade for the food and goods it took to sustain life on the island. Although they were incredibly wealthy as a nation, very few other kingdoms wanted to form an alliance with them, fearing it would put a target on their own backs.

The city toiled, close to collapse. Despite having a daughter who could coax plants to life and a son who shared her gift of gold, the queen couldn't maintain order when her people began to starve. She hired a witch of the old ways to bind her son's powers and then jumped into the sea, never to be seen from again.

After their mother's death, the siblings closed their borders and

209

did not allow visitors to come to their island nation ever again. Stories of the great, golden city became rumors and rumors became myth. Over the ages, not even the youngest children believed the Golden City still existed. If it ever had at all.

"Don't just stand there," Maya said. "The leaders of the city have been anxious to meet you. After all the stories they've heard, try not to disappointment them."

Astrid twisted her head to the side so she could see the expression of amusement on Maya's face. Glaring at her, Astrid stepped through the portal.

Waves crashed, forming a soothing, hypnotic sound as Astrid lay in the sand. Her hands and knees sunk deep into the pearlescent particles. Rolling over onto her back, she stared up at brilliant sun. Water lapped at her outstretched fingers, cooling her. She blinked. This was so different than she had experienced for the past month, she wasn't entirely sure how to react.

Maya fell onto the beach beside her. She stood and made room for the elf and Bear to follow. The portal closed behind with a loud pop. Turning her face to the sky, Astrid soaked in the warmth of the sun as she waited for someone to tell her what was going to happen next.

"Astrid."

She spun around at the sound of her name, her heart already

knowing who'd said it. Max stood at the top of a set of stairs leading to a public street beyond.

Rushing towards him, she flung her arms around him, squeezing him tight. "I'm so glad you're here."

He patted her back and held her firmly against his body. "You never should have gone there."

"I know that now. It was a mistake. I thought I could reason with him. Thought I could bargain for peace. But it didn't work." Her voice broke as tears flooded her eyes.

He cradled her in his arms and whispered that he loved her. That she was safe. That they would make things right.

"This is the queen you've told me so much about?" a feminine voice said from behind them.

Astrid lifted her head from Max's shoulder to see a woman who looked to be about her age with long silver hair and piercing blue eyes. She was slender and graceful, but there was a power in her movements that reminded Astrid of the big cats she'd seen prowling in the documentaries on wildlife.

"Who are you?" She disentangled herself from Max's arms.

"I am the sole reason you got out from beneath Renard's clutches."

Astrid looked to Max for answers.

He avoided her gaze as he said, "Astrid, I would like to introduce you to Councilor Cassidhe Winslow of the Seventh Isle. She is the chair of the council that governs the Golden City."

"Councilor? I don't understand."

"We do not have kings or queens ruling us here. The Golden City is a free one. All who are citizens here have an equal say in what what happens by voting on specific measures and by electing the councilors to govern the city."

"They have a representative government. Think about it, Astrid. It's exactly what we've always talked about. Giving a say back to the people. Letting them be the masters of their own fate instead of being ruled by the will of a monarch. You could give up your crown and give it to your people."

Astrid's head swam. She didn't know whether to laugh at how absurd Max's description of their government was, celebrate that they'd finally discovered a model to create their vision of the future on, or cry because there were too many things happening at once and she needed time to process. Maybe it was a combination of all three.

Max searched her face before saying, "Let's get you to your room and let you rest before any more introductions or big decisions."

He swept the hair out of her face. His dark eyes narrowed on every bruise, cut, or scar marring her features.

"I'm fine, Max." She shifted her face away from him. "I promise."

"Still, you've been through a lot. And there's still much to do. We need you rested and at your best so that you can give us a full briefing on what you experienced inside the palace walls."

Cassidhe snapped her fingers and several guards crowded around her. "Help our new guest to her rooms."

Two of them split from the group and strode towards where Astrid stood with Max.

He stretched out his arm in front of her, blocking their path. "I would prefer to take her to her room myself, Cass."

Freed by Destiny

Bear strode up the stairs, followed by Maya.

"We're not letting her out of our sights. We've lost her once. I refuse to do so again," he said.

Astrid glanced between her friends and Cassidhe. Although they had some form of truce or agreement between them, it was clear the strands binding them together were tenuous at best.

"If they know where my rooms are, surely they could take me. If you're worried we might get lost, you could always send one of your guards as an enforcer." She slipped her hands into Maya's and Bear's. "I just don't want to be separated from them. Not yet."

Cassidhe eyed them. Although she was stunning, there was an intelligence to her expression that gave Astrid pause. She hoped her friends, in their haste to get her back from Renard's clutches, hadn't formed an agreement with this woman that would put them in a bind.

"Very well," Cassidhe said, "but Max stays with me. I want him to provide a full debrief on exactly what happened tonight. You have inside knowledge of what goes on in Renard's court, and we need you to provide it to us. Max will be the collateral to ensure you tell us everything you know."

Instead of taking Astrid, the guards wrapped their hands around Max's wrists. He didn't struggle against them as they guided him to where Cassidhe stood.

"I'll give you give three hours to freshen up and process what you've gone through tonight. After that, we need you to give a full report with as much detail as possible. Even the small details may help us to understand how to destroy Renard's hold on the kingdom."

Astrid eyed the woman sharply. She didn't like how she was addressing her. She wasn't a child. Or stupid. She was the draking queen of the Fae. Besides, she doubted this woman had ever had to fend for herself or work grueling hours. She probably didn't understand what it took to survive the slums, much less what Astrid had endured during her time as Renard's captive.

"We appreciate your hospitality," Maya said firmly as she squeezed Astrid's fingers, "but you will kindly understand that Astrid can have as much time as she needs to process what she's been through. Just because we are guests of your city does not mean we abdicate all of our autonomy."

A steely silence settled around them. Cassidhe seemed to weigh the pros and cons of going against her request. She bared her teeth and Astrid realized her incisors had been sharpened into dangerous points.

"Very well," Cassidhe said slowly. "We will send a tray of refreshments to your quarters and when you are ready, you will join us in our council room. Do not wait long. There is much to discuss. Much to do. Lingering in the safety of you room will place the odds in Renard's favor."

She motioned for her guards to follow her as she looped her arm through Max's and strolled down the road. Astrid watched them, wondering how Max felt about being used as collateral.

There was much for her to tell him. She'd missed him and she hadn't realized just how much until he'd wrapped his arms around her.

Maya took her hand and tugged in the opposite direction. "Come on. I want to get to the privacy of your room before we talk more."

Freed by Destiny

Astrid didn't question why Maya felt the need for privacy, but she had the unsettling feeling that she'd traded one cage for another.

Chapter Nineteen

The moment the door to Astrid's room shut, Maya cupped her cheeks and inspected every inch of her face. She made tutting sounds as her fingers grazed small bruises and cuts caused by the glass shattering in the promenade. Astrid winced, her hands cramping from clenching them so tightly.

"We can use more of the Silver Salum Flower." Dropping her hands, Maya began rumaging in the pouch belted to her waist.

Astrid placed her hand on Maya's arm, stilling her movements. She shook her head. "There's no need to waste the flower for such minor injuries."

"But…"

"Maya, I have lived my entire life being healed by my magic. Now that's it gone, sure, I hurt more and for longer, but I have to get used to not having everything resolve itself so easily. I want to feel this pain. I want to remember what it's like to be alive. Part of living is pain. It helps us appreciate the moments of pure joy more. I don't think this is something I understood until I gave up my power."

Chuckling, Maya shook her head. "You always were stubborn. I just didn't realize it would extend to your own self preservation."

"Seriously?" Astrid gave her a sardonic look. "I feel like that's all I've ever done. Give my life to others, even if it put myself in danger."

"True, but you had every reason to be fearless before. But now… not so much. You have to think differently, Astrid. You have to make other choices."

"Perhaps."

"Well, you at least have to let me clean the deeper cuts. I wouldn't want them to get infected."

She searched around in her bag and pulled out a small first aid kit. Inside were several packages of single-use disinfectant wipes. She tore open the packaging and pressed in against one of the deeper cuts on Astrid's forehead. Astrid hissed, her teeth clenching as the wipe left her skin stinging

"You could have warned me!"

"But it was just so satisfying watching your expression."

"Sadist."

Maya shrugged. "I live behind a computer screen."

Astrid stuck out her tongue at Maya.

Freed by Destiny

"Do you feel up for talking about what happened while you were in the palace?"

Astrid opened her mouth but then snapped it shut again. There were lots of thing she wanted to say. She just didn't know where to begin. It was like everything she'd been through was a tidal wave, rising higher until she could barely see it cresting in a spray of white foam at the top.

It was crushing.

"I think I'd rather hear about how you connected with Kali."

"Oh."

"Oh? That's all you have to say for yourself? Did you know she was intending on staying?"

"Yes. They both were."

"They put everything on the line to get me out of there. The least we could have done was bring them with us. Why didn't you set that plan into motion? Why didn't you convince them—"

"After all this time, you think anyone can convince Kali to do something she doesn't want to? She knows the risks, Astrid. Probably better than either of us."

"Then why? Why do it? Why put herself in a position she knows she can't survive if she's discovered?"

"Why, indeed."

Glaring at her, Astrid crossed her arms over chest. "She deserves better than what Renard will do to her. I think his treatment of her already borderlines inappropriate. I can't imagine what he would do if he found out his favorite daughter helped me escape. We need to go back for her. We need—"

"I need you to stop."

Astrid cocked her head at Maya. "What do you mean, you need me to stop?"

"Creators! Astrid, every time you get something in your head, you are like a bull when it comes to achieving it. But that's not how the world works. You can't just make decisions for others without having to pick up the slack."

"You think I don't know that? I'll give you one thing. While I was in there, I realized that there's still so much I don't know about the world. That most of us who were raised purely within the slums will never know. And I hated every single minute of it."

"And yet you survived. You lived on. And you escaped."

"Fine, yeah. I escaped. I survived. But I do not want them to go through the same things I did. You don't know what he's like, Maya. I thought I did. I thought I knew everything there was to know about Renard. But he... is more cruel and vindictive than I ever could have imagined. I think he would stop at nothing to keep himself in power, including hurting them. Killing them. We can't let that happen."

Maya took Astrid's hands and squeezed. "What I'm about to say to you might come off as a little harsh, but I promise I don't mean it to be. They know who their father is. And they have to make their own decisions about what they're willing to accept. They knew the dangers when they decided to work with me. And you know what? I'm glad they chose to get you out of there."

"Can't you see?" Astrid whispered. "They gave me another chance to fight against their father... but I'm not convinced a victory against him would be meaningful to me anymore. Not unless they're by my side."

"They were never going to stand by your side, Astrid."

Tears stung her eyes. Pulling her hands out of Maya's, she turned away from her. Kali might never stand with her, but deep inside her, she knew Kimari would. Wrapping her arms around her shoulders, she shivered against the doubts storming her mind.

"I don't want to talk about them anymore. Tell me more about our new ally."

"Kali introduced us. She's the grand councilor here. From the rumors I've heard, she can be quite manipulative when it comes to getting what she wants. But, once she's your ally, she is a great asset. Or, at least, that's what I've been able to figure out based on the data I've found about her. Kali spoke highly of her. Apparently, they went to a girls' school together when they were children."

"And you trust her?"

"As much as I trust anyone who isn't you. Or Eldris and Bear. I might even throw Max in there if you were to pressure me. But, honestly, Astrid, this world is too draked up for me to trust people beyond my little circle."

"Let me rephrase. Do you think she is a threat to us, or do you think she has our best interests at heart?"

"I think she wants to you succeed because Kali and Max have both hyped up your drive to create a new world order. Here in the Golden City, they want kingdoms to abandon the old ways and turn towards a way of governance more in line with what they use here. With elected officials and councils that make decisions as a team."

"And she thinks this is a viable solution for Lunameed? Because we already function like that?"

"Do we though?" Maya cocked an eyebrow at her. "You make decisions and expect the rest of us to fall into line. Sure, you take our opinions sometimes, but you still push us to follow your lead. Even if we disagree with you. Look at what you did a month ago. None of us—not a single one of us—wanted you to turn yourself over to Renard, but you were convinced that was the only way you could stop him from murdering our people. So, instead of listening to us and taking our advice, you did what you wanted."

"Wow. Angry much?"

Maya smiled lopsidedly at her. "At least I'm not raging at you like I did the night you left. I was so angry at you for ignoring all of us. Layla still is. She views what you did as a betrayal of not just your role as queen, but also as a direct response to her—and everyone else who put their lives on the line for you."

Astrid considered Maya's words. Hadn't she felt similar emotions during her time within Renard's palace? She was sure it was worse for her friends who didn't know what had become of her. And yet, they never gave up hope. She vowed in that moment that if she ever got the chance to show them the same kind of loyalty they'd demonstrated to her, she would. She would ensure every single one of them knew how much she valued them.

"Well, I'm listening now. And I want to hear your thoughts."

"First, let's get you changed. I want Bear to be here for our conversation because he will have a different perspective from the one I have. Did you know that Rene actually helped the golden queen—before she jumped into the sea—find love? I didn't. Bear told me about it."

Freed by Destiny

"No?"

"Yes!"

"I didn't realize he was that old."

"Apparently, they all are."

"Dang, they look good for their ages."

"Well, thank you, sweetheart. And this is why you've always been my favorite."

Astrid spun around at Bear's voice.

He stood in the doorway, his eyebrows wagging at her as he stepped into the room. "I mean, look at me. Do you think anyone could resist this sexy body?"

She couldn't stop herself from laughing. "One day, Bear, you and the rest of the Fairy Godmothers are going to have to sit down and tell me all about your exploits. I mean, I know I've heard some of the stories in The Wand, but somehow I feel like you left out all the juicy bits."

He pointed at himself. "Who? Me? I would never." He waved at her as if she were just joking with him. "Of course I told everything exactly as it happened in real life."

"Uh huh." She rolled her eyes at him. "Then why did your story about the fae who struck bargains for a living change every time you told it?"

He shrugged. "If you were telling the same story over-and-over again, wouldn't you want to spice it up a bit?"

"Alright, fine. I will give you the benefit of the doubt, but I do expect you to tell me. One day. In the meantime, think you could

223

help a girl out by giving us some more details on Cassidhe? She seems… scary, if I'm telling the truth."

"That's just because you're not used to someone being as blunt about things as she is. Look, the thing you have to know about Cassidhe is that she is a lot tougher than she looks. Like you, she had a tough childhood, but the things she's been through molded her into the ruler she is today."

"It sounds like you're fond of her, Bear." Astrid didn't want to ask the question that was on the tip of her tongue as she waited for Bear to continue.

"I was her FG."

"She had a wish that needed to come true?"

"Don't we all? But in all honesty, yes. That's part of the reason why I'm here. I want to broker trust between the two of you. I want to help her trust you. But, in order to do so, you'll have to trust me. More than you ever have before."

"Okay?"

He sighed heavily.

"Right. Well, then. Here goes everything." He sank onto her bed. "Cassidhe has the gift of gold."

"What?"

"You heard me. Her great-great-great grandfather was the son of the Golden Queen. Although his powers had been bound prior to her death, he passed on his genetic mutation to his children. His gift. His magic. And, although the majority of his descendants lacked basic abilities when it came to manifesting magic, there were a few who demonstrated at least a modicum of skill. All of their powers combined added up to basically what we would still consider non magical—except Cassidhe. She has the ability to turn everything she touches to gold, which is why she is so interested in building a partnership with you. The Golden City will be at risk of collapse if they don't see a strong woman at their helm. So, what do you think?"

"What do I think?" Astrid repeated. "I think I want to know everything you know about her. Help me understand where she's coming from and what her meddling will do for Lunameed."

He shook his head. "Look, I appreciate that you want to know more about her, but I want you to consider something. How would you feel if I went around to all the clients I've helped over the years? Would you honestly want me to share your story with others?"

She scowled at him. "I suppose it depends on the scenario. Is there a chance I would have an ulterior motive that could be harmful to the other person?"

Bear drummed his fingers on his leg as he continued to stare at her. "I understand your concerns. I do. But I can't break her trust."

"What about all the times you and the rest of the Fairy Godmothers told your stories in The Wand? How is this any different?" Anger coursed through her as she glowered at him. She couldn't believe he would do this to her. To their cause. He had to know what it meant to her to know that Cassidhe was trustworthy.

"Those aren't the intimate details of the person, Astrid. Those are just bawdy reminiscences of times spent helping people—fae, sirens, dragons, humans, and so many others. It was a way for us to record our successes, our triumphs. But we never shared the personal side of things. The struggles or the mistakes that our charges went through. What you're asking me to do is divulge information that is not mine to share."

Her breath caught in her chest. After all this time, she couldn't help but feel betrayed by Bear. He was supposed to be one of her closest friends. An ally when things got tough. Instead, here he was telling her no.

"What I fail to understand is how you can continue to stand there and pretend to be my friend. I need to know if I can trust her."

He shook his head. "And I can't give you what you're asking for, but I can say this. I have no reason to believe that she is a threat to you. If anything, I would think that, if given enough time, she could become a close friend."

"You truly believe that?"

"I do."

Astrid looked to Maya. "What do you think?"

"She's tough. She didn't hesitate to answer my call when I hacked into the Golden City's messaging system and sent her a personal request for a video call. She's offered to fight against Renard, which is a feat all in itself. So much of the world is terrified of him."

"Why would she do this? Why would she risk the safety of her people to help us?"

"Maybe, before you get too far ahead of yourself, you should ask her that question directly."

Closing her eyes, Astrid tried to let the doubts swirling in her mind settle. She knew the next decisions she made would have the power to change the course of the world. Join with Cassidhe. Learn from her city's council of leaders. Possibly form a strong ally. It was appealing, even if she was terrified it would blow up in her face. She'd trusted Kimari and look where that had landed her.

That wasn't his fault though, she reminded herself. He'd come to her in good faith. He'd wanted to form a partnership with her. He loved her.

"Fine. I will agree to meet with her with an open mind. But I am telling you right now, if things go south, I will blame you, Bear, for not preparing me for what's to come."

"Deal."

They sat in silence. Astrid envisioned the meeting with Cassidhe and focused on what she wanted to say. She hoped she would be able to elicit the responses she needed to make an informed decision about her next steps.

Chapter Twenty

Bear and Maya flanked Astrid as she strolled through the double set of doors leading into the council chamber. Giant stained-glass windows cast colorful light around the entire room. Rows of empty chairs lined a wide walkway to the opposite end of the room where an enormous round table stood. Eight chairs lined the table, each one containing a different person. They wore gilded robes with intricate patterns embroidered into the fabric.

Max stood behind one of the chairs. He smiled at her as their eyes met across the room. It was enough to reassure her that, perhaps, there was a chance forming an agreement with the Golden City would be the right call.

A small man who looked to be more skin and bone than body stood from his chair. His legs wobbled as he turned towards Astrid and smiled. "My name is Darrian of the House of Flint.

I speak for all of us here when I say I am very pleased you have made it to our island."

The other seven councilors nodded.

"Although I wish we had contacted you sooner, we were not in a position to challenge Renard without first seeing who would be taking his place. Having witnessed your bravery over the past year, we are all in agreement: you deserve a chance to lead."

He pitched forward, as if his knees were about to give out. A servant standing in the shadows behind his chair lunged forward and gripped Darrian by the elbow, steadying him.

"Thank you, my boy," he whispered as the servant helped Darrian into his chair. "As I was saying. We are very pleased to hear reports that you are searching for a new way of governing your people. I believe we can help."

Although his words were exactly what she had been hoping to hear, there was a part of her that distrusted him. That distrusted all of this. It was too easy. Too convenient, considering everything she'd been through.

"You knew Kali. I don't know what your relationship with her was or why you would heed her call when asked, but I do know one thing: I trust her. So, if your trust is good enough for her, then it's good enough for me."

Cassidhe rose, her eyes flicking over Astrid, as if assessing her and finding her wanting on multiple counts. "I know you think you deserve to be here. And, maybe you do, but it is up to the council to decide if you are worthy of our help. We responded to Kali because, like you, we trust her. However, her trust in you could be misguided. It is our job to determine whether your cause is noble."

Freed by Destiny

"We have heard the reports, even from her own advisors," Darrian countered. "She wants to create a new world order for Lunameed."

All eyes turned towards Astrid.

She lifted her chin higher, straightening her back. "I wasn't raised to be a royal. In fact, my childhood was the furthest thing from the life I would have had if my parents hadn't been assassinated by Renard. But through my experiences and struggles, I realized that people need to be given a voice. That we can't have a strong country until our populace is valued. I don't know how we can achieve this goal or what system will work, but I know I don't want to dictate to my people the way Renard has dictated to us. I will not be a tyrant."

She hadn't realized before that moment just how much she wanted a different way of doing things. Sure, she had talked about building a better future for her people, but she had never been able to envision what that would look like.

She still wasn't sure.

But she knew one thing: she did not want future generations to be at the mercy of the whims of a tyrannical ruler.

One of the councilors slow clapped. The soft booms echoed through the halls as he continued slapping his hands together. Slowly, more began to follow suit, until all but two of the councilors had joined in.

"Your passion does you credit," Darrian said, his voice breaking through the sound of clapping.

Smiling broadly, she stole a glance at Max. He watched her with a guarded expression, his eyes roamed over her face, but he didn't say anything. He didn't try to approach her. Instead, he continued to wait behind Cassidhe's chair.

"It does her credit, yes, but how can we trust that she won't just disappear if we help her win this war? You all know as well as I do that the transition of power works better when there's a name they trust at the beginning." Cassidhe pointed at Astrid. "She is that name. She is the face of the rebellion."

Murmurs filled the room as the other councilors spoke together in hushed tones. Their voices built into a triumphant song. Although she tried to follow the tidbits of conversations she overheard, it was difficult to decipher their meaning through the cacophony.

Cassidhe turned towards Max and motioned for him to step closer to her. She whispered something in his ear. His eyes flashed to Astrid, his jaw tightening as he listened to whatever it was Cassidhe had to say. He responded, but his voice was too low to hear his words. Astrid shuffled her feet, trying to keep herself from marching over to them and demanding to know what they were saying.

Finally, Cassidhe clinked a dagger against the glass sitting in front o her. "I believe we should take a vote. All those in favor of backing the fae queen, raise your hands."

Astrid closed her eyes, not wanting to see the results as she anticipated the motion failing. She wondered what they would do with her if they decided against helping her more than they already had. Although they had already put their necks on the line, Renard could be a forgiving man if he saw a personal benefit. However, she doubted he would ever be able to forgive the people of who'd helped her, she knew he would stop at nothing to pulverize them into little more than dust.

Maya nudged her in the arm. "Open your eyes."

Freed by Destiny

Blinking, Astrid stared around the room. She counted the raised hands. There were six. Six members of the council believed in her enough to put their lives at stake to help her. She didn't know how—or even if—she could ever repay them for their kindness towards her. She bowed her head.

"It seems our council is in agreement. We will aid you in your quest to end Renard's tyranny over Lunameed. All we ask is that you learn our ways before returning to your homeland. If you find merit in our way of life, we will help you establish your own representative group that votes on major issues affecting your community. You will be queen only in name," Cassidhe said.

Astrid nodded. "Thank you."

"There is no need for verbal thanks. Show us we have made the right decision in putting our support behind you by winning this war. That is all we ask of you."

Max stepped forward. "If we want to maintain any element of surprise, we will have to move quickly. We took Renard while his pants were around his ankles. I do not believe we will be given a second chance. If we wait too long, he will amass his robots once more and program them to kill."

"Max is right," Astrid said, finding her voice after the shock that the Golden City was actually agreeing to help them. "We have to mobilize as quickly as possible. If we can apply enough pressure, he may come out of the hidey-hole he disappears to whenever there's a fight. We can do things that will coax him into carelessness."

"What are you proposing?" Cassidhe asked, one thin eyebrow arching upwards at a steep angle.

"Attack hard and fast. Make him rally his troops…but also force

Lunameedian citizens into conscription. They will begrudge him more than they already do. And, if we can turn the army against him, we will fight. Our team will win."

She folded one arm across her stomach and tapped her chin with the other hand. She stared around the room at the other councilors. The two who had voted against aiding her stared at her boldly, as if testing her resolve.

"What of his robotic soldiers? From what I understand, you have only been able to hack into his operating system for short bursts of time. What will become of us if he is able to regain control of the strongest part of his forces? I will not risk the lives of my people for folly." Cassidhe turned her gaze to Astrid. "We want to help you, but the cost and risk have to be in alignment with the reward."

"I lived under Renard's power for over a month. I saw how he operates. How he manipulates everyone around him through fear to get what he wants. Even his own children are afraid of his wrath. Of what he would do to them if he ever found them wanting. And yet, they were willing to risk their lives to ask for you all to help me. If even his own children are willing to turn against him now, what makes you think that those working to keep his electronic defenses in order won't do the same?"

She stole a glance at Maya, who shrugged. Astrid made a mental note to ask her about which of her previous colleagues who were still under Renard's employ might be willing to turn against their king. She hoped there would be, at the very least, one. Sometimes a single grain of rice could tip the scale. She'd read that once, somewhere. It was an old proverb—or something—but she knew it was true. Look at what she had done for her people. She was one person, and she was now the face of the rebellion. And Kilian. He'd died saving all those children.

Freed by Destiny

Turning her attention back to Cassidhe, she continued. "There is only one thing Renard understands and that's brutality. He doesn't care what else we do. He doesn't want there to be a chance for peace. Not if it means he loses even a smidgen of what he thinks is his. That's why I'm such a threat to him. I have a power he can't possess."

Her thoughts flitted towards the tracking devices he'd had implanted beneath her skin while she was knocked out. A knot writhed in her belly, bile rising up her throat as she realized he might have taken enough of her genetic material to sequence her abilities. It was unlikely, but still. She didn't want to think of a world in which he had her ability to protect himself and create fire.

"You make a strong case for attacking first," Cassidhe said, "but my fellow councilors and myself will have to discuss if this is the route we are willing to take."

"So, let's talk then."

"Without you and your people present."

A chilly silence flooded the room. Astrid held her breath until her lungs burned with need, hoping one of the other councilors would challenge Cassidhe on this decision.

"If I and my people aren't present, how will our interests be represented here?"

"This council is not at your beck and call. Just because we have voted to continue supporting your rebellion, does not mean we will follow your lead in all things, Astrid. Remember, we are a committee of different voices and perspectives. We govern the Golden City's affairs as a group, not by the whims of a single individual. This is something we hope you will learn during your time with us."

"You espouse unity and equality among your people and yet you exclude the very group of people you claim to want to help. Doesn't sound like you're living by your own rules." Her hands shook as she spoke. She didn't know if it was the fact that they were wasting precious time by deliberating what to do next or if it was the condescending way Cassidhe had explained that she didn't have a seat at the table, but it had kindled a fire within her.

"Astrid." Max's voice cut through the room. He glared at her, his lower lip twitching.

She stared straight back unflinchingly. "I don't see where I told a lie."

His eyes widened before darting towards Cassidhe. Astrid shrugged. She didn't care if the other woman took offense to her words. Cassidhe hadn't taken any precautions or held back in her approach with her. Astrid saw no reason to give her anything other than what she'd asked for.

"The girl's right," a feeble voice said from the councilor's table.

Astrid turned her entire body to the sound. She gasped when she realized that the speaker had been one of the two who'd voted no to her request for help.

The councilor, a woman with a halo of white curls and a gentle expression on her face, continued. "We sit here behind this table and deliberate about what the world could be if it would only follow our example. And yet, when we are presented with an opportunity to take out one of the worst tyrants we've seen since the age of darkness, well…" She tsked. Turning her gaze towards Astrid, she smiled wryly. "You've faced a lot in your short life. More than many of us sitting around this table. I should have voted to back you from the beginning. Blame my poor decision on my old bones not being what they used to be."

"Gwendolyn," the other councilor who voted no, a man with a perfectly trimmed beard and startling green eyes, said. "Am I hearing your correctly? Why is it that I am the only one who sees this… opportunity…for what it really is? We will bankrupt ourselves and weaken our military by putting ourselves at odds with the Lunameedian king. He has done nothing to us. And nor shall he as long as we remain out of his business. Think about what you're agreeing to do to our people. They deserve better from us."

"That is precisely the point, my dear boy," Gwendolyn said. "Our people deserve leaders who will stand up for our beliefs, even when it is difficult, and especially when asked. You may think going to war will bring destruction to our nation, but I assure you, in this case it is quite the opposite. Inaction will be our demise and I, for one, refuse to stand aside and watch us fade into dithering fools."

"Well said!" Darrian clapped his hands and smiled at her. "I haven't heard you speak this passionately since the Red Summer. And that was fifty years ago."

"Well, it's taken fifty years for something to inspire me as much as hearing this young woman talk about what she hopes her nation can become, if given the chance."

"Thank you," Astrid said. She bowed her head towards Gwendolyn. "For believing in me."

"Well, when you're as old as I am and have seen so much stuff in the world, then you'll understand why I was hesitant at first. You do forgive me, don't you?"

"Of course." Astrid's heart thumped loudly in her chest. She couldn't believe the councilor who had just stuck up for her was asking for forgiveness at the same time. This city and its people were certainly a stranger bunch.

"Thank you, Gwendolyn, for your input," Cassidhe said icily. She glowered at Astrid and shifted her stance ever so slightly to present the back of her shoulder towards her. It was subtle, but the message was quite clear. She'd somehow crossed a boundary. "I know you are all anxious to determine our next steps now that we have agreed to help the Fae queen in her quest to cast aside the Lunameedian King. Although it is our typical practice to remove outsiders from our deliberations, it seems there is at least one member of our council who believes one of Astrid's representatives should be present during our proceedings. Should we take a vote to determine if we can make a temporary exclusion to our policy?"

The councilors nodded. Just as they had when voting on whether to back Astrid publicly, each member of the council cast their vote. And it was unanimous.

"You may leave Max here to serve as your voice during our meeting."

Astrid shared a look with Max. He looked just as surprised as she felt.

"Don't I get a say in the matter?" she asked.

"I'm afraid not. We took a vote to let you have representation during our meeting, but again, we are not here to serve at your every whim."

"Let it be, Astrid. Let it be." Max took a step towards her, but Cassidhe laid a hand on his arm, stilling him.

Freed by Destiny

"May I, at least, share some of my thoughts with Max privately before leaving?" Astrid asked. Her voice shook with anger as she enunciated each word.

"Of course, dear," Gwendolyn said.

Cassidhe dropped her hand from Max's arm, but the expression on her face made her look like she'd just discovered a rotten, moldy piece of meat.

Max turned his back on the council and looped his arm around Astrid's neck. Leaning in close, he whispered, "You need to be careful around them, Astrid. They are powerful and have a lot of say in what will happen next. They could make or break our attempt at reforming Lunameed into a kingdom dedicated to creating spaces for all creatures, whether magical or not, to live in harmony."

"I know, but, Max, I don't trust Cassidhe. She seems…" Astrid realized she didn't have the right words to describe what was off about the councilor, but there was something.

"I don't know what you're talking about. She genuinely wants us to succeed. She just cares more for the Golden City than Lunameed. Who could fault her? Our hearts are set on Lunameed because that's our home. Don't judge her for feeling the same about this place."

"That's not it, Max."

"Then what is it? You're jealous because there's someone else who has the power to help us? That we don't need you anymore."

She slid her head out from beneath his arm and stared at him, shocked. "What are you saying?"

"I'm saying you made your choices, Astrid. And you chose to

abandon us for someone who couldn't give two draks about you. In fact, I'm pretty sure he proved that when he let you be turned into a prisoner."

Although their conversation was still in hushed whispers, Astrid was deeply aware that they were still standing in the middle of the council room with everyone able to watch—and potentially hear—them.

"Max, this isn't the time or place for this argument. I just want you to push for them to launch an attack as quickly as possible."

"Ever the risk taker. I see having your rash decision making cause problems for you did nothing to quell this in you."

"What's your problem?"

He glared at her. "My problem is that you left us without considering what it would do to our morale or our ability to win this fight. You gave all our power to Renard and left us with little recourse. And now, you want to come back and…not even a day later… launch an assault on the world's most powerful army? And you think I'm the one having a problem."

"I can see there's a lot to unpack there, but Max, if you could set aside your anger at me for one minute, you'd be able to tell that pushing forward with an attack now is the right choice. For all of us. Please. You are our representative. You have to advocate for what's best—"

"And what if I don't think that's the best option? Did you even consider that as a possibility?"

Astrid's skin sparkled as her anger grew. Who was he to come at her like this? To berate her in front of all these people after everything she'd been through? He was supposed to be her most trusted friend. Someone she loved. Someone she'd given up her most precious ability for.

"How dare you." She pulled away from him and turned towards the councilors. They eyed her with a mixture of curious and enthralled expressions. Bowing, she said, "Thank you for helping me get out of Renard's grips. I appreciate all that you've done, and I hope you take what I say now for what it is. No one else here besides myself and Maya have ever worked closely with Renard. You've heard the stories, the rumors, but you don't know the truth of what he's capable of. I do. And if we are going to have even a smidgen of a chance of stopping him, we have to make a move. Now. So please, if you are committed to helping us, do it."

Cassidhe cleared her throat. "Leo will see to your needs while you wait for our final decision."

Astrid ground her teeth. She hated the feeling of not knowing what was going to happen. She'd worked so hard to ensure they had a chance at freedom. Now, here they were at the mercy of someone else.

A guard emerged from the shadows and swept his arm towards the doors at the back of the room. Astrid shared one last look with Max. She didn't know if he would choose to put aside his anger at her and do what would be right for their people.

All she could do was hope.

Chapter Twenty-One

Leo guided them to a separate waiting area just beyond the council room. Without a word, he closed the door behind him as, Astrid presumed, he stationed himself on the other side. She glared after him.

"You shouldn't have pressured them to fight again so soon," Maya said. She stepped in front of Astrid and placed her hands on her hips as she gave her assessing look. Her blonde hair fell across her face, blocking her eyes.

Bear cleared his throat and leaned against one of the walls, watching them closely.

"What choice did I have? You got me out of there, but it will only anger Renard more. You showed your hand, and he will not stop until he's rooted out everything and everyone who helped demonstrate he does have weaknesses."

"You could have been more strategic. Drak, Astrid. I love you, and I will never stop believing in you. You inspire everyone around you to do and be better. You give and give and give... even when it's foolish for you to keep going. But sometimes you're so impulsive I don't know how to plan for what you're going to do next." Bear glowered at her.

"Yeah, well, those decisions have helped us win battles."

"You're not indestructible. Especially now."

Astrid sucked in a breath through gritted teeth. She didn't need to be reminded of what she'd lost. After living a month without her powers, she knew all to well what it felt like to not have any control over what was going to happen to her. She wouldn't wish that on anyone. Except maybe Renard.

"Thank you for the reminder." She turned her back on Maya and went to stand by an open window. From there, she could see the waves crashing against a sandy beach. Golden sunlight kissed golden rooftops and buildings. Everything glittered.

"Astrid, don't do that. I'm not trying to be mean, or to upset you. It's just... you can't know what it felt like this past month not knowing if you were okay. Or even alive. When I got that message from Kali about an opportunity to get you out of there safely, I cried for three hours. From relief. Do you have any idea..." Her voice broke.

Astrid turned towards her, silver lining her own eyes as she opened her arms to Maya.

Maya rushed into them, wrapping her arms around Astrid. They held each other without saying a word. The longer she held Maya, the more she felt the tension she'd been carrying since arriving at

Freed by Destiny

Renard's palace melt away.

A floorboard creaked behind them. Startled, Astrid jumped, her eyes flying open.

Bear held up his hands. "It's only me."

The expression on his face said more than words ever could. Without another word, Astrid held her arm out and invited Bear to join them. His arms enveloped them both as he squeezed them tightly.

"We wouldn't want you any other way," he murmured into her hair. "But light's end, lassie, we worry about you."

Astrid chuckled against his chest. "Yeah, well, I only do rash things because I worry about you, too."

"We know," Maya and Bear spoke in unison.

"That's the problem," Maya continued. "You give everything you have to other people and don't save any of that preservation spirit for yourself."

Shrugging as much as she could pinned against Bear, Astrid smiled.

"I can't wait for the rest of the FGs to see you alive and well. They've been lost without you," he whispered.

"Trust me, the feeling is mutual. When this is all over, I swear I just want—need—a night where we can go out to The Wand together like old times."

"So, you'll be serving the drinks then?"

"As long as you provide the entertainment."

"Oh, honey, you know the others will give their best performances. Rene has been waiting for a chance to serenade us all again and give us a show with his salacious dances."

"I'm sure it'll be fabulous."

"Always."

"Um, you do know I have absolutely zero idea what you're talking about, right?" Maya said, breaking the hug to look at them both.

Bear and Astrid just laughed.

She couldn't remember the last time she'd laughed like this. Even if it was just for a moment, having this sense of normalcy helped ease away her anxiety about what was happening in the room where the councilors were making their decisions. Where Max, who was clearly still upset with her, was her only hope of convincing them to vote in the affirmative.

"So, you're really not going to explain?"

Smiling, Astrid shook her head and said, "Tell you what. You come out with me when this is all over and we've won, and I promise you won't regret it."

Maya cocked an eyebrow at them both, but just shrugged before she strolled towards a circular couch and sank into the cushions. "When all this is over, I'll want to celebrate with everyone who's willing. So… be ready for that."

"But we have to get Kali and Kimari to safety." Before Astrid knew the words were on her lips, they tumbled out of her.

Maya paused, her hands gripping together so tightly they turned white. Bear shifted from one foot to the other.

Freed by Destiny

"They made their choices, Astrid," Maya said.

"What do you mean?"

"I mean, they could have tried to stop their father at any time, but they chose not to. They don't challenge him."

"You don't know what it's like in his court. No one challenges him. No one would dare."

"But Kimari could."

"What do you think he did when he came to me to begin with? You don't know what it's like to have Renard as your father." Anger coursed through every fiber of her being. She expected Maya and Bear—out of everyone—to have had a change of heart. Maya was Kali's friend. Or, she had been. It was complicated.

She'd had her doubts in the palace for sure, but now that she knew they'd been working to create a plan to get her out, she knew all those moments when they'd been alone and they'd shown kindness to her meant everything. Those versions of them were the real ones.

An image of Kimari's face above hers, his eyes hungry for her, filled her mind. Heat swelled in her belly, a desire she couldn't stop from growing each time he did something to protect her.

"You're right—I don't. But I know our choices define us, and they've chosen to lie to you, put you in harm's way, and manipulate you to get what they want," Maya said.

Astrid scoffed. "What, exactly, do you think they want?"

"What every child wants: the approval of their father."

"And nothing they've done to go against him—to defy him—

means anything to you, then?"

"Why would it? I'll grant you, helping you escape the palace was a pretty gutsy move, but it doesn't change the fact that you wouldn't have been in there to begin with if Kimari hadn't come to you."

"Yeah, he came to me to broker peace between us. To try and end this draking war."

She seethed as she watched Bear cross the room to an easy chair situated across from Maya's couch.

"I don't want to argue with you about this," Astrid said.

"Good. I don't either," Bear said. He folded his arms over his chest and stared at her. "I know you care for them. You wouldn't be defending them like this if you didn't. And I won't even pretend to understand what you've been through."

"But…?"

"But, sweetheart, you have to see that they'll choose him over you."

"I'm in love with him."

She clapped her hand over her mouth. She'd never said them out loud before.

"You can't be serious," Maya said.

"I am."

"What happened between you at the palace?"

Astrid wasn't sure if she would be able to explain. "It wasn't just at the palace. It was before, too."

Bear's hands glowed a brilliant, sparkling rose-gold. "Well, I'll be draked."

"What?"

"One of my abilities to sense when someone has found their match."

"So what? You think Astrid and Kimari are matched set?" Maya asked. "Seriously? There's no way. He's a human. She's a Fae. And, beyond that, what about Max?"

Bear shook his head.

"It's Kimari." He stared at Astrid, a bewildered expression on his face. "You know, I can count on both hands how many times this particular power has activated for me. And all of them, every single one, we're end game."

"As I said: I'm in love with him."

"Clearly."

The door flew open, and Max strode into the room. He glanced from Bear's hands to Astrid's face, his expression darkening as he met her gaze.

She didn't know how much he'd heard, but one thing was certain: he knew she'd just admitted that she was in love with someone else. Someone he considered an enemy.

"So that's it then." His voice was venom dripping down her skin, leaving behind a path of destruction. "You spend a month with him, and you fell in love. I thought... hoped... that you'd just said all those things to me when you left to make the separation easier for both of us, but I guess I should have known better. Did you ever love me? Or was I just a pawn you could manipulate to further your goals?"

"That's enough." Bear stepped between them, his large frame nearly blocking Max from Astrid's view.

"I should have known you'd come to her defense."

Bear placed a steadying hand on Max's shoulder. "You know as well as I do that once a Fae's mate is discovered, there's no stopping the romance."

He shrugged Bear's hand off his shoulder and scowled. "You actually believe Kimari, the crown prince of Lunameed, is her mate? Really? He's nothing more than a playboy pretending to be a hero." He shot a glance at Astrid. "And you! You fell for it hook, line, and sinker. All he had to do was flash you that brilliant smile and play hard to get. Is that it?"

"Max, I know you're angry—"

"Angry? You think that's what this is? Anger? Drak! Astrid, I love you. I wanted to spend the rest of my life with you. I waited for you. Every day, I waited for you to finally decide that you had stood on your own two feet for a long enough time. That you were ready to accept what we are—were—gaw!" He stomped his foot as he struggled to find the right words. "I have loved you since the first moment I met you. I've believed in you. Stood by your side, even when I didn't agree with you. I thought it would be me. I thought, in the end, you would choose me."

Tears leaked from the corners of Astrid's eyes as she watched the anger and disappointment and heartbreak wash over him. She didn't know how to explain to him that she did love him. That she did want him to be by her side, always. That she did want him to remain one of her closest friends. That she chose him.

Just not in the way he wanted.

There had been a time when she thought she could. When she thought she loved him in the way he did her. But too much had happened to her. She'd changed. Now, she couldn't deny the attraction she felt for Kimari. Even if she wanted to, she knew she wouldn't be able to set aside her feelings for him. If Bear was right, she could never truly be fully satisfied with anyone but him. She would always want him.

"I'm sorry," she whispered.

It wasn't enough.

He nodded once, his eyes hardening as he continued to stare at her. Clearing his throat, he stood the tiniest bit straighter. "I came here to tell you the council has decided to attack Renard in two days' time. That's the quickest they could rally their troops and send envoys of elves to their closest allies to ask for support. If they are successful in gaining additional troops, Renard will not stand a chance."

He stared down at the floor. A single tear dripped from the tip of his nose and fell to the floor with a small plop. She didn't know what he was feeling, but she could imagine how difficult it had been for him to hear Bear's declaration after securing her future as the recognized ruler of the Fae. She reached out and gripped his arm. He stiffened at her touch but did not pull away.

"Thank you for helping convince the councilors. We need to do this if we are going to have a chance at stopping him."

He lifted his chin just enough for their eyes to meet. His shone brightly with unshed tears. How she wished she could take away his pain. He'd known when she'd left with Kimari that there had been something between them. She'd told him she wasn't sure what would happen next. Still, she could imagine that hadn't made it any easier to accept that she was choosing Kimari over him.

"I am and forever will be yours to command, Astrid. Even if I disagree with you."

"We are both royals to our respective people, Max. I don't want you to serve me. I want you to be my equal. My thoughts and feelings have not changed. I want nothing more than for us to create a new way of governing our people, together. We don't need a marriage to solidify our friendship or union." She clasped her hand to his. "We just need this. Trust."

The corners of his lips twitched, and Astrid thought he might smile.

Instead, his eyes narrowed at her as he yanked his hand from hers. "Maybe, one day, we will be able to be friends again. Until then, we can remain allies because I know you want what's best for the magical realm. But we are not friends. Or family. Or anything else you want to conjure up in your head about our relationship. I'm sorry—lack of relationship."

"Max!" Maya said, stepping forward. "Don't say things you'll regret the moment you walk out of this room."

He shook his head. "I won't regret them because they're the truth."

She stormed across the room and before anyone could stop her, slapped him across the cheek with the flat of her hand. Wincing in pain, she shook her hand several times, her skin glowing brilliantly as she stepped away from him again.

"She gave up her healing ability for you. Do you know how many nights she stayed by your bed? How many times she said all she wanted was to have you back? To make sure you were safe? She did everything to bring you out of that coma. And here you are, making a demand on her heart? Demand that she return your affection for her? She already told you how much you mean to her. She gave up something not only important to her, but that would keep her safe from Renard. And still, you can't accept that you are her family. That she does love you."

"Back off, Maya. I don't need you to tell me how to feel or what I should be grateful for. Astrid promised to marry me before she pledged herself to him. I think I have every reason to be angry."

"Fine. You can be angry. Do it. No one is stopping you. But what I'm telling you is that you need to get over it. And if you want to continue with this fight, you're going to have to stop acting like a petulant child and suck it up."

Astrid shot Maya a side-eyed glance. She'd only heard her speak this passionately about three things before: technology, Eldris, and bubbles.

"We've been through a lot together, the three of us, but that doesn't mean you get to decide who Astrid ends up with. Only Astrid can do that. And you can choose to either accept your place in her life or let her go."

Astrid didn't realize she'd been holding her breath until Max finally blinked at Maya.

"You're right." His shoulders sagged as he stared at the floor. "I'll leave you now. One of the guards will take you to the council room when they're ready for you."

He didn't look at Astrid as he left the room, and she couldn't help but think this was the last time they would talk to one another so openly. She'd broken his heart. Again. Only this time, there wasn't hope left for them. Her feelings for Kimari had started as a forbidden whisper. Now they were a roaring waterfall. She didn't know how deep it would go, but she was certain the fall would be worth it.

The minute the door closed behind Max, Bear released a sigh of relief. "I never did like that one."

"What?" Astrid cocked an eyebrow at him. Numbness tingled down her spine and to the tips of her fingers and toes. Max was gone. She didn't know how long it would take him to get over her. If he ever would.

"Max. He was always too… controlling. Or tried to be."

She shrugged. Kimari was her end game but losing Max's friendship was like a knife plunging into her heart. A part of her died when he'd left without telling her it would be okay. That he could accept his place in her life.

Maya wrapped her arm around Astrid's waist and pulled her into a tight embrace. Leaning her head against Astrid's shoulder, Maya whispered, "It's going to be okay. You'll see. Max will come around once we get through this."

"You're assuming we can get Kimari and Kali to safety. They're still with Renard. If we attack with bombs, they could be hurt."

"We have to do what is best for our people."

Astrid froze at Maya's words. She didn't want to just be a ruler to magicals. She wanted humans and magicals to live together in harmony, without fear or resentment towards one another.

"I think what's best for our people is to remove Renard from power—without causing undo harm to civilians. Many of them haven't had a role in our suffering."

"Haven't they, though? They lived with the privilege of being human. They didn't have to consider from a young age that they might be separated from their parents solely based on their abilities. They never had to attend the funeral for a friend, too young to even know their street address. How could they possibly know how to handle a gun and knife and rage against their captors? They have never lived without the luxury of their human hood."

"Just because they benefited from the system doesn't mean they should be unjustly punished. Many of these people are just trying to live their lives. They had no idea what Renard was doing in those facilities, and they never thought to ask. I want something more. Something better for the world."

"You say many of them were just trying to live their lives and had no idea about the terror they inflicted there, but that's not entirely true, now is it? They chose to work for Renard in his palace. They chose to ignore the bursts of anger and malice because he was so personable in every other way. They were complicit."

"You think they should die because of their complacency?"

"No…"

"Then you don't want to send a bomb to wipe them all out?"

"If it's a last resort… if they choose…" Maya shot a glance at Bear, her eyes pleading.

He grunted before settling down into one of the chairs. "What Maya is trying to say is that sometimes the means justify the cost. Renard cannot be allowed to remain in power. He will continue researching our powers, in order to secure his supremacy. We must be willing to fight fire with fire if we are to beat him. Unfortunately, that means there must also be sacrifices. Even happy endings come at a price, Astrid."

She fumbled her thumbs as she weighed the pros and cons of

using excessive force for taking out Renard. Too much fire would kill everyone within the palace walls, including the crown prince and princess, if they weren't careful in their approach. Was she really willing to sacrifice them if it meant she would never have to worry about Renard again?

"It's just something to consider," Bear said, drawing her attention back to the present moment.

Gritting her teeth, Astrid paced back and forth before stopping in her tracks and turning to face Maya. "I have an idea, but it's a risky one."

"Let's hear it."

She hoped Penny would forgive her for what she was about to suggest. Or, at the very least, understand. "Maya, do you think you could build a body for my PEA?"

Chapter Twenty-Two

Maya stared at her, blinking. Her mouth opened and shut as if she were trying to formulate the correct words but struggling to do so. "Create a body for your PEA? Astrid, you know we can't remove the physical device from your brain. It's too interconnected with your body."

"Yeah, but you could remove all the data... like Max did before. Only this time, instead of erasing it, you could implant it into a new operating system."

Maya narrowed her eyes at Astrid. "But why would we want to? She'd just be a robot. Like any other. Only... if she retains any trace of your memories, she could be a liability to us."

Astrid steadied herself to tell Maya the truth. "She's an AI. The first one ever created."

"That's not possible…"

"Why not?" Astrid swung her arm around them. "Look at where we are. Do you remember where we started? Do you remember how Max and I found you in that city where Renard already stormed? Because I do."

She turned towards Bear. "We met each other in a draking bar, Bear. Where I worked as a bartender. If we can change, why can't the operating systems of computers learn and grow and change in their own ways. Don't answer that one. Just trust me. Penny is alive. She's real. And I think it's time she had her own body."

Don't.

The single word filled her mind like the buzzing hum of a thousand, swarming bees. She swatted them all away as she squared her shoulders and planted her feet further apart into what she hoped was a power stance. "Don't fight me on this one. I know this is going to sound insane, but I think my PEA possesses some of the powers of the ancient queen Amaleah."

Maya and Bear shared a concerned glance. Then they burst into laughter.

"You actually expect us to believe that someone found enough information on Amaleah to recreate her?" Maya laughed again. "What a joke, Astrid. Truly. Most of those records were lost during the Ages of Darkness."

"I know it sounds far-fetched, but I've spoken to her. I know she's real. Her stories are real."

"No, Astrid." Maya laid her hand on Astrid's arm. "There's no way your PEA contains that kind of information. She doesn't have a strong enough processor. I'm sorry, Astrid, but it's the truth."

Freed by Destiny

"Why do you think I fought so hard to find a way to bring her back? Think about it. Why would Eldridge willingly risk his life to help find the spell that brings back lost things if he didn't believe me?"

"Because he loves you, and because he wants to see you shine. You're the most powerful Fae he's ever met. Beyond that, you're our queen."

Astrid pressed her fingers into the bridge of her nose and counted backwards as she tried to stop herself from crying—or worse, exploding—at Maya's words.

"I don't know how to prove to you that I'm telling the truth other than to ask you, again, to build her a body."

"Okay… say I build a body for your PEA. And say it doesn't prove anything. Then what?"

"Then you'll have proved me wrong and I'll drop the subject."

Maya clasped her hand and squeezed. "Astrid, I know you've been through a lot over the past month. I can only begin to imagine what Renard did to you while you were his prisoner. But this is insanity. PEAs aren't capable of sustaining themselves on their own. They need to be connected to a brain to function. It's how they're designed."

"And I'm telling you, Penny is different. She's special."

Bear shook his head at Maya. Astrid didn't say anything. She could tell they thought she was suffering some sort of breakdown following her escape from the palace, but she knew better. She knew Penny was more sentient than anything else, and she deserved to have a life that wasn't bound to hers.

"I know you're worried about me, and maybe justifiably so, but I know what I know. It's okay if you don't believe me. I just need you to—I don't know—trust me? Or at least give me the benefit of the doubt."

"Astrid…." Maya looked everywhere but into her eyes.

Astrid knew the internal battle she must have been having. Give into a request she thought was insane or risk pushing Astrid away even more.

"Please, Maya."

Maya shot a glance at Bear, who only shrugged. "Fine."

Astrid flung her arms around Maya's neck and pulled her into an embrace. "Thank you! Thank you! Thank you."

Patting Astrid's back, Maya whispered, "It's okay. There's nothing to thank me for just yet. Wait until we see if the process works. But remember, I promise you nothing."

Astrid leaned her forehead against Maya's. "You won't disappoint me. I know it."

Before they could say more, the door to their room swung open and Cassidhe stormed inside. With a flick of her head, the guards trailing behind her took up their post outside.

"I suppose Max has told you that we intend to attack Lunameed as you suggested?" Her tone was icy as she looked down her nose at Astrid. "I was against it, but my colleagues believe that you have the greatest insight into Renard's weaknesses. I hope they're right and you're not leading us into a trap."

"I would never…"

"I don't know you. I've heard the stories, of course. How you were raised without knowing your true heritage. How you rose quickly in popularity among the magicals living in Lunameed. How you have made great and terrible sacrifices to protect them. And yet, when a pretty face entered the scene, you swooned like a schoolgirl. Max told me everything."

"Max is a biased party when it comes to Astrid," Bear cut in, stopping Astrid from exploding on Cassidhe. Her skin sparkled brilliantly as she tried—and failed—to control her anger at the insinuation that she had risked the future of her people over some stupid crush.

"Max has been the only completely honest person I've met from your group," Cassidhe countered. "He understands what it takes to win a war."

"I'm assuming you think you know what it takes, too?" Astrid said.

"I know what it takes to survive. If your story is to believe, you should know how scrappy and hungry for a new world order you have to be to make a permanent change. And yet, there you were, fraternizing with one of Renard's own. Anything you said to the prince could have been taken back to his father almost immediately. Don't you find it strange that he and his sister helped you escape but didn't come with you? They put themselves in danger by remaining. Unless, of course, there was never any danger for them to begin with because they played you."

Although Astrid had had similar doubts bursting at the seams of her mind, she maintained her composure as she met Cassidhe's gaze. "You're right. They might have been playing me for a fool. They could have ulterior motives. Who knows? But you know what, at least I'm not so jaded that I can't give people the benefit of the doubt. All I know is that they tried to give me secret messages all throughout my captivity to let me know they were on my side. And then they followed through on everything they said they were going to. That means more to me than anything."

"Max was right—for someone who was raised in the slums, you certainly are naive."

"No, I just choose to give people the benefit of the doubt. Do I trust them to not break their promises to me? To not let me down? Of course not. But I'm not going to let my underlying operating system convince me that they will always let me down."

Cassidhe paced from one end of the room to the other. Her heels clacked on the floor with each step, making Astrid jerk from the sound. Astrid watched her move, wondering what was going through her mind. She couldn't get a good understanding of how Cassidhe operated or why she did the things she did. All she knew was that she needed Cassidhe to be in their corner if she was going to accomplish the things she needed to. They didn't have to be friends; they just needed to trust one another enough to accomplish their goals.

Eventually, Cassidhe came to stop directly in front of Astrid. "I want us to have a great partnership. Despite what Max has told me and what I've observed of your character, I still believe that you can be the face of a new type of governing system within Lunameed. The real question is: after fighting for so long to regain control and your title, are you willing to give it all up?"

Astrid contemplated her question. Was she willing to give up the power and protection she'd worked so hard to achieve? She wanted to say yes. She wanted to tell this woman that she was willing to forfeit her right to rule if it meant a better future for her country. And yet, she hesitated. Power had that ability. It coiled around people like a snake. And, like the venomous cobras living in the rainforests of Smiel, it would suffocate and crush anything it deemed small enough to break.

"I want what's best for my people," she replied, hedging her words in order to leave a line of communication open between them.

"And what if the Golden City truly believes that having another in the seat of power—or rather many—is the best thing for your people? I've heard how you disregard the opinions of your fellowship, your councilors. How are my peers and I supposed to trust that you will act with deliberation and reserve moving forward when you have yet to demonstrate your capacity to do so? Wasn't it your decision to invite Renard's help to meet with you to begin with? Wasn't that what angered the king?"

"Now hold on," Bear said as he strategically placed himself between Astrid and Cassidhe. "It's true that Astrid might, at times, be a bit rash, but she always follows her heart and does what she believes is best for others. Did Max tell you all the times she made personal sacrifices to save others? Did he tell you how she remained behind until all the people were evacuated from the city Renard bombed?"

"And is that not yet another example of how she disregarded the benefit of the whole to save a few? I'm sorry to say, but it does seem your precious Astrid has quite a lot of explaining to do."

"So this is how Max described me to you?" Astrid felt another layer of her heart crack at the thought. Rash. Poor decision making. Foolish. She wanted to scream at the top of her lungs that she might be those things, sometimes, but it was all done out of a deep respect for the life of others. Even her decision to attempt an agreement between herself and Kimari had been to stop the war between his family and her.

"If I may," Maya said. "It seems that you have been provided a very biased perspective of Astrid. Did Max tell you she recently chose Kimari over him? Did he? Because that might cloud his judgment of her."

"He may have alluded to a decision…"

"Then you should take what he says with a grain of salt."

"Prove me wrong. Show me that she has leadership abilities."

"You council has already decided to help us, " Astrid said. "Why should I prove anything to you?"

Cassidhe glared at her. Her lips turned downwards as she sucked on her teeth. "You should learn to respect those who could help you."

"Respect is a two-way street, Cassidhe. So far, you have treated me with little more than contempt since I first arrived here. Why should I show you something you have yet to show me?"

Cassidhe's mouth dropped open

"Careful, I wouldn't want you to catch a fly in that trap."

Cassidhe snapped her mouth shut and glared at her. "You are in my city, Astrid. I would be careful—"

"Your city? And here I thought the Golden City was known for its collective governance."

The glare Cassidhe gave Astrid would have made a younger version of the Fae queen's blood turn to ice. Instead, she just stood there, waiting for the other woman to respond.

Through clenched teeth, Cassidhe said, "At least I have someplace I know I can call my home. I belong here. Where do you belong?"

Her words punched Astrid in the gut, sending her reeling through an onslaught of emotions. The only physical place she'd ever felt like she belonged was The Wand. Being in that place, with other Fae and the FGs, had meant everything to her. But she knew she would never be able to return there as the same woman who'd left. Too much had happened, and she knew who she was now. She wouldn't be accepted in the same way as before.

Maya's face flashed through her mind. And Bear's. And the rest of the FGs'. Of Max. Her heart hammered as his smile filled her vision. She needed to repair the rift between them before it solidified into a deep chasm she wouldn't be able to cross.

Kali and Kimari were the last to appear. Kimari's face lingered long past when the others receded. She couldn't explain why, but she felt at home with him.

"You can't think of a single place you belong, can you?" Cassidhe smirked at her.

"Actually, I was just thinking about all the people who accept and love me for exactly who I am, even if I can be headstrong and stubborn sometimes."

"Don't forget the rash part," Maya added with a smile.

Rolling her eyes, Astrid returned the smile. "They even love me when I run headfirst into action without really considering the consequences because they know my heart is in the right place. Sure, you have an entire city gilded in gold, but do you have people in your life who make you belong no matter where you are?"

Cassidhe harrumphed at her. "I can see why so many people follow you. You speak with such passion that it's difficult not to believe your words."

They stared at each other. Astrid couldn't help but wonder what else Max had told her in his anger. He clearly wanted to hurt

Astrid, even if it was only emotionally.

"Look, I disagree with the council. They want to help you. I think it's a mistake. But what can I do to fight them? How can I ensure that you won't destroy us in the end? You could be using our defenses to lure Renard's forces out. You could turn on us. Your actions could leave us defenseless."

"Astrid has not left anyone on the battlefield. If anything, she's let herself be put in harm's way," Maya said.

"Exactly. That is the problem I'm talking about. I can give her the benefit of the doubt that she doesn't want to betray us. That she won't hurt us. And yet..."

"And yet, you're willing to stand here and talk about me like I'm not here. I am not a traitor to my kind or to my allies. Who do you think you are, to insult me like this?"

"Ladies, I don't think we're going to come to a resolution if all you do is insult one another and get defensive." Maya placed a steadying hand on Astrid's shoulder. "Please, Astrid, let it go."

"I think you should leave." Astrid growled at Cassidhe. Flamed slithered between her fingers, flickering with violet brilliance.

Cassidhe's eyes widened as she took a subtle step backwards. "Are you threatening me?"

"No, I'm warning you. Back off."

"Enough." Max stormed into the room, his face a mask of disgruntlement. "We don't have time for you to be arguing with one another. Quit trying to outdo the other. You're both... well... you're both strong leaders. And we need all the brainstorming power we can get right now."

Freed by Destiny

He turned toward Astrid. "I have followed you to the end before, and I shall do so again a thousand times over. I've pledged myself to you and to your cause. Our... relationship is not what..."

He choked on his words.

Astrid reached out him, longing to give him comfort. He jerked away from her and took a position beside Cassidhe.

Averting his gaze from Astrid, he looked to Maya and Bear. "We have to devise a plan that weakens Renard's defenses. So far, he's always seemed to be at least one step ahead of us." He turned his full attention on Cassidhe. "You have done so much for the Golden City and are a true testament to what leadership can look like. To the power that a collective can have. I look forward to continuing to learn from you and to add my mark on the future of Lunameed and its surrounding neighbors."

Astrid narrowed her eyes as Max's pinky slid across Cassidhe's wrist. A smoldering tempest swirled within her stomach as she trailed the movement of his caress across the woman's skin. She shouldn't be jealous. She'd just told him that she was certain in her decision that they were better suited as friends than as romantic companions. And yet, she couldn't fight the cold bite the tenderness of his touch on Cassidhe's wrist delivered to Astrid's heart.

To her astonishment, Cassidhe wrapped her pinky around Max's. The curl of their entwined fingers solidified her contempt of the other woman.

Good for him, Penny's voice whispered at the back of her mind. *Be happy for him, Astrid. You broke his heart. And here he is, flirting with a woman who would rather see your head on a stake than see you crowned as queen of the fae. Still, look at him. He looks happy.*

269

Now you decide to show up? she asked back.

Don't take that tone with me. Do you have any idea how long it took me to form as a materialized thought inside your head again? Your thoughts are like a never-ending hedge maze.

"Astrid?" Maya placed a steadying hand on her shoulder, pulling her back into the present moment. "Can you hear us? Are you alright?"

"What?" She blinked rapidly as she tried to remember what they had been discussing before she zoned out.

Maya leaned in close. "Are you okay?"

Astrid smiled. "I'm fine. Truly. I was just thinking about what we can do to make things… better between us." She turned towards Cassidhe. "We don't know each other well, but if Max is to be believed, you and I are quite similar."

Smirking, Cassidhe leaned ever so slightly forward. "We are nothing alike."

It took every ounce of control Astrid had to stop herself from giving Cassidhe a snarky comeback. Instead, she inclined her head towards her and said, "It's okay if you're not at a place yet to see me as a true partner, but I will do everything I can to prove to you that I am a strong ally. And that I want a better world for all magicals and non-magicals alike. Whether you believe me or not doesn't change what I am willing to do to see my vision to the end."

A broad smile stretched across Cassidhe's face. It made her look younger somehow, more approachable. "That is exactly what I was hoping you would say."

"So it's agreed then—we will work together." Astrid stuck out her hand towards Cassidhe.

Cassidhe stared at her hand with a frown plastered across her face. Her upper lip curled as she took Astrid's hand in her own. "Agreed."

And just like that, Astrid secured the support of a powerful ally she didn't even know she needed. She only hoped the Golden City would be strong enough to help her defeat Renard's armies.

Chapter Twenty-Three

Maya blew a bubble as she bent over the metal skeleton of a humanoid robot. Sparks flew from the fine-tip tool she was using to weld two pieces together. Her brow furrowed as she leaned in closer to examine the seam.

Astrid watched her work, wishing she knew what she could do to speed up the process. There were only a few hours left before the Golden City was set to launch its attack on Renard and she wanted, more than anything, to have Penny at her side.

She peered around the room as she waited for Maya to finish up her task. An assortment of broken-down robots lined one of the walls. Electronics she couldn't even begin to determine the use of lined another. Maya stood at an L-shaped worktable that was laden with all manner of tools. She popped another bubble as she bobbed her head to the music she had playing in the background.

"You have to give it time, Astrid. If you want this to be done properly, you can't rush the process," she said. She snapped another piece into place and tested how snuggly it fit into the robot's processor by holding it upside down. The piece didn't even budge.

"We don't have time to give, Maya. You know this better than anyone."

Maya shrugged. "Yeah, well, that might be true, but you've asked me to design and build something highly complex. I can't do that with a snap of my fingers. Even if I could, I'm not sure I would want to. You have something special going on with your PEA and I would hate to completely fry it before we even really have a chance to see how it does in its new body."

"How *she* does in her new body," Astrid corrected. "She has a name, Maya, and a whole personality."

Maya popped another bubble in response before bending her head over another section of the head. She pulled down a magnifier in front of her eyes and tsked as she noticed some small flaw in the metal. Astrid began pacing as she waited for Maya to finish what she was doing.

Are you sure this is what you want?

She didn't know if the thought was her own or Penny's. In some ways, it didn't matter. The idea of being able to physically touch Penny—to hug her—was something Astrid wanted more than anything. She'd lost her once; she would not lose her again. If anything, she would give Penny a chance to learn and grow beyond her current capacity.

Memories can be fabricated.

Astrid groaned. "I can't believe you're trying to make me doubt

274

you."

"Did you say something?" Maya looked up from her work bench. She blew her bangs up on top of her head.

"Uh, no," Astrid replied quickly. "Well, maybe?"

Maya shoved the magnifier away from her eyes and peered at Astrid from across the room. For the longest time, Maya had been the only one she trusted with her secret.

"Well, which is it? Yep, you said something or no, you didn't?"

"I, uh," Astrid stumbled over her words. "Honestly. The truth is, I sometimes talk to my PEA."

Maya's hands paused for a moment, her head inclining towards Astrid, as if anticipating just a little more information. When Astrid didn't continue, Maya dropped her tool onto the workbench. She came around the robot's body to stand beside Astrid.

Taking her hands in her own, she said, "Astrid, we all talk to our PEAs sometime. They've been our constant companions our entire lives, but that doesn't make them sentient. It's all part of their programming."

"I hear what you're saying, but I just don't agree."

"And if this body doesn't work the way you envisioned it would? What then?"

"Then it doesn't work, and we go back to square one."

"Astrid…" Maya looked down at their clasped hands. Her lower lip trembled as her hair fell over her face, shielding her eyes. "I know you've been through so much. More than any person should have to go through in an entire lifetime, much less a little over twenty years. But…"

"You don't believe me. So, what is this?" She yanked her hands out of Maya's. "Huh? If you're convinced my PEA isn't sentient, why are you building a body for her?"

"Because you asked me to!" Maya's skin took on a dewy glow. Her eyes twinkled with tears as she shook her head.

Astrid's heart pounded erratically. She placed one hand over her chest, trying to calm herself enough to continue her conversation with Maya. None of her techniques worked to diminish the anxiety raging within her. It squeezed its fist around her organs until she felt like she was going to pop.

"I don't want to fight with you," Maya whispered.

"Then don't." Astrid folded her arms over her chest and pouted at Maya. "Eldris risked his life to help me find the spell to bring her back. If he didn't believe she was special, why would he do that? Help me understand why you don't believe me. When have I ever purposely led you astray?"

Silver lined Maya's eyes. "We love you, Astrid. And we do believe in you. It's just… we would do anything you asked— have already done so many things—but neither of us knows if this is real or just…"

"Folly."

Maya nodded.

"I see."

"Eldris believed it could be possible. He'd seen glimpses of visions. Things he'd never dreamt of before. Then you said your PEA was special. Sentient. He desperately wanted to believe it was true, that it was possible to create new, technological life. But when you cast the spell and it didn't work…"

"He began to doubt," Astrid finished for Maya. Although realizing her friends' doubts was painful, she could understand why they were hesitant. Sentience had never been achieved within their robots or machines before. Sure, they'd developed some robots who came close, but they still operated completely within the scope of their code.

Penny was different. She had her own thoughts, feelings, and memories. Astrid didn't know how to convince her friends of the veracity of this truth, but she was determined to try. Even if it took waiting until her PEA had been transferred to the robot's body.

Maya didn't look at her as she tinkered a bit more with the circuit within the robot's frame. The only sign that she was still upset by their argument was the tremble of her hands. Sighing heavily, Astrid placed a steadying hand on Maya's shoulder, hoping she could impart how much she appreciated and loved her friend into that single touch, but knowing it wasn't enough. If her time in Renard's palace had taught her anything, it was that there would never be anything she could do or say that would make up for the things her friends had sacrificed to keep her safe. To place her in a position of power.

She just hoped she could prove that their sacrifice had been worth it.

That she had been worth it.

Chapter Twenty-Four

Astrid wandered the halls. Sea breeze wafted through open windows, smelling of salt and warmth. She stood before one of the windows on what she thought was the top floor of the fortress and stared across the Golden City to the ocean beyond. Turquoise waves turned to white foam as they crashed on the glistening sands.

A hazy memory fluttered around the edges of her mind, begging her to relive the moment Max had portalled her to the beach after rescuing her from Kaden. She'd allowed him to move forward with an extraction process to try and access her memories. She'd lost Penny, her last lifeline to her past. Although she'd gained a new family and understanding of who she was, the pain of having Penny ripped away from her still lingered. Even after all this time, she'd made the choice to give her up. She'd chosen to sacrifice her. It didn't matter that she hadn't understood what that would mean.

This new version of Penny still wasn't the friend she remembered. She wasn't the loving, careful, calculating PEA who had been her constant companion her whole life. She was something new. Something Astrid still didn't fully understand.

"I was hoping I would find you alone." Max's voice was gruff and close behind her.

She didn't turn to look at him, didn't trust herself not to fling herself into his arms and cry for the things she'd lost in this battle to become the queen her people needed.

"I was just remembering when we faced the robots in the ocean, after you rescued me from Kaden," she whispered. Her chest tightened as she continued to fight the urge to go to him.

"It has been a long, harrowing road since then, hasn't it?"

He stood close enough behind her that she could feel his heat emanating from him.

She leaned towards the window, creating more distance between them. "I'm not sure I would have chosen everything that has transpired then, no."

He chuckled. "No, I don't suppose I would, either. But I knew what I was getting into when I took you from Estrellala and brought you to my aunt. I knew what would become of you if you were, indeed, the lost queen. I should have warned you…"

"How could you have known what would become of me? You knew it would be difficult. You knew I would face untold challenges and that I would have to make difficult choices. But how could you have known it would be like this? There's no way you could have." She sighed and inclined her head towards him.

Freed by Destiny

"It's okay, Max. I've made my choices. So have you."

Although she couldn't see him, she could envision the way his throat bobbed as he swallowed hard. She could almost hear the steady increase of his heart as he tried to decipher what her words meant. She knew he still loved her. And there would always be a part of her that loved him.

"You've changed," he said, disrupting her thoughts. He placed his hand on her shoulder and turned her around. His brow furrowed as he examined her face. "What happened to you?"

She shook her head. "I survived a month in captivity with Renard, Max. What do you think happened to me?"

His lips pressed into a thin, hard line. "How could I know what happened to you in there if you won't tell me? All I know is that you left with him and… are now committed to him. Even though he betrayed you."

His expression darkened and Astrid knew they were on the verge of descending into another unproductive argument. She'd hurt him, but there was nothing she could do to mend his broken heart. He was her family. She loved him dearly. But the chasm between them had grown too large. There had been too many misunderstandings. They'd chosen different paths.

"Max…"

"Don't. Don't tell me that you love me. And that you're sorry. It won't help."

She snapped her mouth shut. "Fine. I won't say those things again, even if they're true. But you're right. It doesn't matter and they won't help. We're trapped in this cycle of misunderstanding and hurt. I don't want us to be forever trapped there. So let me be clear. I want your friendship, more than anything, but I *need* your

281

support to secure our shared dream of creating a better world for magicals. I can't achieve that goal without you. So, whether we like it or not, we will have to work together to make it happen. Maybe after some time has passed, you and I can become friends again. We can move past the things that have happened to us and be a family. Will it look like you envisioned? Probably not. I think we're past the point where we could be together, even if we tried. I think you know that, too. You just aren't in a place where you can admit it."

He remained stoic as he stared her. She longed to know what he was thinking. To know that he was at least considering what she was saying. Slowly, his lips curled into a grim smile.

"When I first met you, you were terrified of the things happening to you. And you were so… wild. You're still the most stubborn person I've ever met."

She bit her tongue to keep herself from telling him to look in the mirror sometime. She needed him to move past their history and to believe that they could become friends once more. It wasn't that she missed him desperately, though she did. She'd been telling the truth when she'd said that she needed him to achieve her goals.

"I can't tell you that we'll be friends at the end of this story, but I can… I will… promise that I will be there until the darkest hour has passed. Our end goal is larger than any of us."

She closed her eyes. It was the most she could expect from him.

"Thank you."

He lingered, peering at her with a look she couldn't read. There had been a time when she'd known what he was thinking just by being near him. Now, though, he was more stranger than anything else.

He tucked a strand of her hair behind her ear. "We have both seen some of the darkest parts of this world, Astrid, and we are still standing. I have to believe that at the end of this all, we will be, eventually, be able to share a mug together. To reminiscence of the things we've faced together. Of the battles we've won and the people we've lost. And to not hate one another.

"I don't hate you now."

His fingers slipped from her skin as his sad smile returned to his face. "I know."

Coldness spread through her body.

"I only hope he's worth it."

She chuckled and smiled as she looked up at him. "Me, too."

She felt the comfortable air between them, just as it had been so many times before. Then, as if recognizing it as well, Max nodded and turned away from her.

She waited until she could no longer hear his footsteps before turning to follow him back to the main floor of the fortress. Wherever the road led her next, she hoped he would still be a part of her story. But, despite the fact that they had solidified their intent to not treat one another with contempt and to work together to move forward, she doubted they would ever be able to reclaim what had been lost. This time, there wasn't a magical spell that could bring back the companionable aura between them.

What was lost, had been lost forever.

Chapter Twenty-Five

Astrid pulled fingerless black gloves over her hands and stood back to examine herself in the mirror. She'd returned to her rooms following her conversation with Max and was now waiting to meet those who had answered the Golden City's call. She'd pulled her hair back into a tight braid, keeping it out of her face.

Black, form-fitting, lightweight body armor had been left in her chamber along with a selection of weapons. She needed to bear in mind the fact that she could no longer heal herself. Her fighting style would have to adapt to this new reality.

Her features had become sharper during her time in Renard's captivity, as if being held against her will had hardened her. Perhaps it had. Turning to the bed, she examined the weapons. There were guns, a selection of knives, and a few explosives. She trailed her fingers over the hilts of the blades until she landed on a jeweled one. Tiny diamonds and opals glistened from the hilt. The blade's tip was incredibly sharp as she ran her finger over it, drawing blood. She winced and stuck her finger in mouth to stop the bleeding.

She didn't know when she would have cause to use the knife, but she slipped it into a strap on her thigh regardless. She plucked three of the guns and attached them to her body as well without looking to see what kind of weapons they were. She didn't bother with the explosive or the other knives. Her goal was a to use her magic as much as possible. It writhed within her, ready to rear itself on Renard's armies.

Her watch buzzed against her skin, alerting her to a message.

Max: *We're ready for you.*

Whatever happened next, her life was about to change. Either many had heeded her call, or, and this was the more likely scenario, they were still too afraid to rise up against the king. Who was she to call on them for help? Who was the Golden City to ask them to fight in a war they had no part in unless they chose to involve themselves? When she was fully the queen of the fae, would she be willing to put her people's lives in danger to help someone she'd never met?

She couldn't say for certain she would put them in that position, so how could she expect the same from the Golden City?

Her watch buzzed again.

Max: *It's now or never.*

Swallowing hard, she turned towards the door. It was strange, this fear that she would discover no aid on the other side. She'd made it this far with little to no help other than the magicals who had been willing to rebel against their king. Although their forces were small and had considerably fewer resources, they'd been able to do so much.

Still, would their new allies be enough to help them win? Regardless, she would fight to whatever end.

Astrid stood outside the doors to the council room. Her hands shook as she hesitated.

"You've faced worse than what lies beyond those doors," Bear said as he came to stand beside her.

Her lips tugged into a lopsided smile as she stole a glance at him. "I don't know. A room full of politicians sounds worse than facing a horde of Renard's robots if you ask me. Certainly more stealthy."

"Ah yes, the terrors of squaring off against the smooth-talking voices of the people. So awful. Look at this, it's giving me the gooses." He held his arm in front of her face and pulled back his sleeve. His arms were so hairy, it was impossible to see his skin.

"I know. It's simply dreadful."

"Too bad we don't have some ale to drink before mixing with the monsters."

Despite the nerves still messing with her stomach, she smiled. "I knew I could count on you to make me laugh."

"Darlin,' if there is one thing I could do the rest of my life, it would be to ensure you laugh every day."

She slipped her hand into his. "I don't know how many others have heeded our call. When Janae attempted this before, there was no one who came to our aid. Why should we think it will be different now?"

"Because of Cassidhe and the other councilors. They have agreed to help us. They have opened the gates. We can only wait to see if the flood comes."

He shoved the doors open without another word. They clanked against the walls on the inside of the room. Astrid gasped as her gaze fell upon five portals, each held open by a different elf. She was too far away to see what lay on the other side of the portal, but she knew it could only mean one thing: there had been at least a few who had answered her call.

No longer were they alone in this fight.

"Ah, she has arrived," Cassidhe said, motioning for Astrid to join her at the front of the room.

Astrid strolled down the row of chairs. Humans and magicals alike gazed upon her as she walked towards Cassidhe. She stared at them, assessing where they were from and which country they represented. She wasn't well versed in sigils and flags from other places, but she noticed five different symbols represented among them. She nodded at them as she passed.

She peered through the portal directly in front of Cassidhe. Beyond the abyss, an army stretched beyond her vision. Rows upon rows of solders waited at ease. A commanding general stood with some of her commanders at the helm of the forces. She was taller and more muscular than any man Astrid had ever seen, including Bear. The commander turned towards Astrid and smiled menacingly before stepping through the portal.

Bear yanked Astrid backwards as the general materialized before them. He shoved Astrid behind him, a gun drawn and pointed directly at the soldier. Cassidhe flung her body in front of the general and held up her hands.

"What in the *drak* are you doing?" She growled.

Bear didn't say anything as he lifted his head to take a harder look at the general.

"I asked you a direct question," Cassidhe said. "I demand a response."

Max came from forward from somewhere in the crowd and stood beside Cassidhe. "No one means Astrid any harm, Bear. I swear it."

Bear eyed him suspiciously.

"What reason do I have to lie?"

"It's okay," Astrid said. She laid a hand on Bear's arm, lowering his weapon. She met Max's gaze. "If he says they don't mean me any harm, I believe him."

Bear grunted but moved to the side.

Cassidhe readjusted her dress as Astrid stepped forward. "Now that we have that… uncomfortable… situation out of the way, let me introduce you to the Lead Councilor of Winterdom: Lady Brennen."

Lady Brennen stepped forward. "I prefer to be called Nat, if you don't mind."

Her voice was softer and less gruff than what Astrid had been imagining.

"Well, Nat, it is nice to meet you."

"I have heard tales of you over the past year. If they are to be believed, you are a ferocious warrior."

"She is," Bear and Max said at the same time.

Her skin briefly illuminated at the praise, but then dimmed as she stuck out her hand. "I wouldn't say that I'm ferocious. I am just unwilling to compromise when it comes to protecting my people from the tyranny of Renard."

Nat bellowed a laugh. "You will forgive me for saying this, but you are not what I was expecting."

"Well, I think you're in good company. I rarely am."

Nat turned towards Cassidhe. "You didn't tell me she was such a firecracker."

"I didn't know." Cassidhe shrugged.

Nat cocked an eyebrow at her and then turned her attention back to Astrid. "I have been given clearance to grant you the aid of our army, but only if I deem your cause worthy. I joined because of the rumors. It will your merit that earns our support."

"I hope I do not disappoint."

The elf closed the portal to Winterdom.

"Please, take your seat at the councilors' table," Cassidhe said, motioning towards the circular table beyond the portals.

Nat nodded and took the first seat.

Freed by Destiny

Janae, followed by Eldris, came through the next portal. She sniffed when she saw Astrid.

"So glad to have you back with us," Janae said. "I was worried we would never see you again when you abandoned us to turn yourself in to Renard with his welp."

Anger roiled within Astrid's stomach.

"It's good to see you, too, Janae." Despite her best efforts, there was still a bite to her tone as she spoke.

Max flashed her an appreciative smile before turning his full attention to his aunt. "I'm glad you're back with us, aunt."

He embraced her with both arms. She looked frail and small within his muscular arms. Somehow, Astrid never seemed to notice how tiny she was when she was standing on her own. Janae was a presence all to her own.

"Anything that will keep our people safe and give us a chance to finally take Renard out of power, I will do. Even if I am not enthused with who has been selected to lead us to victory."

Astrid ground her teeth.

Eldris stepped past Max and Janae to embrace Astrid. He breathed in deeply as he held her against his chest. "It is good to see you."

"And you," she whispered back.

"I tried to see you, tried to see the path of the future, but it was cloudy and dark." He held her at arm's length. "I am so glad that you made it out of Renard's captivity alive."

She bowed her head. "Our fates are not written in stone."

He shook his head. "No, they most certainly are not. Although, I

291

must say you've surprised me more than any other."

"There are three other countries who have pledged to aid us, or, at the very least, send a representative to make a determination," Cassidhe said. "Janae, please join the councilors' table. We will be joining momentarily."

Janae strode towards the table where Nat sat.

Eldris, on the other hand, leaned in close and pressed his lips to Astrid's ear. "Where can I find Maya?"

A smile played at her lips. Their love was one she hoped to someday have. "She's building a robot for me. Send her a message and I'm sure she'll send you directions to her lab."

He leaned back. "Robot?"

"I'll explain later. I promise."

Although it was clear he would be asking her plenty of questions later, Eldris made his way down the path between the chairs to the door at the back of the room. Astrid listened to his footsteps fade into silence before turning her attention back to the portals.

The portal to the rebels' encampment closed with a pop. Astrid rocked back on her heels as she waited to see who would emerge next. Two portals undulated at the same time. From one of them stepped a massive man wearing golden armor and a robotic hand. A jagged scar stretched from his left eyebrow down to his jaw. He looked her from head to toe and smiled broadly as he licked his upper lip.

"King Vlander, I was anticipating one of your representatives. It is a great honor to have you join us." Cassidhe bowed.

"The pleasure is all mine, I assure you." He grasped Astrid's hand and kissed her knuckles. "It is very nice to meet you, Queen Astrid. I have heard many of the tales of your beauty. None compare to the reality."

Her skin crawled, but she forced herself to smile at him. Until she understood all the intricacies about the relationships he had with the other countries who had answered the Golden City's call, she couldn't risk jeopardizing their support. Before she could respond to him, the next arrival stepped between her and King Vlander.

"Vlander, you never change." A slim man with a tousle of golden hair and eyes that glittered like emeralds placed a hand on King Vlander's shoulder. "Can't you see the girl doesn't want your attentions?"

He waggled his eyebrows at her.

"And how would you ever know what a girl wants, Dominic?" Vlander growled. His face transformed into a horrifying scowl that made Astrid's insides quake.

"Trust me when I tell you that I know quite well what gives a woman pleasure."

Astrid's eyes widened. Both of these men were repulsive, but for different reasons.

Dominic held her hand, sending gooseflesh up her arm as she deftly removed it from his grasp. He smirked at her as she avoided direct eye contact with him.

"I do believe we've made our friend, here, uncomfortable with our banter. Please, forgive me, Queen Astrid. I swear I would never do anything to impute your honor."

She glanced at Cassidhe for guidance on how to respond, but the councilor only subtly shrugged at her.

Astrid had faced the darkest shadows and challenged Renard, even when it could have meant her immediate death. If she had been able to do these things, she could face down a few pigs with grace.

"Not at all." She laughed and nodded at both of them. "Before I was a queen, I was a barkeeper. If you think your banter makes me uncomfortable, you've clearly never spent an evening getting men drunk."

They both stared at her with blank stares. Then, Vlander bellowed a laugh.

"I was not anticipating how funny you would be." He turned towards Cassidhe. "There is so much you left out about this girl, councilor."

"I'll have to remember your tastes next time, King Vlander."

"Yes, you will."

"Well, I could do with a glass of wine. What about you, friend?" Dominic asked as he pulled out a flask from inside his blazer. He shook it at Vlander and smiled.

Vlander accepted the offering and took a large swig.

Cassidhe clapped her hands, and a few servants came forward bearing a tray laden with glasses and bottles of wine. "What kind of host would I be if we didn't have refreshments available for you? Please, join the councilors' table, and I will be happy to ensure your cup is never empty."

Without another word to Astrid, they strode towards the table where Nat and Janae already sat. The servants set glasses before them and left one of the bottles between them to share as they began to drink.

Freed by Destiny

The sight of their merriment left ice creeping up the insides of Astrid's stomach. Her country's future hung in the balance of these people's decisions. And yet, here they were, pretending as if they were for a social call. She didn't like it. Or understand it.

She turned to Cassidhe and placed her hands on her hips. "Who else is coming?"

All but one of the portals had closed. No others opened to replace them.

"Our last guest is one whom I am most interested in introducing to you. They are not active in the matters of humans, but I believe they answered the call because you are fae."

"What do you mean?"

Cassidhe turned towards the elf holding the portal open. "Is she coming?"

The elf nodded.

The portal began to shimmer and undulate as a figure stepped from beyond the abyss. Dark auburn hair tumbled around her shoulders as she lifted her chin to meet Astrid's gaze. Her petite form moved with a grace Astrid had only seen in dancers. When she finally met her eyes, they swirled like the waves crashing upon the sea during a storm. She smiled at Astrid, slightly elongated canines extending over bottom lip.

"I have waited many years for the rise of magicals within Lunameed's borders. It is a pleasure to meet you, Astrid Bluefischer, the Firebird."

Astrid extended her hand to the woman. "Let's just hope we can achieve our goal to create a path for magicals to live without fear once more in Lunameed. Perhaps you can be a part of that endeavor."

"Perhaps," the woman replied.

Cassidhe cleared her voice. "Adira, thank you for coming. I wasn't sure if you—"

Adira turned towards Cassidhe. "I don't believe I asked for your opinion, human. I thank you for inviting us to this cause and for alerting us to your city's involvement in freeing Queen Astrid from her captivity, but I would prefer to hear from the queen from here on out."

Cassidhe's cheeks flushed, but she bowed her head in submission. Her reaction piqued Astrid's curiosity about who the woman was. She didn't smell human. There was a coldness to her, a scent that Astrid couldn't quite place. It was unlike anything she'd encountered before.

"Do you know who I am?" Adira asked.

"Adira," Astrid responded. "Though, I'm not sure the relevancy of your name."

Laughter bubbled from Adira's chest. "Yes, of course. I am the queen of the sirens."

Astrid balled her hands into fists. "But the sirens have been dead…"

"For centuries? Yes, well, that if that were true, how would one be standing before you now?"

"What about your tail? How do you have legs?"

Adira cocked an eyebrow at her and tsked softly. "Has no one taught you the history of the magical world?"

Astrid shook her head. "There wasn't time between our different campaigns against Renard."

"What he's done to the history of your country may never be recovered. For that, I am sorry. Sirens had been on the verge of extinction for millennia. But then, as if by providence, we were given a safe haven to call our new home, far from the shores of any known country. Far from men who had continued to commoditize us. We were given a chance to rebuild and to grow into a mighty people once more."

"But… where?"

"None may know."

Astrid turned towards Cassidhe. "Then how did you…"

"We have our ways of communicating with the sirens, even though they have separated themselves from the rest of the world."

"What Cassidhe means to say is that, despite our best efforts to keep our people together, there have always been those who are called to explore beyond our borders. One such siren has chosen to find his home here in the Golden City. He knows how to communicate with our kingdom. Although he rarely does so, we were quite pleased to hear of your escape from Renard's clutches. Thank the Light you are here now."

"I am lucky to have been given the chance to escape Renard," she said carefully. She didn't know what it was about the siren, but she didn't know if she could trust her.

"Yes." Adira continued to stare at Astrid in such a way as to make her feel as if she could see straight through her.

"Now that we're all here, we should begin. There is only so much time before we are set to attack Renard," Cassidhe said, drawing

Astrid's attention.

Max gripped Astrid's elbow, guiding her towards the councilors' table. He didn't say anything as he deposited her in one of the chairs and took a place standing behind her.

Staring at the gathered group of councilors, Astrid wondered how many of them would actually fight to save her people. They were on the precipice of having everything they needed to defeat Renard. All that stood in her people's way was her. She was the last test. And if she failed to convince the envoys from the other countries to join with them, it could bring doom to them all.

Chapter Twenty-Six

The chatter in the room died as Cassidhe stood in the middle of the circular table. She slowly spun around as she spoke, seemingly making eye contact with each country's representative. Astrid wondered if she'd practiced the speech beforehand or if it arose in the moment. She doubted it was the latter.

"We've gathered here to remove a tyrant from power. Each of you has chosen to heed our call, and for that we are eternally grateful. I know some of you have questions about our strategy. You are unsure whether this is the route we should be embarking on. Others want to know how facing Renard as a unified front will benefit them."

Astrid noted that Cassidhe didn't mention anyone joining the cause because they believed in the mission. It was a hard fact in life that others did things not for the heart of the mission, but for what it could provide to them. Although it stung that their intentions were not in the place she'd hoped they would be, if they were all willing to donate their troops, technology, and other resources—even risk their own lives—perhaps intention did not matter as much as outcome.

"Regardless of why you have chosen to join us here, we will need a commitment from you before you will be allowed to engage in any of our dialogues about strategy. As you know, Renard's reputation precedes him. He is a master at collecting information. He has spies everywhere. And, if he doesn't have a living spy he can count on, he uses his technology to hack into other country's systems. We all know how he is. We've seen it at every council."

Astrid didn't know why this surprised her, but it did. For some reason, she had always envisioned other countries interacting with Lunameed without realizing the extent to which Renard subjugated his citizens. The idea that all these world leaders had sat around and let him run illegal experiments on magicals, hunt down and assassinate a royal family, and who knew what else— not to mention spy on them—left her flabbergasted. She scanned the gathered representatives and noticed that many of them were not watching Cassidhe.

They were all staring at her.

She locked eyes with King Vlander. He gave her what she assumed was supposed to be a smile, but it looked more like a snarl. He was clearly used to being seen as a powerful warlord. She wondered if his might was what won him his crown. She made a mental note to ask Bear and Max for each of the represented country's histories once they had a moment to themselves.

"Yes, yes," Vlander said, interrupting Cassidhe. "We all know why we're here. You don't need to belabor the point, Cassidhe."

Her cheeks flushed. Yet, she didn't lose her cool as she smiled at him broadly. "Well, then, by all means, King Vlander, please, tell us what your thoughts so that we might assuage them."

He scowled at her, or perhaps his face always looked as if he were scowling. Astrid couldn't tell.

"I want to know how we will be compensated for our sacrifices for your cause. You mentioned gold." His eyes drifted to Astrid as he gave her a calculating look. "But there are other treasures more valuable than coin and gems."

Astrid felt Max stiffen behind her. She cocked her head towards him, silently warning him to stand down. The last thing she needed was for him to, once again, attempt to protect her when she didn't need a hero. After all this time, she would have thought he'd realized that she was perfectly capable of protecting and managing herself. Still, she found that he struggled to see how strong she was, even if he said he did.

"And what, exactly, are you fishing for here?" Astrid asked.

"I think you know what I want. Stop playing coy." He stared directly at Astrid as he said this last part.

She cringed beneath his gaze. Who was he to look at her like she was a piece of meat ready to devour? Bile churned in her stomach, threatening to creep up the back of her throat as she forced herself to meet his eyes.

"Cassidhe might know what you're insinuating, but I don't. So please, enlighten me." It was an old trick she'd learned from bartending: play dumb. Force them to become more precise in their words. Nine times out of ten, whoever the creep was that was bothering her would stop because being direct somehow made his power trip less appealing.

Unfortunately, Vlander fell into the one out of ten scenario.

"You look like you'd be a good drak. And, if you are, perhaps there's another way we could come to an arrangement. I'm in the mood for a new wife."

The sound of Max's dagger sliding from the hilt strapped to his waist sent gooseflesh racing up Astrid's arm. She held up her arm, ready to throw a protective shield around the king if Max went too far.

"Vlander, my dear boy, if you think this is how you talk to a lady, you clearly haven't met someone with as much class as Astrid has," Dominic said. He reclined in his chair, his feet stretched out in front of him, beneath the table. "Besides, I wanted to ask for her to commit to a treaty and sealing it with marriage. We can't both marry her."

He waggled his eyebrows at her. "Although I wouldn't be opposed to sharing."

The way these men spoke about her, as if she weren't there and as if she were a toy to be played with and 'shared' without regard for her feelings, left a bitter taste in her mouth. They were pigs and they deserved to be slaughtered. If this was the type of support Cassidhe had been able to procure for her, she wasn't sure she appreciated the help.

She placed her hands firmly on the table and stood. "Thank you for coming. I appreciate you both for being willing to, at the very least, entertain the notion of forming an alliance with me. However…" She stood taller; flames licked around her wrists and curled up her arms. "I will not be bullied into marrying or draking either of you. I might need help in saving my country from the likes Renard. I might need to find help in unsavory places. But I will be damned to darkness if I will ever give myself over to the likes of you."

Vlander growled, his eyes darting between her and Cassidhe. He pointed a meaty finger at the latter. "You promised me she would be amenable to joining me as my third wife. You lied."

Astrid turned towards Cassidhe.

"Is this true?" She crushed her nails into the palm of her hand to keep herself from scorching Cassidhe's face with a pillar of flame. "How could you ever even consider that I would be willing to give myself to someone…"

She couldn't finish her sentence.

Max lunged at the king, his face a mask of rage and contempt. His dagger dug into the king's chair, right between his legs. "If you ever even insinuate that you have those kinds of attentions for Astrid again, I will personally ensure you'll never have another child. Do I make myself clear?"

Although Vlander smiled thinly at him, he nodded.

"Good." Max turned to Dominic. "And you, what do you have to say about your behavior?"

"Honestly, I was just hoping to see if the reality was as good as the stories I've heard about the fae queen who can turn herself into a firebird. Bedding her would just be a rather enjoyable side benefit."

Max's grip on his dagger tightened. Astrid touched him on the arm. His muscles tensed beneath her fingers. Grunting, he sank back on his heels and fell into a glowering stance behind her. She inclined her head towards him, thankful he had heeded her desires, despite his obvious distaste of both the men sitting at the table with her. Even if she found them repulsive and would rather fall into a pit of eternal abyss than spend time alone with either of them, she couldn't afford to form new enemies.

Dominic smiled at her and bowed his head low. "I am glad to report that I am not disappointed in the reality. You are certainly as strong and brazen as I had heard." He pointed a slender finger at the flames still flickering around her arms. "I would like to see you morph into a firebird, if you are willing to show us."

Although the power swirling within her core had swelled during the month she hadn't been able to use her abilities, she had been able to maintain control over her powers. Still, she was afraid if she attempted to control such a powerful gift, she would be unable to contain the explosion as she shifted into her animal form.

"This room isn't suitable for such a request," Janae said, drawing Dominic's attention. "You can hardly expect a flamecaster to demonstrate their abilities while inside. For all we know, she would lose complete control and kill us all."

"You would never lose control, would you?"

Despite his words indicating belief in her abilities, there was an edge to his tone that made her stomach squirm. There was no way she could trust him. Perhaps not ever. And yet, she needed him if she was going to have enough support to defeat Renard. They'd fought against him for over a year and all it had gotten them was the shadow of death. She would not let the loss be her legacy. Magicals had already been through enough. She refused to be another reason why her people's hope was fading.

Just like the firebird of her namesake, she was determined to kindle the flame of rebellion even in the darkest of places.

"If I were to lose control, I can assure you, everyone in this room would be charred to a crisp. Except me. The flames never bother me."

His lips curled into a menacing smile, as if he were a predator ready to pounce on its prey. "You must show me this amazing ability of yours. I would imagine that you are quite a force to be reckoned with."

They stared at one another. Astrid wondered what his end game was. It was clear that whatever his intentions were, they did not involve love. Or even friendship. No, she doubted he wanted anything other than to secure a powerful weapon against his enemies, just like every other person she'd met since coming to this island.

Don't let him goad you into anything you'll regret later.

Penny's voice tickled at the back of her mind, slowing her racing heart.

You've faced worse than his ilk before. Don't let him turn you into someone you don't want to be. This is your chance to show the other rulers that you are not some heathen queen plucked from poverty. You walk a higher road.

Astrid formulated what she wanted to say to him to make him stop. He clearly enjoyed the challenge of bending her to his will, so force would only heighten his desire for her. In this case, she wondered if she needed to use a bit more sugar to coax him into the path she wished to go. Time was running out. If they weren't careful, they would surpass the threshold of surprise and forfeit their opportunity to destroy Renard.

"I wonder, Lord Dominic, if your interest in Queen Astrid arises from your genuine interest in seeing her demonstrate her power or if you have another purpose in pressuring her to do something she clearly is uncomfortable doing." Adira smiled sweetly at Dominic. Her pointed teeth protruded from her mouth, giving her a menacing appearance.

Dominic cocked an eyebrow at her and she snapped her teeth at him. Astrid wondered if she would actually bite him if given the chance or if she only wanted to intimidate him. Whatever her intentions, his cheeks flushed a brilliant red, and Astrid thought she saw a bit of panic swell within him.

Then he stared straight at her and said, "I don't believe you would ever hurt me."

"No? You don't think I enjoy feasting on the flesh of men who anger me? Then you clearly have never met a siren before."

He blinked at her as if trying to determine if she was continuing the joke or not. "There are not many sirens in the mountains."

"Unfortunately, your arrogance is showing again," Cassidhe said.

Astrid whipped her head towards the other woman. She was surprised the councilor was risking the negotiation.

"You honestly expect me to believe that she could overpower me?" Dominic asked.

"Friend, as someone who has had a tussle with a beautiful siren once, I caution you to keep your thoughts to yourself on this one." Vlander pointed at a circular scar on the base of his neck. "I was lucky enough to make it out with my life."

Adira's eyes flashed a brilliant emerald as she licked her lips and continued to stare at Dominic.

The apple of his throat bobbed as he swallowed hard. He stole a furtive glance at Astrid, as if to gauge her reaction to the siren defending her in this way. Astrid held her hand in front of her mouth and yawned. If he wanted to play stupid games, he could face the consequences of his actions.

He folded his arms over this chest. "Clearly, I misjudged the situation." He plastered an overly sweet smile on his face as he turned towards Astrid. "Please forgive me for my bearish behavior. I swear I didn't mean offense."

She dropped her hands to table and glared at him. She was tired of people—especially men—forcing themselves on her. She didn't want his apology. She wanted him to change his behaviors, and not because a siren stepped in with threats of bodily harm if he didn't stop being such a pig.

"I will accept your apology. This time. But let me make myself perfectly clear. I do not condone making women uncomfortable, nor do I believe that people should be automatically forgiven for their missteps just because they can provide something that is needed."

"So you admit it. You do need me." He grinned at her roguishly.

"That would be a no."

"I think we've gotten derailed from the real point of discussion here," Cassidhe said. She flashed Astrid a warning glare before smiling sweetly at Dominic. "There are certain things that are off the table when it comes to this negotiation. Gold and jewels will be provided and backed by the Golden City. If you wish for trade and commodity guarantees, that is also open for discussion. If you want a promise from the Fae queen that she will serve as an ally for future battles with your enemies, I am sure she will be amenable to this. But, if your intent in coming here was to insult her by insisting that she should become what is essentially your property, and I will have to ask you to leave."

The room stood in silence. Astrid was certain that if a bead dropped, it would sound like a cacophony rising in the shadows.

Vlander shook his head. "I did not mean to give offense, Queen Astrid."

Although he had been an absolute pig just a few minutes before, she couldn't help but believe that he was being genuine now. She nodded at him, accepting his apology.

Dominic, on the other hand, turned a deep shade of purple. If he had been a kettle, Astrid had no doubt he would have been whistling.

"I'm sorry to say that this is not the type of treatment I had been expecting." He shook his finger at Cassidhe. "You really should reconsider how you treat potential allies in the future. You wouldn't want to end up costing yourself more than you gain."

Cassidhe, with all the poise and grace of a swan, simply shook her head and waved her hands at him.

Dominic harrumphed and shoved himself away from the table. "If this is your response, then I must beg my leave. The next time you have a proposition of this nature, please consider my answer a no."

A set of guards approached Dominic. Cassidhe wordlessly nodded at them. They gripped him by the arms and jerked him towards the table. He growled and struggled against their hold.

"What the drak do you think you're doing? Let me draking go!"

"I am afraid, Dominic, that if you are unwilling to join us, we will not be able to portal you back to your home until we are certain you are not a threat to our plan."

Freed by Destiny

"What? You can't do this! I'm a dignitary for another country. You do not have the authority to detain me."

"Rest assured, Dominic, you will be treated with the utmost care while you are our guest. However, to assure us that you will not alert Renard of our plans…or anyone else that could prove to be a problem…I will have to confiscate your communication device."

"No. I do not condone this. I demand that you let me return home. *Now.*"

"Dominic, old friend, the lady has given her response. Let it rest. I can personally guarantee that you'll be returned once the attack on Lunameed is complete," Vlander said.

Astrid whipped her head towards the grizzled warrior. He winked at her. Her eyebrows shot up as she tried to understand the shift in his personality from just a few moments before.

"You," Dominic growled with venom dripping from his tone. His eyes narrowed at Vlander. "What do you have to do with this?"

"I am afraid I don't know what you're talking about, my friend. I came here, just as you did, to meet the fae queen and determine if her cause was worthy of the aid of my kingdom. After meeting her and seeing how she holds her own against us, I can see why so many in her country want to displace Renard for her. Besides, I never liked that pompous, self-entitled dingleberry anyway. So, as far as I'm concerned, Astrid and her forces have my full support."

"Take him away," Cassidhe said before Dominic could respond. She nodded to one of her guards. "Give him the soothing tonic to help with his aggression. We'll worry about his memories later."

Dominic continued to struggle against the guards as they dragged him from the room. Astrid watched him go, a sense of unease settling onto her stomach.

See how easily Cassidhe turned on a supposed ally? Couldn't she do the same to you?

Penny's voice whispered at the back of her mind again. Astrid wanted nothing more than to have a conversation with her about everything that was happening, but she didn't receive a response when she thought, *What other choice do I have?*

Chapter Twenty-Seven

She glanced around the table at the remaining members who had gathered to discuss their assault on Renard. Janae sipped from the flask that had been strapped to her waist. She caught Astrid's gaze and smiled at her.

"Thank you for playing along with my plan," Cassidhe said, smiling at Vlander. "Without you, I'm not sure we would have gotten to his true intentions so soon."

Vlander nodded at her before turning towards Astrid. "I am sorry if I made you uncomfortable before. I swear it was not my intention. We just needed to make sure Dominic was in attendance for the right reasons. Clearly, he was not."

"So, let me get this straight. You pretended to be a gross, scummy pig to lure Dominic into a false sense of security, thus getting him to reveal that he wasn't actually here to help us."

"Just so."

She folded her arms over her chest and sank back into her chair. She hated not being in the know about the things that could impact her. It bothered her how easily Cassidhe had let her play bait.

"Would you have let me rip out his throat or stop me before it got that far?" Adira said.

Cassidhe cast a level gaze at her. "No. We are not prepared to ruin our relationship with his family over this… transgression. There is nothing to worry about. He's been placed in a very comfortable room. Once we are certain he cannot ruin our plans, we will return him home."

"After you, what was it you said, 'fix his memory?' What, exactly does that mean?" Astrid asked.

"Ah, that. Yes. There is a fruit that grows on our island that, if eaten, can alter memories. All we have to do is feed him a story about how he drank too much, passed out, and was moved to his room to sleep off the liquor. He will not remember what actually happened."

After having been held captive against her will by Renard, Astrid found Cassidhe's plan completely unsettling. From what she was saying, he wouldn't even remember what he'd done. Without his consent, his memories would be removed. It was a deep violation of everything she believed in.

"You have to give him a choice," she said.

"Excuse me?" Cassidhe said cooly.

"You can't just remove his memories without him having a

choice."

"Uh huh, and what, exactly, do you think would happen if you released him from captivity, knowing we tested his loyalty. His goal was to deliver what he knew of our plans to Renard, Astrid. Surely, you cannot be so naïve as to believe that we can let him go free now?"

Astrid bristled.

"I didn't say to release him. What I said was that we cannot just remove his memories without, at the very least, giving him a choice. He can remain in captivity until he's given a fair trial. Perhaps he will remain forever. Or, he can be released immediately and sent home, but he will lose all memory of our conversations. It seems like the fair and just thing to do, not just remove his memories without his knowledge. That in and of itself is a violation."

To Astrid's surprise, Adira leaned across the table to have a better look at Cassidhe as she said, "I agree with the fae queen. If we have learned anything from our past, it is that we cannot allow anyone to be victims. Especially if we are the arbitrators that could stop it from occurring. My people have a long history of the oppression of magicals in this realm. Do not forget that we were nearly wiped from this world entirely. It was only because of the Dark Emperor that we remain today."

"This is not the time of darkness, Adira, and we are not discussing killing Dominic. But I see your point. You want there to be a fair chance for him to claim his own destiny as so many before him were not given the chance."

Adira nodded towards Astrid. "I am not the one who is owed this credit."

Janae folded her hands together. Although Astrid knew firsthand how harsh she could be, she moved with such grace that it was easy to forget that she was a true warrior behind the mask.

"Astrid has always harbored a desire to be a savior," Janae said. "Of course, she is sometimes misguided in her actions. However, in this particular case, I will have to side with her and Adira. Dominic is a repulsive human being, and I am appalled you invited him to begin with. It is not Astrid's failing for wanting to correct a great wrong you would have been committing by following through with your plans to remove his memories without giving him a chance to explain himself."

Astrid smiled to herself at Janae's boast of confidence for her position. Although they had their share of difficulties, when it came to supporting magicals, she knew she could count on Janae to always be a voice of reason, however militant she and Max might be.

"Fine. It's settled, since you all seem to be in agreement." Cassidhe drummed her fingers on the table. "Now, can we please move onto the discussion how we will launch this attack on Renard? We need to be as coordinated as possible so that we have our greatest chance at defeating him."

"Let's hear it then. How do you think we should attack the draking king of Lunameed?" Vlander asked.

Cassidhe gestured towards Astrid. "For that question, I will defer to her. She lived with the king for a month. Was a friend of his daughter. And, if I am not mistaken, is completely in love with the crown prince."

Astrid didn't know how she'd done it, but in one statement, Cassidhe had, at the same time, given her credit for knowing and understanding Renard and also undermined her authority by insinuating that, perhaps, she was in league with the royal family. Grinding her teeth, she steeled herself for the remarks she was sure the others would make about her ties to his family.

She made sure to make eye contact with each member of the assembled group. "Renard relies heavily on his robotic army to protect him. He uses fear to control everyone in his kingdom. I'm sure you've heard the rumors—perhaps even seen the video of a bomb he used against innocent civilians. Humans. If I hadn't stayed until the very last moment to ensure refugees had been portalled to a secure location, even more casualties would have occurred. He is a cruel man. Even his own children want him removed from power."

"So they can seize if for themselves," Janae said.

"No."

"What the Fae queen isn't telling you is that the crown prince, Kimari, tricked her into believing that he was her friend. That he wanted to form an accord. And, once he was within our secure boundaries and privy to our conversations, his father threatened to kill off magicals one by one until they both agreed to return to him. Kimari does not want his father removed from power. He wants to bolster their strength and use Astrid as a catalyst to get what they could never have: magic. You've seen the reports I've sent you. Even my own nephew was a victim of his experiments." Janae lifted her chin towards Max. "Tell them how they experimented on magicals and left them for dead in a cell after they got what they wanted."

Astrid turned towards him, just as everyone else did. Although his features remained the same, sweat formed at his brows and slid down his cheeks. He avoided Astrid's gaze.

Her stomach churned. He could change the narrative. She had

every intention of protecting Kimari and Kali—or trying to—but Max had the opportunity to turn their potential allies against them.

She clutched his hand. Although he didn't look at her, he squeezed her hand.

"It's true. The king ordered for magicals to be experimented on and I was one of the unlucky ones to be placed in a lab. So was Astrid. I don't know how to describe how terrible it was." He shuddered. "But I do not believe what my aunt says about Renard's children. Is it not possible that they have been the victims of his cruelty and malice? Perhaps even more so than anyone in this room realizes?"

Warmth crept through Astrid. She knew how much it pained him to give any credit to Kimari, given everything that had transpired. But whether because he still loved her or he knew in his heart that it was the truth, he was giving Kimari an out. He was saving him. For that, she would be eternally grateful.

"Look, I have every reason to hate the royal family. Kimari is the reason my betrothal to Astrid ended. So when I say that I believe he wants something better for our kingdom and that he will help us take his father out, I believe that. The same goes for his sister. She may have lied to us about her true identity, but I still believe she, too, wants out from under her father's thumb. They helped us get Astrid out of the palace. They are the reason we were connected with you, Cassidhe."

Astrid held her breath as she waited for Cassidhe to give an indication that this was the truth. Anxiety coiled in her abdomen like a snake ready to attack.

"Kali was the one who asked for my help with the assault on the palace. This is true," Cassidhe said.

"Exactly. Why would she do that if she didn't want to help us?" Max asked.

"Because she's trying to lure us into a false sense of complacency. How do we know they haven't figured out a way to track Astrid, even now? How do we know they haven't turned Astrid? There are too many variables. You forget that I was part of the triumvirate with Leilani and Renard. He didn't just betray the fae. He betrayed us all. So tell me how. How do we know he didn't force Kali to do his bidding? He will stop at nothing to ensure he remains in power. Let's not forget what kind of man he is," Cassidhe said.

"So, you would judge the children on the crimes of their father?" Astrid countered. Her blood broiled as she regarded Janae. She should have known this would be the position Janae would take.

"Let's not forget that second chances are a must if we are to create any type of world that is better than the one we currently have." She slammed her hands down on the table.

Max gripped her shoulder, keeping her in her seat.

She shrugged him off her and kept going. "Sure, we can acknowledge there's a chance Kali and Kimari have done all of this just because of some twisted fantasy of their father to toy with me like a cat does a mouse. It is possible, but it is not likely. Even if it was, I would rather make my decisions based on believing the best in people than in fear."

"Yes, and look how that turned out for your parents."

Astrid's heartbeat thrummed in her ears. She swallowed. Sweat coated her hands. Her stomach churned as she struggled to find the right words to convey exactly how she felt about Janae bringing the death of her family into this conversation. No matter how far removed she was from the events of that night, Renard's actions had shaped her into the person she was. Her adoptive parents had died from the guilt of sacrificing their daughter to save her. She'd been passed around from home to home, never finding a forever family.

Until she'd met Bear. And Max. And Maya and Eldris.

Sometimes, families weren't based on the bloodlines that connected people to one another. They were the ones who supported, celebrated, and consoled. They were the ones who rose up to stand beside someone when a fight was about to break out. And, if Astrid had any say in it, she would claim Kimari and Kali until her last breath.

Nat cleared her throat loudly as she inclined her head towards Adira. They shared a look between them, jarring Astrid from her thoughts. If she had to guess, the two of them were on the same page about something, but what, she couldn't be sure.

"Thank you for your thoughts, Janae," Nat said. She shoved her chair away from the table and went to stand in the hollow space in the center of the table. Her large build filled the room, making Astrid feel minuscule in comparison. "I appreciate all the different perspectives that have been shared during this conversation and I would like to propose a strategy."

The rest of the assembly bowed their heads to Nat and showed their palms to her.

"My armies can launch the main assault along with King Vlander's armies. Combined with the high-tech weaponry I know you have," she said, looking at Cassidhe for confirmation, who nodded, "our armies rival those of Renard. I believe we can distract him enough for a secondary assault launched by the fae, elves, magical creatures, and Adira's sirens. I believe we could break his line of power. This will give Astrid an opening to bring Renard to her mercy."

She turned towards Astrid. "You will have to kill him. We must not leave any chance that he could return to break you once more."

"This sounds very similar to the strategy I've been thinking about since before we launched the rescue mission to retrieve Astrid," Cassidhe said.

"And what of Kali and Kimari?" Astrid asked.

The rest of assembly shared a look.

"You want to kill them, too, don't you? Even after I've given you all the reasons to let them live."

"You have to understand, while they live, they will always be a threat to peace. They have the potential to destroy any progress you make towards a better world."

"Not if they're a part of the solution. We have to at least give them a chance. You agreed to offer Dominic a second chance. Why can't you do the same for them?"

Nat sighed heavily. "You are certainly passionate, aren't you? I can see why you have garnered so much support from your people. But all the charisma in the world won't stop Renard's children from coming to hate you for killing their father. It might not happen right away, but I can promise you this: the longer time moves on, the more they will resent you. You will be the one responsible for his death. They will miss him, and they will blame you. Are you prepared for the backlash that is inevitable?"

"I don't believe this will be our story," Astrid said. "I just... don't."

They stared at each other. Nat did not back down or even blink as she stood before Astrid.

"Since we are on such a time crunch, why don't we table this conversation until after the assault? Who knows, perhaps we will have a different attitude about them once the imminency of the battle is over. I, for one, would like to believe that Kali, at least, is redeemable," Cassidhe said.

"Then it's decided," Nat said. "We all agree to follow the plan I've laid out."

"When?" Astrid asked.

"I need at least an hour to ensure my troops are ready," Nat replied.

"As do I, to bring all who have volunteered to fight closer to shore," Adira said.

"Vlander?" Nat asked, turning towards the king.

"My armies are ready. All I need is a group of elves to create enough portals to send them to their positions."

The tension in the room shifted as everyone gathered took in the depth of this decision. It wasn't lost on Astrid how much they were risking for her. For her people. For a chance at something greater. She just wished she would be able to repay them when the time came. That she would be able to show them the same kindness and trust they had her.

"Whatever happens, thank you for taking this chance on me." Tears threatened to spill down her cheeks as she stared around the room. This was it.

Freed by Destiny

She could only hope they would not be burned to ash on the battlefield.

Chapter Twenty-Eight

Astrid dashed through the hallways after the assembly ended. She needed to find Maya, to tell her everything that had happened. She needed to know if she was anywhere close to finishing the robotic body for Penny. There was so little time.

The moment the conversation ended and the delegates from the other nations had been portalled back to their homes to ready their troops, Max had asked her permission to prepare the soldiers as well. She knew he'd been waiting for this moment for so long, it must have seemed like a dream that it was finally happening. They'd not only amassed enough support from the people of their country, but they'd also found allies among the nations surrounding them. They had a real chance at beating Renard.

She was running so fast that she didn't hear the footsteps approaching her from the opposite direction or check around the corner as she swung around it. She slammed straight into another person.

"Ow!"

Astrid and the other person fell to the ground in a heap. It was all elbows and knees as they scrambled to regain their footing. The person Astrid had knocked down slammed her elbow into Astrid's nose. She felt a crack. Tears welled in eyes and her vision blurred. Hot liquid poured from her nose before Astrid had a chance to press her nostrils firmly. She gagged as the taste of her own blood filled her mouth.

"I'm so sorry!" the other person said.

The sound of ripping fabric tore through the hallway before the woman pressed a strip of cloth to Astrid's face.

"Can you breathe?" she asked. "Are you alright, Astrid?"

Astrid blinked. Intellectually, she'd known she'd given up this ability. She'd made that choice. And she'd received minor bumps and bruises along the way. She'd even consumed a bit of the Silver Salum Flower to heal one of her wounds. Yet, it had taken a broken nose for the magnitude of her decision to finally hit her.

"I'm fine," she mumbled as she dropped her hand from her nose and let her silver blood freely flow down her cheeks.

"By the Creators," the woman whispered as she reached over and pinched Astrid's nostrils closed. "I think I have some of the elves' flower in here. Give me just one moment as I check."

With one hand, she began digging into a pouch slung across her chest.

"I'm fine," Astrid said. "Really."

Freed by Destiny

She sucked in a breath through her mouth and exhaled slowly. Her heart rate returned to normal in incremental steps as she finally took a moment to observe the woman sitting in front of her. She was older than Astrid would have originally thought, with wisps of gray hair straying from the bun at the nape of her neck. A sprinkling of freckles smattered her nose and cheeks, and her eyes were a brilliant green. They held wisdom there.

"Besides, it should be me apologizing to you for knocking you down. Are you alright?" Astrid dropped her gaze down, assessing the woman for broken appendages or anything bleeding.

The woman chuckled. "Always the savior, aren't you?"

"I... don't know what you mean." It was then that Astrid noticed the pointed curve of the woman's ear.

Gently, the woman caressed the tip of her ear and said, "Yes, I'm fae, but how about we keep that between ourselves."

"Who are you?" Astrid tried to remember if she'd ever met this woman before, but she couldn't think of a single instance in which she'd seen her face. Of course, Maya was more knowledgeable of the faces and names of the survivors from Renard's massacre. She had entire databases telling her where members of the noble's families were living, if they were still alive, and what their current status was. She and Max had tracked so many of them to recruit them to her side that she'd forgotten how many were still missing from their tree.

"Samiah Everblood, at your service."

She didn't recognize the name either. "Is that your real name?"

"Of course."

"It's not one of the names listed in our annals..."

"No, I don't suppose it would be. My family immigrated to the Golden City long before the fall of the fae, even before the great accord when the humans, elves, and fae decided to rule as a triumvirate."

Astrid cocked an eyebrow as Samiah. "I didn't know any fae had left Lunameed."

Samiah shrugged. "I'm not surprised. There weren't that many of us who were upset by the decision to join forces with the other two."

"You were alive when the accord was made?" Her stomach clenched at the thought. Although the accord had been made one hundred years prior and had lasted just over eighty years, it was still uncommon to meet many who had lived during that time, even among the fae and elves. Although, she realized that Janae would have been alive then.

"Of course. Fae can live well past the time of elves and humans, if in the correct conditions to support longevity."

An awkward silence followed this statement. Questions bubbled and popped through Astrid, but she couldn't bring herself to ask any of them. Every time she opened her mouth, she felt as if she were going to say something wrong or dumb. She needed to know the answers she potentially held about Renard and why he had become such a monster.

With a sigh, Samiah stood, her knees creaking slightly. She leaned into Astrid as she extended her arm to provide support to her. Astrid still needed to make it to Maya, but she couldn't bring herself to leave the woman just yet. Not when there was a chance she would find out more information about her family that could help her in the long run.

Freed by Destiny

"Did you know my parents?" she found herself asking. "Or my grandparents?"

Samiah shook her head. "I wasn't high enough ranking to have spent any real time with them. I met your mother a few times when we were at the same parties together, but we were not close. There was another woman... I can't think of her name now. She was her greatest friend and confidante. There wasn't much room for the rest of us when we were there."

"Please..." Astrid clutched the woman's hands. "Please, can you tell me... anything you know about them. What were they like? Why did you move here?"

Samiah removed her hands from Astrid's and took a step back. "I understand you want to know more about your parents, but there is truthfully nothing I can tell you. As I said, they were royal. I wasn't." She shrugged. "And I moved here because I didn't believe in the accord. I didn't think we should ever have allowed ourselves to become in league with Renard's father. I can only describe the feeling I got from him as shady. He wanted what he couldn't have. To be fae. To have magic and power beyond what was rightfully his. And he taught his son to be the same way. Only I hear Renard is more a monster than anyone before him."

"You could say that again." Astrid's watch buzzed, but even that distraction couldn't pull her attention away from Samiah. "Are there many expats here?"

"There are several of us, yes. We wanted a different world. One where we wouldn't be at the mercy and whim of a ruling class."

"Was it really that bad?"

Again, Samiah shrugged. "There have been too many wars between the fae and humans for us to trust that they would not continue to harm us. Clearly, we were correct."

She spoke with such conviction that Astrid didn't know what to believe. She had been raised to believe that the time before Renard's betrayal had been a period of peace and prosperity. For everyone.

Her watch buzzed again. She glanced at it. Maya's name flashed across the screen.

"There is somewhere you're supposed to be," Samiah said.

"Yes, but I would rather hear from you."

Samiah shook her head. "I never intended to meet you."

"Why not?"

"Honestly, no one I know here wants to return to the motherland. We've formed our own community here. We have a voice in the election process now and we're gaining ground in building our population. We also know Renard enslaved many of our kind once he assassinated your family." She pressed a hand to her chest and gasped. "I am sorry if I have brought something up that causes you harm, but I want to help you understand. There's nothing left for us in Lunameed. It's not our home anymore. It hasn't been for over twenty years. For some of us, myself included, longer than even that."

"But… there's so much you could help us achieve, if you give us the chance. With your knowledge and experience living here, you could help us form a new way of living. Of governing."

"You would give up your newfound power to the people?"

"Yes. I never wanted it, anyway. I want to see a world in which no one has to suffer because of the—what was it you called it?—

the mercy and whim of the ruling class. I've been there, done that, and I would never want anyone to feel that way if I was in power."

"But you are. In power, that is."

"Exactly. So why shouldn't I use some of my influence to change how things operate in our country? Why couldn't we envision a different way of doing things? Why couldn't we offer everyone freedom? A chance to make their own way in the world? I believe we can. That we must. What do you think?"

The buzzing of her watch intensified as she waited for Samiah to answer her.

Samiah smiled gently and said, "I'm sorry, Astrid, but I don't believe anyone here is willing to fight for you. We gave up on our monarchs long ago. Just because you were not raised within the sphere of influence, doesn't mean that we automatically trust you. What you say now could change with the snap of a finger. We've seen it so many times before. We've been given promises that were broken in the past. But no more. Fight for our brethren's freedom. Remove the murderer king from his position of power. But do not expect those of us who have already made our choice to remain separate from the fae community to fight at your side."

Samiah turned her back on Astrid. Her slender shoulders shook. "I am sorry for what you have lost. No one should have to suffer the loss of their family."

Her voice caught in the middle of her phrase.

Astrid reached out a hand; her fingers dangled just above her skin as she hesitated to touch her. What this fae must have lost before coming here. Astrid knew enough of the history to know that there had been an enormous amount of fighting before the accord.

And yet, she couldn't help but wonder who this woman had been and what her true story was. There was so much she didn't know about the experiences of her people. How could she be a unifying force if she didn't understand their pain and loss? It was obvious to her that she didn't represent hope for Samiah. Her very existence was a symbol of the pain and destruction her people had faced.

Perhaps even at the hands of her parents.

Her watch buzzed again.

"You should go," Samiah whispered. "There's nothing left for me to say to you. Despite everything, I do wish you well, Astrid. Perhaps you can finally be the savior our people always needed. Just don't forget your story. Your legacy."

She ambled away from Astrid, her head held high. Although she was weathered and elderly, she moved with a grace Astrid could only hope she could master as she aged.

Astrid lingered, listening to sound of the fae's footsteps fading into silence. She vowed she wouldn't forget how it felt to be alone. Hungry. Afraid. She wouldn't forget how hopeless it felt to have no power over her own life. If she could, she would ensure no one in Lunameed ever had to feel that way again.

A message exploded from her watch and flashed in front of her face.

Why aren't you answering my calls? Come to the lab. I need you.

Chapter Twenty-Nine

Astrid skidded to a halt in the lab's doorway. It had only been an hour, maybe two, since she'd gone to the council meeting, but Maya had made an extreme amount of progress on the robot during that time.

The frame was metallic and glittered when the light from Maya's intense lamp hit it. Electric music drowned out all other sound as she approached Maya, who was bent over the robot, working on a knee joint.

She tapped Maya on the shoulder as gently as she could. Maya swung an elbow up and at her, the tip of her bone grazing Astrid's cheek. The moment Maya realized who was in the lab with her, she shut off the music and wrapped her arms tightly around Astrid, pinning her arms to her sides.

"I'm so sorry! Are you okay? I didn't hurt you, did I?" She pulled back to examine Astrid's face. Her hair fell into her eyes as she searched for any sign of breakage.

Astrid winced when Maya prodded at the tender spot around her nose where Samiah had accidentally hit her.

"Did I do this to you?" Her shoulders drooped. "I'm so sorry, Astrid. I should've known it was you. It's just… some habits die hard, ya know? I spent so much time protecting myself after I ran away from Renard's lab that I guess…"

"You don't have to explain yourself to me. And no, you didn't do this." Astrid pointed at the bruise she knew was darkening her eye sockets. "I met a fae who's been living here since before the betrayal."

"What? But… how? No one came up on my search. I think they would've shown up."

Astrid shook her head. "I don't think so. She told me she came here shortly after the accord was made. I don't think she was part of a noble family. She seemed to resent the aristocracy."

"But still. I ran an exhaustive list. If they had a record, I would have found it."

"Maybe they don't. Who knows what arrangement they have with the Golden City? Maybe they have become full fledged citizens here and Lunameed no longer has a record of them. I don't know. All I do know is that she was here, alive, and quite mysterious. I swear I asked her so many questions that she couldn't seem to answer for me. That's all I want. To know the truth. To understand."

"I think we have more important things to worry about than some fae we don't even know." Maya jerked her head towards the robot. "I'm just finishing up some of the final touches to make sure her body can articulate like a real person. I want her to have as much functionality as possible."

"How soon will you be able to add the coding from my PEA into her?"

"Well, that's the problem. You underwent an extraction to begin with that wiped her programming. Even after the elves attempted to restore her, there still wasn't anything left. And...I can't remove the PEA from your head because your brain has formed around it. I don't want to go digging through your soft tissue and accidentally kill you. Or worse, remove your cognitive functioning."

"I... don't understand. If Max was able to perform the extraction and everything else, why didn't that hurt me then?"

Maya flicked the bruise on her face, sending a wave of pain through her. Astrid jerked away from her, her hand flying up to her face to cradle the injured spot.

"You gave up what protected you from harm. Or don't you remember?"

Swallowing hard, Astrid nodded. "So what are you going to do?"

If possible, Maya's skin turned paler as she rummaged through one of the pouches looped around her belt. She drew out a bud from the Silver Salum Flower and offered it to Astrid. Bowing her head, Astrid accepted it and shoved the flower into her mouth before taking a swig from the glass of water Maya handed her next. Her body illuminated with light as her broken nose mended.

"How do you feel?" Maya asked.

Astrid swatted away Maya's hand as she tried to poke at her face.

"I'm fine."

"Good. Because what I'm going to propose might hurt. A lot."

"Sounds promising."

"I thought you'd say that, which is why I already sent Eldris to find something we can use to numb you to the pain. And I have another flower that can heal you. So really, there's no risk here, right?"

"Is this supposed to be where I say I'm out? Because it's not happening. I owe everything to Penny. My life. My place as the queen. Everything. I'm not going to let you scare me away from trying everything in my power to give her what she deserves."

"Right. Unless everything you've heard is just a reflection back of your own thoughts caused by an echo from the malfunctioning PEA in your brain."

Astrid gaped at her. She waited for a comeback to materialize, but it never did. Instead, she resorted to staring at Maya with a dumbfounded expression plastered on her face.

"Right, well, I was hoping you would put up more of a fight. But since it's still abundantly apparent that you're set on moving forward with this course of action, I do have to warn you: I was just trying to scare you away from this course of action. You won't feel a thing when I perform the procedure to copy the files from your PEA onto a new device."

Gritting her teeth, Astrid paced across the room. The last time she'd let someone attempt a similar procedure, she'd lost Penny altogether. She couldn't let that happen. She wouldn't.

"You're sure it won't completely wipe Penny from existence again? I don't think the spell will work again on the same lost object."

"Positive. Who's the best hacker and computer whiz you know?" Maya popped a bubble in her face. "I could do this procedure in my sleep if I needed to."

Astrid fumbled with her fingers as she contemplated the risks and rewards of moving forward with her plans. On the one hand, she was putting everyone at risk by focusing her attention on giving Penny a body. On the other hand, if some of her powers were linked to the AI, there was a chance she could be creating a powerful ally she could trust above anyone else.

"Fine, but we have to move fast. I need to be back in the council room in less than an hour to launch the attack. Her fumbling turned into chewing on the nail of her thumb.

"I have a suspicion that once the transfer is complete, the files in your PEA will be too corrupted again and the version of Penny currently functioning in there will be erased. Again. Only this time, instead of disappearing for seemingly forever, I'm going to capture her data source and transfer it to the blank PEA I've already created and implanted into this ol' gal." Maya patted the robot's arm for emphasis.

"Do whatever it takes."

Maya pointed towards an operation table nearby. With a shaky breath, Astrid climbed atop it and lay back.

"I'm going to need you to lay on your stomach, if you don't mind."

"Why?"

"Easier access to the area I need to cut a small incision in. Nothing major, just a small little hole I can feed the wire into."

"You're worried about digging around in my head, but you want to send a wire through my brain?"

"Exactly."

"Wow. And to think I never thought you'd be the one to fall off the deep end."

Maya rolled her eyes at Astrid. "I'm trying to have a meaningful conversation with you about what I'm about to do. The least you could do is try to be more serious." She crossed her arms over her chest. "Or do I need to resort to harsher methods to get you to understand?"

"What kind of harsher methods are you talking about? Because I have to be honest with you, I can sustain a lot when it comes to pain."

"Uh huh," Maya said as she jabbed the sharp, pointy end of the wire into Astrid's hand. "And you're going to tell me that felt good, are you?"

Astrid winced and jerked her hand back to her chest as she examined the spot where Maya had just hit her. Unlike all the times before, she didn't feel the security she normally did whenever she was in Maya's company.

Maya dug around in her belt pouch and pulled out a small bottle of clear liquid. It bubbled and fizzed slightly as she swirled it around.

"Here, drink this," she said as she shoved the bottle into Astrid's hand.

Astrid pulled the top off with her teeth and wished she had the use of her other hand. It was the foulest tasting thing she'd ever consumed, which was saying a lot since she grew up on the streets.

Freed by Destiny

"Swallow."

"I can't," she attempted to murmur. What it came out as was a serious of strange hums and grunts that meant nothing.

Maya pinched Astrid's nose closed and held her mouth shut.

"Swallow," she commanded again.

Despite the dryness permeating her mouth and fear, Astrid was able to force the liquid down her gullet. It burned as it traveled to her stomach, leaving a strangely cold sensation in its wake.

Every part of her body tingled as she waited for the effects of the numbing serum to kick in.

"Let's give it a couple of minutes and see how your body reacts to the numbing potion."

Astrid attempted to open her mouth to reply, but she couldn't quite feel her lips or tongue. The grinding sound of Maya's bone saw filled the room and she squirmed as the vision of it cutting into her head filled her mind.

"No need for that. I won't be using this tool on you," Maya said as she dropped the saw on the table and opted for a microscopic blade.

Astrid didn't remember the rest. She closed her eyes so she couldn't see what Maya was doing. All she knew was that twenty minutes later, Maya dropped a few petals from the Silver Salum Flower into a glass of water and tilted the lip of it to Astrid's mouth.

Astrid sputtered and a drizzle of water ran down her chin, soaking into her shirt. Her head felt like it was going to explode from the pressure building inside. She clutched at her forehead and

343

groaned.

"Shh," Maya cooed beside her.

The clink of the glass being set on a table sounded like a stampede. Astrid flinched and leaned back against the pillows, wishing she could just die from the agony. Slowly, the healing impact of the flower began to take effect. It started as a fuzzy warmth at the nape of her neck and gradually expanded to encompass the rest of her head. A sensation of weightlessness settled upon her before quickly dissipating. She sighed in relief and opened her eyes wide.

"That wasn't so bad, now was it?" Maya asked.

"Do you want the honest answer?"

"Uh huh. I told you it would be painful."

"But did you get what you needed?" Now that the pain had subsided, all she cared about was knowing whether the procedure had worked or not.

"I won't know until I try to add the copy to the PEA I inserted into the robot. Theoretically, it should be a complete copy of all the coding in your device."

Astrid braced herself for the next question. She didn't want to ask it. She didn't want to be told the truth, if it was something she wasn't prepared for. Her stomach twisted in knots and she resisted the urge to bolt away from Maya.

Running wouldn't do her any good. Besides, she needed to finish preparing for the attack. Every day, it was a new pressure weighing her down. Sometimes, the burden made her feel like she would bend so much she would snap. But she never did. She just kept on pushing forward.

"Did you erase what coding was still left on my PEA?"

"Yes. I was correct, earlier. When I made the copy, some sort of fail safe engaged in your PEA and it completely wiped all the data. I know because I went back to make a second copy and it was a blank slate. Almost as if it was a brand-new device, which clearly it isn't."

Astrid sucked in a breath. If the fail safe had wiped her PEA again, it could mean that the copy could be corrupted. That she could have lost Penny. She didn't know if she could survive that loss a second time.

"You have to test it. Please. I can't go into battle not knowing if Penny is still... alive. Still there." Tears welled in her eyes, unbidden. They slid down her cheeks, streaking them. She didn't even attempt to hide them. "You have to tell me. No matter what."

Maya's shoulders sagged and she bowed her head away from Astrid. "I won't be able to do a full diagnostic in the next five minutes, which is all the time you have to get to the council room again." She cupped Astrid's cheek. "Don't worry. I promise, if she's in there, I will find her. Even if it means breaking some sort of encryption code or figuring out a puzzle to unlock her. I will make sure she's at least partially viable to take on an immortal body."

"Why can't you just run the diagnostic now? Surely it can give you preliminary data that will tell you if she's at least on the device or not. Please, Maya. I won't be able to fight at my full strength if I don't know. Even if it's bad news, that's better than not knowing."

Maya sighed. "The best I can do is see if there is any data on the memory stick."

Astrid pressed her hands together to keep herself from fidgeting as she waited for the computer to read the disk Maya had inserted. Crossing her fingers, Astrid prayed that Penny would still be alive. She shielded her eyes with her hands and waited. Multiple computers beeped at her as Maya worked from different stations. Peeking through the space between her fingers, Astrid stared at Maya as she worked on connecting the memory stick to a computer.

She leaned in close to Maya and whispered, "Whatever you do, don't let her die."

Her skin turned sallow as she twisted her entire body away from Maya.

"Just tell me."

A series of seemingly random beeps followed. Astrid dropped her hands from her face and stared at Maya. "What's going on? Please, just tell me."

Maya leaned towards her computer screen as she examined the output from the stick she'd inserted into it. Wordlessly, she read the lines of data flowing across the screen.

"That's interesting," she whispered, sitting back.

"What is?"

"It looks like the coding is all there, still."

"You're positive?" Relief filled her. This was exactly the type of news she had been hoping for. "This isn't a prank?"

Maya blew a bubble and popped it as she stared at Astrid. She didn't even blink as she stood before Astrid motionlessly.

Freed by Destiny

"Okay. Alright. I get it. I know I never should have asked you that question to begin with. But, come on, Maya. You know I've been waiting for this moment since I decided to let Max extract my memories from my PEA. Now you're telling me that data is there, all of it. That I can bring Penny back... but you seem unsure."

"It's just... there's a lot of code I don't understand. A lot of commands that seem to have been overwritten dozens of times, yet still linger. I've never seen anything like it."

"Maybe it's because Penny is an AI," Astrid said.

"Maybe." Maya tapped her cheek thoughtfully as she continued to watch the code scroll up the screen. She shook her head and tutted beneath her breath.

"What are you thinking?"

"Honestly, I'm not sure what this all means, but I doubt I'll have her up and running before the battle. There's too much code here to upload into the new PEA. Maybe, in a few days, we'll be able to see if the copy worked."

Astrid bowed her head. She had been hoping for a different outcome. Still, she smiled when she looked up at Maya again. "I know you have your reservations about all of this. Thank you for sticking with me."

Maya shrugged. "I'll set the coding to upload into the robot's PEA to see if it works. But I need to help with the effort to hack into Renard's soldiers again. Every time I've been able to do it, he changes the firewalls around his network. It gets more and more difficult to access them each time."

"I know you can do it. You're the best draking hacker this world has ever seen."

Maya's skin burst into a glittery illumination that filled the entire room with light.

"Stop it." She punched Astrid lightly in the arm. "I don't want to blind you."

"What? I'm only telling the truth. You deserve so much more credit than what some people would give you. I am very glad to have found you. And not just because you're the most kick-ass computer whiz I've ever met. I don't know what I would have done without you."

Her words seemed to sober Maya. She lowered her head and chewed on her bottom lip before saying, "Please be careful out there today. Promise me you won't intentionally put yourself in harm's way."

Astrid pointed at herself. "Who, me? I would never!"

Maya rolled her eyes. "And I'm sure everyone believes that story."

"Well, they should, because it's the truth!" Astrid crossed her arms over her chest and pouted for dramatic effect.

Maya shook her head and placed one hand on Astrid's shoulder. "Still. I want to hear you say it."

"I can't make that promise, Maya. You know me, maybe better than anyone else. If there's a chance, even a slim one, that I can protect our people, I'm going to take it."

Silver lined Maya's eyes as she let her hand slip from Astrid's shoulder. "I was worried you would say that. I guess I shouldn't be surprised. You might be stubborn as an ox and rash, but one thing has never changed about you: you want to protect and save people more than anything else."

Freed by Destiny

It was Astrid's turn to glow at the praise. "I try."

"You do. And we all love you for it. But, Astrid, you have to remember you're not invincible anymore. If you get hurt..."

"If I get hurt, I promise I'll seek help immediately instead of letting myself continue to deteriorate."

"But it might not be enough! What if you take a blow that kills you instantly? You can't..." Maya sighed heavily. "Just...just promise me you'll try to keep yourself out of harm's way. I don't expect you to come out of this completely unscathed. I just want you to try and not get yourself killed."

Sticking her hand out, Astrid waited for Maya to shake it. "Come on now, don't leave me hanging. I promise I won't do anything to put myself in undo danger unless it's absolutely necessary. There, does that suffice?"

Hesitantly, Maya took Astrid's hand. "I guess that'll have to be good enough."

Both Astrid and Maya's watches buzzed at the exact same moment. They met one another's gaze and embraced one last time.

This might be the last time they ever saw one another.

"I love you," Astrid whispered against Maya's ear.

"Ditto."

Astrid chuckled against her friend's hair as she released her from the embrace. Whatever happened next, at least her last memory of Maya would be a happy one.

Gripping the robot's shoulder, she whispered, "Come back to

me," before striding from the room. All she could hope was that she would be there for Penny when her consciousness uploaded into her new body.

Chapter Thirty

Astrid made a quick pit stop at her room before heading to the council chamber. To her surprise, someone had laid out an outfit for her. She trailed her fingers across the fabric. It had been made from the finest body armor. It was supple, yet sturdy. If she had to take a guess, not that she wanted to test this theory, she estimated that it would be able to survive multiple hits before even beginning to deteriorate.

Undressing quickly, she slid into the form-fitting body suit that served as the under armor for the outfit. It slid over her skin like silk, but she could tell the material was designed to provide an extra layer of cushioning and support if she were struck by a larger bullet.

The actual armor fit snuggly against her skin and layered on top of one another like dragon scales. She swung her arms around and stretched them high above her head. The armor moved with her without weighing her down or limiting her mobility. Smiling, she turned to leave her room to find Max standing in the doorway watching her.

"How long have you been there?"

He shrugged.

"We have to join the others."

He nodded slowly. "I know."

She motioned to the hallway. "So… are you going to get going or…"

"I just wanted to tell you that I'm glad we got you out of Renard's grasp. And I'm glad we're launching this assault. To whatever end, at least this will all be over soon."

"And then the real work begins."

"Maybe it'll be what we always talked about. I'm sure it won't be perfect, but at least it will be ours."

"It definitely won't be perfect. I don't think there is such a thing. But I think we have a good foundation to build something so much better than what we currently have. We just have to trust one another. And forgive the humans."

Max scoffed. "You're only saying that because you fell in love with one of them."

She shook her head. "No, I'm saying it because it's the truth. You've seen how Renard treated his own people if they weren't part of the upper echelon of society. We can offer them a chance to be whoever they want to be, free from the mistrust and hate he fueled for the magical world. You know I'm telling you the truth."

"I don't know if our people are going to be willing to forgive humans for everything they've put us through."

"I'm sure there will be some who can't look past the horrors we've endured." A vision of Samiah's face filled her vision. "And there will be some who seek a new home outside of Lunameed's borders. And there will be others who choose to stay and are never able to forget or forgive the past. That's fine. All we can do is fight for everyone's chance to live a life freely without worrying about what will happen to them. That's what we're fighting for today, Max. That's why all these different nations have decided to join with us. So what if it's not perfect."

He smiled broadly at her. "You never cease to amaze me, you know that?"

"Yeah, well, I hope I can continue to amaze you once this is all over and done with."

"You will." He caught her hand. "I can't even envision a world in which I'm not in awe of you."

He smiled down at her and her heart began to race. Her stomach flip-flopped as he leaned in closer. She didn't want to have to reject him again. Not right before the battle. She didn't want the last thing to transpire between them to be an argument.

"Max…"

"I know you've made your choice and it's not me. I just… wanted you to know that it's okay."

Her insides continued to squirm, but she leaned away from him so that she could meet his gaze squarely.

"I've been thinking about everything...and I know you never intended to or wanted to hurt me. And... I guess... I didn't want to go into this battle without you knowing that it's okay. I'll be okay."

A smile tugged at the corners of her lips. She hadn't realized it before, but this was exactly what she needed to hear him say. Throwing her arms around his neck, she pulled him into a tight embrace.

"I was worried..."

"Me, too."

They held each other. Astrid let herself believe that their friendship could survive past everything they'd faced. She needed to believe that he would be there for her on the other side of this war. Closing her eyes, she breathed in his scent, memorized the way his arms felt around her. Her life had been marred by so much loss. Her birth parents. The Diones. Potts and Kilian. Penny. But she'd found something in Max and the rest of her friends that she'd been searching for her entire life.

Family.

She would hold onto them as tightly as she could, because she didn't know if this would be the last time she ever saw them.

Bear cleared his throat behind them. "Am I interrupting something?"

Letting go of Max, Astrid stepped away from him and said, "No, not at all. We were just telling each other goodbye, in case one of us doesn't make it through the battle.

"Wow. Ouch. And here I thought we were having a moment, but I guess not." Max winked at her and she laughed.

Bear held up his hands. "Well, don't let me stop you from saying goodbye. But…" He tapped his watch. "Time is ticking and we need to get down there."

"Right," Max said. He walked past Bear. "I'll see you down there."

Astrid moved to follow him, but Bear caught her arm, stilling her. She cocked an eyebrow at him.

"Do you really think one of us isn't going to survive this battle?"

Shrugging, Astrid turned away from him. If she met his gaze, she wouldn't be able to stop the tears from filling her eyes. And if they did that, she wouldn't be able to keep them from spilling down her cheeks. She didn't want her potentially last moment with Bear to be one where she was crying and he was trying to console her. She was too badass for that. So, instead, she gritted her teeth and stared at a dark spot on the hardwood floor.

"It's possible. We already lost Potts, Kilian, and so many others before it was their time. Who's to say…"

"It could happen."

She snapped her head towards him at the gruffness of his voice. She would utterly break if he was the one to start crying.

"Don't say that."

"Well, it's the truth. I can tell that's what you're thinking. I'm not going to sugar coat it for you. Renard's army is the largest, most well-funded one in the whole of the world. But that doesn't mean that we have to give in. And it certainly doesn't mean we have to give up hope that we'll be able to overcome him. In fact, I think we will. I mean, I don't want to brag, but you have an entire gang of fairy godmothers on your side. What does he have? Some robots? Ooh, so scary."

Despite the tension of the impending war, she laughed.

"Well, now, that's music to my ears." He smiled at her. "Whatever happens out there, I know you're going to survive. That's part of who you are. It's built into your very essence. And if you're thinking of proving me wrong, just know that I will hunt down your draking ghost and spend the rest of my life haunting you— not the other way around."

She flung herself into his arms and hugged him tightly. His arms crushed her against him so hard that she could barely breath. She didn't care.

"Now, let's go kick evil booty."

Pressing her lips into a thin line, she gave him a look that clearly stated, 'that's really what you wanted to say?' Bear didn't even acknowledge it. He just turned and began walking towards the council room, whistling as he went. Astrid watched him go. Although he'd given her a moment of levity, she couldn't squash the feeling that this battle would mean more loss. She just hoped she could survive losing another member of her family.

They all thought she would be the one to survive, but what they didn't understand was that sometimes, living in the shadow of death was worse than not existing. She had wandered in darkness for so long that, now that she'd finally stepped into the light, she didn't know if she could go back.

She just hoped she wouldn't have to find out.

Chapter Thirty-One

Screens had been set up all around the room so that Cassidhe, Astrid, Adira, and Janae could watch the assault launched by Nat, Vlander, and part of the Golden City's army. Astrid's leg shook as she stared at the screen directly in front of her. So far, all they'd shown was the elves creating portals into an open field just outside the city wall. She wanted to be out there with them, not made to stay behind while the action took place someplace else.

Adira laid a hand on her knee, stilling her movement. Astrid glanced at the siren, who nodded at her. A glimmer of her elongated teeth flashed beneath her lips as she turned her attention back to screen without a word. Astrid continued to stare at her. All her life, she'd thought sirens were extinct. And yet, here one sat.

"Why have you kept yourself hidden all this time? I mean… I know there have been occasional rumors, but I always thought they were hoaxes."

"There has been a long history of sirens, merpeople—whatever your people want to call us—being hunted and killed. There was a point in time when only one of our kind was left. If it hadn't been for the Creators, we would have been lost to the sands of time."

Astrid cocked an eyebrow at her. "You have records going back that far? How is that possible? Everything was destroyed during the Great Darkness…"

Adira shook her head. "Our home was established long before the fall of the empire. Although we didn't keep anything pertaining to the world outside of New Ulna, we can trace the rise and fall of our people all the way back to the city's founding."

"But how is that possible?"

"We separated ourselves from the rest of the world, Astrid. That's why you believed we were extinct. So few of our people leave New Ulna to pursue their own endeavors that we've been able to keep our secrets safe. No outsiders have been to our city in well over three thousand years. Nor will they ever without an express invitation from me. Any of our people who leave the safety of the city know that the one rule that cannot be broken is to never reveal our secrets."

The magnitude of what Adira was offering by being a part of the campaign against Renard struck her. She was risking her people's very way of life, just to help Astrid stop Renard.

"You shouldn't be helping me."

Adira shook her head again. "I'll admit, it was a difficult decision. Yet, I would make the same choice again. Trust me when I tell you that we have discussed, at great length, coming forward with the truth of our existence and our people are in agreement. Now is the time for us to fight. I've heard about the terrors Renard has inflicted upon magicals in your kingdom. If his malice were to spread, I would hate to imagine what he would do to my people."

Her words kindled a kernel of curiosity deep inside Astrid. "Are sirens powerful?"

Adira sank further back into her chair. "It's not about our gifts, Astrid. Look at what he's willing to do to his own people. If he is that cruel and callous to them, what will he do to someone like me? He will use us as lab rats and then leave us to die. We will not be a part of his campaign for power, nor will we let him attempt to conquer the world without a fight. I'm not doing this for you. We couldn't care less about the ways the world is run on land—with one exception: how do your choices affect the seas?"

"But you could hide. If your city is well disguised as you make it out to be, then how would he ever be able to find you?"

"You said it yourself. His technology continues to advance and, in some cases, outstrip the abilities of even your most powerful beings. He was even able to capture you. So tell me, Astrid, would it be prudent to stick our heads in the sand until he discovers our great city? I think not."

Astrid hadn't considered that these other nations had decided to join with her, not because of some great loyalty or trust in her, but because they had their own agendas and fears. She didn't know if that made her trust them more or less.

"I am sorry if I've upset you," Adira said. "It was not my intent. The stories of your bravery have reached my city. Your greatness is sung by all who have seen you in action. They were your strongest supporters when we called everyone home to vote on whether we should join this fight or not."

"Oh, I wasn't…"

"One of our many gifts, dear one, is our ability to sense the emotions of others. I saw the doubt creeping into the recesses of your mind. But you shouldn't worry. Even if we're not here for you, we are still here. We are still fighting."

The armies began marching through the portals. Astrid turned from Adira to watch the procession. Her eyes scanned the skies, searching for any of the tell-tale signs that Renard had released his robots to attack the army, but, because the person holding the camera was moving around so much, the feed was grainy and difficult to decipher. Leaning in closer, she noticed a small speck of darkness in the background. She ground her teeth together as the speck turned into a rock-sized smear.

"That's him" she whispered. "Those are his soldiers," she said more loudly.

Standing, she pointed skyward.

The others in the room remained silent as the dark spot continued to progress towards the portals. Astrid thrummed her fingers on her knee as she waited for a protective shield to go up, but nothing stopped the first wave of blasts launched by the robots. Hundreds of soldiers screamed in unison as a blaze of white light filled the screen followed by nothing.

Coldness clung to Astrid's innards as she waited. She turned to Janae.

"Why didn't one of our soldiers produce a magical shield to protect them?"

Cassidhe's face had turned pale and ashen. Her eyes never left the screen, as if she were waiting for the haziness to clear and the soldiers she'd sent to the battlefield to reappear as if nothing had just happened. Astrid glowered at Janae as she waited for an answer that never came. Exasperated, Astrid released a low growl and strode towards the front of the room.

Pointing a finger at the screen, Astrid said in a shaking voice, "He didn't even hesitate. He just sent his soldiers on a kill mission. I doubt any of the soldiers he sent survived." She met each of their gazes. "How did he know we were attacking? He had his soldiers ready to go. He shouldn't have had enough time to prepare. That was our strategy: to attack when he had fewer resources at his disposal for war. How did he know?"

Janae tapped her fingers on her chair's armrest, her lips pressed into a thin line. "There have always been spies in our camp, Astrid."

Astrid whirled on Janae, flames licking at her fingers. "You think it was one of our own who did this?"

To Janae's credit, she did not back down. If anything, her back straightened even more as she faced Astrid down. "I'm saying that we don't know who it was. It could have been anyone. From any of the camps. So don't come here and try to insinuate that I put one of our people up to this. We have always had spies in our camp. Drak, Astrid, even one of your most trusted allies ended up being a member of the royal family. How were we supposed to see through the mire if even you can't do that?"

A fireball formed in Astrid's hand. Her fingers curled tightly around the thread of magic containing her fire in one place. "It was a complicated situation with Kali and you know it. But you also know she helped me escape from Renard. Surely you can see that she's matured a lot over the past few months. She told me everything she is today is because of the influence being around magicals had on her."

"Look at you. Look what Renard has done to you. You used to be such a powerful force. You took down entire fighter jets with your abilities. But look at you now, sitting on the sidelines while others attack and are killed. All in your name. All to win you the throne. Their lives are the price of our freedom. But if you had been there, you might have been able to save them."

It didn't matter that Janae had always prodded her about her decision to fight rather than lead from the sidelines. She'd fought with her about going to the front lines. Now, here she was shaming her for agreeing to take a back seat. Astrid couldn't stop herself from inching towards the black hole forming in her mind. If she fell into it, she wouldn't be able to stop herself from spiraling.

"Janae, is this necessary?" Adira bared her teeth at Janae, her eyes narrowing. "We cannot let Renard form a wedge between us. We don't know that there was a spy at all. He is known for his hackers. Perhaps one of them intercepted one of the transmissions Cassidhe sent inviting us to join forces with her. Or perhaps one of the countries who chose not to join provided him with a heads up."

"It is possible that one of them told Renard I had invited them to meet, but I was careful not to include any details that might reveal our plans. Besides, we had not fully set our timeline when I sent those invitations. It is more likely he is tracking our communications and put two-and-two together." Cassidhe shot a furtive glance at Astrid. "We all know you gave up your healing ability to save Max. I am surprised at you, Janae, for encouraging her to put her life at risk when she's barely recovered from being under Renard's grasp. These two things combined are the reasons we chose to keep her behind. It was a great loss to have him attack the way he did, but it was one we were prepared for."

"How, exactly, did you prepare for that kind of loss?" Janae shot back.

Cassidhe shrugged and turned her attention back to the screen, as if waiting for the visuals to return.

"Cassidhe, if you had something up your sleeve and didn't tell us before the battle, I expect you to tell us now," Janae said.

"If you would please be patient, all will be revealed." Cassidhe tapped her fingers on her arm as she continued to watch the screen. "And I would remind you, Janae, that you are a guest here. It would be wise for you to treat me and the rest of my council members with the respect we deserve."

Janae's mouth gaped open, and she glared at Cassidhe with venom. After a moment, she sniffed and lifted her chin. "You should be careful, Cassidhe. I wouldn't want the rest of our allies here to see the true darkness that lies within you."

"Enough." Adira growled. She cocked her head at Cassidhe. "We just watched Nat and Vlander's armies be obliterated by Renard and the two of you are bickering like a pair of old sea hags. So, either tell us what's going on, Cassidhe, or let us mourn the loss of our allies in peace."

"There's no reason for mourning," Cassidhe said just as her watch buzzed loudly. She punched one of the buttons on her wrist and a projection of the battlefield expanded before them. Nat's face filled the screen.

Astrid gasped. Although there had been a small part of her that had hoped Renard hadn't completely destroyed their first line attack, she also knew the power of his robots and how difficult they were to kill. And yet, here Nat was. Alive. She could hardly believe it.

"That was some trick you suggested," Nat said breathily, as if she had been running. Her hair clung to her sweaty skin.

"So his armies continued flying towards the Golden City then?" Cassidhe asked, completely nonplussed by the fact that she was talking to someone they had, only moments before, thought dead.

"Yes. He took the bait, just as you said he would."

"What is she talking about, Cassidhe?" Adira growled between clenched teeth. "And no more of your games. Tell us plainly what is going on."

"You didn't tell them!" Nat balked.

"I didn't want to risk Renard finding out."

Astrid narrowed her eyes at Cassidhe. She was certain that was a subtle dig at her for wanting to protect Kimari and Kali. She was so blinded by her hatred of the entire Titus line that she actually believed Astrid was a spy. A traitor to her kind. As if she would ever put her people at risk for any of Renard's family members.

Except, she already had. She'd abandoned them to his devices when she'd gone with Kimari to the palace. She'd known full well that she might not ever be released. And yet, she'd gone. Perhaps Cassidhe had been correct in doubting her. The thought nagged at the back of her mind like a fly.

"What did you do? I don't understand. We saw his robots launch a missile strike at you. You should be dead," Adira said.

"Ouch. You know, Adira, if you wanted me dead, you should have just said so."

Adira approached Cassidhe and leaned into the camera so that her eyes were level with Nat's. "Tell me what is going on."

Freed by Destiny

"We faked the army going through the portals."

"What? How?" Astrid glanced at Janae to gauge her reaction to this news. Her lips were pressed into a hard, thin line, but she didn't say a word as she watched Cassidhe closely.

"Nat's telling the truth. I knew we couldn't fight the robots in a direct battle, so I convinced Nat to prep her army and pretend like they were attacking. In reality, they used a group of fae from your army to create a realistic projection." Cassidhe jerked her head towards Astrid, "Clearly, our plan worked."

"How did you recruit members of the fae?" Astrid asked. She was genuinely curious how Cassidhe had gained access to her people in such a short time. Especially since they didn't know her.

"Max gave the order."

"Of course he did," Astrid muttered. Louder, she said, "I'm glad your scheme worked, but next time, perhaps you can tell me how you plan on using my own people."

Cassidhe shrugged. "Once we win this war, we shouldn't have any reason to put your people's lives in danger like this again. You said it yourself—you want a better world. Once you have the tools to lay the proper foundation, we expect you to follow through."

Turning her attention back to Nat, she said, "Was anyone injured in the missile strike? Are all the fae you used to create the illusion alright?"

Nat's features darkened at Astrid's question and she shook her head.

"How many?"

"Eleven."

"See, not so many that you have any reason to be upset about," Cassidhe said.

Ignoring her words, Astrid laser focused on Nat. "Any other casualties? How many other injuries?"

"Three other casualties. All elves we were using to generate the portal. So far there have only been twenty-three injuries, mostly minor but a few more serious. This is a resounding victory, Astrid."

"I wouldn't call using illusions and tricks to hide away from Renard's armies a victory. Were any of his robots destroyed in the attack? If not, I would view this as a major loss. We cannot afford more lives to be lost if we don't gain ground against Renard." Astrid held up her hands in a placating fashion. "I can admit that I'm relieved not everyone was killed during the missile attack. And, thank the Light there weren't more casualties. But drak it all, if we are going to sever the head of the beast, we have to be bold in our maneuvers. Have any of you ever fought against Renard before?"

Nat shook her head. Astrid peered at the other women standing around her. Everyone except Janae shook their heads.

"Right. Exactly. So the only people in this room who know what Renard is like are me and Janae." She turned towards the elf. "What do you think we should do next?"

Janae raised her eyebrows, but she kept the rest of her emotions in check as she cleared her throat and said, "In this regard, I have to agree with Astrid. It is not a victory to cower behind our magic while his missiles destroy us. It was only a few casualties, this is true. But every soldier we lose now means one less we have in our arsenal when we launch our larger attack. We cannot afford to lose more when we do not also do damage to Renard."

"Besides, I thought the plan was to wage a full frontal attack so that the rest of our troops could attack him on his weak side." Astrid crossed her arms over her chest and glared at Cassidhe. "What changed?"

"Actually, this one was my idea," Nat said. "I've been paying close attention to Renard's strategy for a while and realized that he might not even engage with our troops if he viewed them as too large of nuisance. So, I recommended that we pretend like our troops were entering the field to see how he would react. It was a gamble, but it's one I would take a million times over if it yielded the same results. I'm sorry we didn't tell you before, especially since it involved your troops. We figured since Max gave the order that he had already cleared—"

"Well, he didn't."

"Enough. We don't have time for the bickering," Janae said. "We have a monarch to remove from power and a war to win. Let's just focus on that. Please."

In the distance, a siren blared. It was faint at first, as if it were more a bird's whistle on the wind than anything else. Then, as if it were a hurricane breaking against land, it began to roar.

Chapter Thirty-Two

"We can't stay here!" Cassidhe yelled over the cacophony of the sirens. She motioned towards a door at the back of the room.

"What's happening?" Astrid asked.

She gripped Cassidhe's arm. The projection from her watch turned into fuzzy static and then dimmed as a concussive blast shook the walls. Glass shattered all around them as the windows broke. Astrid threw up a layer of protective magic all around them as stones from the ceiling came crashing down around them. Her body quaked as they struck against her shield.

"Cassidhe?" Janae asked. She stood tall despite the crumbling ceiling and walls.

"The city is under attack."

"But… how? How did his soldiers get here so quickly?"

Fear clawed at Astrid's stomach, turning her insides to mush as she fought off the wave of fatigue that washed over her from using her magic. After a month of not being able to tap into her abilities, her stamina had decreased significantly. She was not sure how much longer she could maintain her connection with her protective magic.

"He has his own portalling devices."

"And you're just now telling us this?" Adira asked. She snapped her teeth at Astrid. "You didn't think that was something we should know heading into this battle?"

"Honestly, I thought you all knew. It's not as if it was a well-kept secret."

"Tell Nat and Vlander to bring the troops back. Tell them now."

Astrid shuddered as a particularly large rock fell smack dab in the middle of her shield. It was large enough to have crushed them if it had fallen on them.

Cassidhe and Janae both began typing out messages.

"How are we going to get out of here?" Cassidhe asked. Gone was the mask of composure. Her eyes were wild as she stared at the chaos all around them.

"On my mark, we're going to move as a team towards the doorway." Astrid nodded towards the door at the back of the room. "That will be a secure enough location for me to catch my breath. I can't maintain this shield forever."

Sweat coated her brow and dripped into her eyes as she spoke. There was nothing she wanted more than to let herself drop the shield. Her knees shook from the pressure of maintaining it. Yet, she would be dooming them all if she did.

"On my count," she said. Her voice broke. "One. Two. Step. Step."

As one, she and the other three leaders shuffled over the rubble towards the door. Cracks formed in the floor beneath them where large blocks of stone had smashed into it. Astrid was careful not to step too heavily on the largest of the cracks. The worst thing that could happen next would be for the floor to cave in before they made it to the door.

Janae slipped, her leg sliding down a rather nasty piece of rock. Blood gushed from the wound, turning the floor slick. She hissed in pain. With shaking hands, she ripped a length of her blouse off and used it to tie around the cut. Although her hands moved steadily as she tied a knot on top of the deepest part of the cut, Astrid noticed the furrows in her brow and the way she stood unsteadily as she rose to her feet.

"Are you alright?" Cassidhe asked. She stretched out an arm for Janae to take as she stepped over a chunk of the ceiling that was double her length.

"I'm fine," Janae said. "Let's keep moving."

Cassidhe's eyebrows rose, as if she were surprised by how gruff Janae was being, but her attitude didn't surprise Astrid at all.

"We need to keep going," Astrid whispered through clenched teeth. Although the largest of the rocks had already fallen, she was worried she would drop her shield and then another fracture would occur. She didn't know if she had it in her to generate a new shield without a moment's rest.

By the time she reached the reinforced doorframe, her mind had turned hazy and her body numb. She collapsed to the ground, panting. Her stomach seized and the contents of her breakfast coated the floor.

A warm hand held her hair back as another patted her back. Astrid closed her eyes, trying to force her stomach to calm itself. She did not want to give these people—who were meant to be allies—any sign of her weakness. She couldn't afford to lose their support.

Assuming they survived.

She couldn't discount that there was a distinct possibility they would all perish even before they'd made it out of the town hall. For the roof to have caved in the way it did and the blast to have knocked them so hard, Renard's soldiers had to be close. For all she knew, they were already in the building.

Searching for them. For her.

"We have to keep moving," she said before wiping the back of her hand across her mouth. "Is there someplace safe we can go? A safe room or…"

To her surprise, it was Cassidhe who dropped her hair to shift into Astrid's frame of view.

"There is, but I'm not sure we can get there."

"What do you mean?"

"It's below sea level and if that blast did this," she said, sweeping her hand toward the destruction around them," then I don't want to think about the amount of ruin the room will be in by now."

"So you're telling me that, with all the gold you could possibly want, you didn't hire a professional builder to design a room that was safe against attacks like this?" Astrid stared at her incredulously. "What do you use all your money for anyway?"

"We never thought we'd be attacked."

"Ooh, shocking. Any other privileged viewpoints you'd like to share?" Astrid rolled her eyes.

"We don't have time for this." Adira rested her back against the door frame and peered around the rubble. "I have never met Renard, but my people honor the histories of this world. If he is anything like the kings and queens of darkness described in the past, we should assume he has spies everywhere."

"Just so," Janae said. "It could even be one of us."

The other three turned towards Astrid. Her head pounding and her magic pulsing inside her, she stared back unflinchingly.

"If I was the spy, why would I be fighting so hard to save you? Why would I be pushing to take Renard down? Go on. Explain it to me. I'll wait."

"It's not like you asked to be saved," Cassidhe said. "I trusted Kali when she asked me to help get you out of the palace, but for all I know, this all could've been part of your plan. Gain our trust."

"Do you even hear yourself right now? Renard killed my parents. He destroyed the Fae way of life. He's been draking experimenting on magicals. Torturing them. Leaving them for dead. And here you are, accusing me of aligning myself with him? Of spying for him?"

"Yes, and the moment you were set free, you still chose his son over one of your own!" Janae growled.

"And there it is. Tell me, Janae, what are you truly upset about?

The fact that I fell in love with a human or that you are losing out on an opportunity to consolidate your own power?"

Before Janae could answer, pounding on the other side of the exterior wall drew their attention. Astrid gripped the handle of her gun and pointed it at the wall. If there were robots on the other side, she would fight until her last breath.

A spray of rock preceded the blinding light of day blasting through a hole in the wall. Astrid squinted, trying to see what—or who— was on the other side.

"Astrid? Are you there?" The voice was hoarse and gruff, as if he'd been screaming, but she would recognize that voice anywhere.

"Bear!"

She lowered her gun and leaned towards the hole. His motorcycle floated in midair, rumbling as he maintained altitude.

"We have to get you out of here," he said. "The city is under attack. We…"

His voice broke off as a streak of red light exploded against his shoulder. As if in slow motion, she watched as a spurt of silver blood gurgled from the wound and then began gushing. He blinked at her, his eyes unfocused.

"No," she whispered as she lunged forward, reaching for him.

Her fingertips grazed his as he slid from his motorcycle and plummeted to the ground.

Chapter Thirty-Three

Astrid's wings erupted from her back as she dove out the hole. The others shouted at her to stop. Their voices were little more than whispers against the pounding of her blood and the rush of the wind as she propelled herself towards Bear.

Summoning what little magic she could tap into, she formed a protective barrier around him, praying it would be enough to break his fall. She used it to press against the wound to staunch the bleeding.

Limply, his body tumbled through the air. All thoughts faded away except one: she needed to save him.

Energy blasts shot past her. One of them grazed her left wing. She screamed in pain but didn't pull any of her protective power back to herself. She wouldn't be able to support two shields.

Bear thudded against the ground, sending a shudder up Astrid's spine from the impact against the shield. More shots from her attackers rained down on her. Without her healing ability, each time she was struck left her weaker and more vulnerable. She didn't know how many robots there were or if she would be able to fend them off. All she knew was that she had to try.

Pressing her wings tight against her body, she shot forward, increasing the velocity of her fall. Her ears popped from the speed of her descent. At the last second, she flung her wings open, breaking her fall and leveling her body out so she could come to a rolling stop on the ground. She leapt to her feet and raced towards Bear. He didn't move or open his eyes as she dropped to her knees beside him.

"Bear?" Her fingers trembled as she tugged at the pouch containing her Silver Salum Flower petals. She couldn't get it open. Hot tears streamed down her cheeks as she continued to fight against the zipper keeping the pouch closed.

A blast from above exploded next to her, singeing her pants. With a loud sob, she expanded the shield protecting Bear to include her as she finally undid the pouch. As soon as the pressure on his neck was released, a gush of silver blood came pouring out.

Crushing the petals, she pressed them to his lips and into the wound.

"Come on," she whispered. "Don't die on me. Please, Bear. I need you."

Laying her head on his chest, she listened for any sign of a heartbeat. She longed to feel the motion of his chest rising with breath. There was only stillness. The drumming of her own heartbeat filled in her ears. Pounding her fists on his chest, she yelled, "You can't die on me. Do you hear? I forbid it."

Freed by Destiny

A cascade of blasts battered on the shield, cracks splintering across it as she struggled to keep it up. Clinging to Bear's hand, she stared up at the band of robots hovering above her. She waited for them to fire again, to attack her, but they remained perfectly still. Lifting her gun, she fired at one of them. The blast exploded in the center of the robot's chest, melting its frame. Sparks flew as wires broke. The robot sputtered in the air before taking a nosedive the ground.

"Astrid." Renard's voice boomed from one of the robots. "I am surprised at you. After everything I've done for you, this is how you repay me? Fleeing from my home. Planning to attack me."

He tsked and the sound reverberated throughout her entire body. "I want you to know, this was not the future I had planned for you. I really did want for you to be a member of my family."

Too fatigued from maintaining her shield and worried about Bear to care, Astrid fired rapidly at the remaining robots hovering in the sky. With each one she shot, a new one replaced it from a hoard farther away. Screaming, Astrid leapt into the air, her wings stretching wide as she rose higher into the sky. Flames curled around her body, burning brighter and hotter as she shot towards the robots. All thoughts of exhaustion melted away.

There was only anger.

Renard's booming laughter echoed from the robots swarming around her. The hoard had closed in on her as she flew. Despite her lack of energy, she forced the firebird within her to release.

The world was consumed in flame. Her vision clouded red. Her wings cut through the robots, melting them in half as she plowed into them. Still, Renard continued laughing at her. With a roar, she swooped the other way and cut down another segment of his forces. Their glowing red eyes dimmed as Astried cleaved their bodies in two.

"Do you think defeating a handful of robots can stop me, Astrid?" Renard asked. His voice echoed through each of the robots, overlapping itself, engulfing her.

"Face me yourself then," she said. "Stop hiding behind your soldiers like a coward. Do you see me hiding away? You're not a leader, Renard. And, one day very soon, you will lose the tenuous control you've been able to obtain, because you know what you are? A slug, too lowly to deserve what you have."

Renard's laughter abruptly halted.

"I had considered, after this… attempt had been squashed and you had been punished, to let you redeem yourself by offering my son an heir. I, for one, still want to blend our two races together. To see a new generation presented who can rightfully lead us from this cycle of hatred. But you just will not let me, will you? You just keep pushing. It's hateful, Astrid, and not a good look. Your mother, the Creators protect her soul, would be so disappointed in you."

"How can you say that when you stripped me from any chance of ever knowing her?" Astrid growled.

Explosions in distance drew her attention to the sea. Ships anchored in the bay fired at a group of robots attacking them. Missiles and streaks of light slammed into the mass of soldiers. They fell from the sky and filled the water with their metallic bodies before sinking beneath the waves.

"You might beat me," she said. "You might even win today. But you should know now, more than ever before, your day is done. We will keep rising up against you. You're done, Renard."

"We'll see about that."

Freed by Destiny

The robots surrounding her lifted their arms and fired at her at the same time.

A pillar of ice formed a dome around her. It exploded into shards as the robots' blasts struck it. Gasping, Astrid flew higher to avoid being cut by the ice. She peered around the city, searching for who had protected her from the robots. A small band of fae stood, shoulder-to-shoulder, on the roof of a building just a few feet away. They summoned another dome of ice, trapping a group of the robots within it as Astrid swooped down to melt another group. She didn't know how much longer she could maintain her firebird form. She just knew she had to keep going. For her parents. For the fae. For Bear.

Portals began opening on the rooftops all around her. Fae, elves, and human soldiers clamored from them. They attacked in waves, launching magical strikes along with missiles at the swarm of robots still lingering in the air around Astrid. She threw up a wavering layer of protective magic around her body as she dropped from her position and angled herself towards Bear.

She needed to know if he was truly dead or if the Silver Salum Flower had worked.

A hard, cold hand wrapped around her ankle and wrenched her back. She screamed as the robot pulled her to its chest and wrapped its arms around her.

"It would be poetic, would it not, for your own people to kill you in their hate of me," Renard said through the robot.

"If they do, my death will be a sign to all who follow of your incompetence. Can't you see that using these tools against me are only a sign of how weak you are? Why do you think so many other nations joined forces with me to fight against you?" She smirked at the robot, knowing Renard could see her on the other side. "You've never faced a day of danger in your life, have you? You've always let others do your dirty work for you. Drak, Renard, you couldn't even come find me yourself. You had to send your lapdog to do it."

Her head swam with all the things that could go wrong with this gamble. He would either take the bait and come in person to see her death, or he would crush her now. It was really a coin toss which way he would land.

The robot's hold on her arms loosened.

"You want to see how powerful I am?" Renard growled. "Then I will show you."

In unison, the robots regrouped into a mass high up in the clouds. Astrid watched them warily, trying to determine what they would do next. She didn't want to think about the destruction they could commit on the city, on innocent civilians, should they wish to begin targeting people instead of her or the armies. When they continued to hover in the air high above the rest of them, her mind whirred with all the possibilities of what he could be planning.

They all came back to one: he would destroy the city. Kill everyone. Do anything to keep his power. He didn't care who he hurt in the process.

If this was to be her last moments of life, she wanted to spend them with her friends.

With one final glance at the robots, Astrid descended towards Bear's body. From what she could tell from her place in the skies, he hadn't moved at all. Her hands shook as she approached him.

"Please don't be dead," she whispered as she reached his body.

His skin was ashen, his lips blue. Tears pooled at the corners of her eyes. Renard had taken everything from her.

Her parents.

Her heritage.

And now, he'd taken Bear.

Anger built inside her, spilling out of her like a tornado. Her scream echoed through the streets. Her body quaked as the sound faded into silence.

Too afraid to touch him and have her deepest fears confirmed, yet too hopeful that there was a chance he was still alive, Astrid continued stand next to him. Her head pounded as she fought to maintain her composure. She knew Renard was using his robots to watch her.

Her people needed her to remain strong. The burden of carrying them was too great. And yet, she could not let herself put them down.

"Astrid?" a timid voice said from behind her.

Astrid swung around, raising her gun to point it directly at Maya's head. Unperturbed, Maya simply pushed the barrel away from her face.

"Is he…" She trailed off.

"I don't know." Astrid's voice caught. Wrapping her arms around her shoulders, Astrid looked away from Bear. "Could you… see. I tried. But I…"

Wordlessly, Maya knelt beside Bear and took his hand into her own. Pressing her other hand to his lips, she waited to see if she could feel his breath on her fingertips. Next, she examined the wound where Astrid had rubbed in the Silver Salum Flower. She tutted softly to herself.

"What is it?" Astrid asked. She pressed her nails deep into her palm as she attempted to keep herself from bawling. If Bear was dead, now was not the time to mourn him. Not when everyone else's lives were at stake. "Just tell me. Is he still alive?"

With one single word, Maya made Astrid's heart stop.

"Yes."

Before Astrid had a chance to celebrate, or even comprehend that Bear was still alive, the horde of robots shifted closer to where she stood.

"Did we hear that right?" Renard's voice boomed from a new robot. "Is the fairy godmother still alive?"

Wary of their intentions, Astrid stepped closer to where Maya knelt beside Bear. The shield wouldn't be strong enough to hold the robots off for very long, but she was determined to not let him harm her friends again.

"You broke your promises to me, Astrid, and now I will make you watch as everything comes crashing down around you. It's what you deserve."

Summoning a giant fireball, Astrid launched it at the closest robot. It jerked backwards as its exoskeleton began melting.

"Get him out of here," Astrid whispered to Maya. "Keep him safe."

She didn't look away from the robots as they stared down at her. She didn't know what they were waiting for or why Renard was hesitating to act. She was vulnerable and at his mercy.

Freed by Destiny

"I'm not going to leave you here to face down a horde of robots on your own," Maya said gruffly. "You don't have to carry the weight of this battle on your own, Astrid."

"What's this? A lover's tiff?" Renard blared from another robot. Astrid couldn't tell which one. "And here I thought you'd returned to the elves because of that bastard Max Beauregard. Wasn't he the one you were pining over, even though my son was offering you a better future? You broke his heart, you know. And you will be punished for it."

Ice curled around Astrid's heart. She closed her eyes in hopes that her thoughts wouldn't be conveyed outward. Relief at Kimari having successfully lied to his father intertwined with doubt. It was possible she had been the one duped by him, not the other way around. But, if there was one thing she was determined to believe, it was that Kimari loved her.

She wouldn't let him down by giving his father any hint that he wasn't on his side.

"You can tell your son that he is the last man I would ever want to marry."

There was a short pause and then Renard said, "You can tell him yourself the next time you meet. Of course, you'll most likely be in chains and begging for his mercy. I'll let him be the one to decide your fate. It seems only fair, considering what you've done to him."

Astrid stepped away from Maya and Bear. She lifted her chin higher and said, "I'm not afraid of you or your family, Renard. And you can't force me to be. But it does seem like you're afraid of me."

Although she maintained a composed expression as she spoke,

her insides quivered at her defiance of him. She knew, first-hand, what he was capable of.

"We'll see," Renard said through all the robots.

From the corner of her eye, Astrid saw Max leading a small band of soldiers towards her.

He held up fist as she smiled broadly at the robots and said, "What do you really want? You seem reticent to kill me. What I am to you? A plaything you can toy with? Or are you afraid killing me would be enough to stir our citizenry into action?"

One of the robots lifted their hands and fired at her. The blast dissipated as soon as it struck her shield, but the faint blue light protecting her, Maya, and Bear shattered with the impact. Astrid rocked forward. Her breath exploded from her, her head spinning. Every part of her was sore.

She refused to back down.

"I could keep this up all day," she whispered, her voice hoarse. "And I will keep protecting the people I care about, my people and this whole draking world, until you can't hurt them anymore. I don't care what you do to me. I will die before I let you hurt anyone else."

Sweat dripped down her brow as she spoke, forming gooseflesh across her skin as an ocean breeze swelled and chilled her. Shivering slightly, Astrid puffed out her chest.

A loud pop followed by a suction of air whipped through the street. A portal formed in the middle of the sky, directly above the horde of robots. Max leapt from it, his eyes meeting Astrid's as he tumbled through the air. Bright light filled the street as a bomb exploded.

Chapter Thirty-Four

Astrid skittered backwards, the force from the blast taking her off her feet. The robots, broken by the blast, plummeted from the sky. Bits of metal struck the ground all around her. Groaning in pain, she clutched at her ears. Silver liquid leaked from one of them as a soft ringing drowned out all other noise. Her head swam, everything seeming to swirl and sway around her. Dust filled the air, making it difficult to breath. She searched the street for Maya and Bear, desperate to know that they were alright. Maya was pressed against a wall further down the street and cradling Bear to her chest. Although she was gray with dust, Astrid didn't see any silver coming from her or Bear's bodies.

Sighing in relief, Astrid began searching the debris of broken robots for any sign of Max. He'd been so close to the bomb, she wasn't sure how he could've made it out without being harmed. Panic coiled within her like a snake ready to strike when she didn't find any sign of him. Wobbling as she stood, she inched her way towards the heart of the explosion where a crater marred the street.

She closed her eyes as she stood at the edge of the crater. She didn't want to see him laying among rubble, his body broken, blood leaking from his lips. The vision of it filled her mind as she leaned over the hole. Her heart racing, she opened her eyes.

He wasn't there.

She didn't know how he had escaped. She looked around, not trusting that this was the reality of the situation.

"You will not win," the metallic voice hissed through the rubble, startling her.

She whirled around, expecting to see a robot pointing a gun at her. All she saw was swirling dust.

"You think this stunt is enough to even hurt me? Everything you love, everyone you've fought so hard to protect, will be destroyed. I will relish in watching you watch."

Looking down, Astrid saw the dented, blackened head of a robot. Its central core hung from its neck and its eyes glowed red as it stared up at her. Astrid didn't give Renard the satisfaction with a retort. She just sneered at it before lifting her foot and stomping directly on the core. The robot's red eyes flickered. She stomped again. A loud crack ruptured the air as the red faded to darkness.

Sniffing, Astrid hobbled her way towards where Maya still rested against the wall with Bear.

"Are you okay?" she asked as she knelt beside them.

Maya's lips were cracked and a stream of blood ran down her

chin. Astrid reached forward and cupped Maya's cheek.

"Maya?"

She blinked at her and a small smile tugged at her lips. "I'm fine. Just... dazed."

Her eyes were glassy, and Astrid didn't like how much she was struggling for her words, but they didn't have time to waste. They needed to get out of here. Looking down, she examined Bear for any sign of new injuries. He grunted when she prodded at the place he'd been wounded.

"If you keep touching it, it'll never heal."

She threw her arms around his neck and hugged him tightly. He grunted again, but wrapped one arm around her middle, hugging her.

"I was so worried about you," she whispered, burying her face in his beard. "I..."

"Shh," Bear murmured. "I'm fine. See, all spick and span. I promise, I'll be good as new once I have some time to rest."

"What happened?" Astrid said, lifting her head to look at Maya. "I don't understand how Renard knew—how he was able to mobilize so quickly."

"I think, although I'd have to run a test to verify, but I believe there's a hack on our communication line. It's the only thing I can think of that would've given him enough information to strike like this."

"Maybe we shouldn't have invited the others to fight. At least then there would've been fewer people who could've turned against us."

"I don't believe we were betrayed. I've been monitoring all communication that comes and goes from the city. Nothing has transmitted to Renard directly."

"But they could have sent a coded message to someone back in their home nations to relay to the king. Or someone from one of their countries could have tipped him off. There are so many more options than just being hacked, Maya."

"True." She chewed on her bottom lip. "But I want to give our allies the benefit of the doubt. We have no reason to doubt them."

"We have no reason to trust them, either," Astrid countered.

"Fair enough."

Astrid shook her head, making the world swim again. Her hand trembled slightly as she dug into her pouch and pulled out a small handful of Silver Salum Flower petals. She weighed her bag as she contemplated how terrible she felt. If the world continued to swim, she would have difficulty talking, much less flying. And, if she was going to have any chance at beating Renard, she needed to be at her best.

The bag felt light. She only had enough of the petals left for one, maybe two doses to heal any injuries she might sustain during battle. Sighing, she pulled a small water bottle free from its designated pouch on her hip and dropped the handful of petals she had in her hand into the bottle. She chugged the water. The effect was nearly instantaneous.

Her mind cleared and the aching in her muscles subsided. She stretched, letting herself revel in the movement before clearing her throat and staring out over the wreckage. She still hadn't seen any sign of Max, and that realization made bile creep up the back of her throat.

Freed by Destiny

Six portals formed in an arch around her. She leapt to her feet and lifted her gun. It wouldn't be enough to protect them if it was Renard's army, but she would stand as long as she could against him.

A giant figure emerged from one of the portals. Long, pointed claws and massive wings filled her vision before she met Andra's gaze. The harpy snarled as she shook from the sensation of being on solid ground once more.

"I can fly hundreds of miles and be exhausted, but not feel ill. Why is it that the moment I walk through one of those draking portals, I feel like I'm back in the research lab?" She shook her wings and rolled her head from side-to-side.

"What are you doing here?" Astrid asked. This hadn't been part of the plan. The magical creatures were supposed to attack the palace.

"Renard is on his way here. In fact, he might already be here."

"What?" Astrid had heard a lot of unbelievable things in her life, but this one topped the others. She had taunted him, but she had never imagined he would rise to her bait.

Unless he was one hundred percent confident he could squash them.

Her chest tightened beyond comfort and her hands twitched. Dizziness washed over her. She swayed, her body unable to determine how to remain straight.

"We came because the final battle will not be fought in Lunameed. It will be here. He's come here. For you." Andra's feathers ruffled as she spoke, her eyes flashing yellow as she snarled. "If I get the chance, I will rip his throat out myself."

Astrid's eyebrows rose to her hairline, but she refrained from commenting. Although she didn't want to kill him for the sake of revenge, she did want to eliminate him from power. If that meant taking his life, she would.

"You might get the chance. Our forces are... scattered. I'm not sure what happened."

Andra took several steps forward as more magical creatures entered through the portals. Nalia raced to Astrid's leg and climbed to her shoulder. She nuzzled her head against Astrid's.

"You shouldn't be here," Astrid said.

I couldn't let you rage war against Renard without me, Nalia communicated telepathically. *Besides, if you died and I wasn't here at least trying to protect you, I could never forgive myself.*

And I could never forgive myself if I let you come with me and you end up getting hurt. Or worse.

Well, unless you command me to stay behind, I'm coming. So there.

Chuckling, Astrid ran a finger down Nadia's spine. The baby dragon hummed deep in her chest, the rhythm reverberating across Astrid's body. The ache in her chest subsided with the rhythm. She pressed her forehead against Nalia's and breathed out slowly.

Astrid pulled back and looked to Andra. "Have you heard anything about Max?"

She knew it was a long shot, but she couldn't shake the image of him leaping from the portal, throwing the grenade, and then... nothing. She couldn't remember if she'd seen him escape or not. And, although she hadn't found his body, a sense of dread settled into her bones.

"No, I'm sorry. We just received word from Maya's direct line that she wanted us here."

Astrid turned towards Maya, a question in her eyes. "What does she mean? How could you have been the one to contact them? You've been here. With us…"

A prickling at the back of her mind nagged at her. What if the traitor had been Maya all along?

Maya shook her head.

"I know that look," she said, "and I'm going to need you to stop those thoughts dead in their tracks."

"But I wasn't…"

"You bet my draking arse you weren't. Think back to how long you've known me. Remember all the times I saved your arse? Do you think I would have done that if I were a spy planted by, of all draking people, Renard? No." She hoisted Bear to his feet. Although she was slender, she didn't tremble under his weight.

"You said it yourself: it's likely someone close to us. Who better than the head of tech and cybersecurity department?"

Maya stared at her blankly. Her cheeks glistened a brilliant white light.

"How dare you," she snapped. "I've done everything I can to help you succeed, and here you are, accusing me? Besides, I didn't say it was someone close to us, Astrid. I think it's more likely that we were hacked! I should've stayed—"

"Ladies…"

"What!" Both Maya and Astrid yelled at the same time. They turned their heads to Andra.

Andra growled at them. "It's obvious neither of you is a spy. I know Kali's betrayal cut you both deeply, and it is suspicious how Renard seems to know our plans even before we communicate them outwardly, but you have to stop yourself from falling into his traps. This is what he wants, the chaos between you."

Guilt rippled through Astrid. Andra was right. Renard was a master manipulator. All she had to do was look at how his children acted around him to see that they were terrified of how he would change the rules or attempt to turn them against their friends and loved ones. This was no different. If he planted enough seeds of doubt, it would be easier to deteriorate their bond. Easier to break them. Easier to win.

Before she could tell Maya she was sorry, Maya enveloped her in a tight embrace. "I shouldn't have lashed out at you."

"No, I shouldn't have accused you."

"Right, now that that's taken care of," Andra said, her voice growing impatient, "we have a battle to win."

As she spoke, another wave of magical creatures appeared through the portal. An elf stepped through each one and closed their respective portals with a wave of their arms.

A flash of a nightmare zipped through Astrid's mind. A night sky swirled with wind and clouds. The sister moons were dimmed by their cover. Stars were the light of her ancestors watching over her.

Her hands turned clammy as she remembered the comet streaking across the sky and striking her.

Freed by Destiny

A shiver ran down her spine.

"Are you alright?" Maya whispered, squeezing her shoulder.

She shook her head. She didn't want to admit that the dream could've been a premonition. And the comet, a missile.

"You look pale," Maya said. "What's going on?"

Astrid shook her head. "Nothing that you can help with." When Maya continued to look at her with concern, she said, "Truly. I'm fine."

Although she could tell Maya didn't believe her, Astrid was determined not to let her know of her fears.

"Where's Eldris?" she asked, hoping to change the subject entirely.

"He went to join Max…" Maya trailed off.

"We should move," Bear said. Although he was still gray, he didn't wobble as he stood on his own two feet.

Astrid leapt towards him, wrapping her arms tight around his middle. He stumbled backwards a few steps but returned the embrace once he'd regained his footing.

He patted her back and said, "We have to find the others. If Andra's correct and Renard is here, his tactics will become even more brutal. I don't believe he was lying when he said he wanted to break you by making you watch as he kills your loved ones."

She nodded against his chest and, using the back of her hand, wiped away the unbidden tears clinging to the corners of her eyes. Turning towards the magical creatures, she said, "Thank you for being here. I am honored to fight by your side."

Although not all of them had the ability to talk, they bowed to her or released a sound of what Astrid took to be approval. Nalia, still perched around her shoulders, rubbed against her cheek.

They believe in you.

Although those four words had been said before, they somehow meant more to her after living a month in Renard's clutches.

To whatever end, they will follow you.

Nalia's words surged through her, bolstering her confidence. No matter what happened next, they were here together. They had not given up when things got difficult. And, despite everything, they still believed.

"Let's go find the others," Astrid said as she turned towards the main building where Cassidhe, Janae, and Adira were still most likely trapped on the top floor where the council room was.

She'd been so concerned about Bear and then Max following the battle with the robots that she had almost entirely forgotten about them. Her wings stretched out from her back as she jerked her head towards Andra to fly with her. They ascended towards the crumbling building.

She pointed towards the opening she'd flown through to save Bear, her senses heightened as she waited to see if the council members were still inside. Through the rushing of her blood in her ears, low voices carried on the wind.

She dove back through the hole, careful not to clip the sides of the building. There, huddled in the same spot she'd left them, were the three other leaders. Janae frowned at her, her eyes hardening.

"Where's my nephew?" she asked before Astrid could say a word.

Freed by Destiny

Astrid blinked at her. "How am I supposed to know?"

Janae bared her teeth. "I felt his presence… and then…" She shook her head. "We all heard the robots ask about him. You have to tell me. Please. What happened to him?"

Although the knot in her stomach tightened at Janae's words, Astrid steadied herself. She might not like Janae, but she still respected her. Besides, she had more of a claim to Max's welfare than Astrid did.

"He threw a bomb into the robots… I couldn't find him after."

Janae closed her eyes, her lips pursing. She pinched the bridge of her nose between fingers and remained like that for an uncomfortable moment. Astrid watched her, understanding how she must be feeling. Until they found Max again, Janae would carry her worry for his well-being across her shoulders. Astrid couldn't fault her for that. She would be doing the same.

When Janae finally lowered her hand, she met Astrid's gaze. "I pray that we find him, but we cannot let ourselves be overcome. There is much to do."

They didn't always see eye-to-eye, but Astrid couldn't help but feel in awe of Janae.

"All of our communicators are down," Cassidhe said, breaking the moment.

Astrid cocked her head towards her. "Mine was working…"

"It's not now. I've been trying to reach the others." She shook her head. "Renard must have figured out a way to block our signal. We are alone here."

Shaking her head, Astrid said, "We're not alone."

She gripped Cassidhe around the waist and dove out the window. Cassidhe's scream nearly burst Astrid's eardrums as they dropped a few feet and then leveled out again.

Cassidhe punched her in the shoulder.

"Hey! Owe!" Astrid said with mock pain.

"Was that strictly necessary?" Cassidhe asked.

"I don't know what you're talking about." Astrid smirked. It was petty and childish, but she would cherish Cassidhe's shocked expression for a lifetime—or at least until she replaced it with something better.

She dropped her off on the ground near Maya before looping around and flying back to the opening where Andra was waiting.

"I'll be right back," she said as she slipped inside the building and picked up Adira. She flew to the opening and handed her off to Andra. The siren balked at the harpy's sharp claws but didn't say anything as Andra flew towards the ground.

Astrid went back into the building one last time to get Janae.

"Let's go," she said, reaching out a hand towards the elf.

Just as Janae's fingers closed around Astrid's, a series of small explosions rocked the already unstable building. Astrid pulled Janae into her arms, just as the entire building collapsed.

Chapter Thirty-Five

Janae buried her head into Astrid's shoulder as a weak protective shield formed around them. The shield rippled with the impact of beams and stone toppling onto them. Although it was strong enough to stop the debris from completely crushing them, it wasn't enough to stop the pulse of the impact.

Astrid whimpered as her magic faltered. "I can't…"

"I know."

They slammed into the ground. Astrid's shield remained intact following the impact before dissipating. Giant slabs of stone and heavy beams formed an arc above them. Astrid stared up at the narrow gap between her body and the rubble that would surely crush them both to death and laughed.

Janae elbowed her in the side. "I don't think now is a time for amusement, Astrid."

Janae was right, but Astrid couldn't stop herself from laughing at the absurdity of the moment. Here they were, about to be crushed to death, and somehow, miraculously, they'd been spared because of a freak arc formation in the rubble.

"Well, I'm glad one of us is amused by our current predicament," Janae said.

There wasn't enough room in the small opening and Janae was forced to continue laying on top of Astrid, just as they'd fallen. Astrid tried wiggling her feet to see if there was any opening at the end of the rubble. Her foot nudged against the stone, shifting the delicately balanced debris above them. Dust fluttered down, coating Astrid's tongue, making it difficult for her to breathe. She coughed, her eyes watering.

"Don't move or you'll crush us yet," Janae said.

Although the lighting was dim, Astrid could tell Janae was grimacing at the subtle shift of the caved in rocks above.

"We're going to get out of this."

"Overconfident as usual, I see," Janae said. "Why is it that you can never just… accept your lot in life? You constantly push. And you take others down with you."

"By others, you mean Max," Astrid said. Her heat strings pinged a little at the insinuation that she would ever do anything intentionally to hurt Max.

"You convinced him you loved him."

"I do love him," Astrid growled. "Just…"

Freed by Destiny

"I knew from the start that you weren't good enough for him. You led him on. All the while, you were holding out for a better offer. I never should have given you my consent."

"And if you hadn't taken me under your wing and mentored me, where would you be? Face it, the elves were getting nowhere in their quest to remove Renard from power until you helmed me at the front of battle. You didn't even know about the research centers until I came along. So sure, be bitter about the fact that I hurt Max. That's fine. It's not anything I haven't already told myself. But I can't help that, despite loving Max, it's not the same kind of love he has—had—for me. And, quite frankly, it's none of your business what we decide or how we come to terms with the changes in our relationship."

She released the last bit of air in her lungs as she finished talking. She still didn't understand why Janae disliked herso much, but she refused to let herself be broken by anyone. Not anymore.

"He is my heir."

"Yes, and he doesn't want to be. Have you even ever asked him what he wants? Do you know how many conversations we've had about building a world different from the one we grew up in? No? I didn't think so. He doesn't want to lead the elves the way you do."

"Fine. You know him better than I do. Congratulations. You're so special. That doesn't change the fact that you made him believe you were in love with him and then you gutted him."

Astrid tsked loudly. "I literally gave up one of my most powerful abilities to save him from death and you think I did that because I...what? Have a savior complex? Look, I don't know why you dislike me so much, but you have never made me feel completely accepted by you. Even in the moments when you showed me kindness, you were always tough. So, forgive me, but I don't really feel like explaining my feelings for your nephew. That is, other than to say, butt out. Oh, and let me repeat myself one last time. I do love him. He is my family. And I would give up my healing ability again if it meant he could live even one day longer."

"And yet you're willing to break his heart."

A tension-filled silence hung between them. Astrid wished she wasn't pressed almost face-to-face with Janae, but they were practically smooshed together.

Janae sighed. "I may have been too hard on you. It's just… you remind me so much of your mother. There are times I see her reflected in you."

"And that makes you hate me? I thought the two of you were friends." Astrid huffed. Her head swam and her throat ached from swallowing too much dust. The air was becoming thinner with every word they uttered and every breath they took. Astrid had no doubt that, at some point, they would be completely out of breathable air.

"I don't hate you. I just… see her flaws in you. And I don't want you to repeat them. Did you know that she and Renard once had a fling?"

Astrid's hands turned clammy. "I may have heard something to that effect. Renard told me she chose my father…"

"Yes, she chose your father," Janae said. "And do you know what happened? It drove Renard down a path of darkness. Don't get me wrong. He'd always been a spoiled little brat, but when he and your mother were an item, he wasn't as cruel. She could have stopped him becoming the man he is now."

Freed by Destiny

Astrid's chest popped upward as she stifled her nervous laughter. "It sounds an awful lot like you're trying to blame my mother for Renard's poor decisions. Sure, could she have maybe let him down a little easier? I mean, maybe? But we've seen what Renard is like when he doesn't get his way. And look what he draking did to her. He killed her."

"And I have every belief that she would still be alive if she hadn't chosen…"

"Don't you dare insinuate that she made the wrong choice. Drak you, Janae. People love who they love. They make decisions based on what they think is right in the moment and you have no right to judge them—anyone—on how they live their lives. Besides, are you trying to tell me you think Max has the capacity to become an evil tyrant who physically harms those who get in his way? I don't think that about him, and I'm surprised that you do."

"That's not what I was saying at all."

"Then what were you trying to say, exactly? Because it sounded an awful lot like victim blaming and viewing Max in a rather negative light."

Although Astrid couldn't see Janae's face, she could envision her pursed lips and cold eyes. She'd seen the expression far too often not to know what it looked like.

"Fine, Astrid. You're right. I'm wrong. I'm sorry if I ever made you question your parents' decisions. But I can promise you this, it was done in the service of helping you learn from the mistakes of the past. I do not want you repeating them."

"And that's fine, but, maybe, next time choose different words."

Although tension still hung between them, poised to explode at

411

any moment, an immense of relief flooded through Astrid for finally speaking her mind.

Rubble shifted above them, sending a shower of dust onto her face again. Her eyes stung as particles scraped against them. She coughed, her lungs burning and her throat aching from the thick coating of dust threatening to suffocate her.

"Astrid?" Bear called as more dust fell between the rocks. The slab of rock shifted lower, grazing the top of Janae's back.

"You can summon your protection magic any time now," Janae said as she pressed into Astrid.

Astrid tugged on the tendrils flailing about from the core of her magic. They were wispy and weak and did not respond to her calling upon them. She groaned, spittle flying from her lips as she pushed every ounce of her strength into forming a brace against the collapsing rocks perched to crush them beneath their weight.

"I'm coming," Bear said as the sound of rocks being lifted from the pile echoed through the cracks. "Just hold on."

She gritted her teeth, tears leaking from the corners of her eyes as she tried to keep her magic in place. Blood trickled from her nose, but she didn't dare attempt to lift a hand, lest she disrupt the flow of her magic into the shield.

"I can't…" she whispered.

"Keep holding on," Janae said. Gone was the terse tone she'd been using only moments before. Now that death was upon them and she didn't want to die by being crushed, she had taken on the mothering persona she'd so often used with Astrid during their time training together.

"Astrid?" Bear called out. "Please tell me you're okay. Give me a sign, darlin'."

Astrid could not force herself to speak. Her magic waned, leaving her as quickly as she had summoned it. With a flash of brilliant white light, her shield completely dissipated.

Chapter Thirty-Six

Heat formed a tight circle around Astrid's body. She screamed as the ground beneath them caved in and they dropped into freefall. She clung to Janae as she attempted to release her wings before it was too late.

Hard, metal arms slammed into her back, catching her. A robot's face stared down at her, green eyes scanning her as she fought to lift her gun out of the tangle of limbs.

"It's alright," the robot said.

She tightened her protective magic against her and Janae's bodies.

"Astrid, it's me."

A thought clicked in her brain. The robot had come from underground. Where Penny had been made. Where she had been downloading into her new body.

Astrid stopped fighting against the arms holding her and looked into the robot's eyes. "Penny?"

The robot nodded.

Astrid gasped. Every fiber of her body hummed as she pressed her forehead to Penny's chest. The whir of the processor reverberated through her body instead of a heartbeat. Still, she was thankful she could have Penny in any form.

"Can one of you explain to me what's going on?" Janae asked. In the dim light of Penny's glowing eyes, Astrid could see Janae glaring at her.

"I asked Maya to build Penny—my PEA—a body. And... it worked."

"Why would anyone..."

"Because I'm an AI. I know you have a lot of questions, Janae, but let me assure you, I am the real reason Renard assassinated Astrid's family. He was after me."

"I don't..."

"My mother and Renard were working together to see if they could create an AI as powerful as the ancient heroes," Astrid said. "They decided to mirror this one's personality off everything they could find about Queen Amaleah."

"That's utterly impossible. All those records were lost during the Great Darkness. How could they have possibly..."

"I'm just an algorithm of the things they thought should be included. Although, I believe that something Leilani did infused a portion of magic in me that bled into Astrid's abilities. Perhaps that is why she has more power than any fae in over a century."

Janae's jaw dropped and then promptly snapped closed again.

"I know it's a lot to take in," Astrid said gently.

Janae didn't answer.

"By my calculations, the ceiling to the basement will be caving in within the next three minutes. Perhaps now would be a good time to get us out of here."

"Yes, please," Astrid said.

Although Penny's voice carried notes of her former tenor, threads of the voice she'd heard in her waking memories were woven into her intonations. Add the robotic cadence of her speech, and Astrid was left wondering just how much of her PEA remained as part of the core processing of the PEA. There was a part of Penny that seemed so familiar, even now that she was in a body of her own. And yet, she wasn't the same nervous, hyper aware AI she'd been before she'd been wiped from her processor during the memory extraction process. Before she'd been reformed using the spell to bring back things lost.

Jets on the bottoms of Penny's feet blazed as she propelled them upwards.

"Hang on," she said as she lifted one of her arms and blasted a hole through the ceiling.

Astrid threw up a weakened shield just as a pile of pebbles and dust fell on top of them. Penny punched through the last of the beams and stone above them and into daylight.

Bear fell to his knees as Penny dropped to the ground in front of him. Reaching out to Astrid, he tugged her into his arms and held her closely to his chest.

"I thought you were gone," he whispered. "I was sure you were."

"Shh, it's okay. I'm okay." She patted down her body. "See. All here. Still intact."

His eyes roamed over her body, searching for any sign of injury before darting to Penny. Without hesitating, he stepped between them.

"Who are you?" he asked.

Penny stuck her hand out for him to shake. He stared at her, his lips twitching. Astrid placed a hand on his shoulder and squeezed, drawing his attention back to her.

"I asked Maya to build a body for Penny. This is the result." She gestured towards Penny, who waved. It was so humanlike, Astrid almost believed that she was a biological creature. But she knew all of Penny's reactions were a result of her programming, albeit highly sophisticated and able to learn.

Maya, who had been standing between Cassidhe and Adira, tending to their wounds, stepped forward and said, "I wasn't sure it would work. I've never seen a PEA this sophisticated before. I mean, sure, I saw traces of this programming when I first examined Astrid's PEA… but this…" She swept her hands towards the robot. "She learns from her mistakes and generates new understanding of people just by observing them. I've never seen anything like her before."

Andra came to stand beside Astrid. Her wings folded flat against her back as she stared at Penny before saying, "We can't stay here. Renard knows this is the last place you were at. He will come for you. You know better than any of us that once he's had a taste of control, he will not give it up easily."

Andra was right Astrid shivered as coldness skimmed over her skin, leaving gooseflesh in its wake.

Andra sniffed at the air.

"A storm is brewing," she said.

As if on cue, lightning illuminated the sky in an arc of brilliant purple.

"Come on," Astrid said, nodding down the street. "We need to find the others and regroup. Figure out our next steps."

She wanted to go search for Max in the crater caused by the bomb again but knew her attempts would be futile. He wasn't there. She didn't know where he was or what had happened to him.

"Does anyone have a working communicator?" Maya asked.

Andra led the way, her broad shoulders towering above the small crowd as she moved forward. Adira caught Astrid's arm and squeezed, stopping her from following. When Astrid met her eyes, they pled with her to stay. So she did.

Penny lingered behind as well. Although she busied herself with examining the crater a few feet away, Astrid had no doubt she was in range to hear every word shared between herself and Adira.

"This storm is siren brought," she said.

Astrid cocked an eyebrow at her. Members of the Fae could manipulate the weather, but she knew nothing of the magic sirens contained. So much of the world around them had been lost during the Great Darkness.

"Sirens do not have a lot of magic," Adira said. "We can shift between our tails and our legs. We can talk to sea creatures and breathe under water. But a few of us can control the weather above our seas and oceans."

"Why are your soldiers summoning a storm?"

Adira shrugged. "Probably for the very reason you think. We're under attack. Although Renard shouldn't have known about their existence, let alone they would be joining a fight like this one, it is apparent that something has gone terribly wrong."

"Clearly."

"Do you want to join them?" Astrid asked.

"You're a good leader," Adira said. "I know Janae and Cassidhe have given you a hard time, but I can tell they admire your desire to keep not just your people, but the whole of the world safe from Renard's clutches. I promise we will be with you when the time comes."

Astrid smiled and bowed her head at Adira as she went racing to the beach. She flung her body into the ocean, her legs glittering like a sunset on reflected water before sea foam flew from the waves like clouds.

"You handled that well," Penny said. She came to stand beside Astrid. "I attempted to connect to the server Renard is using, but the security systems he has in place are too robust to break through at this point. It does seem he is the one blocking our communicators from connecting with one another though. I found an unusual frequency coming from his account, which I can only assume is what he's using to stop us from communicating."

Astrid wrapped her arms over her chest as Penny spoke. She stared out at the towering waves and the purple lightning and tried to think through a strategy that would get everyone she loved out of this situation alive. She doubted Renard would be lenient with her this time. She'd embarrassed him, demonstrated the weaknesses in his rule.

"Penny."

"Yes, Astrid?"

"Do you ever wish… I had paid attention to you when you begged me not to extract our memories?"

Penny hesitated. Her eyes roamed the seas, mimicking Astrid. "If you had heeded my warning, I would still be as I once was. I see now that the encryption code your mother placed on me was limiting my abilities from reaching their full potential."

Turning towards her, Astrid reached out and took Penny's hand. It was strange, trusting something that looked so similar to the ones she'd been fighting for over a year.

"You never stopped fighting to bring me back," Penny said. "I exist because of you."

"Even though you weren't initially sure you wanted that, either."

"No." A low rumble emitted from Penny and Astrid could only describe it as an attempt at a chuckle. She smiled.

"So, I think the moral of this story is that you should always trust and follow my lead, even if you don't agree. Okay. Great." She smiled broadly at Penny.

Although Penny couldn't change her facial expressions because of her mechanical body, Astrid could sense her displeasure in the way she held her body stiffly.

A freezing wind whipped across Astrid's exposed skin, stinging her. She shivered and returned her attention back to the sea.

"There were Fae here, helping me earlier," she whispered as she remembered the way they'd formed the ice domes around her, protecting her from the robots. "Where could they have gone?"

In the commotion and fighting that'd followed, she'd completely forgotten about them. And Max had been with a small band of soldiers when he'd come to help them. They, too, were missing.

A sinking sensation writhed within her. Something wasn't right. If they'd been here, they would've joined her. Unless they couldn't. Unless Renard had done something to them.

"We have to look for them," she said.

Without waiting for a response from Penny, Astrid bolted towards the alleyway she'd first seen Max walking down. Her heart sank. Bodies covered the ground. Bluish froth dropped from their lips. Astrid knelt beside the first Fae and laid her hand on her throat, trying to determine if she was still alive. The body was cold to the touch.

She turned towards Penny. "I don't understand."

"Poison," Penny said.

"But how? How did this happen?"

"If I had to guess, it would be that someone within the group released a localized aerial toxin."

She shook her head. "That isn't possible."

"There is a high probability that Renard was able to successfully infiltrate your rebellion. As you accepted more Fae and humans into your camp, the likelihood that one—or more—of them would be a spy for Renard increased."

Astrid pinched the bridge of her nose as she realized what Maya and Bear had tried to tell her earlier. Whoever the spies were, they had made a mess of everything. If she ever found out who they were, she wouldn't stop until they'd received justice.

Since the Fae who'd summoned the ice hadn't resurfaced as well, she decided she didn't want to go looking for them if all they found were more dead bodies.

"Come on," she said to Penny. "We need to go rejoin the others. We need to tell them what we found."

Penny nodded.

As Astrid began walking away from the alley, the hair on the back of her neck stood on end and she had the sensation they were being watching. She spun around, hoping to see the fae who'd helped her before. Instead, there were only the dead bodies and darkness.

Chapter Thirty-Seven

Astrid leaned in closer, sensing there was something lurking in shadows, just out of sight.

Something big slithered across the ground and she jumped backwards.

Penny lifted her arm, a gun rising out of a panel on her forearm, and pointed it at the dark part of the alley.

"Who's there?" Astrid called as she took another step backwards. "Show yourself."

A tentacle flapped onto the ground in front of her. Its girth was nearly the same as her own.

"Oh, drak," she whispered as she took another large step away from it. "What is that?"

The creature's body moved into view as it dragged itself across the dead elves. It towered above them, the top of its head just shy of the rooftops of the two buildings it was wedged between. Its beak snapped as it ripped into the elves' flesh, devouring them.

"A kraken. My best estimation is that it fled the sea because of the fighting happening there," Penny said.

Astrid's stomach roiled as she watched the kraken eat the elves before bending over and retching on the side of the alley. She didn't know if they should stop it from eating the elves, flee, or kill it. She looked to Penny for any suggestions.

"We should go."

"You don't think it'll follow us?" Astrid asked. She didn't trust that it wouldn't kill more of her army to alleviate its hunger.

"You see how slow it's moving," Penny said. "On land, it is slow moving. I would be more afraid of trying to flee if we were in the water. As it is, we can worry about it later."

Astrid didn't need to be told twice. She backed away from the kraken, her senses heightened.

In the distance, as horn blared, tugging at her attention even as the kraken's eyes lifted from its meal and stared directly at her.

It slammed one of its tentacles directly at her. Using the remnants of her protective magic, she formed a shield around herself to stop its suckers from latching onto her.

Penny fired at its arm. The first blast left a gaping hole in the kraken's flesh; black goo seeped from its wound. It flailed its other tentacles in all directions. They slammed into the walls of the narrow alleyway, dislodging stone and brick to fall all around them.

Freed by Destiny

Penny wrapped an arm around Astrid's middle and yanked her out of the alley. She cried out as they dropped from the sky and skidded across the ground. A large dent was prominent on Penny's back from where a rock had been propelled at her.

The kraken lumbered towards them, more quickly than what Penny had described as possible. Astrid cried out as she fired several shots at it. Only one of her blasts struck the beast, and it barely grazed its tentacle.

"A little help here," Astrid said as she released another volley.

Penny tried to push herself off the ground, but her arms collapsed beneath her.

"Penny!" Fear gripped Astrid as she watched Penny struggle to rise to her feet. She hadn't believed that her PEA could be harmed while in her robotic body. But, she realized, she'd been able to destroy Renard's robots. She had no reason to believe that they had better materials from which to construct a robot than Renard.

"We're going to get out of this," she whispered as she tried to create an exit strategy. "Just hold on."

"I think one of my wires is pinched," Penny said. "I will attempt to fix now."

She reached behind her back and prodded at the crater. Her joints screeched slightly as she tried to pop the indentation back out.

The kraken had advanced upon them. It stretched out its tentacles, aiming to crush her.

With a scream, flames erupted over her body and she released her wings. The kraken's eyes followed her as she zipped into the air, forming a blazing arc in the sky. She knew she was giving away their position, but it didn't matter. They would either be killed by the kraken or they would be sitting ducks. In this case, she would rather at least have the chance to survive.

Forming a fireball in the palm of her hand, Astrid hurtled it towards the beast. The fireball struck the kraken straight in the left eye. The kraken flailed its tentacles wildly about in the sky. Astrid darted left then down, then forward, barely weaving between the massive arms as it tried to hit her.

"I'm sorry," she whispered as she sent another fireball at its head. Goo and a foul odor spilled from the gaping hole she'd formed in its side. She launched another fireball at it, almost immediately. This one, too, hit. More goo oozed from the kraken. She didn't want to kill it. Didn't want to be forced to injure it. But it wouldn't stop advancing on them. It was leaving her no choice.

With a roar, she flew directly at its eye and pressed her blazing hands against its body. It released a startling shriek as the heat of her body melted its flesh. Flames licked up its head, spreading rapidly as she fed more and more of her fire magic into taking the beast out.

One of its tentacles slammed into her side, knocking her from its head. She crumpled to the ground, her ribs cracking. Groaning, she prodded at her sides and winced in pain.

She didn't have time to consume more of her Silver Salum Flower. The kraken had turned to Penny, who was firing at it as she continued to lay on the ground.

Fighting through the pain, Astrid stood and ambled forward, blasting the kraken with her gun as she tried to conserve some of her power.

"Get out of here," Penny said. "Leave me. As long as my core processor is still intact, it can't kill me."

Freed by Destiny

Astrid had already lost Penny once. She refused to lose her again. Even if it was just temporarily. Besides, there was no way of stopping the beast from completely destroying every aspect of Penny's body, including her operating system.

Sliding her gun back into her holster, Astrid let her fire magic burn through her, transforming herself into the firebird.

A loud pop split the air around them as several portals opened. Astrid hurtled upward, terrified they belonged to Renard and not her allies. From one of the portals, Layla emerged, clad in body armor and carrying a massive gun. She stumbled forward a few steps as she took her bearing after being transported through time and space. The kraken zeroed in on Layla.

"Watch out!" Astrid screamed, just as one of the beast's tentacles smacked Layla in the back. She somersaulted through the air before slamming into a building several feet away.

Soldiers emerged from the portals in droves. Astrid released a sigh of relief as she realized they bore the sigils of Nat's and Vlander's armies. They had finally arrived to aid in the fight.

Her relief was short lived as the kraken swept its arm through the first section of soldiers, sending them flying backwards. The rest of the army, still too disoriented from portalling to react quickly, clumsily drew their weapons and haphazardly fired at the beast. Several of the shots barely missed Astrid.

Fearing for all their lives, Astrid dove towards the center of the beast's head. She punched the creature's skull and kept diving until she was completely enveloped within the kraken's head. Thick goo swirled around her as she pushed through it's body. Disoriented, she shifted direction. Her lungs burned from the lack of air. Her mind turned fuzzy. Forming a thin layer of protective magic tight against her body, Astrid increased her speed, hoping it would be enough to release her from the inside of the kraken's body.

Her fist slammed into something solid. Fire poured into her fingertips as she pushed against whatever she'd struck. She prayed to the Creators of old that she was up against an external portion of the kraken and not some internal organ. Her fire weakened the gelatinous goo oozing between her fingers. She dug through it, even as her arms became heavier and her eyes began to close.

Her hand punched through to open air. A firm hand gasped her wrist and yanked her forward. She collapsed to the ground, panting as her lungs refilled with air. Slime covered every inch of her, congealing in her hair as she crouched while she regained sense of where she was and what she had just achieved.

Dull noises hummed all around her, but she couldn't understand what they were saying. Lowering her head to her legs, she drew deep, slow breaths. Steadily, her mind cleared.

"Are you alright?" Layla said. Her face came into view as she lowered herself to Astrid's level. "Can you hear me, Astrid?"

She wiped her hand across Astrid's brow and tucked thick strands of her hair behind her ear.

She turned towards someone Astrid couldn't see and said, "I don't see any injuries."

Astrid cleared her throat and said, "I'm fine."

Layla turned to look at her again, her eyes full of concern. "Are you sure?"

Instead of answering, Astrid stood and went to Penny. Her legs wobbled slightly as she walked, but she kept her head held high. She didn't want to let her people see her struggles. She'd saved them and she wanted to maintain the trust they had in her for a little bit longer.

"We need to get back to the others," she said to Penny. "Do you remember which direction they went in?"

Layla placed a warm hand on Astrid's shoulder as she came to stand behind her. "Astrid, I think we can afford to take some time for you to get cleaned up." She wrinkled her nose. "Besides, you smell like a fish that's been sitting dead in the sun too long."

Nat stepped forward, her broad form distinguishable even through the haze still hovering in Astrid's vision. "I don't mean to argue with your friend here, but we actually don't have time to waste. We need to find the others. We haven't been able to communicate with anyone for more than an hour and Renard is here. We saw his robots scanning the city for any sign of us. He'll surely know we're here by now."

"Do we have something we can put Penny's body on?" Astrid asked as she gestured towards the robot. "We just need to get her to Maya and then she can fix…"

"We can't take a robot with us," Vlander said. "They're all part of Renard's regime. Why would you think this one is any different?"

"Because it was one of our team members—Maya—who built her," Astrid said, her eyes narrowing at the king. "You have nothing to fear from her."

He glared at her but didn't argue.

"The others went that way," Penny said, pointing down the main road. "They turned left at the next intersection, but I didn't see where they went from there."

Nat motioned for a few of her soldiers to pick Penny's feet up and another set to do the same with her torso. The front end lifted her too high and a clanking sound echoed from inside her.

"Please be careful," Penny said. "I think I might have a loose part that I don't want coming completely undone as you're carrying me to Maya."

Although the soldiers scowled at her addressing them, they shifted her weight so that it was more evenly distributed between the front and back.

Layla looped her arm around Astrid's shoulders and tugged her towards the road. "If we're not going to get you cleaned up, the least I can do is make sure you get to our rally point safely."

"We don't have an official rally point."

"Well, then, wherever it is the robot is taking us."

Although Astrid still wasn't sure how to act around the woman who was supposed to die in her place, she was grateful she'd appeared when she did. If it hadn't been for the armies distracting the kraken, she doubted she would have been able to defeat it. Even if it had meant getting completed doused in its organic matter. She sniffed, the foul stench of spoiling guts filled her nose.

"You know, I never thought I would be able to smell myself, but it seems I was entirely wrong," she said, chuckling a little as she allowed Layla to bear the brunt of her weight as they walked.

"Don't get me wrong, I don't care if you're covered in this gunk, but since I have to be close to you, I wanted to save myself from having to smell you."

"Oh, I see," Astrid said, her lips curling upward. "And that's the reason you're helping me walk?"

"Well, I couldn't very well let you get all the credit for saving the day." Layla's face turned serious. "You remember our bargain, don't you? Renard's mine, if it comes down to killing him to win?"

Astrid's stomach tightened. She didn't want to have to kill Renard on the battlefield unless it was absolutely necessary. Let him have a fair trial so the people felt as if they had a say in the future of not just their kingdom, but their lives. However, she also understood Layla's need for revenge. For justice.

"If it comes to that, then yes."

Layla smiled, her eyes darkening and peering far away as if she were seeing something that wasn't there.

"Hey," Astrid said, "I know getting revenge on Renard for his crimes against our families has been your goal…"

"It's not just my goal, Astrid. It's my whole purpose. My destiny. He stole the life that should've been mine. And there is nothing he could ever do that would recompense for that. Do you understand?"

A part of Astrid knew that Renard needed to be killed. He was too dangerous alive. He'd already prove that time and time again. And yet, she couldn't bring herself to admit that she longed for his death, perhaps just as much as Layla did.

"Whatever happens, we should be proud of how far we've come," Astrid said, hedging her words. "Besides, I don't believe that you exist solely to destroy Renard. I think—"

"I don't care what you think," Layla snapped.

Startled by her sudden change of attitude, Astrid pressed her lips together and shifted her face away from Layla. She knew the type of trauma she'd endured growing up because she, too, had felt the sting of loss. They were two sides of the same coin, the main difference being that Layla's parents had willingly sacrificed their child while Astrid's had asked them. She didn't know which was worse.

The ground shook beneath their feet. Astrid met Layla's eyes and found concern mirrored in them. Lightning streaked across sky, illuminating the darkness descending upon them. In the distance, booming sounds became louder, as if it were approaching them at a steady pace. Astrid stared up at Layla.

This could only mean one thing.

Renard had finally found them.

Chapter Thirty-Eight

Dozens of human soldiers, each bearing the sigil of King Renard, strode down the street. They marched in unison.

Astrid shoved herself away from Layla and squared her shoulders. If it was a fight Renard wanted, then it was a fight he would get. She was tired of hiding. Exhausted from it, actually. All she wanted now was to finish this fight before even more lives were lost.

The soldiers stopped when they were a few hundred feet away from her. They pounded on their chest and chanted a war cry.

"Astrid," Layla hissed from the corner of her mouth. "What are you doing?"

"If I am going to die today, Layla, I would rather it be while I'm fighting than on my knees begging for my life."

"Easy for you to say. We all know Renard wants you to be kept alive. He probably has something more sinister planned for you. But the rest of us…" Layla shrugged. "He wouldn't care at all if every single person who has ever aided you was destroyed."

"Since when did you become so afraid of death?" Astrid asked. "You always seemed so nonchalant about fighting before. What's changed?"

"Nothing," Layla said, holding up her hands. "I swear. It's just, if I die on this battle, then I'll never get the glory or satisfaction I deserve from taking out Renard."

"Is that really all you can think about?" Astrid asked. "Killing Renard?"

"Honestly?"

They stared at each other.

"Fine. We can retreat down the street Penny thinks the rest went down, but I'm taking up the rear."

Layla motioned for Nat and Vlander to join them.

"Astrid wants to make a final stand right here."

The other two leaders shared a look among themselves. "Astrid, this is not an ideal location to fight. We're in a narrow length of road. There are buildings on either side of us that can be used by his robots as cover when they fire upon us. And they can attack us from both ends."

Sighing, Astrid said, "We can keep moving, but we need to keep a portion of our soldiers ready to defend our backend if we keep going. I know this is asking a lot of you, but you chose to fight with me because you wanted an opportunity to take Renard out.

Freed by Destiny

This is that chance, and we are squandering it by being disjointed and lacking follow through on our original plan. I get it—you wanted to try and fool him. Well, guess what. It didn't work. He played us."

They stared at her blankly.

She huffed and then said, "I will, of course, acquiesce to whatever our group decides, even if I think it's folly."

"Fine, we'll leave a squadron at the back to ensure they don't attack us from behind. But we have to move as quickly as possible." Nat glanced at the buildings to either side of them and then up at the sky. "I can smell the rain coming and I have a bad feeling about what's happening here."

"We knew it would be difficult when we joined Astrid's cause," Vlander reminded her. "To whatever end, we will continue fighting. We deserve to give her this much."

Nat nodded. "You're right. If Renard defeats us here, he will stop at nothing to destroy our respective nations. We cannot stop until we have rid him of this world or have died trying. Anything in the middle seals our peoples' fates."

"Then let it be so."

"Then let it be so," Nat repeated.

Astrid was still in awe of the fact that they had decided to join her at all, especially now that their lives, and the lives of their people, were in great risk of being taken.

A whistle echoed through the street, drawing their collective attention. Astrid dreaded seeing yet another portion of Renard's army facing them down.

She searched the street for any sign of who had whistled at them. As far as she could tell, the street was abandoned. She peered up and scanned the buildings. For the first time, she realized the Golden City's citizens were in their homes. Faces popped into windows. Curtains were pulled back by quivering hands. Lights dimmed as soon as she saw them.

She looked back to where Nat and Vlander stood. It was clear that they, too, had seen had seen the civilians hidden away in their homes. It was one thing to intellectually know that they were risking lives to remove Renard from power. It was an entirely different thing to see the faces of the children who would be dead if they didn't succeed.

"Go," Astrid said. "Get the others. Leave what soldiers you can. But I cannot—I will not—leave these people to suffer because of us."

Flames flickered between her fingers as spoke. The headache and the fatigue slipped away. Her power was still inconsistent and weak, and she wasn't sure how long she would be able to sustain a fight.

They didn't argue with her as they ushered the majority of their forces forward. They left a dozen soldiers with Astrid, who formed an arc around her. Drawing their weapons, they formed an unbroken line between the oncoming army and the rest of their people. In unison, they took backward steps down the street. Renard's forces approached slowly, as if egging them on.

Astrid continued to scan the skies, searching for any sign that robots were approaching. A single drop of rain splattered on her forehead. She wiped away the wetness.

The downpour followed. Wind howled through the streets. Renard's army abruptly halted their approach. Astrid, shivering from the rain, looked above and behind her, but saw nothing to indicate why they had stopped their progression.

Then, before she had an opportunity to move, or even scream, a shadow passed above and dove straight for her. Its clawed hands wrapped around her waist and wrenched her upwards. Mechanical scraping grated against her ears as the robotic dragon lifted her higher. She writhed in its grasp, struggling to free herself. Nothing she did seemed to have any impact at all. Her arms were pressed firmly against her sides, and she was unable to use her gun without hitting herself.

The dragon veered to the left. Astrid twisted in the dragon's claw. Her heart sank. What seemed like the entirety of Renard's army stood on the beach. A fleet of ships were anchored in the harbor.

"No," she whispered. She couldn't go back to him. Not now. Banging her fists against the dragon, she begged for it to release her. She didn't care if Renard was watching and listening to her on the other side. Her blood rushed to her head, turning her lightheaded. She couldn't give him the keys to his success and condemn the rest of them. Her cries turned to quiet sobs as she realized there was no hope of escape. She was his once more.

The dragon's body jerked upwards. Astrid screamed as it released her from its claw and she went plummeting downwards. Her wings sprung from her back, catching her just as she was about to strike one of high-rise buildings beneath her. She whirled around to see what had disrupted the dragon's flight path. There, straddling the dragon with his dagger plunged into its neck, was Kimari.

Chapter Thirty-Nine

Astrid flew towards the dragon. It writhed beneath Kimari as he dug his dagger in deeper, forcing the dragon to slow before reaching down and wrenching out the processor from within its skeleton. The dragon continued to glide through the air for a few seconds longer before it began hurtling towards the ground at an increasingly fast pace.

Kimari continued to hold onto the dagger as the dragon tumbled, tail over head. Swooping down, Astrid flew parallel with Kimari. She stretched out a hand towards him, her fingers grazing his shoulder. He turned to her, his eyes wide with shock before filling with a smoldering desire that permeated every part of her. Releasing his hold on the dagger, he flung himself at her.

Wrapping her arms tight around his middle, Astrid clung as they dipped low. The muscles in her back and arms strained with

Kimari's extra weight. She grunted as Kimari's feet grazed the top of one of the skyscrapers. He ran across the roof as she slowed her momentum enough to stop flying.

A loud boom echoed through the city as the dragon struck the ground. Fire and smoke rose from its remains.

"What are you doing here?" Astrid asked as she spun around to face Kimari. Her wings pressed close to her back. "You're not supposed to be here. Your father..."

"My father can think and do as he pleases. I never should have stayed in the palace when you were rescued." He hung his head. "I wanted to go with you, but I was so afraid of what he might do if I left again."

She reached for his hands. "You don't have to explain yourself to me. Not anymore. I know what you and Kali risked to get me out of there." She closed the gap between them. "I'm sorry I doubted you. You tried to warn me that you would need to pretend to still be in alignment with your father and at very first sign of a potential betrayal, I turned on you."

"You had every right to question whether you'd made the right decision in trusting me. I am my father's son, after all."

"You're nothing like your father."

He cradled her cheek with his hand as he leaned down to press his forehead to hers. His voice cracked as he said, "My greatest fear is that I am exactly like him."

She tilted her head towards him and pressed her lips against his. Warmth spread through her, a fire that ignited every nerve in her body. He wrapped his other hand around her waist, pulling her closer to him until she couldn't tell where she ended and he began.

Freed by Destiny

"I'm sorry for everything he's done to you," he whispered when they finally pulled apart enough to breathe. "I'm sorry for the world he's created because of his never-ending appetite for power. I'm just—"

She pressed her fingers to lips, stilling his words.

"I know," she whispered.

He kissed her fingertips as she withdrew them from his mouth. She leaned into him, pressing her ear against his chest. The steady rhythm of his heartbeat quickened as she trailed her nails down his back. He nuzzled his head into her hair and sighed.

Astrid gave herself a moment to savor being in his arms once more. She still didn't fully know where they stood with one another or whether their relationship had a strong enough foundation to work out, but there was something inside of her that kept drawing her back to him. A thread that, although it shook and wavered, refused to snap.

She pulled herself out of his arms and said, "We have to go. We have to help the others."

His expression darkened.

"What is it?" she asked. She wasn't sure she actually wanted to know the answer, but she needed to have the facts before she could make an informed decision. He knew something that she wouldn't want to hear.

"He has Max."

The air rushed from her body. Every part of her went numb. She should have known it was a possibility. It made sense. He'd attacked the robots and somehow, despite the bomb going off, he'd been taken by them. Still, she didn't want to know what

Renard had already done to him.

"Why didn't you tell me this to start with?"

"I..." He floundered for his words. "Honestly, I was just relieved to have found you before my father's newest toy brought you to him."

She shook her head as the numbness was replaced with anger. "You let me waste time with you. You... you let me kiss you when Max was down there." She pointed her finger at Renard's forces. "He's suffering while I'm up here..."

She cursed beneath her breath, unable to finish her sentence.

She flinched as his footsteps approached her.

"I know. I'm sorry," he whispered. "Do you have any idea how relieved I was that I got to you first? I'm sorry that I let my emotions get away with me. But Astrid, not knowing if you were okay after you left the palace killed me. I trust that...he... kept you safe, but it wasn't the same as knowing that you were alright."

Heat from his hand hovered just above her skin.

She spun around to face him. "I was worried about you, too," she whispered as she wrapped her arms around him. "But if you ever withhold information like this again, I swear I will scorch you."

His chest rumbled beneath her cheek as he laughed. She didn't like that he hadn't told her about Max right from the beginning, but she could also understand how relieved he must have felt when he'd rescued her from the dragon.

"Deal," he said and then kissed her forehead.

Freed by Destiny

She wanted to linger there, in his arms, with her worries at the back of her mind instead of the front, but she knew they couldn't stay here forever. If they chose to shirk their responsibilities to their people, Renard would win. And he would find them.

The only way out of this alive was to remove him from power.

"I have another bad piece of news," Kimari said.

She frowned at him. "What's that?"

He pointed towards the direction where she'd been pulled from the street by the dragon. "Those soldiers were never going to attack you, Astrid. They were sent there to herd you towards my father's armies. He's not planning just a battle. He's planning a massacre."

She ground her teeth.

"So, what do you suggest?" she asked. The rain hadn't ceased yet and a chill settled into her bones as she stared out over the city. "I don't even know where half of our allied troops are. We got separated from Maya and Bear. I haven't seen Eldris…By the Creators, I don't even know what happened to the sirens."

She turned towards him then. "Are they okay?"

"They took out nearly half of our armada," Kimari said.

She nodded but tilted her head towards him. "That doesn't tell me if they're okay or not, Kimari. Just tell me. Please."

"I… don't know how many survived. My father declared it a victory, but…" He trailed off as he looked past her towards his father's army. "I'm not sure we can beat him, Astrid. He's built more robots—different from the ones you've faced before."

"Like the dragon."

He nodded. "And worse. There's something… off about them. I can't quite put my finger on it, but they seem to move beyond their coding quite a bit, as if they were learning how to adapt to the world. As if they were actually learning."

She covered her mouth with her hand as she gasped. After twenty years, he'd finally figured out how to replicate, at least in part, what he and her mother had developed. She doubted any of his creations were as caring and thoughtful as Penny was.

"Your turn," Kimari said. "What you do you know about his robots?"

"Twenty years ago, our parents worked together to develop an AI. They coded her to believe she was an incarnation of Queen Amaleah. My mother saw what your father's real intentions were with the creation, so she stole it away and—"

"Your PEA," he said, cutting her off.

She nodded. "My PEA."

"All this time I wondered why my father was so obsessed with finding you. I thought it was because he knew the fae were restless under his rule and viewed you as a way to appease them. But… what he really wanted this whole time was to find what he had lost."

"He killed my parents because of my mother's betrayal." She spat the words as if they were poison on her tongue.

Only the wind rushing past them and the rain splattering all around them broke the silence.

"Now, more than ever, I know my father shouldn't be in charge of ruling anyone. I need you to know—to understand—I'm not just joining you because I love you." Kimari's cheeks flushed. "I mean, what I wanted to say was… the only way I can make amends for the shortfalls of my father is to make sure he can never harm anyone ever again."

"And how, exactly, are we going to do that?"

He smiled at her. "I have an idea, but it involves using you as bait."

Chapter Forty

"Bait?" Astrid blinked at him. "You seriously expect me to put myself in a position where he could recapture me. Besides, didn't you just destroy a whole draking robotic dragon to keep me from your father? And now you're telling me you want to bring me in?"

He shrugged. "Well, do you have a better idea?"

She cocked an eyebrow at him. "And what, exactly, do you think we can do once we're down there? At best, he'll accept your word and just lock me up. At worst... he'll kill me and imprison you. I'm not willing to take that chance. Besides, my primary goal right now is saving Max and I don't see how this would accomplish that."

"Because it will give us access to him. If I've learned anything from growing up as his son, it's that he gets cocky when he thinks he's in total control. With good reason, I know, because he's historically made things work out in his favor."

"You honestly believe you can kill your father?" she asked, crossing her arms over her chest as she stared at him in disbelief. "Kimari, I can't let you do that. You know I can't."

His jaw tightened as he stared down at her. "How else am I supposed to make right everything he has done wrong?"

She shook her head. "Maybe we're not supposed to right all the wrongs in the world. Sometimes, letting go is the best thing we can do. You know what, I refuse to let anyone tell me that I have to make amends for what Leilani did by stealing the PEA and implanting into me. I know she thought she was doing the right thing. I can feel it in my bones every time I think about what Renard did to her... to us... to the whole of the fae people after she betrayed his trust. But I will never compromise what I believe in to make recompense for what she did. And you shouldn't do that for your father, either. His sins are his own."

Kimari wrapped his arms tight around her.

Sliding her arms from being squashed between their chests, Astrid returned the hug. "I say all of this knowing that it's the best plan we have."

He stiffened in her grasp. "You're sure?"

"Positive."

"Okay then," Kimari said. "Let's go save your elf."

Freed by Destiny

Kimari chained her wrists together but didn't lock them. Even still, the weight of the iron made her skin crawl. She hated that she was being forced to set aside her pride in an attempt to goad Renard into a false sense of security.

At least the rain had washed away most of the goo from the kraken, so that was a small win. She still smelled like the underbelly of a beached whale though.

They hadn't taken the time to find her allies and tell them about their plan. She hadn't wanted to risk Renard injuring Max beyond repair and it hadn't taken much for Kimari to agree that acting as quickly as possible would be the best for everyone.

Still, as Astrid trailed behind him with the chain links clinking, she couldn't help but remember the first time she'd been captured and taken to Renard. She'd barely begun to understand her true power at that point. Kimari's actions during that time made a lot more sense now, too. Although he put on the air of being just as uncaring for her feelings as Renard had, it was his way of trying to protect her. Even then. She just hadn't recognized it yet.

She prayed that was how he reacted today. She needed him to put on the best act of his life if he was going to be able to explain how the robotic dragon had been destroyed and yet, someone his father had not explicitly sent to retrieve her had somehow made it back unscathed. She should have punched him in the face a few times to make it more believable, but it was too late for that now.

Guards wearing the red and gold colors of the Titus line milled about the road. They averted their eyes from her as Kimari yanked her chain, forcing her keep up. She couldn't tell if it was from fear or deference that made them look away.

In the short time he had made footfall on the Golden City's island, Renard had already assembled a dais on which he could sit and be raised higher than his soldiers. Astrid smirked when she saw his ornately carved chair standing in the center of the dais. It was sad how necessary it was to him to be placed at the center of all things. Wasn't it enough that he was king? Apparently not, given that that he was so focused on everyone around him worshipping him.

Kimari stole a glance at her as a they approached the dais. Although his expression remained calculated and harsh, there was a hint of concern in his eyes that reassured her that she could trust him. She was literally putting her life on the line with this decision, and she prayed she wasn't showing just how foolish she really was.

"What's this?" Renard asked as he sipped from a wine glass with dark liquid sloshing over its sides. Setting the glass on a side table, he leaned forward. "Has my son returned the queen winger to me?"

Astrid flinched at the insult.

"Father," Kimari said as he bowed. He yanked her chains downward and she fell to her knees.

They'd practiced this move a few times on the rooftop of the skyscraper, but doing it now, when she was before Renard, left her feeling small and insubstantial. Grinding her teeth, she forced herself to keep her head bowed. Perhaps the show of reverence would put Renard in a better disposition, make him sloppy. It was all Astrid could hope for.

"Look at me, boy," Renard commanded.

Astrid lifted her eyes enough to see Kimari stand and face his father. His back was ramrod straight. He held his hands behind his back, and they quivered ever so slightly.

"How is it that I sent my dragon to go retrieve her and instead, I see that it's offline and now, miraculously, you're here with her? Explain yourself."

Kimari balled his hands into fists. "I followed the dragon to make sure it worked. It was attacked by some of her soldiers." He jerked his head towards Astrid. "When it was taken down, I tracked where it fell and retrieved her from the wreckage before her people could get to her."

"And how, in the bloody darkness, did you achieve that?"

Kimari held up a small object. "How else? I used one of the transporters to send me to a specific place in time and space."

Astrid held her breath as she waited to see how Renard would react to this declaration. Although Kimari delivered it with a persuasive tone, it sounded false to Astrid. She doubted Renard would be fooled.

To her surprise, he opened his arms wide and beckoned for Kimari to join him on the dais. Astrid watched as he approached his father with trepidation. Each footfall seemed to move in slow motion. Her chest burned from lack of air as she waited to see what Renard would do next.

Movement behind the king drew Astrid's attention. Her jaw dropped open as Kaden and Kali stepped on the dais. Kali wore her hair in long braids that had been pinned to top of her head.

She wore sleek body armor from neck to toe, with only her head uncovered. She scowled when she saw Astrid chained in front of her father. Her eyes darted to a tent off to the side and then back at Astrid.

Not knowing what Kali was trying to convey, Astrid turned away from her. The worst thing that could happen would be for one of the guards to notice the communication happening between the two of them and report Kali to her father. Astrid didn't want that kind of blood on her hands.

"You have proven yourself," Renard said, gripping Kimari's hand.

In the same instant Kimari's shoulders relaxed from the tension of waiting for his father's approval, Renard wrenched his arm behind his back and pinned him against the floor. His other arm was trapped beneath their combined weight. Kimari struggled against the hold but couldn't get his hands free.

"To be a great disappointment," Renard finished with a snarl. "Have I not given you everything? The best education, food, clothes, opportunities for military glory. I even agreed to let you bed and marry that filthy little winger."

He inclined his head towards Astrid.

"And how do you repay me?" He jabbed his elbow squarely into Kimari's back. "You betray your own family... your own king... for her."

He glared at Astrid as he spoke, spittle flying from his mouth.

"I should have known you wouldn't be strong enough to keep your feelings separate from your duty. How long have you been lying to me, Kimari? Hmmm?"

Freed by Destiny

Kimari grunted. His usually placid face was wracked with pain as Renard pulled on his arm. Astrid could practically feel the sinews in his shoulder stretching and tearing. Flames formed between her fingers, and she lifted her hands to launch the fireball straight at Renard's head.

Before she could launch the attack, a soldier slammed her to the ground. He punched her square in the nose. She felt the crack before she felt the blood gushing from her nose. Tears welled in her eyes as she pressed her other hand to her face. The soldier spat in her face as he pinned her hands above her head.

Kicking upwards, she nailed him right in the crotch. His face scrunched up in pain. She sent her magic up her arms. Flames raced across her skin, scorching his flesh until tiny blisters formed all along his palms. His lips contorted into a grimace. Astrid maintained the steady flow of magic into her hands.

"Stop!" Kali screamed.

Astrid jolted, releasing the soldier from her flames. She peered past the shoulder on top of her, and her stomach dropped.

Renard had Kimari tied with his hands behind his back. A dagger was pressed firmly to his throat. His eyes raged as he glared at her. She'd never seen anyone look as furious as Renard did in that moment.

"I swear I'll kill him," Renard growled. "Stop fighting against us. You already made your choices. You could have had a great life with us in the palace, Astrid. We invited you to be a part of our family and you sneered in our faces. Broke your promises to me. To my son."

He jerked the dagger closer to Kimari's throat and a thin speckle of blood bubbled from the slender scratch he left behind. Astrid

457

grimaced at the wound.

"Tell me what I have to do to make you let him go," she whispered.

"I'm sorry, did you say something? I didn't hear the words, 'please, your great and impeccable leader, please let him go.'" His eyes danced with glee as he leaned in closer to her. "Go on. Beg for his life. I'll wait."

Astrid tried to discern if this was another one of Renard's tricks or not. He dug the tip of his blade into another spot on Kimari's throat. More blood seeped to the surface and trailed in a small river down his neck. Astrid dropped her hands to her side and let her body go limp. He jerked his head at his soldiers, two of which stepped forward and secured iron manacles around her wrists. This time, they were locked.

"You see, I am a reasonable man," Renard said. He gripped a handful of Kimari's hair and tilted his head back.

As if in slow motion, Astrid watched as he lifted his hand with the dagger. It flashed white as it caught the lights illuminating dais. Little rainbows danced in the sky as the blade reflected the light outward. He met Astrid's eyes across the short distance between them, a strange, carnal smile dancing on his lips as he brought the blade down.

Chapter Forty-One

Astrid screamed. Her eyes closed as she was yanked backwards. Her ears rang and her heart ached. All she saw was the movement of the dancing light through the air as Renard plunged his dagger into Kimari's throat. She waited for the gurgle of his blood as he began choking. She did not want to watch him die. She couldn't bear to watch as another person she loved was taken from her.

Instead, what she got was a strange yelping sound and the clatter of the dagger hitting the ground.

Her eyes snapped open.

Renard gripped Kali by the wrists. With unbelievable strength, he lifted her from the ground, her feet dangling above the platform.

"You, too, Kali?" His brows knit together as he peered up at her.

"Daddy, please," she whispered.

His expression darkened.

Tears streamed down her cheeks.

"He's my brother," she whimpered.

"And I'm your king." He backhanded her, her head twisting. Blood oozed from her lips and nose as Renard dropped her like she was nothing onto the ground. Her body slumped, her neck still at that odd angle. Astrid's heart ripped open as she realized what had happened. There, in front of this entire army, he'd killed his daughter.

The beloved of the kingdom.

The favorite child.

Her friend.

Something dark grew inside her, twisting its way from the deepest pit of her power and swelling to the top. She released a scream and with it, a black tendril of power that flapped around her, warding off the soldiers as she superheated her hands enough to melt the iron from her wrists. The molten metal burned her flesh, but she didn't care. All she wanted was to hold Kali. To tell her that she finally understood what was going through her head when she'd rescued Astrid from the palace the first time. This woman who so easily could have been one of her greatest enemies, had sacrificed so much to save her life on countless occasions.

And Renard had just killed her.

Her rage overflowed, incinerating all the soldiers standing too close to her to avoid her flame. Even her hair simmered with fire as she approached the dais. Kimari, injured and bruised as he was, crouched next to Kali. With his hands behind his back, he couldn't even hold her as her life slipped from her body.

Astrid was too focused on the two of them to see what happened next. All she heard was a strangled cry and the squelching of a weapon piercing a person's body.

Kaden drew his own dagger from the Renard's back. Blood smeared across the metal.

Renard blinked at Astrid, his lips parted as if he were going to say one last thing before he tottered over. The dais shook from the weight of his crash.

The tendrils of her power faltered as the reality of what had just occurred settled in. After all they'd been through, everything she'd faced, Kaden had finally turned against his master. She remembered one of the first conversations she'd had with him, all those months ago when he'd taken her to what was supposed to have been a secret hideout. He'd seemed almost... tender.

And conflicted about his role in all of this.

She'd seen the darkness in him when he'd threatened to kill all those who had supported her. She'd thought she'd killed him. Yet, here he was, betraying his king to save her.

Except, he wasn't looking at her. He was staring at Kali. Her face was pale, her eyes unmoving. The dagger slipped from his grasp as he collapsed to knees beside her. He hadn't saved Astrid at all. He'd killed his king to avenge his princess.

Chapter Forty-Two

Beneath the wails from Kimari and Kaden, Astrid heard the shuffling of a body moving across the floor. Shifting her attention back to Renard, she realized Kaden had not successfully killed the king. As the other two's focus was on Kali, Renard had been stretching his arm towards the dagger Kaden had dropped.

Without hesitating, Astrid lunged towards the dagger and clutched it in front of her. In a swift movement, she slammed the blade deep into Renard's eye. Blood spurted from the wound as she wrenched the weapon free. She stabbed him again, this time in the heart, just to be sure he wouldn't move again.

She swayed as she attempted to steady herself for what was to come. Her fingers fumbled on the pouch containing the last dose of the Silver Salum Flower she'd reserved for herself. Without hesitating, she pulled the last of the petals free and crushed them in her palm. Cupping her hands together, she collected enough rainwater to soak the petals before bending down and tipping the water onto Kali's lips.

No one said a word, not even the soldiers, as they all waited to see if Kali could be saved.

Astrid cut the rope binding Kimari's hands behind his back. Tears rolled down her cheeks as she stared at Kali's still lifeless body.

Beside her, Kaden sobbed. His eyes were red-rimmed and snot trickled from his nose. He placed his hands on either side of Kali's head and snapped it back into place. Pressing his lips to her forehead, he kissed her gently before smoothing back her hair.

"I'm so sorry," he whispered over and over again.

Astrid laid her hand on his back as he began rocking and back forth, his sobs becoming louder.

The flower wasn't working.

Thundering footsteps echoed from behind them. Astrid turned her attention back to the road just in time to see hundreds of soldiers advancing towards them. Portals opened on the skyscrapers on their sides. Behind them, a giant wave rose from the seas. What remained of the sirens grouped together, swords and tridents raised.

"Let her go, Renard!" Vlander yelled from somewhere deep within the army. His voice echoed on the wind and Astrid knew it had been amplified by one of the Fae.

Renard's soldiers looked to Kimari for direction. His chest rose and fell, his hands covered in his sister's blood. His eyes wandered to his father's body as his shoulders began to shake.

"I'm here," Astrid whispered, stroking his back. "It's going to be okay."

He jolted, his entire body stiffening. "How can you say that when Kali is dead?"

His voice carried so much venom in it that Astrid was taken aback. She, too, was reeling from this loss.

"I know you're hurting right now. I know you don't want to have to face what is coming next. But I need you to take command of the army. Of the nation. This is what Kali wanted. Don't let her death be in vain."

She hated that she was using Kali's death to spur Kimari into action, but they couldn't let their suffering detract them from needed to come next."

He stared at her, his face stricken and pale, before finally releasing one long, slow breath. Scooping Kali's hands into his own, he kissed them and laid them delicately across her stomach before rising to his feet.

"Wherever you have the elf, release him," he ordered the soldiers closest to him. "I thank you for your service to my father, but we are done here."

The soldiers hesitated.

"Do not make me repeat myself again," Kimari said.

He sounded exactly like his father. It was enough to motivate the soldiers into action. A pair of them left the main area, presumably to retrieve Max from wherever he was being kept.

Kimari descended the dais, his footsteps measured as he strode towards Astrid's allies.

"Astrid will not be harmed," he said, his voice tight. "We are releasing the leader of the E.L.Fs back to you. My father, King Renard, is dead."

The news of Renard's death started as a murmur that increased into a roar. Layla, in wolf form, rushed forward, a wild look in her eyes. She bounded past Kimari and didn't stop until she reached the dais. Her fur hackled as she sniffed Renard's body. Growling, she backed away from him and came to sit beside Astrid. Pearlescent canines peaked over the side of her mouth as she glared at Astrid.

"I know," Astrid whispered. "I'm sorry."

Layla shook her head.

"What's its problem?" Kaden grumbled as he peered at the wolf with a mixture of exhaustion and interest.

"That wolf is the real Layla Dione in her shifted form." Astrid sucked in a breath. "I had promised her that she would be the one who could kill Renard if his life was to be the price."

Kaden blanched at her words, and she regretted adding that last part. She just wanted him to understand the complexity of the emotions both she and Layla were experiencing. She knew Layla was just as pleased as she was that Renard would never be able to harm another magical, yet the loss of being the one to exact justice and take revenge left a void she wasn't entirely sure how to fill. Not yet anyway.

Kaden turned to Layla.

"I'm sorry for taking away that opportunity for you. But..." He swallowed hard, his throat bobbing as he looked down to Kali. "I couldn't let him get away with what he did to her."

Freed by Destiny

Layla cocked her head at Kali and sniffed at Kali's lifeless form. Her long, pink tongue darted out, swiping a streak across the princess's cheek.

Kaden shoved Layla away from her and glared at Astrid. "What the drak is she doing?"

Shrugging, Astrid turned to her and asked, "Layla?"

She nudged at Kali's face again and growled at Kaden when he tried to push her away. Leaning down, Astrid pressed her ear to Kali's chest and stilled at what she heard.

A heartbeat.

Lifting her gaze to Kaden, she whispered, "She's still alive."

Chapter Forty-Three

Three Days Later

Astrid sat beside Kali's bed, a book in her lap and a bowl of grapes beside her. Nalia curled around her feet, her body warming Astrid's feet against the chilled air of evening.

She, Kaden, Maya, and Kimari had taken turns over the past three days keeping watch over Kali as her body slowly healed. No one had been able to explain how the Silver Salum Flower had seemingly brought her back from the dead. The hypothesis they had was that she had still been alive when Astrid had administered the petals and, when Kimari had reset her neck, that had allowed her to heal properly. Regardless, Astrid was just grateful that she was still alive. Even if she hadn't woken up yet.

Turning a page, she plopped a grape into her mouth as she read the next few lines. *People should have a say in their destinies. It is the only way for them to become truly free. And it must be an unalienable right to be a master of oneself.*

She sighed. Of all the books she could have been given, Cassidhe had chosen one about the benefits of a free society. Although it was dull as a rusted pipe, she appreciated the sentiments shared in the text. Many of them mirrored what she had been thinking about over the course of the past year. She knew she would need help in establishing the society she wanted her children and her children's children to grow up in.

She'd bid farewell to Max and Cassidhe, who'd gone back to Lunameed only that morning to begin drafting documents for the new government they were going to propose to her and Kimari. Maya and Eldris had joined them, citing their need for some time away from the fighting. Maya had taken Penny with her to continue working on repairs and upgrading her body. Now that she could utilize Renard's labs, she was confident she would be able to build a better, more durable version of her. Bear and the rest of the Fairy Godmothers had dispersed to find new charges in need of a little magic.

Although she was happy to see her friends return home and go off to explore new places, Astrid was left wondering how she fit into the new world order. She'd spent more than a year of her life thinking only of this one purpose—to remove Renard from power—so now that it was done, she was overwhelmed by a sense of being lost.

A soft knock on the door drew her attention away from her thoughts. Kimari paused in the doorway. She smiled at him and cocked an eyebrow. He came to stand beside her, his fingers brushing against hers. They hadn't had a moment alone together since his father had been killed. Every hour for two days straight had been spent in debriefing what had occurred with her allies, preparing for Kimari's coronation, and then the actual ceremony to present him as the new king of Lunameed.

Throughout it all, Astrid had found herself wondering what he was thinking. If he had forgiven her for pushing him to step up when he'd clearly been worried about his sister and grieving the loss of his father. It didn't matter that he'd been planning on dispatching him, himself. It was still a loss. Still a shock.

His fingers trailed up her arm and skimmed across her collarbone. She shivered as gooseflesh prickled on her arms.

"I couldn't stop thinking about you," he whispered.

Heat kindled in her belly as she stared up at him. Her lips parted as she struggled to find the right words to express how much she had been thinking about him, too. Bending down, he kissed her gently. His lips were soft against hers, as if he was afraid he might shatter the thread connecting them just by showing her love. His tongue slid across her lower lip, sending a shiver down her spine.

Ahe dropped the book to the floor as she wrapped her legs around his and pulled him closer to her.

"Ugh. Get a room. Preferably one that isn't mine," Kali whispered, her voice hoarse.

Kimari turned towards her, a smile brightening his face as he clutched at her hands. "Don't you ever scare me like that again."

She smiled weakly at him. "I'm not entirely sure what you're talking about, but sure."

"Kali," Astrid said cautiously, "do you remember what happened to you?"

Kali's brow furrowed and her lips pursed. She shook her head. "I just remember Father threatening to kill... you," she said, glancing at Kimari, "but I couldn't let him."

Kimari swallowed hard and his hands trembled as he clung to his sister.

Astrid prepared herself for the inevitable truth: Renard had attempted to kill his daughter and he'd almost succeeded. But, before she could explain what had happened, Kaden came to stand in the doorway.

"We all thought you were dead," he said matter-of-factly. His body filled the doorframe as he lingered there. "And when I saw you fall, blood seeping from your mouth, I...just... snapped."

He turned away from them and cleared his throat. When he looked at them again, his eyes were bloodshot and puffy. "I killed your father. I'm sorry."

Everyone in the room paused in silence as his words sunk in. Part of Astrid still didn't believe that the horror Renard had inflicted upon them was over. She didn't think she would until they'd hunted down every research lab in the country and shut it down. Or until they'd established a new government, where even the lowliest voice could have power. Or until she and Kimari could really discover what they were to one another without Renard's presence casting a shadow of doubt over them.

Kali nodded and said, "I understand and I'm sorry you had to make that choice." She held out her hand to him. "But you've always been a part of our family. He was going to kill Kimari. And Astrid. And Max. I couldn't let him destroy the people I care most about in this world. So, when I say I understand why you did it, I mean it."

Freed by Destiny

He approached her and took her hand. Kissing it, he said, "I hope I can make it up to you. One day."

"There's nothing to make up. You did what you thought was best in the moment and that's all anyone could ever ask for."

They stood in silence, thinking about the things they had lost, but also what they had gained.

"So," Kimari began, "what happens next?"

"What happens next?" Astrid repeated, a smile playing at the corners of her lips. "Anything we can dream."

The End.

More Books by S.A. McClure

The Lost Queen Chronicles
Royal by Blood Book 1
Chosen by Fae Book 2
Crowned by War Book 3
Destroyed by Vengeance Book 4
Claimed by Steel Book 5
Freed by Destiny Book 6

The Valka Chronicles
Spellbreaker
Starseeker

Broken Prophecies Series
Kilian: A Broken Prophecies Story
Keepers of the Light
Destroyers of the Light
Harbinger of the Light (coming soon)

Apprentice's Wings Series
Wings of Gold & Snow

Fortuna Saga
Spade